Return to Power
The New Illuminati
Part 2

Return to Power
The New Illuminati
Part 2

By

DAVID–MICHAEL HARDING

Return to Power
The New Illuminati – Pt 2

Copyright © 2016 by David Harding

Photograph of the author by
William Tillis and Harold Hutchinson © 2011

Cover by Kerwin Designs

DavidMichaelHarding.com

Printed in the United States of America
October 2016
First Edition

1 3 5 7 9 10 8 6 4 2

ISBN-10: 098572854X
ISBN-13: 978-0-9857285-4-0
Library of Congress Catalog Number: 2016954044

Novels by David-Michael Harding

How Angels Die

Cherokee Talisman

Losing St. Christopher

The New Illuminati

**Return to Power – The New Illuminati
Part 2**

Short Story Collection

The Cats of Savone

Find free reading excerpts and preview upcoming
novels at the author's website -

DavidMichaelHarding.com

For Kathryn

Support & encouragement does not come without cost

REBELLION TO TYRANTS IS OBEDIENCE TO GOD.

– Thomas Jefferson

1

Sam Ciampiano had thought it was only a game. There was a big, paper covered, hard, one-dimensional board of squares with bright colored headers emblazoned with street names. Dollar signs dotted the board and play money was tucked here and there – purposely hidden or left to peek out and watch the game until pressed into service. The board folded neatly in half along a black cloth seam that was worn and frayed to gray by use. The cardboard box that held the board and the multi-colored money was the same – battered and bent at the edges, torn at the corners. Some of the game pieces had lost themselves over the years, but the game was still playable. The tokens were interchangeable and essentially meaningless as he remembered. His father had fancied a rather large military embossed brass button ahead of the tiny original pieces. Sam never let on he knew, but the big button was easier for the senior Ciampiano to move with his gnarled fingers – some of which had never been properly set when broken against the forehead of a man who had the temporary good fortune of having ducked just right. Sam himself had once played an entire game as a frail safety pin simply because he did not want to be the shoe. The memory struck him as comical now that he was living in the world's biggest shoe, just north of the heel.

Thoughts of the board, the pieces, and the playing of the game reminded Sam of his life in a way he figured few others who ever shot the dice considered. He was a reflection of the game board – a little battered and worn, frayed at the edges – and also felt as if a few pieces were missing. One piece was a substantial part of his heart he was coming to understand might never be found again.

While he wasn't stuck on Mediterranean Avenue without chick nor child and caught at the mercy of another player steeped in green and red plastic houses and hotels, he had crossed the literal Mediterranean, though he didn't recall collecting two hundred dollars as he passed Gibraltar. His Mediterranean Avenue had been the final maritime leg of a cramped and harried exit from Tampa and had, over the course of two months, discreetly deposited him in this coastal town within the Province of Bari.

Sam didn't know where the next roll of the dice might land him, but for now he worked, rested, and willed himself to enjoy his freedom in a simple unassuming way. The past and the future churned behind his eyes, the scruff of a light beard, and beneath a short billed, dark blue fisherman's cap as he sat on the steps of a five hundred year old stone fort in Monopoli, Italy.

He looked out across the cobalt water of the Adriatic Sea to the east. King Charles the 5th – Emperor of Rome and the King of Spain, Italy, and most of the known and New World – had the fort built in the 16th Century. It had been long abandoned as a parapet of defense for Monopoli and the centuries had seen the massive structure assume a myriad of services, including a historically brief return to its military origins during World War Two. A plain smooth concrete machine gun bunker stood nearby in stark contrast to the fort's ancient carved blocks of stone. The fort would no doubt remain long after the elements had washed the concrete and steel bunker into the depths of the sea.

For now, the fort and its heavy bolted doors were still and the only witnesses as Sam tied countless three inch fishing hooks to their thick leaders for the next day. He would be out on the water well before first light catching the local cash crop. The fish would be traded for a few Euros to the cooks who would be waiting along the shore when he and a dozen others like him, in small brightly painted wooden boats of blue and orange and red, came in. Much like his time spent selling newspapers back in the States, this job required an early riser. And also like the newsstand, he'd often sell out early if the catch or the headlines were right and garnered enough attention. Regardless of his haul, Sam saved the best fish for the *Osteria Perricci*.

Perricci's Café was on a street barely eight feet wide. It was more sidewalk than street, but it had a street's name, *Via Orazio*. The restaurant made up twenty-five feet of the first floor of a row house that had no obvious end and filled the block three or four stories high in a haphazard fashion that resembled an unsquared deck of cards. Construction of the houses through the centuries slapped the face of any building code. It was that way through the whole of what locals called Old Town – the aged coastal neighborhood that surrounded the small single-handed fishing fleet, the fort of Charles the 5th, and the oldest of the churches. If and when any city inspector came around looking for building violations they were sent away with their boxes checked and their stomachs full. If they came by too often, they went away hungry, but with boxes still checked, usually by fingers still swollen inside splints meant to keep the pinky immobilized until it could heal from being crudely disjointed. The same applied to the health *ispettore* who presumably oversaw the cleanliness, fit, and output of the kitchen heart of the café which would cook Sam's catch. For an inspector sighted in on *Osteria Perricci*, a trip to *Via Orazio* was brief and he seldom passed within the shadow of the café's deep maroon double doors. As soon as any resident saw him, they were on him like gulls buzzing baitfish, screeching a threatening alarm as if his presence was a personal affront to their sensibility. Everyone in Old Town Monopoli ate at *Perricci's* from time to time, as they did a myriad of other local, innocuous, nearly invisible eateries, and to suggest the quality or cleanliness was less than *primo*, even by the *ispettore's* mere presence, was a poor reflection of the neighborhood and the decency of *Via Orazio's* residents. It simply would not be tolerated.

Sam heard and saw these attacks – and attacks is what they were – from the one foot wide iron railed balcony of his single room, two floors above the *Osteria Perricci* kitchen. Mr. and Mrs. Perricci, the owners and only waitress and sole cook, were pleased to offer the finest and freshest *pesci*, complements of Sam's morning constitutionals into the Adriatic, to their usual guests in exchange for Sam's room and board. Some months before, Sam had passed beneath the iron balcony escorted by the Perricci's oldest son, fifty year old Antonia Jr. On that first day, the men had hurried by Junior's daughter, Palma Isabella, as she swept unseen dust away from the front of the café. Palma, named for her grandmother, was in her early twenties and the picture of Italian beauty with dark hair hanging long and loose like a frame of raven walnut around dark but glistening bright eyes and a smile that shattered mirrors for their inadequacy at reflecting perfect angles of grace.

The man with Junior Perricci was handsome with a profile chiseled from granite. Isabella could see his muscles ripple even beneath an oversized shirt as he walked with the balance of a dancer. Over his broad shoulders was a large black canvas zippered bag. Her father's hands were empty and he motioned quickly to Sam as they walked by and into the restaurant.

"*Zio*," Junior said to his daughter. "Uncle."

Sam scarcely looked up at the beautiful, innocent dark eyes that looked for his. As Isabella brushed the mane away from her face and smiled politely, she thought it curious to see an American in her father's company.

Zio. That was enough for now. To Isabella, uncles came and went from the small room upstairs every year or so. None stayed long and each disappeared unnoticed. She treated them graciously, but would never ask anything further about them. The uncles never offered more than a courteous good day or thank you. If any, young or old, had thought anything of her as she became a woman, it was fleeting and unannounced. To do otherwise would have been foolhardy at best for men on the run and deadly at worst for offending their protectors.

Junior kissed his mother and introduced Sam with a wave of his hand, but no name. "This is a friend of ours."

Palma smiled and nodded. As her husband stepped from the kitchen the wordless scene repeated itself, but this time Isabella was the door. Her grandfather nodded at his introduction and asked Sam in Italian if he spoke the language.

"*Un po'*, a little," Sam said respectfully as he saw his father in the old man's face and mannerisms.

Antonello Sr. nodded again and motioned Sam towards him. He offered to take his guest's bag but felt the heft and thought better of it. Instead he led the way to the stairs which led up from the kitchen. Junior and Sam followed. Isabella followed them all with her dark eyes before she drifted back to her broom in the street.

Upstairs in the small room the three men talked briefly. Junior translated what he could, but his English was no good and Sam's Italian was leaving many gaps. After three minutes of frustration, but before any misunderstandings, Junior stepped out on the tiny iron balcony and yelled to his daughter.

"Isabella! Come quickly! *Vieni! In fretta! In fretta!*" and he clapped his hands as though it would make her faster.

As it was she was at the door to the upstairs room before another attempt was made in either language.

"You are a guest of my family, Mr. Ciampiano," Junior began again with Isabella translating close behind. Her English was unpracticed, but sound.

Antonia Sr. perked up. "Ciampiano? He is Italian? Where is his family from?"

Isabella translated.

"*Mio padre*. South of Palermo. Ficuzza," Sam said in broken Italian.

"Sicilian? Always the Sicilians," Antonia said as he shook his head.

"His friends are our friends in Ficuzza," Junior said, waving off Isabella's translation. "Mother's town. We have an obligation."

"*Certo*. Of course. But American. Why American?"

"The favor comes to Ficuzza from America, Papa. Don T."

Isabella translated on her own something Sam had known from the moment he stepped unseen through the back door of The Columbia Restaurant in Ybor City.

Sam had slipped into the vast wine cellar beneath the restaurant unnoticed and waited. He knew the maître d', a long-time fixture at the restaurant and aged friend of his father, would soon be down to select wine for a diner as he did so often with equal parts care and regularity. It was only a few minutes before Sam heard the cellar door open and the humming of the maître d' as he descended the steps.

"Mr. Guzimon?" Sam called gently, not wanting to alarm the old man. "It's Sam Ciampiano."

"*Il Piccolo Martello!* The Little Hammer! Ah! Your father – such a man!" He stopped short. "Why are you down here? Do you need wine?"

"*Grazie, no.* I need to speak to Don T."

"Ah." The maître d', a small man made smaller and almost frail by age, hesitated only a beat. "Yes. Yes. Of course. *Un minuto.*"

Sam stopped the old man as he turned to go. "You haven't selected your wine."

"They can wait."

In a small back dining room of the sprawling restaurant, Mr. Guzimon spoke discreetly in a big man's ear. He in turn whispered to the head of a small table of men enjoying a light lunch appetizer of Spanish Bean soup. When the head of the table heard the message he set his spoon down gently and wiped his mouth with his cloth napkin.

"Excuse me a moment," the Don said as he laid his hand on the shoulder of the man seated at his right. "Come with me," he said in a low voice as he stood and left the rest of the men to their soup as they questioned each other with only their eyes.

Without a word, Sam exchanged warm hugs with the Don when the pair from the back room descended the stairs and met him in the cellar.

"*Martelletto*, what do you need?"

"I have to get out of the city – the country. Can you help me?"

The old men looked at one another for a moment before returning to Sam with tighter eyes. The one from the right hand began to ask. "What has happen–"

"No," his boss said firmly. "Go. Send me Guzimon."

When the man cleared the top of the stairs, the head of the table put his big hands on Sam's broad shoulders, squeezed, then patted Sam's hard face. "You are a good man, *Martelletto*. Your father was a good man. I know you come here with respect and in great need. Why is not so important."

"*Grazie*, Don T."

"This is a great country, Sammy. To leave it is a big thing."

"It is impor–"

"Shhh. Not a word – to me or anyone. I will learn soon enough. You know the ways of the street. Guzimon will take you to a safe place. Some time, later maybe, he will come and take you to the port." The Don looked at the palms of his own hands and held them out as if for inspection. "These hands will... Arrangements will be made. Passage. It will not be comfortable, but you will be safe. When you arrive, do exactly as my emissaries request."

"You know I will."

"I do know. I do. When I have learned enough and know it to be safe, I will send a word for you."

"It may never be safe, Don T."

"I understand. But you will be safe, *Martelletto*."

"*Grazie*. I'm sorry to come like–"

"Nonsense. If you had gone anywhere else, I would be offended."

Sam wanted to say that he was so grateful and could never repay the kindness, understanding, effort, and risk, but he also knew that it didn't need saying. Don T beat him to it and released him of the burden.

"Your father paid this fare for you many times over. This is my payment in return and still I am indebted."

Mr. Guzimon was coming down the stairs.

"Take him through the old tunnel," the Don directed. "Bring him food. Pack a healthy bag with cheeses and breads that will keep. See to it he has wine. And books. Find me good books."

"Yes, my Don."

"It is a long trip, *Martelletto*."

"Don T, I have to ask. There is a black bag hidden inside the couch at my father's house. I could use it."

"Your house may have many eyes on it."

"I'm sure of it. Mr. Abreu, my neighbor. He could get in."

"I know him," Mr. Guzimon said.

"See if he will do me this favor," Don T said.

Mr. Guzimon nodded.

"Goodbye for now, my Little Hammer," the Don whispered. "We will see each other again."

Sam hugged his benefactor and was rewarded with a kiss on both cheeks and a wad of cash, all Don T had in his pockets.

Sam looked at the money and eased it back. "If I can get the bag from my house, I will be okay."

"We will get the bag, but this is walking around money to keep your pocket warm." Without waiting for an argument that respect would not permit, Don T directed Guzimon. "Take him."

Guzimon touched Sam's arm. "This way, *Martelletto*," and the pair disappeared in the maze of the wine cellar.

In the oldest portion of the basement, beyond the current aging wine, was a small storeroom that appeared as discarded as its contents. The light switch was an antique black Bakelite knob that connected fabric covered frayed wires that ran up the wall and passed in ceramic tubes through the ceiling joists. A single dirty bulb, held up by cobwebs as much as ancient wire, hung in the center of the room. The bulb glowed to life. Dust covered wooden wine crates, some still showing wisps of dry rotted straw packing, were strewn and stacked about. The odd indistinguishable kitchen apparatus, unused for decades and as lost as its original purpose, completed the cluttered room.

Sam followed Mr. Guzimon to the far wall and watched him open a tiny door that was nearly invisible before it was disturbed from beneath its coat of dust. The maître d' looked at the size of the door and the size of his charge. Sam was thinking the same thing.

"It gets bigger inside," Mr. Guzimon said as he tugged the door open.

Inside was another black knob light switch similar to the vintage one in the storeroom. It was turned with a loud click and several lights came to life and showed a musty narrow corridor built of brick with a low vaulted ceiling. The passageway was about five feet high, three feet wide, and looked to be at least eighty feet long.

"It will take you beneath the street." The maître d' clasped his hands as though to pray. "Ah. In the old days it was used to move coffee beans from the roaster to the café. They kept the roaster across the street for fear of burning down the café. They nearly did so, many, many times." The old man waved his hand at the tunnel as if blessing it. "Sometimes," he smiled. "Sometimes other things passed through the tunnel."

Sam smiled in return and put his hand on Mr. Guzimon's shoulder before ducking through the door.

"Thank you, Mr. Guzimon."

"There is a room at the far end. We will bring you up through whichever building is most clear. I will be back with something to eat and wine after I see to Mr. Abreu."

Sam hustled through the tunnel to the sound of Mr. Guzimon closing the small door behind him. At the opposite end, as he'd been told, was a small room with a dusty desk, but a bed that appeared fresh. He walked the small room then sat down. His eyes scanned for anything useful then settled into the palms of his hands to reflect on the last several hours and to wait on the protective, guiding hands of others. Don T and Mr. Guzimon were vital and his safety and escape rested on them alone now, but number one on the short list in his head was a petite brunette looking at him over the counter of his father's newsstand from beneath a wide brim floppy hat and shrouded in huge cheap sunglasses that nearly covered her face.

"Sam," Karen said, not at all like a question and without looking up from the newspapers she absently flirted with in her hands.

The voice brought him away from his book more than his name. He looked across the counter at the sunglass-cloaked face that was ignoring him.

"Karen?" he said with equal parts disbelief and surprise.

It was a question that wasn't seeking an answer. Sam knew the woman behind the lame disguise was his recently burnt out flame, Lieutenant Karen Auburn. That was a given. If there had been room for a follow-up question, it would have circled around why she was in Tampa at his newsstand and not at her JAG desk in Washington.

Karen didn't look up, but knew what to say to shock Sam's focus away from her sudden appearance to her true purpose. "You're being watched."

"What?" he said smiling though his eyes instinctively scanned every inch of the street, the cars, and began darting along rows of windows several stories up in the buildings across the street.

"You heard me. Maybe not yet. Or maybe they're here already. I don't know. But listen to me. They're coming. I don't know when or how, but they're coming."

"Who's coming?"

"FBI. Military. Probably CIA. Local PD. The Bureau has the intel, so they'll be running it. If it plays out like I think, this bitch named Nuary is hot footing it for Tampa right now. She could have called ahead and might have for surveillance, but she'll want to be here for the arrest. You've got to get out of–"

"What are you talking about?" Sam muttered, though the softness of the question revealed a measure of recognition. His eyes ignored Karen's fumbling through the newspapers and looked again to the cars and windows across the busy street.

"I know, Sam," she said as she looked up at him for the first time. For some reason, perhaps uninhibited now as unseen watchers closed in or to demonstrate the urgency of what she was saying and also the sharp and bleeding point of the accusation, Karen tore off her sunglasses and leaned toward him until her face filled his eyes. "The driver rolled into the driveway and you moved him back to the wall. That wasn't released, but you know it happened, you were there. It was you."

Karen had just described the scene outside the Mayor of San Francisco's mansion following Sam's assault on behalf of the New Illuminati. The mayor's sins had found him and he would never walk normal again, but now, somehow, for the first time in his life, Sam was caught. This wasn't a test by Special Operations Command to see if he'd crack or turn on the mission. This was Karen. A JAG officer yes, but his Karen, his one-time lover and the girl who still inhabited his dreams. She had been a smile in a hard life nearly void of laughter and now she was pointing an accusing finger directly at him.

He recoiled slightly as his mind raced ahead. "I don't know what you're—"

"Goddamn it, Sam! Blackbird. Blackbird! The FBI brought me in on some computer manipulations and the assaults in San Francisco and then here in Tampa. Christ, Sam – Tampa? Really? Tampa?"

"You're—"

"I'm right, that's what I am, and you know it. And my guess is you have a few minutes to a few hours to get out of here before an FBI SWAT team drives a tank over these newspapers." Karen brushed at the papers and sent a couple off the counter inside to the floor on Sam's feet. He knelt for them, straightened them, and put them back on the counter.

He was as compelled to deny as she was to convince. Both showed cards they'd have played with no one else.

"I'm lost, Karen. I haven't talked to you in months and you show up ranting about things I know nothing—"

"Stop it!" She checked herself and looked around as she fumbled over a newspaper with a hand that was trembling uncontrollably. "Sam... Please..."

"Karen. I don't know what you're talking about."

She couldn't hold the ruse. With her sunglasses gone – flung aside among the papers – Sam watched her eyes fill and the tears easily overwhelm the berm and pour down her cheeks.

"They had us run a scan of anyone mustered out with your... your background. There aren't many, Sam. And only one in Tampa. And they think it started here. TNI. The Illuminati thing. The local District Attorney and the regional FBI are all over it. I got the report first, but they'll have it by now. Sam, please. I know. And they'll know. They're coming. You have to run. Please."

"From what?" he smiled, which infuriated her. "I haven't done anything."

"You sonofabitch, Sam Ciampiano. You stupid sonofabitch."

"Karen, I appreciate you trying to do something here, but I didn't do anything."

"You didn't go to San Francisco?"

"Never."

"The Senator in Tampa? Five blocks from here?"

"I read about it in the papers," he said as he motioned to his wares on the counter.

"They'll pick you up."

"They can't prove a thing."

"They don't have to."

This froze him. "What do you mean?"

"They'll see what I see. The pieces fit. What doesn't, they'll make fit. Every politician across the country wants someone's head for this. They don't even care about a trial. They're seeing the boogeyman behind every tree. They'll make an example of you. They'll kill you, Sam." The tears came in waves as Karen's lower lip quivered and her shoulders began to lurch in her crying. "You'll never get out, Sam. They need it closed and you'll be the fall guy. It won't matter if they get anybody else. You're their headline. You'll be their Oswald. Their patsy."

Sam looked around. If someone was watching, Karen's disguise was long melted under her tears. He tore a paper towel from the roll at the end of the counter and pressed it into her hands. It was the first time they had touched in months. Sam put his hand over hers and steadied it down into the papers. He felt the concern in her hands masked by the trembling. "Hey. Hey. They have nothing. Come on, Karen. Thank you. Thank you so much, but they have nothing. I'm okay."

She wiped her eyes, blew her nose, crushed the paper towel harshly and threw it harmlessly into Sam's chest. She snatched the cheap sunglasses from the papers and adjusted them to cover her red eyes. "You're not okay. On your best day, you're not okay. You lost your dream. I was there, remember? I saw it." The sunglasses couldn't keep up with the tears and she tore them off again to wipe at her eyes with her bare hands. "Now you're into this other thing with God knows who else–"

"You're getting hysterical, Karen," Sam said as he tore another towel off the dispenser.

She ripped it out of his hand before he could hand it to her leaving him holding a torn corner.

"They saw you Sam! The mayor, the driver, the bodyguard. Remember the cop at the door of the bathroom when you punched the Senator in the face? You walked right into him. Even the Senator will say she saw you. She'll say whatever the Bureau tells her to say to end this."

"No one got punched in that bathroom."

"It doesn't matter, Sam. Don't you get it? It's close enough. They'll find you on surveillance in the airports. Something. All the victims will swear it was you just to try to stop what's started."

"No one got punched in the bathroom," Sam said again as he looked at Karen hard, but she didn't hear him over the sound of rushing tears.

"Do you even know what's happening? Do you read any of these?" she said as her hands collapsed palms up on the newspapers. "Do you read the stories, you jarhead?"

Sam took the abuse. He didn't smile, but offered up a weak defense. "Jarheads are Marines. I was Army."

As before, Karen seemed not to hear. "People are assaulting crooked politicians from county commissioners and mayors to members of Congress. Offices are being firebombed, Sam. Someone's going to get killed. Jesus, don't let it be you. I don't want it to be you. Please go. I'll help. Come with me. Leave now. Please, Sam. Please."

"Karen. Karen? Did you hear me? The Senator wasn't punched."

"I know. I know. She was tied up. I was just talking about the assault. I read the report. She was... never... punched..."

The words fell noiselessly on the worn out counter and were lost in the thousands of printed words on the newspapers. Sam was still looking at Karen as her eyes focused through the tears until she saw her old lover's face clearly. It came together. Somehow she had held out the slimmest hope she'd been wrong — that Sam wasn't involved and he would offer her the air-tight alibi only a JAG attorney could really appreciate. They'd relax and he'd fawn over her for trying to rescue him though he hadn't needed it. They would go to dinner again and fall in love again and would one day look back on her mad dash to Tampa and laugh. It would have all worked itself out and left them smiling and kissing and sweating — collapsing in each other's arms across Sam's bed. But it wouldn't happen. Sam knew the Senator wasn't punched.

"The...," Karen baulked and wiped her cheeks with her hands. "The stories given to the press said—"

"I know," Sam said. "Like at the mayor's house where the guy rolled onto the driveway. Some things get released to the papers, some don't."

Karen swallowed hard, but the lump wouldn't go down. The person in front of her was the most wanted man in the country.

———————

2

Special Agent in Charge of the Tampa Office of the FBI, Calburn Denti, had just answered the phone. The bend of his elbow would leave the only visible crease in his starched and pressed white shirt. The receiver wouldn't disturb his manicured gray hair, but the voice on the line ruffled his last feather.

"Denti," he heard a woman preempt his hello. "This is Alyn Nuary." It was his boss in Atlanta. "Did you get my email? Is there movement? I need eyes on this guy ASAP – as in yesterday. Have you at least got the local PD on site?"

Cal had yet to speak. "Good morning and no to everything you said."

"What do you mean, 'No?'"

"No, as in I haven't seen your email, and probably because I haven't seen it, no to movement, eyes, local PD, everything. What's up?"

"Read your mail, for Christ's sake. This is urgent!"

Alyn Nuary hunched over her tidy desk as though she could get closer to Denti's throat through the phone. She was as neatly coiffed as Cal, but compliments of high end retailers Cal would have ignored. For Alyn, the money was an investment, just as it had been for her augmentation, Botox, and hair styling. Her smile was as phony as her perfect teeth, but to the men who laid her back in exchange for opening doors for her rise up the Bureau ladder, it didn't matter. She was gorgeous, ruthless, and an excellent shot.

Cal clicked to his email and saw the latest arrival. The time of the email was 8:07 am. It was now 8:09.

"Are you kidding, Alyn? Were you dialing when you hit 'Send?'"

"Read! Read! I developed a solid lead on the Illuminati. I need surveillance set up right now!"

"*You* developed a 'solid lead?' Have you been watching CSI again? Where'd this come from?"

There was a pause in which Calburn could hear Nuary sigh. It was not a signal of relief, relaxation, or even exasperation. Rather, it was much more akin to the gathering wind of a storm.

"You know, Denti. You're going to reach for my buttons one day and I swear to you, you'll pull back a bloody stump."

Cal was busy reading her email and ignored the threat that would have easily grown teeth if Nuary didn't need the experience and real investigative smarts of someone like Calburn Denti.

"Ciampiano," he said as he read. "Who's he, how'd he turn up, and what's the connection?"

"Keep reading instead of having me do your work for you."

"Tampa? Tampa is the connection?"

"Do you have something else?"

"I've been working some things with the District Attorney down here."

"And?"

"Not much yet," he lied. "But it's getting legs."

"How come I haven't seen the reports?"

"LaRoy wanted everything to go through him, remember the Washington meet?"

LaRoy was John LaRoy, Nuary's boss and Assistant Director of Criminal Investigation for the FBI. He was old school to the bone and gruff, but a cop's cop.

"I know you and LaRoy go way back," Nuary said. "Dinosaurs usually do, but I'm way ahead of both of you fossils. You told me a while ago that this entire Illuminati business started in Tampa with some nonsense county fiasco. Well, I'm handing you a warm body in Tampa to support your otherwise frivolous conjecture. Are you going to take it?"

"I'll look into your ex-Ranger."

"You'll do more than that. You'll get a set of eyes on him ASAP. His address is in the email. Get someone over there. I'm working up a dossier on this Ciampiano and he's looking better for it every minute. We'll pick him up as soon as I get there. My plane leaves Atlanta in forty minutes. Meet me at the airport."

"You're coming to Tampa behind this?"

"I want to talk to this character."

"Alyn, let's watch him a while. Maybe he'll lead us somewhere. I doubt he has the tech background."

"I don't give a shit what you think, Denti. Get someone on his house. I'll be there in two hours." The phone clicked in Cal's ear.

He didn't hang up the receiver. Instead, he touched the speed dial and heard the phone ringing in Washington, DC, on the desk of John LaRoy.

"LaRoy," answered a voice that did nothing to hide its annoyance at being interrupted.

"John? Cal Denti. Do you have a minute?"

LaRoy's voice changed as if a secret switch had been hit, as indeed it had. LaRoy was coarse with an old sense of humor, but his temperament was easily swayed by experience and credibility. Calburn Denti had both in spades.

"Always, Cal. Whatcha working?"

"The New Illuminati, but I'm not alone."

"You got that right. I've got every cyber-geek in the Bureau working all angles I know to track these boys down."

"How about Alyn Nuary? Did you sic her on anything hot coming in?"

"No, why? Her panties in a wad?"

"She just hung up in my ear."

"That's not news. She must do that, what, once a week?"

"You're right, but today it wasn't before she asked me — check that, told me — to start trailing an ex-Ranger down here named Ciampiano. I was wondering if that name came from you."

"Not mine. Ex-Ranger, huh?"

"Right."

"Remember the uniforms from our Washington meeting?"

"Lieutenant Auburn and Major Caulden. I remember."

"Auburn's JAG and Major Caulden... Caulden reeks of CIA, but you'd never prove it."

"CIA? They're in this?"

"Everybody's in this one, Cal. If this guy's military, the name might have come from them."

"Not without going to you with it first."

LaRoy dawdled and poked through his email. "That's true."

"Nuary would side step you though. I was wondering where she got the name and what was behind it before I jumped through any hoops."

"She is your boss, Cal," LaRoy said as he saw an email from his forensic unit.

"She's incompetent, John," Cal said without his voice rising a note.

"She's good at politicking and shaking her ass in front of the right dicks," John said as he flipped through the attachments from the forensic unit.

"That's quite a way to refer to your direct reports."

"Just an observation. Nothing personal. Hold it," LaRoy came up short. "Here's your Ranger. He's on a list of former military we've been pulling together. The only ones who got this list are me and Karen Auburn at JAG. She must have sent it on to Nuary."

"I don't know, John. I got the impression Lieutenant Auburn wouldn't do something like that without talking to you."

"Maybe it's a girl thing. Her and Nuary."

"Auburn's not a girl. She's a Lieutenant. Never happen."

"You're right and I knew that before I said it. That damn Nuary gets me thinking sideways for all her bullshit."

"This doesn't sound good."

"Oh, don't worry, Cal, I'm not going around the bend. That high dollar call girl has been a burr under my saddle since the day they promoted her."

"Not Nuary. This Ciampiano thing. If only you and the Lieutenant received the package, how'd Nuary get that name?"

Cal let the silence fill the gap. He knew what he was suggesting and LaRoy knew it too.

"I've got somebody on my geek squad who's thinking with the little head instead of the big one."

"That'd be my guess, John."

"Dumb sonsabitches. I need a favor, Cal. I need you to roll with this one. Tail this Guinea if that's what Nuary wants. After she plays her hand, I'll circle back and plant my foot in her skinny ass and her dumb ass boyfriend in forensics, as soon as I find out who he is and, trust me on this one, I will find out who he is. Little prick."

"I know you will, John, but I didn't call you to launch an internal investigation. I just wanted to be certain you have what I have."

"Roger that. Thanks."

"Nuary's on her way. She said she'd be here in a couple hours. If this Ciampiano pans out, she'll be calling you to gloat about five minutes after we pick him up."

"That she will. She'll probably call the Director first, maybe even the White House."

Both men laughed, but it was short, tight, and caught in their throats. Regardless of how Nuary got Sam's name, what LaRoy had read in the last few minutes and Cal surmised from the urgency, it was probable Ciampiano was connected to TNI. His background – ample to LaRoy for its simplicity and vagueness – suggested he might be the muscle end of the vigilante group.

"Hey, Cal. How's the DA doing? My buddy, Jack Aaron? Still a crotchety sonofabitch?"

"That he is."

"And still a good cop, I bet."

"He is that."

"Remember your little trip up here on the KC-135?"

"I do."

"And the name I had to pry from Jack's pocket?"

"Clayton Rand. The Tampa tech whiz kid and millionaire."

LaRoy was leafing through a manila folder and looking at all the info that had been collected on Clayton since Jack Aaron had reluctantly dropped the scrap of paper holding his name on John's desk.

"Call the DA. He did a helluva job pulling Rand out of his ass. See if he can find a connection between Rand and this Ciampiano. Give him something to do while you babysit the Ranger for Nuary."

"She won't like people outside of the Bureau on this."

"Screw her. Tell her the DA developed a parallel lead, but keep Rand to yourself for now."

"Don't tell Nuary about Clayton Rand?"

"No. That leak I've got in Forensics? It might run both ways. Let's play it close to the vest. We've been watching Rand since Jack made his little speech and coughed up that name. The geek squad calls it a digital peephole, but they've got nothing so far."

"Which would be exactly what we'd expect."

"Yep," LaRoy muttered as he scribbled a few notes on a yellow notepad. "Sic Aaron on the connection and then go along with Nuary."

"Understood. I'll call you."

"Good. Thanks, Cal."

As he'd done following the click of Nuary's hang-up in his ear, Cal didn't hang up his phone. Strict land lines were a rarity in almost any space, but internal Bureau calls still utilized the nearly antiquated, but reliable and secure hard wired phone lines for office to office calls where possible and practical. Cal touched the release, heard the familiar dial tone, and hit the speed dial for the Tampa DA's office. After a short gauntlet of admin assistants, he heard Jack's voice.

The local District Attorney was the polar opposite of Cal in dress and appearance, but more the same in work ethic and street sense than either was likely to admit. Jack was heavier. Drank and ate too much. Spurned exercise. He lived alone and wore the same crumpled shirt on consecutive days, but always with a tie, generally a different one, which constituted to Jack a change of wardrobe.

"What's the matter, Denti?" Jack snorted. "You want a parking ticket fixed?"

"Not hardly."

"Just pay the fine, you cheap shit. Christ, you government workers are all alike."

"You might want to rephrase that, Mr. DA. You're a government worker. Remember the election?"

"Right. The residents of Florida know they need proper police protection under the law because their local FBI office isn't worth a shit."

"You're a prosecutor, not a policeman."

"I have a gun," Jack continued, highly animated. "Do you have a gun?"

"Yes, and a badge too."

"Oh, I've seen those FBI badges – tiny, scrawny little things. Look like they came out of a Cracker Jack box. I'd be embarrassed to pull that scrap of tin out at a real crime scene. You ever been to a real crime scene, Denti?"

"Did you have ten cups of coffee?"

"No, why? Don't tell me you're buying. I'll have a heart attack."

"Are you done?"

"Not yet. You still getting your wife's anniversary present at yard sales?"

"How about now? Done now?"

"I've got one more for you. You are so cheap–"

"Save it. I've got something for you."

"What do you have to say, smart guy? Give it your best shot, G-man, but it better be good. You suck at snappy comebacks. What do they say? Don't mess with dragons, or let sleeping dragons sleep, or something like that," Jack said as he geared up for what he presumed to be an unusual retort from his foil.

Cal shook his head and couldn't suppress a smile. "What?"

"You want to trade insults? I'm just saying I'm the sleeping dragon and you're out of your league."

"Wow. How does Marcus maintain his sanity? Don't meddle in the affairs of dragons, and let sleeping dogs lie. Neither of which apply. Can we move on here? I owe you and I'm paying up."

"How?"

"You gave my boss a name – Clayton Rand. He wants to reciprocate."

"I thought your boss was some leggy bitch in Hot-lanta."

"That's true. I meant John LaRoy in DC. Remember when you cried all the way to Andrews Air Force Base strapped in the KC-135?"

"Oh... Good one. You're getting quicker. I'm proud of you. At least I didn't wet my pants like you did."

Cal ignored him. "We've got a name for you now. His background fits the muscle end of the Illuminati and here's the kicker – he lives in Tampa."

All the humor in Jack's voice vanished. From the onset he had reasoned that The New Illuminati had been born and cut its teeth in Tampa. They, with Clayton Rand playing a major tech role, had diced up hometown politicos as an act of local patriotism. Only later did they graduate to the national stage and even then they came home when the latest assault on a sitting US Senator happened six blocks from Jack's office. He had always believed The New Illuminati had started here with Rand. Now the FBI was saying it had another likely player and he lived in Tampa as well.

Jack was sitting ramrod straight. He hunched up and over his cluttered desk, head down, pen in hand over a hastily snatched transcript of a Grand Jury proceeding that was flipped to its blank back so quickly it tore. Jack's feet were tight under his chair – staggered as if they were in a pair of starting blocks at the beginning of a race. The name Cal Denti would say next would be the echo of the starter's pistol.

Runners take your mark. "He got a name?" Jack asked as his pen touched the paper.

"Sure does." Set... "Sam Ciampiano." Go!

3

Sam was settled in the hidden room beneath the few streets and old cigar factories that comprised the neighborhood known as Ybor City. The maître d' had long ago supplied him with an ample dinner, assorted books, and a duffle bag filled with wine, cheeses, bread, and crackers. He lay back on the single bed. His eyes blinked and focused on the ceiling as though the scenes in his head were being projected there. His old high school friend, Clayton Rand, was leaning on the worn out counter of the newspaper stand. The conversation replayed and Sam saw the unspoken words in Clayton's eyes again, just as he had on the first days. Karen skated across the ceiling screen – first as she was on the day he had chased her up the street and frightened her nearly to death. The next pictures were of her visits to Tampa. Behind her were the sand and sun of the Gulf of Mexico. Then the sun set quickly on the imagined screen on the ceiling. Sam thought for only a moment about the mayor in San Francisco and the senator in the ladies room. He heard again the crunch as the mayor's knees broke followed by a pitiful moan uttered through the gray duct tape that was preventing Sam's target from screaming like a man on fire. For an instant, Sam could smell the urine that puddled around the Senator's expensive shoes as she collapsed under the compression of Sam's chokehold. Then Karen reappeared with frantic eyes that held pieces of a puzzle that were the New Illuminati. Sam's own eyes drifted closed.

On the street above his head Mr. Abreu was at the threshold of the rear delivery entrance of The Columbia. A huge battered suitcase, held together with a frayed sun-bleached piece of clothesline rested behind him in a rusted grocery cart which seemed to be giving up under the weight of its consignment. Mr. Guzimon answered a hasty knock and without a word, each man took an end of the suitcase and wrestled it free from the cart.

"Ah, how did you manage this?" the maître d' asked.

"She's a might stout, I grant you," Sam's elderly neighbor said with authority. "But so ain't I when it comes to young Ciampiano."

The suitcase and both old men stepped into the restaurant and immediately headed down to the wine cellar. They stopped to rest midway on the steps.

"I ain't asking nothing, see?" Mr. Abreu said between trying to catch his breath. "But they's a copper minding the boy's house. I seen him up the street — sticks out in our neighborhood like a priest collar in a whorehouse."

Guzimon smiled, still breathing hard himself. "Copper. I've not heard that term in a great number of years."

Mr. Abreu waved his hand and fought for another breath. "Picked it up in New York, I think. Maybe Chicago. Too many years ago. Police wore cheap badges made of copper. Punks... Punks these days don't even know where 'cops' comes from. It was the old timers back in the Apple and Chi-town."

The maître d' nodded and straightened himself. "Ready for another go?"

The answer was Mr. Abreu's coarse hands grabbing his end of the ancient suitcase. Throughout the remaining struggle down the steps and through the wine cellar they didn't speak though they did stop to rest. When they came to the anteroom to the tunnel they sat the bundle down for good. Mr. Abreu said nothing as Guzimon opened the small door with no hesitation for what he was revealing. When he clicked the antique Bakelite switch, Mr. Abreu leaned over the suitcase and looked down the throat of the dusty tunnel.

"I didn't know she was still open. I figured the street department or the trolley car had caved her in by now."

"Sound as a dollar," the maître d' said as he patted the curved laid-up rounded brick wall then brushed his hands together to erase the dust.

At the opposite end of the tunnel in the hidden room, a small red light behind a rusty wire cage came to life along with the tunnel lights. The red light shut down the mental projection Sam had been replaying and he swung his feet off the bed.

Mr. Abreu and the maître d' heard the hinges on the far door moan as Sam opened the door and peered down the tunnel.

"Your fine neighbor has brought you a parcel. Perhaps you might lend a hand."

By the time Sam had hustled the length of the tight passage, the two older men were knelt over the suitcase tugging the knots of the clothesline apart. Sam stood up from the tunnel just as the big suitcase was opened. Inside was a thick black canvas bag. The straps were triple sewn and heavy – meant for weight and abuse. Sam put a big hand on Mr. Abreu's shoulder.

"Thank–"

"Hush up," Abreu said as he brushed Sam's hand away. "Don't go soft on me." He pointed down at the big bag. "Had a helluva time lugging that bitch outa your couch. That was a smart spot. Took me a few minutes to cipher on how to fish it out. I got your couch all buttoned up tight again. They won't know nothing was ever there."

Sam nodded. He knew no one had looked in the bag and neither man would ask, but the questions in their eyes were unavoidable.

As Sam leaned over and hefted the heavy bag with one thick arm, the maître d' moved the conversation away from the delivery. "Mr. Abreu tells me there are police on your street. Just watching."

Sam's neighbor winked. "I give 'em the slip."

"There will be more coming," Sam said as though asking for forgiveness.

"Hell with them. They're dumber than a box of rocks," the old man said as he retied his empty suitcase. "All the same, I best be getting on back. I'll keep an eye out. You take care, young Sam."

Mr. Abreu slapped Sam on the shoulder and turned to go, but was stopped by Sam's outstretched hand. The old neighbor who had seen the tough little boy grow into a man sat the mangled suitcase down and took Sam's hand so slowly the maître d' thought Abreu's arm was injured. Mr. Abreu and Sam shook hands and nodded their respect. There was no goodbye.

Before Mr. Abreu had started back up the alley behind The Columbia with his forlorn grocery cart, Mr. Guzimon was guiding Sam and his black bag back into the tunnel. "I'll be down promptly at three am through the other side. The door is bolted from the inside. Open it for no one save myself."

"*Grazie.*"

"Ah. Is there anything further you will require?"

Sam tapped the bag in front of him as he hunched over with it enough to pass through the undersized door. "I'm all set."

"Very well. At three then."

Sam scurried along the tunnel holding the bag. When he passed back into the hidden room the lights went out in the tunnel behind him.

The black bag came to rest on the small bed and Sam tugged on its heavy zipper. Inside was the weight that had caused Mr. Abreu such trouble. Cocooned in soft padded cases were two rifles, a shotgun, and two pistols, along with several smaller black or desert tan pouches. Each weapon was spotless beneath its lightly oiled cloak and would have passed for new to anyone other than Sam. He knew each to have been fired so often as to be perfectly broken in and as balanced and comfortable as an extension of his hands. As the wrapped bundles slipped from the black bag they were laid out on the bed with the care and gentleness of a priest arranging the sacraments.

While he needn't have checked the firearms – knowing unmistakably how they were prepared and stored – recent events drove up his already hyper-vigilance and he began undoing the protective cases. The first rifle unfolded from its case as if it were being born.

At first there was just the hint of a sand colored polymer shoulder stock with several adjustable elements as a long rifle was eased from its pouch. The stock and grip wrapped around a heavy but simple bolt action receiver. Above the bolt was a matched scope – long with thick mounting rings holding it so tight it was essentially permanently affixed to the top of the rifle. The gun was a sniper's dream – an American made Remington customized into an M24 military 300 magnum long range killer machine. It would have felt bulky in a lesser grip, but with its heft came painstaking accuracy at a thousand yards if the wind cooperated.

The other long guns had features that suited scenarios other than what the M24 provided. The pistols had their own pluses and minuses – trading off distance and accuracy to the rifles for their ability to be concealed.

Pawing through the bag Sam found smaller cases that held laser sites, suppressors, several fully loaded magazines, and other add-ons for the firearms. He also let his fingers run over almost countless boxes of the assorted ammunition for all the guns. The ammo easily doubled the weight of Mr. Abreu's struggle, but Sam left it all in the bag. With little effort, Sam found the last bag he was after.

It was a desert tan camo rucksack. When the heavy black canvas bag gave it up, Sam turned and sat on the edge of the bed next to his collection. He opened the main zipper pouch and pulled the bag open. Inside were tightly wrapped bundles of currency. Cellophane packages of hundred dollar bills – five thousand dollars in each half inch stack – came out and landed on the bed. Then came a few packs of twenties along with short bundles of Euros. The foreign money, wrapped like the Benjamin Franklins, spilled across the cot in colorful contrast to the predominantly bland green and grey of the US paper money.

The last things in the pack were identification. He flipped through his blue coated US passport. For all the countries he had visited with Delta Force, it had no stamps. Wherever he was headed at three AM, likely the passport would no longer be a saving grace document so many millions saw when they held their own. For Sam, the booklet was a ticket back to the United States – something, if Karen was right and he knew she was, would mean a lengthy prison stay or worse. It would have to go. For now he slipped it in his back pocket.

A thick manila envelope yielded a few forms of ID with his picture and over different names. One of these had paved the way to San Francisco and his rendezvous with the mayor. These, as well as some of the money, had come from his father. Neither Ciampiano had been much for banks. Sam Sr. out of necessity and Junior out of learned reflection.

"You never know," he heard the senior Ciampiano echo as Sam looked at two driver's licenses, one from Florida and another from New York. Each had his picture, but another name.

"Yep," Sam answered. "You never know." These he would keep. For now anyway.

The money and the IDs were returned to the rucksack minus a partial stack of hundreds that wrapped itself around the cash Don T had pressed in his hand. Sam stood up, checked the loaded magazine of a Heckler & Koch .45 caliber pistol, racked a round into the chamber, and stuffed it in his waistband at the small of his back. A second loaded magazine for the big pistol was jammed in a back pocket opposite the passport. Everything else was reinterred in their separate cases and tucked back in the black canvas bag. As he zipped it closed and set it near the door, he thought about his father's house. In all likelihood, he wouldn't see it again. There were pictures there he would have liked to have, especially the baby picture of him and his mother that was always in his father's dresser. He'd miss little else.

As he stretched out on the bed the H & K bit his back. It was eased out and placed on the mattress near his head. On the streets above him, movement was nearing a quiet frenzy as the FBI et al descended on Tampa and launched their search for him. It seemed days ago already, but Karen had hugged him, kissed him, and cried for her loss and his safety behind the lowered flap of the newspaper stand only hours before. By now, she'd be buried in her pell-mell dash north.

At the Virginia border, Karen put the battery back in her cell phone and wished she had somehow gotten a disposable one for Sam. There had been a thousand thoughts and wishes in the last twelve breakneck hours. Few would have made a difference. None would be safe now. Even her own safety was a question.

"What happened to Ciampiano?"

"How'd he avoid the dragnet?"

"Was he tipped off?"

"By who?"

"How?"

"Why?"

"Is the Illuminati operating inside the Bureau?"

Likely, the local agency would be blamed. In fact, hours before – just miles before she crossed the Florida-Georgia line – City of Tampa detectives and local FBI agents had taken up positions to monitor Sam's house and the newsstand. Somewhere in southern Georgia, an airplane going south, carrying FBI Regional Director Alyn Nuary, had passed twenty-eight thousand feet over Karen's speeding northbound car. While Karen ran from the trap, her counterparts were closing in. None of them knew Sam had left the Ciampiano house likely for the last time when he had drifted out at 4:30 AM that morning to open the newsstand. Less than twenty-four hours later a knock at the door of Sam's subterranean hideout would signal his leaving Tampa and the United States as well.

———————

4

C al Denti met his boss, Nuary, at the airport. The pair had dispensed with small talk chatter at least a year earlier when their weekly meetings had degraded to shouts bookended by silence. She had hung up on him with regularity and he had disappointed himself by employing the same playground tactic. Although Alyn was a stunning woman to look at, Cal couldn't stand the sight of her. Through her limited tenure in the Bureau, he had watched her name appear on promotional lists over people far more qualified and deserving. Nuary was the poster child for sleeping your way to the top. Perhaps worse than her ass shaking, she was a Teflon thief who stole good work with impunity and blamed others for failures. Cal had kept hoping her next rung on the ladder would be her last, but it didn't happen. He wasn't shy about his sentiments and toyed with her inexperience which infuriated her. But without people like him Alyn was rudderless so she managed a very uneasy alliance.

This time, she didn't regurgitate rudimentary directions as though she was talking to a rookie fresh from the Academy. When Cal heard this example of leadership via a telephone call or conference he swore she was reading from the Bureau's manual on investigation 101. Nuary scarcely talked at all for most of the trip from Tampa International to downtown. Her fingers and eyes were skating over her cell phone instead. Cal smiled at his apparent good fortune that she was unable to both text and talk, though she did make bumbling nonsensical attempts he dutifully ignored. Between the tones and pings of her phone, she relayed what was happening and what was expected.

"What's the depth of the surveillance?" she asked.

"Depth?"

"Are we following him? How many rings of coverage are around him? How many yards out?"

"We have agents on his house and his business. No sign of him yet."

"He has a business?"

"A newspaper stand."

"I didn't think they existed."

"It's the only one I've ever seen outside of New York City. The District Attorney has some info about Ciampiano. We're going to stop by his office."

"Set up a conference call. It's quicker."

"But not as effective. The DA – Jack Aaron – is old school. He wants to talk."

"Older school than you?"

"Yes. I'm high-tech compared to Jack. You'll love him."

"Jesus. Another dinosaur."

Cal parked in a four story garage attached to the City of Tampa's Government offices and the police station. Gone with the chit-chat were also the courtesies Calburn Denti would have extended to any other woman. Knowing she wouldn't know where to go even had he held a door for her, he entered the building from the third level of the garage ahead of her. On an earlier occasion he had been derided as patronizing for opening a door for her. She was more than capable, she had explained, with the implication her capabilities extended into every other known avenue of the professional world. Cal knew different, but never held another door for her apart from perhaps a dragging foot as he might well have done had Jack Aaron been trailing him shouting obscenities.

Cal nodded to the Tampa Police officer who was working the electronic doors. The young man waved him through the scanner, but pointed to Nuary.

"She's with me," Calburn said.

"May I see some ID, Ma'am?"

Nuary was bothered more by the salutation than the stop.

"This is Agent Nuary," Cal said before he caught himself and thought better of the oversight.

"Thank you, Agent Denti, but I'll still need to see ID, ma'am."

Alyn drove her hand into her purse as her eyes rolled. When her hand disappeared, Cal picked up the slightest adjustment in the young policeman's posture. He turned to the side, presenting a smaller target, and his hand, very casually, almost unnoticeably, came up alongside his big automatic pistol. Nuary didn't notice as she jerked out a sandstone colored ostrich skin wallet and flipped open her shield and identification.

"Will this suffice?" she spit. "You don't have much clout around here, Denti."

"It's not him, ma'am, it's—"

"Director Alyn Nuary. FBI. If it's not too much trouble."

"It's not him, Agent Nuary. It's stan—"

"That's, Director Nuary."

Calburn stepped in and took note of the officer's name on his shirt. "Officer Vireo? Are we cleared?"

The patrolman took Nuary's wallet and examined the ID. "Are you headed to the DA's office, sir?"

"Yes."

Vireo jotted their names down on a crude ledger along with Jack Aaron's and the time. He flipped the fancy badge holder closed and handed it back to Nuary. "Welcome to Tampa, Director Nuary. Please sign my log."

The response was a clip of the wallet from the young man's hand and the turning of her back. "Lead the way, Denti," Nuary continued as she scribble her name on the sign in sheet below Cal's. "Let's get this little meet and greet of yours behind us."

"Thank you, Officer," Denti said as he fell in front of his boss and made for Jack's office.

Cal flicked a finger toward Nuary's purse. "Is that shield holder government issue? It's quite..., oh, I guess, fancy."

"Handmade ostrich. And the word you're struggling for would be 'stylish.'"

"No. I was leaning more toward 'non-regulation.' The Bureau has a historical protocol for–"

"That sounds about right, coming from you. Those long sleeve button-down white shirts would make Mr. Hoover proud."

"Yes it would. We call it 'a tradition of excellence.'"

"I call it archaic."

Calburn reached in an open doorway and knocked. Jack Aaron looked up through, over, and around stacks of case folders.

"Jesus, now that's a first. Did you really just knock? I didn't know it was time for your weekly lesson on how to be a policeman. Maybe this time–"

Cal stepped in under the verbal assault and Nuary followed.

"Jack Aaron," Cal motioned behind him. "Alyn Nuary. Regional Director from Atlanta. And my boss. Try not to embarrass me."

"Shit. If she knows you at all, she knows you can do that all by yourself." Jack stood and shook Nuary's hand very firmly. "Welcome to Tampa, Madame Director. Or do you prefer Agent, Special Agent, Ms. Nuary, what? You call me Jack, deal?"

"My pleasure, Jack. Alyn would be fine."

"Good. Good. Pull up a chair. Have a seat, Cal." Jack hustled around his desk to the door. "I want to get Petey."

"Marcus Pete," Cal said as he tried to keep his boss in the uneven ebb and flow that perpetually surrounded Jack. "The District Attorney's office chief investi–"

"Petey!" Jack bellowed up the hall with the subtlety of an air horn. "Put your pants on! We got company."

"Chief investigator," Cal picked up. "Excellent man. I've been trying to recruit him for years."

Nuary nodded all but unconsciously as she scanned her phone and twiddled her fingers over digital keys. She didn't look up as Jack shuffled back around behind his desk, but talked to him just the same.

"Jack, Denti said you have something more on this Ciampiano. We're not finding a cell phone or a land line to petition in the Pen trap to capture his calls. What is he, off the grid or something?"

Jack leaned all the way across his desk until he was awkwardly looking up at Alyn. He captured her attention and she lowered her phone. "Not quite," Jack said. "He has a house – his father's. Inherited it. His old man's deceased."

"A house, but no phone? Nothing comes back to that address."

"I'll have my boys look into it, but I'd guess the old man worked a deal with somebody in the neighborhood years ago. He probably runs a line from another house."

"What?" Alyn asked, not following.

"It was pretty common back in the day." Jack leaned back in his chair. "A hundred years ago when Cal was still dragging by the hind tit, we did the first serious phone taps in that neighborhood on the old mob. They saw one prosecution and started throwing up wires all over hell's half acre. Probably one of those old lines."

Alyn was stunned. "Dragging from what?"

"The hind–"

"Jack? Jack," Cal short circuited the conversation toward the human resource department. "Can you look into it?"

"Sure. Sure."

The Director was recovering, but had made a mental note, she would return to quickly. "Does he have a wife at home counting quarters from his big business venture?"

"No wife."

"Girlfriend? Drinking buddies in faded fatigues waving Rebel flags?"

"Nope."

"Family local?"

"Not officially."

Nuary hesitated and leaned forward. "How's that, Jack?"

"Not a blood family, at least not blood like most folks think of it."

Nuary looked at Cal for help.

"The father was also Sam Ciampiano," Jack continued as though he hadn't noticed Nuary's confused look and strained patience. "He ran a numbers racket forever out of his newsstand and was muscle for the last of the old-time wise guys."

"A criminal for a father. It's starting to come together."

"Probably not," Cal said. "Our guy was the All-American boy. No record. Joins the Army out of high school when he could have opted for a football scholarship."

"Dumb too. Makes poor choices. That fits the profile," Nuary mumbled.

Cal paused. Jack stopped with his mouth open and finger pointed, but Cal had the comeback.

"Might be that 'tradition of excellence' thing again."

"Hardly," Nuary pissed as she returned to her cell phone.

Jack rocked in his chair and dropped his staged finger into a weave of his hands and rested them in his lap. He took a deep breath that was mostly sigh. "Sounds like you two have had this conversation before."

"A time or two," Cal said, dismissing the disdain. "What can you tell us about Ciampiano?"

"That he's not here."

"Not here? Where here?" Nuary asked as she abandoned her phone again.

Jack pointed to his desk. "Here. Tampa."

"You sound pretty certain, DA."

"Yep."

"Can I ask why so certain?"

Jack's chair leaned him forward. His hands folded again but sat uneven on his piles of folders. He slouched down on them just the same. "Because I've lived in this town for over sixty years and me, or no one else, has ever seen the flap of that newsstand down before one o'clock."

"I take it that the place is closed now? Is that what you're saying?"

"Tight as a drum."

Marcus Pete tapped the door as he walked in. He wore a neat olive green suit with a matching shirt and tie. Marcus was his usual stark contrast to Jack's rumpled shirt and skewed tie beneath a collar that flashed worn threads at the crease alongside his neck.

Jack launched into introductions.. "Petey, this is Director Alyn Nuary of the FB of I. She's Calburn's boss so don't embarrass him.

Alyn, meet Marcus Pete, a decent enough investigator if you don't give him anything too tricky."

"Director," Marcus said as he shook hands with Nuary.

"Investigator Pete."

"How are you, Marcus?" Cal asked.

"Very well. Busy with your Illuminati players."

"His players?" Jack snapped harmlessly. "This was our case before the Feds even knew they had a dick in their ass."

"Jack... C'mon...," Cal said as he reminded him of Alyn with his eyes.

"Oh, yeah. Sorry about that, Alyn. We get going like a bunch of sailors around here–"

"We?" Petey looked for elaboration.

"Don't concern yourself, DA," Nuary blurted. "You think Ciampiano has fled?"

"Not just fled, but spooked. Tipped off maybe."

"How's that?"

"Why else would he close early? Cal says he's an Army Ranger – Special Forces. Probably Delta. He can probably see a trip wire a half mile away in thick brush. Something spooked him."

Nuary made another mental note regarding her underling passing out too much information to the locals.

"If not something, then maybe someone," Cal said and the words hung for a moment.

"Maybe," Marcus said. "We're not sure who, but if this is coming together like we think, it could be that our boy Clayton Rand felt some heat and passed it on."

Though strangled by Botox, Alyn's manicured eyebrows went up as far as they could. "Who's Clayton Rand?"

There was a dance of eyes and rapid change of partners around the room. It fell to Cal as the mediator, but Jack saw the gap and bailed him out.

"Petey here and our geek squad developed a maybe on a guy who looks good for the startup of this nonsense. I took it to the Bureau in Washington for some help in watching him. Nothing concrete yet, but we think he looks real good for it."

Nuary turned noticeably in her seat to Cal. She was hot. "You know about this Rand?"

"I do."

"And you failed to report it to your superiors? That's dereliction."

Jack had heard and seen enough. "It ain't like that, Alyn. I took Rand to Cal in absolute confidence. I needed a wheel in Washington to move on my search warrants."

"We've executed search warrants on this Clayton Rand person?"

"Not exactly," Petey offered. "We needed search warrants for the Pen traps on his cell phone and computer traffic. We've been tracking his electronic intel."

"And?" Nuary said unable and unwilling to conceal her annoyance and growing anger.

"Nothing yet. He's smart."

"Which makes us like him all the more for it," Jack said, continuing to be careful to leave Cal out. "This guy's not making any mistakes."

"Do we have physical eyes on him?" Nuary snipped. "I mean, you've done so well with Ciampiano. We don't even know where he is."

"There's surveillance on his house and office."

"But a guy like this," Petey said. "He moves through the cyber world more than the real world. Our tracking there tells us where he is within a few yards."

"So you have an address I take it?"

"Of course, Alyn," Cal spoke for the first time in several minutes.

Nuary pulled her phone out as if it were a notepad. "I'm ready."

"They're already tracking him," Cal offered.

"Is the address too much to ask?"

"Of course not. It's in one of these files," Jack said as he began rifling.

"The GPS coordinates will do for now. Do you have a recent printout?

"Our geek squad does. I'll get it. We've been watching him, waiting for him to tip his hand."

"Did you say 'geek squad?'"

Jack grinned as he punched a speed dial on his phone. "Just a term of... What is it a term of, Petey?"

"Term of endearment."

"Yep, term of endearment."

"I'm sure they feel that way about it." Nuary looked through Cal. "It's a phrase I've heard before."

Jack was talking to his phone. "Oakes? What's the Global Phasing numbers–"

Petey tried to help. "Global Positioning–"

"GPS. Just GPS," Nuary seemed to warn.

"GPS!" Jack blurted out to the sole member of his very adapt forensic unit, Helfer Oakes, on the other end of the line and one story below. "Hold on." Jack tore a corner off a piece of a page from a folder that had meant something to someone on another day. He grabbed a pen that had the tracks of leaking ink on it. "Go ahead." And Jack began to scribble as Alyn squirmed and grew red faced beneath her makeup. Marcus lowered his head at the repeated spectacle of his boss's peculiar genius. Cal smiled and leaned back comfortably.

"I got that part," Jack was saying. "Twenty-seven point nine, what? Nine. Three. Six. What? Six. Is that one six or two? ...No, I mean one six... What'd you say, Oakes?... Nine, three, six, six... I asked you if it was one six... Not, one, six. One six. Christ. Petey? Take this," Jack said as he held the phone out. The room could hear numbers being recited. Along with the phone Jack pushed the scrap of paper and the leaky pen across the desk. "Jot down the numbers for Alyn, here."

Petey squatted enough to use Jack's desk and scrap of paper. "Hey, Helfer. It's Marcus. Start over, would you please? Just one time. Straight through. I'll read it back."

He did just that and as he read the numbers back, Nuary typed them into her phone. She had a second request. "And would you ask if they have a Protocol Address Verifier set up on Rand?"

"Helfer, do you have a Protocol Address Verifier set up?... He says yes."

"An oasis in the desert. Thank you."

"Thanks, Helfer. Yep." Marcus reached across Jack's desk and hung up the phone. "What's the GPS for? We're tracking him through his cell phone movements."

"Surveillance," Nuary said.

"We have that set up, Alyn," Cal said as he leaned back into the conversation and his smile vanished. This was serious and he knew it. "We've been watching him for a while."

"Aerial surveillance. We've pulled in MacDill Air Force Base and others."

"Drones?"

Jack sat up straight. "The Feds have drones over my city?"

Alyn slipped out a pretentious smile. "High altitude monitoring platform."

"You got any missiles on this high altitude monitoring platform of yours?"

"I'm not at liberty to say."

Jack turned away from Nuary as she stood abruptly and brushed her fitted skirt flat.

"Cal. Help me out here," Jack muttered. "We're watching a couple of deep right wingers here, not the head of Al Qaida. Make sure you don't have some loose cannon with his finger on the switch, will you?"

"The most recent head of Al Qaida is dead," Nuary said. "We killed him. With a drone."

"Well, don't blow Rand's house up until we get a chance to talk to him."

"Talk to him? You say you can't even find my guy. This Rand character is probably gone and you don't even know it."

"We'll find Ciampiano," Cal said. "You just gave us the name this morning. He won't be far."

"Right," Nuary said as she glared at Marcus and Jack. "I gave you Ciampiano. I didn't give him to the locals."

"What?" Marcus said.

"All I've heard so far is how you can't find him. Don't know where he is. He got tipped off. Nothing but excuses."

"He'll make a digital wave somewhere before long," Marcus said as he recovered. "We'll find him. Jack's right about the newsstand. We don't know yet why he closed early, but we'll find out."

"What was that remark about 'the locals?'" Jack quizzed as though genuinely puzzled.

Nuary looked up from her phone. "I alerted TSA before I left Atlanta. All the airports from Miami to Jacksonville are looking for Ciampiano."

"There's how Ciampiano got tipped off," Jack shouted. "For Christ sakes! TSA? Another federal agency run amok. They steal watches for a living!"

"Jack," Cal said. "Go easy."

"Easy? You Feds blow in to town and think you're taking over. Forget about it."

"We're preparing Federal charges," Nuary said. "The warrants are federal. You're trumped."

"Bullshit. I used local warrants on Rand and we're getting search warrants for Ciampiano's place right now."

Alyn held up her phone. "Ah, you and Denti need to step out of the dark ages. I already have them. Right here. Federal ones. Let's go, Denti. We could use your help, Jack – crime scene tape, traffic control – if you want to tag along. But it's my party now."

"Bullshit it is."

"Federal officers are assembling at your office, Denti. SOCOM is standing by at MacDill. We'll have teams hit Ciampiano's house and business by end of day. Forensics will take it from there."

"SOCOM?" Cal said as he stood up. "Special forces don't execute warrants. Does LaRoy know about this?"

"I sent him a text. He'll watch from the sideline until we see what the search warrants yield."

The name sparked Jack, who was demonstratively agitated – a short step from normal for him. "John LaRoy don't strike me as a guy who watches anything from the sideline," he said. "You're wildcatting this, aren't you, Nuary?"

"Oh, you know LaRoy? I thought so."

"We've met."

"I bet you have."

Alyn was up and at the door and Cal was being pulled by an invisible rope. He looked back at Jack and held his pinkie and thumb to his head as a phone and mouthed that he'd call.

"Go have your fun, Agent Nuary," Jack shouted toward the door. "But you can't use Navy Seals as your private SWAT Team. That dog won't hunt. Not even in Washington! LaRoy will put your ass in a wringer and I'll work the crank."

Alyn stopped and spun. Her earrings caught in her hair. "This is a Federal investigation. You're done. Understand? If you need help with the big words I can make it clearer. Pull back. Drop out. Or I'll have you charged with obstruction."

Cal was easing Nuary to the door. "Fight nice, Alyn. Let's go."

Nuary actually pushed Cal away. "You too, Denti. You want to spoon feed the locals and cut me out? I'll transfer you. You'll be scanning mail on the Canadian border. Sonofabitch."

Marcus was stunned. Cal was embarrassed for the agency and moved around Nuary to the door. "I'll call you, Jack."

"Jesus H. Christ. You are something else, Nuary. A goddamn bleached blonde meat grinder, aren't you? You better go back to Atlanta and play cop on your fancy ass phone there. You're not going to like Tampa. It gets hot down here."

"Go fuck yourself, DA."

Alyn ducked out the door. Calburn was some distance up the hall headed for the parking garage. She pulled her cell phone out and began typing. Behind her, Marcus stuck his head out the door then looked over his shoulder back to his boss.

"What was that?"

"That, Petey," Jack said as he leaned way back in his chair and folded his hands behind his head. "That is a rare animal. Exotic really."

"What?"

"Silicone bitchium botoxius."

Marcus laughed out loud, drifted back into Jack's office and sat where Alyn had been. The seat was hot. "I didn't know you were a student of biology, boss."

"These is technical terms, my boy. I don't suppose they make much sense to a person without formal training."

"Oh, I can make out pretty good the genus and species alright."

"You're about to get a whole lot better at it."

"How so?"

"Direct observation of the critter."

"I'll pass."

"And miss out on a valuable training experience? No sir-ee. You're going to jump."

"Jump?"

"Yep. When she calls you."

"You've lost it. She rattled you that bad?"

Jack eased back to his desk. "Not at all. But she might turn you around. Better get ready."

"For what?"

"That phone call."

"No, I don't think her claws are retractable and I like my eyes where they are."

"She doesn't want to get in your pants, Petey. She wants to get in your head. Despite what she said, she wants what we have – the Tampa skinny on Rand and this new character. Ciampiano."

Jack got up and snatched his wrinkled sport coat off an old stained oak coat tree leaving Petey sitting in the warm chair. "Go down and see Oakes. Tell him nothing – and that means nothing, zero, zilch, nada – goes to the Feds without coming outa my mouth. Tell him just like that, hear me?"

"I hear you."

"Thanks, Petey. You the man."

"Where you headed?"

"The Columbia Restaurant."

Petey glanced at his watch and got up. "Are we having an early dinner before the raids?"

"Not this time. You go find Oakes before that FBI whore flashes a little thigh at him and he goes stupid on us."

"And you?"

"I gotta see a fella about a dog."

Calburn was already behind the wheel of his federal car. He started it as Alyn languidly crossed the garage. The engine noise stopped her as she touched a speed dial and stepped away from the car's soft rumble. Cal reached for his own phone and called John LaRoy.

Alyn had Jason Meyer, her lover of convenience and mole in FBI forensic science unit, on the line in more ways than one.

"I already sent you what I have on Ciampiano," Alyn said, being certain she was facing away from Cal. "Add this Rand to the list. Work your magic, darling."

"Your list is growing. I sense a long weekend ahead full of friends with benefits alone time."

"I'm right here for you, baby. Just get me what I want. When I go to the head of the class, you come with me."

"You take the promotions, Alyn. You know what I want."

"I'm all yours. Just get me something on these two. Oh, and add a cocky old fart named Jack Aaron. He's the District Attorney down here. See if he's got any dirt under his fingernails, will you, sweetheart?"

"District Attorney? He's elected. There's dirt."

"Good boy."

"I suppose the results come back to you and not LaRoy?"

"I didn't say that."

"You don't have to. I know you."

"But since you brought it up. It's a lead of mine – nothing to do with the Illuminati case."

"Sure it doesn't. That's the only star you've got your sexy ass wagon hooked to at the moment. And I'm the horse pulling the cart."

"But you're a stud horse, Jason."

"You don't put any shade on it. I'll give you that."

"And you're my stud horse, no one else's. So yes, this intel comes only to me."

"Anything particular?"

"This ex-Ranger. The locals are saying he's pretty much off the grid, but no one is that far off – not living in a city anyway. Can you access the towers for cell traffic and Wi-Fi around his house and his bullshit newspaper shop?"

"Newspaper shop?"

"Can you believe it? I didn't know they still existed outside of New York. I sent you the address."

"That will take a warrant. Patriot Act. Ever hear of it?"

"On its way."

Jesus, how do you get those so easy? Oops! I forget who you are, or rather, what you are."

"Don't go smartass on me, Jason. I've had all the shit I'm going to take today. I'll forward the warrant. You get busy."

"Yes, ma'am."

"You're the second flunky to call me that today. I didn't like it then and I don't like it now."

"Alright. Alright. Christ, Alyn. There must be competition in the shark tank or something. You're pretty worked up."

"Get on it. Check triangulation, or whatever it is you do, between Ciampiano's house and store, and Rand's place and office. See if we can get the two of them together."

"Anything for you, gorgeous. But remember to delete the trail. I don't want John LaRoy knocking on my door."

"Relax. He's another dinosaur on the verge of extinction. He just doesn't know it yet."

"You be sure to tell him that when you see him. I'd like to hear how that goes for you."

"Get busy, Jason. I'll be in touch."

Cal's call with John LaRoy had been briefer.

"I feel like a tattletale in 3rd grade," Cal was saying.

"No need, Cal. Somebody's gotta try and keep her in check. Navy Seals? Did she really say that?"

"She said she was pulling in Special Ops Command out of MacDill."

"She has more balls than most men. And a lot less sense."

"The nonsense and her sex-ploits were funny for a while, but she's crossed the line. She's dangerous. And she's alienating our buddy Jack down here."

"How is the cranky old bastard?"

"Ticked."

"Nuary can do that to a person. You'd know better than most."

"True enough, but we need him. Our Ranger's AWOL. Jack's got good street eyes and knows every nook and cranny of this town. If this is really where all this Illuminati business started, he needs to be involved."

"How'd this Ciampiano go missing already?"

"I don't know yet."

"You got any suggestions?"

"Toss Nuary a red herring. She's got to back off."

"Toss her one? Hell, she's apt to toss me one. However she got that ex-Ranger info tells me she's plugged into a pretty secure stream somewhere. I'll find out, but right now, she's got the advantage."

"Can you at least call off the drones?"

LaRoy was uncharacteristically quiet.

"Oh, shit, John, are you kidding? We've gone that far?"

"There are a number of wheels turning in this town, Cal. And the people turning them are damn nervous. Nervous people make bad decisions. Final ones."

"John. There has to be something. These aren't terrorists."

"Depends on your definition."

"And political affiliation."

"That too, but whoever or whatever they are they've really kicked the hornets' nest this time. We're not talking about Tea Partiers mudslinging with panty-waist liberals, Cal. We've got physical assault of a sitting US Senator, bombings, and a dozen other charges."

"And the threat of a helluva lot more exposure."

"That's a part of it, but it's our job to protect everybody – guilty and innocent."

"Even if the guilty ones are giving the orders and directing drone strikes against their own citizens?"

"Where'd that come from? Have you been sitting in the hot sun with DA? You're starting to sound like him. Nobody said anything about a strike. It's aerial recon. Observation and monitoring – and right now, I'll take all of each I can get."

Cal took a breath. "I'm not getting like Jack. I'm thinking about our Constitution."

"All enemies, foreign and domestic."

"There should be another line."

"How so?"

"Even if they're elected."

"That's a Jack line if I ever heard one."

"Maybe so."

"Look, Cal. I'll see if I can put the brakes on the SOCOM boys, but if she's got the warrants she claims, in addition to screwing a federal judge somewhere, she's screwed your DA buddy Jack pretty well."

"She's on her phone right now. I'd like to know to who."

"Don't let her get to you, Cal. That's her best trick."

"She says we're executing warrants tonight."

"If she's gotten the warrants, I suspect she will."

"I'd rather sit on these guys and try to pick up some tracking patterns and intelligence."

"I'll tell you what I can do. I'll get that Lieutenant from JAG, Lieutenant Auburn, down there. I'll tell Nuary that as this Ciampiano guy is ex-military, JAG needs a presence. Karen's top shelf. She'll keep the gold digger in check."

"Nuary's going to chafe."

"Karen's up to it. At the very least, she's military – use to discipline and chain of command. Anything that bitch does, we'll know about it."

"Okay, John."

"You keeping Aaron in the loop?"

"After I talk him down from ripping Alyn's fake eyelashes off and seeing if she can feel pain beneath the Botox injected into her face."

"I like that. That's funny. You're coming around, Cal. Twenty-first century assault humor."

"Thanks."

"I'll get the Lieutenant headed south. Nuary will execute her warrants. If you get this Ciampiano in custody, he might cop to the whole ball of wax and rolls on Rand. Let forensics do their thing on his house and get back to me. Between forensics and maybe an interview, we'll know if we're barking up the wrong tree."

"That's possible, but my sense is we're getting close. Ciampiano being among the missing adds to it."

"And Jack?"

"He's all in. In fact, I think he's got other cards to play. That's why we need Nuary collared."

"Gotcha. Stay close to him."

"With Nuary around?"

"Let Karen babysit Nuary. You stick with Jack. I remember he was a little wishy-washy on Clayton Rand's name coming out of his pocket and landing on my desk. I haven't forgotten that."

"I remember. But we gave him Ciampiano today. I think we're even and he'll play it straight."

"He's your guy. You know him best. Stay in touch, Cal."

"Sure thing."

"Have you made a pass at Alyn yet?"

"That's not funny."

LaRoy laughed and they both hung up. Nuary was hanging up as well and was at the car. As she slid in she let her skirt ride up a tanning bed's artificially baked bronze thigh. She left her skirt as it was.

Deep coded primal instinct made Cal look at the sexy tease, but he recovered quickly when Alyn smiled at him.

"You're going to wrinkle your skirt, Director," he said as he slipped the car in gear.

Nuary left her thigh exposed. "Try to keep your eyes on the road. Drive."

Cal slammed on the brakes and shoved the car in park as he spun toward Nuary in one motion. "Look, Alyn. Everyone knows your game, but don't play it on me. Why don't you go back to Atlanta and let us run this? You have no idea what you're doing."

Nuary reached over and grabbed Cal's crotch. He was stunned but peeled her hand away instantly and shoved her hard across the seat and away from him.

Alyn tossed her head back and laughed through a veil of her messed up blonde hair. She adjusted her breasts blatantly. "I knew you've been wanting to feel these for years, but not so rough next time."

Cal glanced at her in disbelief. "What is wrong with you?"

She ignored him. "If you grab my pussy, you'd be fired by tomorrow."

"I'll see if I can't reciprocate," Cal said as he tossed the car into gear again and squealed the tires.

"Hardly. You'll get laughed out of town. You know how it goes, Denti. A woman blows a pimple-faced high school football star – the kid's a hero to his buddies and all the old guys wink and say they wish they could have banged that one hot teacher they had. A man plays grab-ass with a senior who's extracurricular activity is pole dancing, but she's a day short of graduating? Now, that guy is a pedophile and goes to prison for ten years. Never works again. Ends up on a barstool somewhere. That'd be you, Denti. Never work again."

"We'll see."

Alyn laughed again. "You going to run to LaRoy? Tell him, 'That bitch Nuary tried to grab my cock!' He'll laugh himself under his desk."

"I don't think so."

"And he'll stay under his desk." Alyn stopped playing and was angry. "You can't touch me and neither can LaRoy. He knows it. I've banged most of Washington. That's the beauty of being a woman, Denti." Alyn relaxed and spoke softly as if relaying a great philosophical revelation to her student. "Sex. You have it. You give it away. And you still have it. It's really amazing when you think about it."

"You need help, Alyn. And someday, someone's not going to find all your bullshit so cute. You're going to get in serious trouble."

The car screeched around the corner out of the garage and sped for the local FBI office.

"Are you threatening me, Agent Dente?"

"I'm trying to help you, but my thought is that you're beyond it."

"Above it, not beyond it."

Cal shook his head and drove. Alyn smiled and finally tugged her skirt back into place.

A few blocks away, Jack smiled at the pretty hostess who met him in the foyer of The Columbia Restaurant. He pointed around her before she could deliver her practice welcome. "Just the bar thanks," he said.

He waved two fingers to his forehead as a lazy salute when he saw the bartender then tapped those same two fingers horizontally on the bar as a measurement. There was no one else saddled up to the heavily carved spotless bar and before he had settled on a comfortable stool with a short back rest, a short smooth glass holding the measured whiskey was coming to rest on a well-tossed coaster.

"Thanks, Jimmy. The boss holding court in back?" Jack took a healthy sip. "Oh, that's good."

"What boss?"

"Don T."

"Don't think I know him."

"Cut the shit. He here or not?"

"Haven't seen him."

"Can you go look again?"

"I'm tending bar here," Jimmy said as he tossed a bar towel over his shoulder and motioned to the obvious.

"That right?" Jack took another drink and looked around at the non-existent afternoon bar crowd. "I think the crush will wait."

"I don't know nothing."

"I know that, Jimmy. You don't know nothing. No one does in this joint. They never do. Everybody knows that. Just wander out back and ask the boss if he has a few minutes. Do it for me."

"He don't like to be bothered."

"He'll like it a lot less when I have to subpoena his payroll records to see how many hours you're working off the books. *Capisci?*"

"Jesus–"

"No, just the Don. Ask him – nicely – if he can spare me a minute. I'll cover for you out here."

Jimmy's departure was languid. The conversation had ended, but he was loath to admit by moving too quickly, that he'd do the prosecutor's bidding. His passage through the swinging kitchen door signaled his retreat, but before the door quieted, the maître d' appeared from around the far side of the bar.

"Hey, Guzimon," Jack said as he saw him. "You old geezer. I figured you'd have retired by now."

"Ah. No retire for me," he said as he walked the length of the bar on the patron's side. Jimmy came back through the swinging doors to his post behind the bar, but stayed well away from Jack and Mr. Guzimon.

"How come? Don T's retirement plan a little too final? Over the years, I've seen people leave here and never be seen again. You know anything about that?"

"Ah, I enjoy the working. What can I do for you, Mr. Aaron?"

"Nothing. You can't do nothing." Jack tossed down the last of his drink and motioned for Jimmy and shoved the empty glass toward the bar back. "I'd like a few minutes with your boss though. He around?"

"I'm afraid not."

"Sorta guessed that'd be the case coming in. What do you call it? *Omerta* or some such damn thing." Jimmy refilled the glass and Jack nodded his thanks and took a healthy sip. "You've been here forever, Guzimon. You remember a fella named Ciampiano?"

"Not that I recall."

"Sure you do. He ran the newsstand a dozen blocks from here for a hundred years. Kept a clean book too. Sound familiar?"

"Ah, sound? I don't hear anything."

Jack pulled down half of what was left in his glass. "Now that's funny, Guzimon."

"I did not attempt to be funny. I'm sorry."

"You don't remember him, huh? It's funny because I saw him at this very bar a thousand times back in the day." Jack was tapping the top of the bar as the whiskey went to work and warmed his stomach.

"Ah, no. I don't remember."

"It's ok," Jack said as he took out his business card and jotted the name 'Ciampiano' on the back. "Maybe you could give this to Don T." Jack left the card on the counter and finished his drink as he stood up. "Ciampiano. See if he hears anything ringing, know what I mean?" A twenty came out of Jack's pocket and took a place next to the business card. "That cover the cocktails, Jimmy?"

Jimmy picked up the money and the card. "Barely."

"Well the service was a little off," Jack smirked as he turned away. The sound of his business card being torn in half brought him back.

Jimmy tossed the pieces of the card on the floor and stuffed the twenty in his pocket.

"You gonna ring those drinks up, Jimmy, or just put the Don's money in your pocket?" Jack bent and picked up the torn card. "I don't think he'd like that, do you, Guzimon?"

"Arrest me," Jimmy spit.

"Never. I'll leave you to the Don," Jack dug. "My guess is you wouldn't be tending bar. You could go to Miami or somewhere. Make a stop in the Everglades and see the gators. Up close. That's a good place to vanish, wouldn't you say, Guzimon?"

"Ah, I don't know such things."

"No, you don't know much, but you know Ciampiano."

"Why say such a thing?"

"Because you didn't want to know who he was or what I was asking about him for. People are curious critters. You mention a name, people just naturally want to know why. But not you."

"Ah, I mind my business."

"But your business is Don T's business. And he knows everybody and everything that happens in this town. He knew old man Ciampiano real good. And so did you. I was born at night, but it wasn't last night. Give me a little credit."

Mr. Guzimon held out his hand for the torn card. "You have been a good customer many years, Mr. Aaron. I will pass on your card."

Jack chuckled. "A good customer. Funny way to put it, but I'll take it." He handed over the pieces and turned to go a second time. "Oh, and be sure to tell the Don how the card got in that shape. I've known him forty years – chased him for at least thirty – and if there's one thing he hates worse than thieving bartenders, its disrespect. Quirky how a guy like him can be that way. Anyway, sleep tight, Jimmy. Thanks for your help, Guzimon."

"Ah. I don't think I helped you."

"Oh, sure you did. See you around."

While Alyn worked her skirt and Jack his contacts, Karen was crossing the Carolina border and wiping bright tears off her cheeks. She had cried several times since she left Sam and for several different reasons. Mostly she cried for what would not be. She had seen the last glimpse of her Sam beneath his upbringing, military training, and coarse quiet exterior while they said goodbye in the darkened newsstand.

When Sam finally believed Karen's warning and she felt the crushing realization that she'd been right about him, Sam dropped the newsstand's flap and brought her inside. They collapsed in each other's arms and kissed with a passion that had been unbridled by the notion that it would be the last time. That was when the tears first changed from frustration at him to loss.

"Go, Sam. Run! I know you can. You know you can. Hurry. They're coming."

"I will, but you're coming with me."

New tears.

"They're not after me."

"Not yet."

The words sank in quickly.

"I'm right," he said. "And any good attorney knows it too. What would you do if you were trying to find me? You'd be all over me, my house, electronic connections. You've been seen with me, at my house, we've talked on the phone, email. They'll find you in a minute if they haven't already, Karen. You're coming with me."

"I'd slow you down."

"Not a bit. I've got some friends of my father's I can go to. They'll get us both out of here."

"Where?"

Sam hesitated – years at his father's side and Ranger training kicking.

"Come and see."

"Can't you tell me?"

"After you tell me you'll come."

"You still don't trust me?"

"Karen, think like the prosecutor you are. You can't tell something you don't know."

It rang true in her head like a bell.

"I won't know where you are or if you're alright."

"You will if you come with me."

They held onto one another in the artificial dusk of the newsstand – the only light slipping through the cracks around the closed flap.

"I can't go. I shouldn't go. I can help you more from here."

"From jail? They'll find the trail between us. They'll–"

"We haven't seen each other – haven't talked in months."

"Will it matter to them? They want a body count on what was done and if they don't have me, they'll take it out on you."

"I haven't done anything."

"You came here."

"Give me some credit, Sam. I took the battery out of my phone before I left Virginia."

Sam nodded and fought for words to change her mind. Inside his own, a clock was ticking.

Behind her lover, Karen caught a single green light glowing from Sam's little used laptop. "You better get rid of that," she said as she pointed.

"They'll see the traffic anyway," Sam hesitated, lost. "I'll dump it."

"No one's watching me yet," Karen said softly. "But they will. I know. I have to go."

Sam's arms and resolve were weakening under the weight of what was happening. "I'm sorry. I'm sorry, Karen," he choked, inches from crying for the first time in memory. "I love you. I love you."

She instantly melted in what remained of his strength. Their mouths fumbled in the dim light until they locked together. Sam's strength was renewed by the passion. He ran his hands over her until they settled on her hips. He pushed into her and slipped her to the wall. Karen buried her fingers in his thick arms then fell to his pants. In an instant his long cargo shorts were open and her flouncy skirt was up around her waist. He lifted her to the edge of the counter and there on the day's newspapers they began to make love. In a moment the papers slipped and slid away beneath their thrusts until Sam gently took her to the floor.

There was a lover's craving on the plywood among the papers, but no frenetic crush until the final throes. Time prevented anything more and while the caress satiated single wants, it left in its wake an emptiness and longing that foreshadowed a lifetime of unmet desire.

When they eased up from each other and the floor, the tears came again. "We have to go," Karen said with a voice that shook and cracked. "They're coming."

The lovers dressed quickly and went to the door. When Karen reached for the simple lock, Sam held the door closed with a hard push. He pulled a small but razor sharp knife from somewhere Karen couldn't see. In the soft light he pulled his driver's license from his pocket. He laid it on the counter and held it down with one hand and sliced at it quickly and efficiently with the knife. The knife stayed on the counter while two halves of Sam's license were in his hands. He held them together up to Karen.

"Won't you need that?" she asked.

"Not where I'm going. Listen," he said as he pressed one of the irregular pieces into her palm. "This is a ticket. It'll take you to jail if they find it, but it'll also get a message to me when the time is right."

"How?"

"You remember where we went to dinner that first night?"

She thought only a second. "Yes."

"I'm breaking all my own rules... But I... I don't think I could take what's coming if I knew you weren't in it somewhere."

"Sam..."

"When the old maître d' seats you, give him this and tell him you'd like to select your own wine from the cellar. Don't ask anything else."

"I understand."

"Karen, be as careful as you can."

"Me? You're telling me to be careful?"

"It's going to get ugly. They'll take everything you have."

"I know."

"If it gets too bad...," he said as he squeezed the piece in her hand.

"I'll be alright, Sam. Now go."

"You first."

They kissed, almost franticly.

"I love you, Karen. I have from the beginning. Go. Go!" He gave the order as sharply as if he were directing a parachute jump into a night sky.

Karen slipped out the door and pushed it closed behind her not knowing if her chute would open.

Sam couldn't breathe. He closed his eyes as his mind felt her disappear beyond the plywood door into the sunshine and the concrete highway headed north. Almost as quickly as Karen was gone, old training and thoughts flooded him. He tried to focus, but was staggered. The computer was snatched up and the knife shoved back in a pocket with his half of his license. He almost fell out the door and walked away from the newsstand. The battery from his laptop went in a garbage can, the laptop in another. He knew it really didn't matter if it was recovered. The data was still out there on a server somewhere waiting for the FBI to find it and its notes to Karen. He kept walking until the familiar alleys of his childhood took him into the arms of a maze no one could follow. Forty minutes later he was in the wine cellar of The Columbia Restaurant.

Hours and hours had passed. Sam ate a little, but had no appetite. He paced the small room and flipped through the books Mr. Guzimon had brought, but was unable to focus. Instead he watched the silent replay of his life on the ceiling of the hidden room. Above him, on the streets of the city, things were anything but silent. The sirens didn't begin until the initial trap had been sprung. Thick boxy black SUVs and vans carrying FBI agents and fortified SWAT teams in helmets and Kevlar bulletproof vests covered with thicker ceramic armor swarmed Sam's house and the newsstand. The newsstand's old plywood door offered no resistance and no early evidence. Its straight one room had been cleared of any immediate threat in three seconds. Bomb technicians came in next, but also cleared the simple old building in record time.

The last wave was a four person forensics team operating under the eye of Jason Meyer. They began filtering each scrap of paper and crevice in the old wood frame. The battered linoleum covered countertop had nothing to say from beneath the day's newspapers that remained scattered across it. Any immediate whisper from the entire newsstand suggested only that whoever left it unattended, did so in a hurry. There were crumpled fresh newspapers on the floor and money in a metal box beneath the shoulders of the old counter.

The forensic team would search on their hands and knees, testing each floorboard. Eventually the floor would be torn up to reveal decades of dust caked spider webs that revealed nothing. Sam's home was undergoing the same scrutiny, but a few tidbits were being given up from its plain walls as if out of fear for what the walls had witnessed done to the splintered fragments of both the front and rear doors.

Two identical SWAT teams of identical black clad men in riot gear rushed up the street from opposite directions. Mr. Abreu had been watching his street from alternating front and back upstairs windows from the moment he'd returned from the wine cellar of The Columbia. When the obvious undercover police car pulled off the street, the old sentry knew the cavalry was coming. He saw the black vans creep up the street and disgorge black robed raiders onto the sidewalk. They were in a controlled tight sprint as they neared their target, with one group steering off to attack from the rear. The old man had to admit their timing was very good. Both front and rear doors imploded at the same moment.

Mr. Abreu listened but heard no further crashing. At least the cops weren't destroying the boy's place. He could hear them yelling, "Clear!" "Clear!" "Clear!" as they rushed from room to room. It wasn't but a few minutes and, apparently disheartened they had found no one to shoot or gang tackle to the ground, the black suited civilian soldiers began reemerging from the house looking disappointed as they stripped off their armor and loaded all their accoutrements and automatic rifles into appropriate vans that had rolled up for that purpose.

Just ahead of the vans came unmarked cars. Some were federal and carried Alyn Nuary and Calburn Denti. Others were city cars driven by uniformed patrolmen and brought Jack Aaron, Marcus Pete, and local police.

"You don't remember this, Petey," Jack was saying as they came up the street and watched along with Mr. Abreu, the retreating black wave of the SWAT teams. "I told you I used to be a State Trooper, right?"

"Maybe once or twice... an hour."

Jack seemed not to hear as he watched forty some odd men with pumped up arms and thick necks loosely assemble around another addition – a SWAT vehicle that resembled a military tank. "When I was with the troopers, we were spread pretty thin. That was before the sheriff's departments really took off. Most counties were undermanned and didn't have a lot of training. If something jumped off, backup might be twenty minutes away. Hell, you couldn't just sit on your ass twiddling your thumbs waiting for somebody to bail you out."

"It was a different world, Jack."

"True. People – even bad guys – especially younger shitheads, marginal bad guys you might call them, they had respect for the uniform, but we managed things different. We didn't give assholes time to think, but we also – and this is important, Petey – we didn't make bad situations worse."

"What do you mean?"

"We'd get a call about a guy with a gun, threatening somebody, whatever. I wasn't special, we all did the same thing, but if a call came in like that, we just went. We were careful, cautious, smart, but we went, usually by ourselves."

"Brave guys."

"We didn't think of it that way. It was our job to keep the peace and protect the public. It probably sounds hokey, but we did what we had to do. And it worked. That's what bothers me with all this bullshit," Jack said as he motioned through the windshield at the SWAT units and the black tank transport. "This looks like an Army battalion. It works against everybody."

"What are you talking about?"

"Too much force. We've replaced talking to a guy with driving a tank through his door. No wonder these things usually turn to shit. Whatever happened to talking a guy down? Now we just point a grenade launcher at him."

"These are dangerous–"

"I know dangerous and most of this stuff could be, but doesn't have to be. You ask a guy a few questions and see how she goes. Or you can scream at him and see how that works out for you."

"You're starting to sound like a liberal, Jack."

"Hardly. Just saying. You can always get tougher, but it ain't easy to put the bees back in the hive once you poke it with a stick. We got along pretty damn good without tanks for a helluva long time."

"People don't respect the authority of the uniform anymore, boss. And they have bigger guns, and more of them. Things change."

The car was stopping behind the armored personnel carrier. "Yea... Things change," Jack said as he opened the door.

Alyn Nuary stopped the opening door and nearly pushed it back closed on Jack's leg. Cal was behind her.

"Ciampiano's not here," she said as she adjusted a big Glock .45 under her tailored jacket. "The bomb squad will be a while clearing the place. Another demolition team is sweeping the newsstand downtown. They'll be done by the time we get there. Tag along if you want." Nuary spun and was headed to a waiting car.

Cal stepped up to Jack's window. "I'll meet you there."

"You want to ride with us, Denti?"

"No, I'll try to keep a lid on her," Cal said as he glanced over his shoulder at Nuary.

"You sure? Must be tough to hold on."

"What do you mean?"

"Riding double on a broomstick."

Petey laughed out loud along with the patrolman driver.

Cal shook his head and chuckled. "That was good."

"I'm full of 'em," Jack smiled.

"Full of something. I'll meet you at the stand."

Jack's arrival a few blocks away at the newsstand was a repeat of the scene at the Ciampiano house. The SWAT Team had collected their disappointment and were leaving. The bomb technicians had done their job and had turned the old building over to Meyer and the forensic team. Alyn had already spurred Jason on and was standing with Cal at the doorway looking in as flashes captured digital images of every inch.

Jack and Petey – Jack's hands buried deep in his pockets – walked up behind the FBI agents.

"The Bureau get a confession yet?" Jack ribbed.

"We might if we had a body to talk to," Nuary spit back. "He went AWOL under surveillance of locals."

"Shit. You knew about him before we did. Don't forget to put that in your report."

"He'll turn up," Cal said quickly then addressed Meyer. "Can we get a quick look inside?"

"They haven't dusted for prints yet."

"We won't touch anything. We're looking for a lead on this guy. He could be nearby."

"Have at it," Jason said as he looked at Alyn and slipped by out the door.

Alyn stepped in first, but stopped and looked around. Her uncertainty as to what she was looking for showed. Cal bowed outside and motioned Jack ahead of him.

"Age before beauty."

"Shit. You couldn't find evidence if it walked up and slapped you in the puss. You just want me to bail you out – same as always."

"How do you manage it?" Cal said to Marcus.

"It's a gift," Petey said as he followed Jack into the newsstand.

Both men stopped briefly at the doorway to negotiate around the stalled Regional Director of the FBI. "Excuse us, Mrs. Hoover," Jack said as he looked to the placement of his feet.

Alyn didn't have a suitable comeback or a comeback of any kind. All she could offer was a snide smile neither Jack nor Marcus took notice of. Cal however, saw and heard it all from the doorway and grinned.

Marcus motioned to the disheveled and torn newspapers on the floor. "Looks like a fight."

"What's the date on them?"

Marcus leaned down, but was mindful to not touch the papers. "Today."

Jack nodded.

As Marcus stood he looked at the counter and scanned the rest of the stand. "No other signs of a struggle. This guy is an ex-Ranger, right? "Maybe he–"

Jack held a finger to his lips. "Shhh, Petey," Jack said as he pointed from his face to Nuary. "You're under surveillance."

Sure enough, Alyn was all but leaning forward, hanging on Petey's every word. Jack's mouth jumped into a Cheshire cat grin. He cocked his head to the side like an imp and froze. Caught, Nuary turned away and stepped to the door. She pointed sharply at Cal then over her shoulder without looking back at Jack and Marcus.

"Looks like Ciampiano was in a struggle. Get the forensic unit back before the locals here screw everything up."

Jack shrugged his shoulders and shuffled his feet talking loud enough for everyone to hear plainly. "Sorry, Barney," he said to Marcus. "Let's head back on down to the Mayberry Courthouse and wait for the phone to ring. Looks like the real cops from over in Raleigh have got this under control. Say. Why don't you call Thelma Lou and we'll all take in the picture show."

Marcus had his head down, but was grinning. Jack continued to watch his step, but followed Alyn to the door as he droned on in an exaggerated good old boy accent and sway. "I reckon we could swing by the diner for a malted milkshake, take a drive out to the lake after the show, look at the stars a'shining on the water..."

Marcus looked up to follow his boss out and came face to face with a well faded newspaper photo in a dusty wooden frame hanging on the back wall. The framed grainy picture was of Sam Ciampiano Sr. standing behind four young boys with newspaper sacks over their shoulders. The caption read, "Return of the Newsboys." Marcus read the names of the boys after a two line description of the newsstand's revival of street corner newspaper slingers. The names stopped him and erased the smile.

"Hey, Andy?" Marcus said as he stared at the picture.

"Give it up, Barn. Let's head over to Mount Pilot for–"

"Jack." All the humor was gone and the name snapped like the crack of a whip.

Without a characteristic word of complaint, gripe, or question, Jack drifted toward his investigator.

Marcus had not strayed from the picture. He didn't touch it except with his eyes which were devouring it over and over as he moved back and forth to find the perfect distance. Too close and the graininess obliterated the faces. Too far and the boys were featureless and non-descript. The names however, were crystal clear from any distance.

When Jack was beside him, Marcus pointed to the list and let Jack silently read along with his finger. *"Pictured with Mr. Ciampiano from the right are newsboys; Sam Ciampiano Jr., Clayton Rand, Raphael Bordaine, and Carl Rand."*

Jack did just what Marcus had done and moved in and out to get the best view of the young faces. He looked at Marcus, blinked quickly in apparent disbelief, then returned to the picture. "Jesus fucking H. Christ," he muttered. "Cal? You're gonna wanna see this."

5

Raphael Bordaine walked back into his office thirty-four stories above Tampa Bay's blue-green water. There had been a short meeting that held little consequence. Business was good, the markets strong again. Traders, brokers, agents, companies, and even the shareholders were making money. That somehow equated to all being right in the world, however, that was subject to change and was about to do just that in prompt progression.

Outside, the sky changed often and exchanged reflected colors with the bay as a cooler sea wind played tug-of-war with a warming land breeze and nudged clouds back and forth over the face of the sun. Even without the full-time sun, it was a nice day. Tampa had to work hard to produce something less than pleasant. Even the rains, soft or torrential, only came to scrub the city's face and made for good days, apart from a few spoiled plans that had held in wait boating excursions across the wide bay and out into the deep waters of the Gulf.

Inside, Raphael lowered himself into his chair behind a broad light oak desk that served as a platform for five wide screen monitors. Most scrolled assorted tickers, tracking the movement of individual stocks and broader markets. A very short pile of mail rested on the corner of his desk. The miniscule stack was evidence of a virtually connected world having all but sounded the death knell for snail mail. Next to the few pieces was a small yellow padded envelope – packages having, for now, held out against digital transfer. Like a child at Christmas, Raphael went for the largest bundle first and opened the package. Inside was a tiny flip phone – simple, plain black, old fashioned style – with big keys and a tiny inactive screen.

He tossed it from hand to hand and turned it over. He pushed his straight hair, left to grow long of late, behind his ears as he looked down and around the phone and its packaging. Nothing revealed anything further. When he flipped the phone open, the little screen came to life. It was already powered up and it flashed a message that listed several missed calls.

Raphael closed the phone and set it aside while he examined the yellow torn packaging again. There was no insert and only a partial return address from Tampa he didn't recognize.

The phone vibrated on his desk.

Raphael looked around the office as though caught between poor acting in a silly comedy and the tension of a high crime drama. He picked up the humming phone and opened the face with both hands. An incoming number came up on the small backlit screen. He brought the phone up to his head slowly.

"Hello?"

There was no answer and the phone buzzed again in his hand.

Raphael held the phone down, looked at it, and felt another vibration. There was a green button labeled 'Talk.' He pressed it with no small degree of hesitation and held the phone back up.

"Hello?"

"Ralph, it's me."

"Clay?"

"Yea."

"You nut case. I was trying to figure out–"

"Listen, friend. Shhhh. Just listen. There's some trouble."

"Trouble? What's–"

"Listen. Don't call me, email, or come to the house."

"Why?"

"The police are watching me."

"Are you fucking–"

Raphael stopped, jumped up from his desk, held the phone down along his thigh, and went to his door. He tried to be casual, but was no good at it. As the door closed he leaned against it heavily and yanked the phone up, but spoke in a coarse whisper. "Are you kidding me? Goddamn it, Clay. I told you. I told you!"

"You told me."

"Jesus Christ! Are they watching me?"

Again, Raphael replicated a poor film character. Though he was five hundred feet in the air, he hustled to his bank of windows, looked out, around, and down at the street.

"Ralph. Get a grip. I thought you were unflappable. A pillar of–"

"Shut up, you idiot! I told you not to start this nonsense. What's going to happen now, Einstein?"

Clayton's voice was relaxed. "How should I know? I'm no mind reader."

"God, you are glib."

"I prefer confident."

"The police are watching you. You send me secret phones. And you're confident?"

"Very."

"Then why the dummy phone?"

"Just protecting my buds. They have nothing to connect you to this thing. I figured it'd be best to keep it that way, but I needed you to know a few things."

"What things?"

"Like what to say when they show up."

"Show up? They're coming here?"

"No." There was a predictable pause. "Not yet anyway."

"Unreal..."

"Breathe deep, Ralph. I'm only giving you a head's up. They'll review all my electronic associations. They'll find you through my digital traffic. You'll come up a winner, but when they come to talk to you, you don't know shit."

"I *don't* know shit!"

"See? Aren't you happy I kept you out of it?"

"You're a pal, Clay."

"We've been friends since we were kids. Share an affinity for old movies, cold beer, and hot women. That's it. We went off to college, came home, and went to work. I do programming. That's all you know."

"That's all I know."

"That's all you know. It's nothing they won't know already. They'll try to trip you up and say me or someone else said you're involved or this or that – that they have a text you don't remember – but it'll all be bullshit. They'll try to bluff you into making a mistake. Don't go for it."

"Don't go for it."

"That's right. Don't go for it."

"Don't go for it. That's a helluva thing to leave me with. Don't go for it. Oh, my God."

"Relax and breathe–"

"You idiot!"

"Ralph. Adjust that brilliant mind of yours – ignore the corruption of Stanford and stick to the script. We never had any discussions. You don't have an inkling. No idea what they're talking about. Maybe you could throw in, "That doesn't sound like, Clayton." Or, "He wouldn't be involved in anything like that." Something sweet. But don't overplay it. Keep clear of it."

"Great advice." The sarcasm was dripping. "Thanks."

"You're welcome. We good?"

Raphael took Clayton's advice and pulled in a deep breath and tried to relax. He sat down at his desk, spun his chair and looked out over the reflecting gray of Tampa Bay. "As good as we can be, right?"

"For now. I can track them tracking me so if the wind changes, I'll adjust the sails and call you on this phone. If I call you on my regular one, don't lose your mind. It wouldn't do to not call my best friend as the cops are crawling up my ass. Help me stay in character. That's all I ask."

"Okay..."

"Thanks, Ralph. They can't touch me. As soon as they show up, I'm going mute. But I'd like to know what led them to me."

"Clay, I'm worried about you, man. If you don't know how they got on to you, that's not a good sign."

"I'll find out soon enough. They think they're hunting me, but—"

"Clayton?"

"Yes?"

"I really don't want to know. Not this time. Not anymore. Fair enough?"

"Fair enough."

They left a comfortable space that signaled the end of the call.

"You pissed?" Clayton asked with a slower deeper tenor to his voice which let Raphael feel the real depth of tension and moreover, Clayton's concern for himself and his friend.

Raphael was not pissed. He was afraid. This wasn't stealing candy bars from the little league snack stand. But he couldn't leave Clayton alone. "I'm not upset. I promise. I'm... I'm anxious."

"Understandable, but—"

"Clay? You know that bit in *Big Jake* where the Duke says, 'Anything goes wrong – my fault, your fault, nobody's fault.?'"

"I might."

"Well, you'd better, because if this turns to worse shit than it is, you get to play Richard Boone and I'm John Wayne. Just so you know," and he eked out the slightest chuckle.

"You got a deal there, pilgrim," Clayton said in his best slow drawn out impression of John Wayne.

"That's sounds more like a scene from *Liberty Valance*."

"But I still do a great John Wayne."

"You should stick to *Big Jake*."

"What's wrong with *Liberty Valance*?"

"John Wayne ends up dead."

A dark Virginia State line whizzed by beneath Karen's car with no regard. She exchanged glances between the highway and her phone and its recently replaced battery. While the phone cycled through its assortment of screens, beeps, and tones as it was resurrected from its power deprived death, Karen collected herself for the umpteenth time. Dried tears still itched on her cheeks, but the lights of cars on the beltway and the city beyond were bringing her around. She held the phone against the wheel and waited for it to complete its rounds through cyber-space and retrieve any messages. When it signaled the search and recovery was complete, Karen's eyes again darted from the road to the small screen. She had missed a call from John LaRoy, Assistant Director of the FBI. The time stamp told her less than an hour had passed.

She knew he'd be calling. Almost a day before he would have received the same package of intelligence that had prompted her reckless dash to Tampa and Sam. Because of Sam's military record, LaRoy would pull in JAG and Karen to assist. Despite twenty-four plus hours of straight driving to Tampa and back north, she was likely headed right back south. This time as a Naval investigator working alongside the FBI instead of a crying fearful lover.

"Where are you, Lieutenant?" LaRoy asked Karen as a hello.

"On the beltway. What's up?"

"I hate to spoil your night on the town, but I'm going to. Meet me at Andrews. We've got something on that Illuminati thing. The Tampa office – Calburn Denti – you remember Cal?"

"I do."

"He's kicking in doors. I'll want you nearby."

"Do we have a flight time? I'm an hour away with traffic."

"Flight time? Hell, we don't even have a plane, but we'll be on whatever's leaving next even if I have to boot the co-pilot."

"We could fly standing up," Karen's tired mind surprised her.

"We could do that. We could do that. Something will be headed to MacDill. If there isn't one, we'll make one. I have a few friends at the Joint Chiefs if we need them. Pack light and meet me there. A couple hours should do it. You good with that?"

"I am."

"Meet you on the tarmac, Lieutenant."

Karen hung up and waited for the time to show on her phone. She made a note and immediately began to agonize over how she was going to tell LaRoy she knew the target of the investigation and by "knew," she was meaning in the Biblical sense. Somewhere around South Carolina on this leg of her blurring roundtrip, she decided it was only a matter of time before her name attached itself to the case and landed on LaRoy's desk. At first he would mistakenly overlook her name and assume she was working on evidence discovery motions or chain of custody. It might take three passes and a placidly frantic call to his digital forensic people before he pieced it together. LaRoy was a good cop – a good man. She would save him the trouble and perhaps save herself as well.

There was nothing at Sam's house to connect Karen to him. Cal Denti wouldn't find a gilt framed eight-by-ten glossy signed, "Love, Karen," next to Sam's bed. He wasn't that sentimental. There wasn't a shoebox of wrinkled letters, ticket stubs, and bent pictures beneath the bed or tucked in the corner of a high shelf in a closet. Lovers no longer kept treasure troves of memories like that. The shoeboxes had become electronic inboxes and tweets and the incriminating return addresses on the upper left-hand corners of scented letters had become IP addresses. Lingering perfume had been replaced by speed. The recurrent folding and re-reading of a piece of paper that had been in their lover's hand or pressed against their lips was usurped by disposable contact that touched base with boring rapidity.

After the search of Sam's house came up empty – empty of Karen and any other evidence she reasoned – Sam was too smart for that – the Bureau would begin methodically peeling a digital onion. Sam Ciampiano's life was at its core. Along the way, the forensic investigators would uncover Karen Auburn. There would still be the time honored neighborhood interviews, but the resulting details would be few and sketchy at best. Karen's downfall would come through digital DNA. The dots of her and Sam's life would connect via the bits and bytes of their electronic fingerprints and be as certain and incriminating as the ones on the tips of their fingers.

In all likelihood, Sam would have destroyed his computer right away, but that would only delay the inevitable. When the searchers had not found the devices they would have retreated behind their own and continued searching from the comparative comfort of their office chairs. It wasn't a process like radar or sonar or even triangulation like two forest rangers in high watch towers scanning the horizon for smoke, but the result would be the same. Karen's electronic interaction with the most wanted man in America would be discovered.

The truth would begin bubbling to the surface when records of Sam's legitimate life were examined. He only had one credit card. His father had used only cash. From Sam's internet account, it was a short and easy walk to his virtual address. His emails, phone records, and every internet site he ever visited would unravel like a cheap sweater. In the simple pile of data left behind, threads pointing north would be easy to filter. In no time, Karen's love notes and phone number would skate across the computer screen of an FBI forensic expert. It was data mining in reverse and relatively simple compliments of the Patriot Act Karen had utilized herself many times. In the end, Karen would find no footing for complaint, just as anyone who had ever bought a tabloid – glossy or pulp paper – with a titillating celebrity cover story could not complain about their own legalized loss of comparative privacy.

The inevitability of the uncovering of her relationship with Sam had sunk in hours before. Now, as she waited inside the clearance area within sight of one of the mammoth two mile long runways at Andrews, she ran through scenarios of how to tell LaRoy. It was possible, though improbable, he would have her arrested on the spot, though the charge would be nebulous. Members of the Military Police had examined her credentials on the way onto the airbase and others milled near every door nearby. It could be they might be driving her off the base minus those same credentials and in handcuffs. In her best scene, she would have her accesses suspended and not too discreet electronic and physical surveillance attached. At either end of the spectrum her career was over.

Her virtual world would be dissected and excised along with Sam's as the relationship was scrutinized. Dates and locations would be catalogued and cross referenced. The upside is that nothing could place her at any crime scenes or with any documented knowledge of the Illuminati. What she would be deemed guilty of was being the lover of unpublished public enemy number one. Innuendo alone would be sufficient to convict her of something.

She leaned forward in a seat that was at the end of an attached bank of similar ones and watched through a huge window into the dark as a prop plane taxied nearby. She rested her elbows on her knees and lowered her head into her hands. Her eyes closed. She was exhausted and felt as though she were still racing up and down I-95. She closed her eyes. There would be no tears now. She was empty and they would be wasted anyway. LaRoy wouldn't care about tears.

The next thing she heard was the muffled drone of aircraft engines whining nearby. Beneath the sound was LaRoy's voice. Karen had fallen asleep in her own hands. John LaRoy touched her shoulder again.

"Hey, soldier. Rough night?"

In the fog between sleep and awake, Karen jerked up and focused ears and eyes.

"Jesus, Karen, you look like hell. You sick?"

"Yes. No. No, I'm fine."

LaRoy motioned through the glass to a smallish jet idling in the dark, strobe lights flashing rhythmically on the tips of the wings. "That's us. A courier flight south. Looks like we won't have to stand up after all."

"Good. That's good," Karen said as she stood up and cleared the cobwebs from her head. She rubbed life back into her face and brain. "John?" She hadn't called him that before. "I need to tell you something before we go. It's crucial."

"Tell me on the plane," LaRoy was stepping away. "They're warming up."

Karen reached for his arm and caught him at the elbow. "You'll want to hear this first. You may not want me on that flight."

"Nonsense. I need you, Karen. Let's go. This guy–"

"Ciampiano?"

"Yea, Ciampiano. He's ex-military. I need JAG to–"

"I know he's ex-military. Spec ops."

"Sure. Sure. I figured you would have pulled him out of the report. Same as me."

"Not the same, John. I know Ciampiano."

LaRoy hesitated for the first time and tried to rephrase Karen's words though he had heard them clearly. "You mean, you know we're looking at him."

"No." Karen drew closer and her eyes pierced his. There could be no semantic parlays. "I know him. Personally. We've met. More than met."

"What?"

"I've known Sam Ciampiano since he left the service."

LaRoy literally took her arm and all but shoved her back in her chair. He deposited himself beside her – close and rough. "How the hell do you know Ciampiano?"

"I represented him."

"When?"

"Just before he was mustered out."

"What was he charged with?"

"It would have been aggravated assault, but–"

"That sounds like our boy."

"But he was never charged."

"Why not?"

"Something called, Blackbird."

LaRoy thought for only a moment. "Makes even more sense. That's our top echelon special operations. Covert black ops stuff."

"Everything disappeared, along with Sam.   That is, Sergeant Ciampiano."

LaRoy's eyebrows went up along with his cop's antennae. "Sam?" he said as the probing question it was.

Karen didn't answer.

"Talk to me," LaRoy said, in the tone of an order.

"Sgt. Ciampiano assaulted–"

"But you call him Sam."

"I have, yes."

"Go ahead."

"He assaulted another sergeant."

"How bad?"

"Bad."

"He try to kill the guy?"

"No, but he nearly tore his arm off according to the preliminary report I read."

"That would be his training coming through. Still sounds like our boy. Keep going."

"It was quick. Like a reaction," Karen said motioning with her hands as if waving off the severity.

"That's the training. Our assault in San Francisco on the mayor snapped both arms." LaRoy paused. "I'm sure you remember that."

Karen didn't answer, but LaRoy knew she remembered and understood the connection he was drawing in his cop's head.

"So you took his case and got to know him through the course of the investigation and trial?"

"I didn't get the chance. An Army Major came in twenty minutes after I met Ciampiano and took him away. The charges were dropped, and all the paperwork disappeared. The next time I checked on it, everything was gone and he'd been mustered out."

"Blackbird."

"It would seem, but there's nothing in his record about Special Operation Command, training, or deployment."

"What's that tell you?"

"I wasn't sure."

"So you dug into Ciampiano?"

"I did."

"How deep?"

It was Karen's turn to baulk.

"How deep?" LaRoy repeated with a voice that tightened with his brow.

"I looked up his last known address – next of kin," Karen answered truthfully.

"Let me guess. Tampa?"

"Yes."

"And?"

Another hesitation.

"Karen," LaRoy said as he stuck his face out and leaned even closer to hers. "You're a JAG attorney. You know better than I do how this is going to play. I like you – always have. You're a helluva talented officer, but I'll say this one time." LaRoy snapped with his eyes and the toss of a stout finger through the glass to the waiting plane. "I'm getting on that plane in three minutes. That's gives you two to tell me about you and Ciampiano. That third minute will be spent walking to that plane or calling the MPs.

"That's not a threat and you know you don't have to say word one to me. You can lawyer up. You know it and I know it. I get it. And I'm not making any promises here. Depending on how this rolls out, things could get pretty rough for you. I'm not promising nothing extra.

"But I'm guessing you know all that. You've already decided to tell me what I'm going to find out sooner or later. Sound about right?"

Karen nodded and swallowed hard, but returned LaRoy's look with one nearly as deliberate.

LaRoy glanced again at the plane, idling its engines faster than before as if reaching for a crescendo that needed no more buildup. He looked at his watch. "What'll it be, Lieutenant?"

Karen looked at the noisy plane then back to LaRoy. "I went to Tampa shortly after I learned Sam left the Army. I... I was looking for something I thought I saw in his eyes that day he said 'Blackbird.' I'll save you the candlelit dinners, but I fell in love. We fell in love."

Another day – minus the roaring plane, his thumping chest, and spinning brain – LaRoy would have rolled his eyes. Instead, they never moved from this woman who was teetering between investigator and conspirator.

"I went to Tampa whenever I could. We emailed and talked a lot in the beginning, but... you'll see that for yourself."

"In the beginning, you said. What's your status now?"

"We ended it several months ago."

"How come?"

"Too far apart. Long distance."

"Long distance?"

"It doesn't work out for most people," Karen was convincing.

"Long distance doesn't work out... But you track him a thousand miles because of a glint in his eye?"

"He became more withdrawn. Post military life was difficult for him."

"Was he violent?"

"Never."

LaRoy sat back and quipped somewhere between question and fact. "But he rips people's arms off."

Karen's resolve quivered. "I know."

LaRoy shot a look at his watch. "I don't suppose a man like Ciampiano ever talked about the Illuminati."

Her eyes tightened above lips that were rock solid. "Never."

"You didn't talk about it?"

"Not once."

"Are you involved in any way? Any way even remotely possible?"

"No, John. I was not and am not. Never."

"Here's the kicker – do you think he is?"

The JAG lieutenant took over. "He fits the profile."

"But what do you think?"

"Given his background, it's possible he–"

LaRoy stood up and looked around, choking Karen's answer off in her throat. He watched the MPs a few seconds then gave another few to the revving plane. "Karen, same question, but this time you answer, not the JAG Officer. Do you think Sgt. Sam Ciampiano is involved with the Illuminati?"

"Yes."

"Any recent contact?"

Now it was time to lie. "None."

"Sure about that?"

"I'm sure."

"No contact?"

"None."

"If it comes up different, they'll be hell to pay."

"It won't."

"You're sure?"

"I'm sure."

"Sure?"

"Sure."

"Christ, you sound like a goddamn mynah bird," LaRoy said as he spun away toward the tarmac. "Get on the plane." He punched the door open, stepped into the dark, and shouted. "But we're not done!"

In Tampa the dark was being held back in front of Sam's house and around the newsstand by banks of massive floodlights atop tall poles. Coils of wire fed the elevated lights from noisy diesel generators running flat out below. The power plants were dark blue, emblazoned with logos of the Tampa Police Department, and their lights turned away the night as far as they could reach.

Within the artificial daylight, explosions of more light signaled the documenting photography of forensics investigators. Everything at each site sat for the photographers. Every angle was shot in the event that something new may one day surface and reveal evidence in a picture that before had been given little credence.

Technicians of all ilks came and went as screening for evidence linking Sam to the Illuminati continued through the night. Uniformed officers from Tampa PD maintained the perimeter. The FBI managed the properties. Cal Denti and Alyn Nuary hovered nearby, alternating from the house to the newsstand until the hour and lack of Sam's presence caused Nuary to head for a local hotel. Cal hung on a while longer and queued the upcoming daylight hours surrounding the ongoing processing and search. He had had copies of the old faded picture from the newsstand made and was sitting in his car with the door open. He was just outside the glare of the floodlights showing on the Ciampiano newsstand looking down at the copy when Jack Aaron and Marcus Pete came up.

"Hey!" Jack slapped his hand down on the hood of Cal's car. "You awake?"

"I'm awake."

"Where's your girlfriend?"

"At the Radisson. Getting her beauty sleep."

"She warming up the rack for you?"

"You're an ass. I'm going home."

"When?"

"Well, since you're here, I think now is good." Cal pulled his door closed as Jack and Marcus came closer.

"Don't be a dumb shit, Denti. Open up," Jack said as he rapped his knuckles on Cal's window.

Cal started his car and stared blankly through the side window as Jack began to rant and flail his arms.

"Don't take off now! Jesus, we've got work to do!"

Cal revved the motor and pointed to his ear as he shook his head no. "I can't hear you," he said, which Jack and Marcus heard plainly.

"Bullshit. Open the door. Just like a government employee," Jack shouted to Marcus. "Going to bed when the heavy lifting starts."

Cal revved the motor again and put the car in gear, but held it with the brake. He let it lurch a little under Jack's hands on the window.

"Knock it off, you federal freeloader! My taxes paid for this car!"

The jerking stopped, Jack smiled, and Cal took his foot off the brake. The car did a short series of inch long starts and stops.

Jack looked at Marcus again. "What an ass. Goddamn third grader."

"You or Cal?" Marcus said as he buried his hands in his pockets and walked around the front of the car to the passenger window. It immediately came down and Cal leaned toward him across the seat.

"What do you think, Marcus?"

"Of you two or the case?"

Cal laughed a little. "I know. I blame it on being tired. Generally I strive to maintain some decorum."

"You mean, not stoop to his level."

"Exactly."

"I know," Marcus said as he leaned his elbows on the open window. "I often struggle with my dignity around him."

Jack shouted across the roof of Cal's car. "Hey. Hey! Don't talk to him, Petey. He's a moron!"

Cal put the car in park and shut it off. He slid across the seat and held the picture of the 'Newsboys' out to Marcus. "What would you like to do with this?"

The District Attorney's Chief Investigator ignored his boss – who was sliding around the car and coming up alongside him – and squatted down by the car door. He reached in the window and touched Clayton and Sam's figures in the picture. "I'd like to pick up these kids and do simultaneous interviews."

Jack was over his shoulder. "They're not kids now. That picture is twenty years old."

"At least," Cal said, as though the horseplay with his car's brakes had never happened.

"We know our Illuminati guy is tech heavy," Marcus thought out loud. "That's Rand. So we interview them at the same time with... wearing... wearing a headset – an earpiece and a microphone."

"What?" Jack said as he too leaned on the car.

"A headset. Some kind of earbud and mic so whoever is doing the interviews can hear the other conversation. Almost ask the same questions at the same time then use their answers to formulate the next questions and trip them up. Use them against each other – live."

Cal leaned over further until he could see up beyond Marcus to Jack. "Is that legal, Mr. DA?"

Jack thought a moment. "They'd both be Mirandized... The question is whether someone outside of the investigating agency can be a part of the interrogation. Interesting, Petey."

"They wouldn't be on speaker. Rather, it would be for us to have the instant communication of the Q and A."

"How's that benefit us though?" Jack asked from above.

Marcus was turning from Cal in the car up to Jack and back as he worked through his impromptu theory.

"Rand's a techno-freak. That's what he knows and, more importantly, what he respects. We use it against him. It... It doesn't even need to be real. We have computer monitors in the room – running code – flashing through screens, and others he can't quite see."

"What?" Jack asked again.

"Think the exact opposite of every old cop show or movie. Or every skit of a detective trying to coax a confession out of somebody. The cop talks and talks – trying to build a bridge to reach the guy and get to the truth. Maybe he's nice, maybe he's not so nice."

"Good cop, bad cop," Jack said as though he'd uncovered a riddle.

"Right, but that was then. Now, with the Illuminati, we go the opposite way. No games. No relationship construction. Just screens and hard drives whirling with us typing on touch pads as we talk into our headsets."

To save Marcus's stretching antics, Cal slid across the car's front seat and popped the door. Marcus kept talking as he stood up to let Cal step out.

"And pressing our earbuds as though we just heard a confession," Marcus was saying while he pushed his finger against an imaginary head piece. "Nothing but electronic bytes and data, whether we have it or not. Instead of Dragnet and Sgt. Joe Friday's bare interview room and empty table, we overload Rand's senses with all the stimulus we can manage."

Cal had a short question.

"And?"

"Right," Jack chimed in. "How are you going to get anything out of him with the one-side mumbo-jumbo?"

Marcus set his feet to give him a moment to think it through more than for any stunning reveal effect. "When he's comfortable or hopefully a little overwhelmed, we touch our headset, look at the computer screen, and ask him as simple as anything, "Who's Sam Ciampiano?" and wait."

Cal and Jack looked at each other. Jack shrugged. Cal folded his arms, looked up at the night sky and sighed. "I like the process, Marcus. You're thinking. In all likelihood, Rand knows we've been eavesdropping on him. He's too good not to know. But he doesn't know we have Ciampiano's name. Granted, this Ciampiano isn't a lock, but he looks good for it thus far. And this," Cal said as he handed the newspaper copy to Marcus. "This is our hole card. Even if Rand knows we're looking at him, he doesn't know we're looking at his little friend."

Marcus waved the photo copy. "Here's our leverage."

"That's not a very big stick, Petey," Jack said he rubbed the effects of a long day and late night from the back of his neck.

"Granted, but it's what we have. What are you thinking, boss?"

Jack continued stretching and rubbing. "I think Rand cries for his lawyer as soon as he sees a badge."

"There goes my techy interrogation if that happens."

"Maybe," Cal said as he reached over and took the photo of the Newsboys back from Marcus. He looked at it and tapped Clayton's picture with a finger. "Jack, if he exercises his right to counsel, I'd like him to know we have this, and hopefully Ciampiano. How would the District Attorney's office feel if this was put in front of Rand? Violation of his rights? Mind you, no questions. Just set it there. With Ciampiano's name highlighted next to his."

"Might be argued as intimidation," Marcus answered for his boss.

Jack chuckled. "You better go get some sleep, Cal. You can't put a gun to a guy's head either – even if you don't ask him questions."

"That picture is hardly a gun."

"You better hope it *is* a gun," Jack bantered back. "We all better hope so."

"It certainly is intriguing."

"Remember who found it. Takes a good cop to find evidence like that."

Cal and Marcus both laughed. They were all tired. "Jack, it was stuck on the wall," Cal said. "Nice police work, Mr. Holmes."

"Well, you didn't see it. Hey, by the way, are you giving me this case? I figured I'd have to arm wrestle you to see if you file federal charges before me."

"There'll be federal charges, but I'm also certain you'll want a piece. There's enough to go around."

"We better get a body in cuffs first, don't you think?"

"Rand will be easy to grab. This Ciampiano looks to be a bit different."

"He's on the lam already thanks to your girlfriend and the TSA," Jack complained.

"We don't know that," Cal said though his voice wasn't even convincing himself. "Maybe he's on a date."

"Sure he is. And when he gets home and sees all the floodlights and ten cop cars at his house he'll walk up and ask us what's going on."

"If he's on a date," Marcus said as he resigned his tech theory and shoved his hands in his pockets. "He's on the bus or in a cab. The guy doesn't own a car. At least nothing registered in his name."

"Anything else come in on him?"

"Very little. He's almost living off the grid."

"That would suit our vigilante group, wouldn't it?"

"It sure as hell would," Jack said as he turned away.

"Calling it a night, boss?"

"Pretty soon. You girls go on home. I'm going to drift back to the house and see if your forensic guys have missed any pictures stuck on the wall."

"Go home, Jack. Your forensic guy is there. The young fella. I told my people to keep him looped in."

"Helfer? He might be green as grass but he could teach your geek squad a few tricks. He found Rand. Your fed boys couldn't pour piss out of a boot if you wrote the directions on the heel."

Cal ignored the toothless slight. "And John LaRoy is on his way down from DC."

Jack yelled over his shoulder as he reached the sidewalk. "How come? He don't trust you with real cases yet?"

"No, he said he wanted to keep an eye on you."

"That could be so. See you tomorrow."

Marcus looked at his watch. "It's been tomorrow for three hours."

Jack was beyond the newsstand now. He was characteristically yelling as he turned and walked backward into the dark toward his car. "That's good, Petey. If your career doesn't take off you can get a job putting the time and temperature up on the bank sign. Maybe be a weatherman too."

"Thanks for the vote of confidence!"

"It's not tomorrow until it gets light out. Go get some sleep. I'll want you ready to work tomorrow. We've got fish to fry."

The District Attorney vanished.

Marcus pointed to the oft used prop in Cal's hand. "Do you believe those kids are The New Illuminati?"

Cal looked at the print in the dim light. He adjusted it to see the picture more clearly as though it were the first time. "I don't know, Marcus. I truly don't. We've got a few fragments separately and this relationship between Rand and Ciampiano is compelling."

Marcus twisted a kink out of his neck. "Jack's got the scent, you know what I mean?"

"I do indeed."

"We picked up on Rand because there was no one else who could do it. That's thin in a courtroom."

"Real thin."

"And this ex-Ranger isn't any better. He's really just an ex-special forces who happens to live in Tampa."

"Right again."

"You probably can't tell me, but I hope you guys have something else."

Cal walked around his car to the driver's door. He held up the picture. "We've got this."

"Yea."

"And your boss. Don't tell him, but if he's got the bit in his teeth, I'll go along with him. He's that good."

"The bit in his teeth?"

Cal opened his door. "Ask the old man. Goodnight, Marcus."

"Night, Cal."

The car started, but Cal leaned across the seat to the still open window on the passenger's side. "Hey, Marcus?"

"Yea?"

"Give some more thought to your tech interview of Rand. I'll have to see what LaRoy says. I don't want to pick him up yet. When we do, I'd like you in the room with me."

"That'd be great."

"Your boss will cry and stamp his feet," Cal smiled in the dashboard light. "But he'll get over it. Talk to you in a few hours."

Marcus gave a nod and a slight wave as Cal pulled away before he wandered over under the floodlights and looked in the open door of the newsstand. He let his mind wander as he looked over and around the evidence technicians who were now bagging the day-old newspapers to examine later and fingerprinting the countertop. A few blocks away, Jack was standing on Sam Ciampiano's porch looking through the windows at a similar scene.

The generators were still running in the street throwing a blanket of harsh awkward light against the house. Shadows of uniformed Tampa PD officers moved up and down the house as they walked the sidewalk in search of relief from stiffness and boredom. The patrolmen collected in groups far enough away from the generators to be heard and traded theories on what it was they were guarding.

Jack looked from the windows to the cops in the street and back to the house. He was as tired as anyone, maybe more so, and lost himself examining the old town architecture of the Ciampiano's open tiled porch. He followed the multicolored bright six inch squares along the porch and up the side of the door. The patterned porcelain made the molding and trim that would be replaced in later designs by carved wood and eventually the bland termite resistant stucco. In the fog of dwindling activity and fatigue, Jack ran his hand up the tile of the door casing and felt the relief of the repeated design in the squares. Three-quarters of the way up the casing his hand stopped at the metal mailbox. It was old – though not nearly as old as the house – with rust peeking through the corners and seams from under several layers of black paint that showed brush strokes from a crude application.

His hand stayed on the texture of the colorful tile, shown quite well by the harsh lights though it was nearly three in the morning. His eyes however reached back to the street and the uniforms. They had collected at the far reaches of the light near the edge of the Ciampiano property line to chat free from the blaring drone of the generators.

Jack moved a step to the side and stopped with himself between the officers and the Ciampiano mailbox. He opened it, but it was not the squeaky metallic sound he expected. Years of heavy paint had tightened the hinge. The lid moved up only as far as it was lifted and stayed there until a hand, presumably heavy with mail, pushed it back down.

With the lid up, Jack eased closer and leaned only enough to the side to allow a few rays of the artificial sun to peek around his shoulder and expose the contents of the mailbox. He didn't expect another picture of the New Illuminati – perhaps a more recent one. Instead, he was looking out of a combination of tiredness, curiosity, and worn habit.

A multi-page flyer from a local grocery store cluttered up most of the box. There was a stiff car dealership ad with a cheap fake key attached that promised 'Occupant' a new car if it started. There were no bills and no letters. Nothing that would help in the search for the history of Sam Ciampiano or in the present, find him. Then a hint of golden yellow caught the bright light. Tucked within the pages of the grocery coupons was a small package.

Jack slipped the package out by the tip of a corner, looked into the mailbox again to check for other hidden gems, and then examined the parcel. He read the partial return address, gently slipped the package under his coat, and walked away.

———————

6

A dozen blocks away, well beneath 7th Avenue, there was a gentle rap on the thick plank door to Sam's hidden room. He was off the twin bed and at the door before the last soft knock. As he stood to the side from ingrained habit – out of the line of fire should any be coming – he listened and heard Mr. Guzimon whisper.

"*Po' Martello?*"

Sam slid the heavy steel latch that would have been more at home on a cattle pen. The door opened stiffly like a prize fighter getting out of bed the day after a title defense.

"*Buona sera, Piccola Martello.*"

Sam smiled weakly and nodded a hello as the maître d' came into the safe room.

"I know you did not sleep, but have you been comfortable?"

"I have."

"Ah, and the bags," Mr. Guzimon said as he pointed to both Sam's black canvas and the duffle he himself had prepared. "They are what you require?"

"*Bene. Grazie,*" Sam said apologetically. "I didn't try the cheese–"

"Ah. No *importante*. You will like them. And the *rosso vino*. *Delizioso*. The very best. You will see."

"*Grazie de nuovo.*"

"Ah. Nothing!" the maître d' said as he stood back and waved his arm with the flourish of a dancer to the open door. "Shall we go?"

When Sam reached for his bags he remembered the remnant of his sliced driver's license in his pocket. He pulled it slowly and held it out to his benefactor.

Mr. Guzimon stared at it and wrinkled further a brow that was permanently so.

A sheepish look replaced the gray one on Sam's face. "There's a girl."

The maître d' smiled and placed both hands over Sam's and the torn scrap. "Ah. There always is."

"She may come by some day. I don't know."

"Ah. She will come. But, *Martelletto*, you – and your father before you – you know the rules of this game. To have this ticket would mean I know of you. To even know of such a ticket means I know of you."

Sam's thick hand fell away and the license with it. "Yeah. Not smart."

"Love makes us not smart, *Martello*. And not smart is dangerous. Very dangerous."

The words were a pronouncement of the obvious and washed away the soft look in Sam's eyes. "You're right," he said as he reached for his pocket. "I'll get rid of this."

"Wait. Let me see it, *per favore*."

Sam held the piece out to the maître d', but the old guide didn't touch it. He cocked his head to the side to see the cut paper better until Sam adjusted it to ease the crook out of his benefactor's neck. Mr. Guzimon drew his finger in the air above the license as though he were tracing the jagged outline.

"Ah. *Bene. Bene*," he said as the tracing finger now touched his temple. "When she comes I have this piece in here. *Martello*, in all the years I wait the tables for Don T, I no once use a paper. No matter the number of plates on the table, I no use a paper and I get the orders perfect every time. People like that. No paper. I get nice tip." The maître d' smiled. "I don't put tips on tax forms." He winked. "But now I remember things for you. I remember this piece of paper when she comes. *E il nome, per favore?*"

"Karen."

"Ah. Karen. Karen. Pretty name." Mr. Guzimon waved away Sam's hand and the license with it. "Come now, *Po' Martello*. It is time to go."

Getting underway for hundreds of missions had been not unlike this very moment. Sam instantly had his black bag slung over his shoulder. The duffle bag of food and books dangled from a hand beneath the heavy web strap of the bag of weapons. The other hand would stay free to pull the pistol from the small of his back or test the mettle of a man and the strength of a jaw that might attempt to stop Sam's escape from Tampa.

The diminutive maître d' went to the small door that would lead Sam through the tunnel and back to the wine cellar of The Columbia. There was no conversation about the building above the safe room. Sam's soldier's instinct whispered that had anyone seen his guardian enter the building, they would not see him leave it until the maître d' wished them to and it would be well after Sam was wherever Don T intended him to be.

When the pair emerged into the wine cellar they found it as still as it had been for generations as it cradled and calmed the aging wine. The floors of the restaurant above the bottles were quiet. Sam didn't baulk or listen for steps. He followed every direction with the immediacy of an order as though following a commander into battle.

The kitchen was empty and dark. A slight light, caressing hanging stainless steel pans and massive colanders, reflected gently to Sam's eyes. The men passed through and hesitated only long enough to open the barred and bolted back door. In the alley that had escorted Mr. Abreu and his rusty grocery cart several hours before, now sat a midsized box truck with a massive faded strawberry painted on each side. In a couple of hours trucks like it would begin stopping in their early morning rounds to drop of fresh fish, meat, and local produce to the restaurant. This truck, however, was picking up, not delivering.

Mr. Guzimon worked the claw that comprised the heavy latch of the sliding overhead door on the back of the truck. Sam shoved the noisy door up a couple feet, tossed his bags in, and slid beneath it, but the maître d' stopped him mid-slide.

"Ah. No, *Martello*. Help me up."

The door coiled open above them as Sam gave a hand and easily lifted his guide into the box of the truck.

"Here," the maître d' said as he found a cargo light switch. "Close the door."

Sam pulled the door closed while Mr. Guzimon waited a count then turned the light on. The poor light showed a floor to ceiling bank of trays in a rack that had held tons and tons of produce through the life of the truck and now held a secret. Sam's guide unsnapped a few restraining ties and rolled the rack across the box of the truck with Sam's help.

The maître d' bent and adjusted a tie-down ring bolted to the floor. Rather than tug up on the metal bracket, he pushed down and turned the ring. Twin deadbolts pivoted under the floor and a section of plywood popped up. The old man looked at Sam. "It is more steerage than first class carriage, but it is a short trip. This leg anyway."

Sam managed a smile, but it was as dim as the cargo light. "How many legs are there?"

There was a gap before the answer. "You have to go the long way home, *Po' Martello*. The very long way."

"Where does 'the long way' end?" Sam said as he looked around the box of the truck as if to say, "We're alone here."

As the maître d' talked, he shuffled Sam's bags into the hidden compartment which took up the massive dummy gas tank and then some. "I will take you to the docks. Our Don has made passage for you to Tunisia and on to Trapani. You know Trapani?"

"Sicily."

"Ah. *Bene, Martello*. Friends of ours from Ficuzza will meet you. They will see to you from there. Do as they say, as I know you will."

"Of course."

"Ah. *Bene*. In you go."

Sam adjusted his bags and crunched himself down into the covert compartment. The maître d' tried to help him. "You are bigger and harder to pack than... You are just bigger," he said as he shoehorned Sam down. "We will be at the ship in fifteen minutes." He patted Sam's arm then pulled the hinged secret plywood door back in place, closed Sam in, and latched the unique D-ring. As Mr. Guzimon pressed himself up he gave a reassuring knock to Sam, locked beneath the floor in the dark belly of the truck.

The short trip promised was just that – and gratefully so. The compartment was never intended for human cargo, though Sam's escape wasn't the first time it had been pressed into service for such, and it was loud and rough. The maître d' knew it to be both and drove as gently as he could to not bruise the fragile 'strawberries' painted on the side of the box truck. When the truck's engine stopped dockside, Sam listened for the sounds of shipping. He waited as though he had a choice. His life was in the hands of others.

The hands of Sam's watch glowed in the pitch black. It was twenty after three. It was nearly as dark outside as Mr. Guzimon had parked between stacks of shipping containers which made the truck disappear in the deep shadows as if in a magician's trick. Sam heard the old driver exit with obvious care, followed by the gentle raising of the rear door. The panel above him popped open. The air was cooler on the docks and made more so by the unintended heat Sam had generated in the tiny hole. He had been much more uncomfortable for much longer on flights and missions around the world, but then he had been the hunter, not the hunted. This chase made his heart beat faster.

"Ah. There are a few passenger compartments on most of the big boats," the maître d' was saying. "Anyone can book a passage – if they can leave with little notice and at four in the morning."

Sam listened intently and nodded as he reached back into the secret compartment and pulled out his bags.

"You must also," Mr. Guzimon continued, "be willing to sail for weeks at a time to get to your destination and share your meals with a crew who may speak little English. Ah, they can also be a bit unsavory. This is no problem for you, I understand. But you must stay in your room throughout. Speak or see or be seen only by the captain. I don't know such things well. Maybe at least two weeks to Tunisia. I cannot say when the boat will move on to Trapani.

"The captain himself will leave meals outside your door, which you will keep locked. He will give you to a friend of ours when you have crossed from Tunisia to Sicily. As I have said, do what they ask of you and all will be well.

"Let's go, *Po' Martello*. The coast is clear."

The two men slid from the box of the truck. Sam had both bags slung over one shoulder. They did not run, but moved quickly along the edge of the huge containers toward a monstrous ship over a hundred yards away. When they were close, the maître d' stopped Sam with a touch on his arm and pointed to an opening in the ship at the opposite end of a gangway. A dark figure moved methodically back and forth across the opening like the pendulum of a clock.

"It is a funny expression, no? 'The coast is clear.' It is from war times, I believe. Checking the shoreline for German U-boats. You know, my father was an Army soldier for America, *Martello*. He followed the same path you are following tonight – United States to Africa to Sicily. He visited his grandparents near Palermo after the invasion. He wanted to leave the Army and stay there, but his grandfather made him honor his word to the Americans. He went ashore at Anzio in Italy a few weeks later. He is buried there. He was a good man."

"Like his son," Sam said in the dark.

"I suppose, yes. To some. Ah. Look there, *Martello*. On the ship. Walking back and forth. That is the captain. Go to his big boat. I leave you in his capable hands."

"*Grazie.*"

"Ah. No need. Don T does not forget his friends. Nor do I, *Martello*. Nor do I."

Sam nodded an unspoken thanks and extended his free hand.

"Our friends will pass word when the time is right," Mr. Guzimon said softly as they shook hands firmly with Mr. Guzimon clutching Sam's thick shoulder. "I will send along news as I can, when I can, but be patient, *Martello*. It will be a long time I am afraid."

"I understand."

"Goodbye, young Sam." And the maître d' stepped away into the shadows.

The captain never spoke or made eye contact with his passenger. Sam made for an explosive consignment. If something happened to him, the captain would have to answer to Don T and his associates in the shipping business. While passengers on freighters existed, they were rare and as Sam's name would not appear on any manifest, his discovery could lead to the captain's termination. Still, losing his job would pale to what would come with a seemingly gentle wave of the Tampa kingpin's hand for the seemingly or real betraying of a trust. This was hazardous cargo.

Neither man spoke in the dark shadows as Sam cleared the gangway and stepped onboard. The captain merely ceased to pace and walked away, down metal steps clad in thick layers of coat after coat of deep red corrosive resistant paint. Sam followed. Certain it had been by design, Sam neither saw nor heard another person. Beneath his feet however, he could feel the rumblings of the big ship.

The interior passageways were narrow and sported a medium gray paint that contrasted nicely with the heavy rust inhibiting deep dull red on the outside sea facing walls and stairs. As the captain produced a six inch thick brass key several decks below, Sam was introduced to a third color.

The door was more hatchway than doorway in the land bound sense. Beyond the captain's key was a small windowless room, perhaps only eight foot square, whose relations had sprung from the family tree of a prison cell much more than the stateroom of a ship. The walls and ceiling were a pale industrial green – made famous or infamous in aged hospitals and prisons on the heels of a long forgotten study that claimed soft green was tranquil and had a calming effect on people under stress.

A heavy duty switch enticed a single bare bulb on the ceiling to life. Between lightbulb and switch was a length of exposed metal conduit covered with untold layers of the placating green. A three by seven foot piece of steel was welded to the wall and served as a bed. The mattress was thick and clean and a stack of fresh linen and several blankets were neatly folded at the head near a fluffed pillow with dark blue and white stripes Sam recollected from old movies.

Welded along one wall was a simple metal writing desk with a straight backed wooden arm chair whose worn deep brown leather covering padding was squashed on the seat and armrests. There was a newer digital clock radio on the desk. It too was affixed to the wall – like most things – in anticipation of rolling seas.

Next to the desk were four rows of books – mostly dog-eared paperbacks – on shelves that leaned back deeply into the restraining wall. On the floor in the corner was a three inch raised lip of steel that served as the bulkhead for a grotesquely simple showerhead sprouting from the wall and a well-aged and stained porcelain toilet. There was nothing else in the room.

"Please keep in this room," were the captain's first words. Even then he did not look at Sam.

The ranking officer did not appear as one would envision the captain of such a massive cargo ship to be. He was a crisply dressed and small man who carried the complexion and accent of the Philippines.

The captain laid the big brass key on the desk. "I bring meals to the door. I strum my fingers fast – like this." The captain rapped four fingers several times in rapid succession as though playing a snare drum on the desk. "Only open to that call. It is me. Know I have left a meal."

"Yes, sir."

"We will be underway quick now. Weather is good. We make first port in sixteen days," he said as he stepped through the door with his eyes still on the floor. In the companion way he held up, one hand on the top of the hatch. "Yankee?"

"Yes, sir?"

"You know you not on my ship?"

"I do."

"You will play the radio low?"

"I will."

"From first port it may be several days before we sail to Trapani. That is where we see each other again. Not before. I bring you up and you leave ship. Okay, Yankee?"

"Understood."

"You will want to stretch. Go at night, near this room. Only this deck. Make no noise. Down this corridor to starboard is the rail. No one on this deck, but do not be seen please. You will scare my crew." The captain smiled a little. "They will think you a pirate." The smile melted. "And do not fall over. I cannot answer to Tampa for you falling off my boat."

Sam nodded as he only now lowered his two heavy bags to the steel deck that comprised the floor.

"You lock door please," the captain said as he pulled the hatch closed behind him and left Sam alone.

The big brass key worked smoothly and was returned to the welded desk. Almost without thought, as if it was expected, Sam sat on the bed, leaned forward with his elbows on his knees and looked around the small room in earnest. Like the door, the room bore the simplicities necessary with margins of space and the demands of a ship. As he had thought when the door was first pulled open, this was more cell than room and it had less to do with the color and more to do with the confines.

He pulled his bags closer on the floor and unzipped the heavy black one. The weapons were left inside, but access would be quicker. Sam understood he was still vulnerable despite Don T, the maître d', and now the captain's efforts. If what Karen had warned was true – and he could not bring himself to doubt her – he might never escape. The FBI could board at any time. The risk wouldn't end until they were underway. And then it would hang over the ship until it cleared coastal waters, which would take time as it sailed south through the Straits of Florida before tacking east into the open Atlantic. Even then, Interpol might be waiting in Tunisia or Trapani.

Sam shook his head involuntarily and rubbed his face hard with both hands. The funk that had waited in the cell/room wouldn't serve him well. He'd shake it and remain focused and optimistic. Not optimistic for himself in the long term perhaps, but cautious that Don T's network would insure his escape to a final destination Sam didn't yet know. While he shook himself free from the current doubts and circumstances, thoughts of Karen flooded him more than had the ship instantly buried itself in the bottom of Tampa Bay. While he would slip away into a void unknown after enduring this cell for a month or so, Karen would not be so lucky. When the Feds found Sam, they would find Karen and her cell would have bars.

Beneath his feet, in the walls, and in the ceiling above him, Sam felt more than heard the deep rumbling of the ship's gargantuan engines. There was a scraping thud as tugboats eased alongside. Between the tugboats and a transient captain to pilot the tight confines of the docks and the channel out to deep water, the ship began to move.

Three thousand feet above the creeping vessel, a prop plane from Washington was making its final approach to MacDill Air Force Base. John LaRoy had said nothing for the last three hours though he found himself staring at Karen often as though somehow watching her could answer the questions he wrestled with. Exhaustion from her recent race to the city coming up beneath her feet begged her restlessly sleep since the plane was airborne. When the rattle of the landing gear coming down shook the floor beneath their feet, Karen woke to LaRoy's finger in her face.

"Give me your phone," he said over the sound of the engines.

Karen heard him fine and complied with no hesitation.

"This plastic piece of shit is going to the lab. I don't know how yet. You know that, right?"

"Yes."

"No warrant. No due process. No goddam nothing! Understood?"

"Yes."

"I'll say I found it. You lost the goddamn thing. Got it?"

"Yes."

"And you don't get outa my sight in Tampa. Hear me? You want to take a piss, you ask me. We'll go in the men's room – I don't fucking know!" LaRoy jammed Karen's phone in his suitcoat inside pocket and crushed the heels of his palms hard into his eyes. "Goddamnit!"

LaRoy and Auburn cleared security at MacDill and were shown to simple overnight rooms on the base. LaRoy had been on the phone although it was four am. He had contacted the duty officer and a two man detachment of security were waiting at Karen's room. They would stand guard for what little remained of the night. LaRoy's people – Nuary and Denti – hadn't answered, but he left very curt, disgruntled messages. Out of desperation he called the local District Attorney, Jack Aaron. Jack answered on the second ring.

"Jesus Christ, I should have known you'd be up. John LaRoy here. How are you, old man?"

"Tired."

"You just get up?"

"No. Haven't been to bed yet. Work to do. You Feds don't know anything about it."

"I might," LaRoy said as he thought about Karen under guard in the next room.

"Cal said the big guns were coming down to see what turns up?"

"I'm already here."

"No shit, huh? Denti and your girl Nuary punched out at five o'clock."

"Nuary maybe. Not Cal."

"Since you're here you can take me to breakfast."

"I need a few hours."

"Oh, bullshit."

"Jack? Listen a second, you old sonofabitch. The worm is turning in this cocksucker and I don't mean maybe. Shit, shower, and shave then get with Cal and come out to MacDill at nine am."

Jack heard something new in LaRoy's voice.

"Okay, LaRoy."

"And Cal says you've got a good investigator. Bring him."

"Anything else?"

"Your forensic guy – the one who found Clayton Rand. Chuck him in the car too."

Jack slipped back. "Do we have to do everything for you Feds? You want me to bring coffee and donuts too?"

"You told me that this shit storm started in Tampa. Well, it's back in your lap, you're the odds-on favorite, and you're running on the rail." John took a breath. "The ex-Delta sergeant. Is he talking?"

"Talking? He ain't even sticking his head out."

"We don't have him?"

"Not even close."

"He could be in Washington," LaRoy said as a hint of desperation crept into his voice. "The search warrants turn up anything?"

"A couple things."

"Are you going to make me ask?"

"There's a connection between your Ranger and my guy Rand. Looks like they were friends when they were kids."

"That's curious, isn't it?"

"I thought so. Cal agrees."

"I'm convinced. So round up Cal and your boys and meet us at MacDill at nine."

"Us?"

"Lieutenant Auburn flew down with me from JAG."

"Good looking head," Jack popped. "Seems to know the score."

"She does indeed. See you at nine."

John had nearly hung up when Jack's plea stopped him. "Hey! You said our Ranger might be in Washington. What makes you think so?"

"Body count."

"I'm thinking I must have missed the latest news cycle."

"Where are you, Jack?"

"Sitting in my car. Downtown. I'm watching your evidence techs to make sure they don't screw up."

"Go home and flip on the news. Do you know the name Candice Beech?"

"Beech? Beech? IRS? A hearing or something. Is that the bitch who tried to talk her way out of the latest scandal then took the 5th when it was somebody else's turn to talk?"

"That's her. Well she won't be appearing before Congress for any follow-up testimony."

"She lawyer up?"

"No. More permanent. Someone put a bullet in her eye while I was catching a plane to Tampa. She's dead as hell."

Jack nearly laughed. "You can hide behind the 5th Amendment, but that sonofabitch sure ain't bulletproof."

John pulled the phone closer and hunched over. "Damn, Aaron, are you still cheering for these guys? If you are, I swear I'll–"

"Relax, John. It's a joke. What do you expect? The goddamn IRS? Everybody hates those people. And they thumb their nose at Congress? To hell with 'em."

"Jesus Christ...," John muttered as he thought again about Karen. "Jack, don't mess around. I mean it. This is damn ticklish. Damn ticklish. By tomorrow there'll be fifty more agents in Tampa. If one hears you talking, I won't be able to keep your ass out of jail."

"Alright. Alright. I'll keep still."

"Get some sleep," LaRoy said as he rubbed his own eyes. "I'll see you at nine."

"At nine," Jack said and disconnected. He sat back deep into the seat of his car. His pistol on his belt bit him in the soft spot under his rib. "Oww," he said as he adjusted the compact revolver. "I'll leave you home if that's how you're going to act."

Jack pushed the car door open and swung his feet out to the pavement. He leaned forward on his knees. Across the street the generators were still pushing light over the Ciampiano newsstand. "One looksee," Jack said to no one as he struggled to get out of the car. "I'm beat."

In front of the stand was a marked Tampa PD car. Two officers sat inside – a young patrolman behind the wheel and a grizzled veteran on the passenger's side nearly asleep. As Jack approached, the driver's window slid down.

"Pretty early start, DA," the uniformed young officer said.

"Naww. Late night. I'm checking to make sure the Feds don't screw anything up."

"Is this our case? I thought with all the FBI windbreakers floating around we were only making sure the yellow tape stays nice and tight."

"Could be. I'll let you know," Jack said as he reached the curb to the sound of the passenger window powering down.

"Hey, DA?" the older officer was saying. "Isn't this an awful lot of effort for a bookmaker? Old man Ciampiano ran numbers as long as anyone can remember, but he's been dead a while. Was his kid into something else?"

Jack stopped on the sidewalk in the glare of the lights and noise of the power plants. "I dunno yet. Must be something to it or the Feds wouldn't still be here."

"And our District Attorney wouldn't be up all night."

The power window closed.

Jack hesitated a noticeable moment longer and thought about the elder Ciampiano before he shuffled his tired feet to the back of an open FBI evidence step-van. Two techs were seated on stools having coffee inside.

"How goes the fight, men?" Jack pulled his identification. "District Attorney Jack Aaron. Any smoking guns?"

"Just yesterday's news," one tech said with a smile as he gestured to the now day old newspapers resting in evidence bags on the floor of the van.

"Say... Now that's funny. Damn funny. 'Yesterday's news.' Good one. You mind if I take another look around?"

The second tech motioned for Jack to help himself.

At the door to the newsstand Jack buried his hands in his pockets. It was an old habit to not inadvertently disturb evidence. If he wanted to though, the hands came out and poked and prodded answers from the innocuous with the tip of a pencil or pen. As he stepped inside he noticed the disturbed newspapers from the floor had been taken – presumably for fingerprint or other testing. He himself had probably spied the best piece already in the photograph from the newsstand wall. As he walked back to the now empty space on the wall, he thought ahead to Clayton Rand and the ex-Army Ranger trying to squirm out of knowing one another and The New Illuminati when he'd slide the photograph of the two of them across an interview table.

At the far end of the stand Jack was looking at the frayed black vinyl barstool with its duct taped patch work. Someone had spent a lot of time – likely years – perched on this stool. The badly stained Mr. Coffee machine was behind the stool on a crude counter tacked to the wall beneath where the incriminating picture had been. Next to the coffee maker were a few ratty paperback books. One seemed less worn and it stuck out in its freshness. Jack cocked his head to read the spine. *Sweet Thursday.* John Steinbeck.

"Steinbeck. Guy can't be all bad." Jack looked back quickly to the open door as if to look for John LaRoy checking Jack's moral pulse against any alleged members of The New Illuminati. Not finding him, Jack looked again at the stack of books – more so out of literary interest now than evidence of a crime. He slipped *Sweet Thursday* from the stack and began to thumb through it. A few pages had dog ears and on them Jack found lines highlighted. "Yep," he said as he read the marked passages. "Good line. No argument."

He rifled the pages as though he was holding a deck of cards. His eye caught a glimpse of writing on the title page. He stopped at the cover to leaf page by page back to the inscription which was in blue ink from a delicate hand, "I found this classic for you, oh, and I posed for the cover! Love, Karen."

Jack held the page place with one hand and flipped to the cover and saw a pretty girl with medium length brown hair in a purple dress posed against the pale yellow of the cover. "Good looking head..." and the investigator's mind ran the name from the writing against the picture on the cover and his own words. John LaRoy's passing comment regarding the JAG lieutenant came back to him.

The book jumped in his hand as it flicked back and forth from the title page to the cover and back again three times in a blurry succession while his mind equaled as many flip-flops.

"No chance," he said in a whisper to himself. As his words tried to convince him, his eyes darted sideways to the newsstand door. Beyond the flap sat the idling Tampa patrol car and outside the door was the FBI forensic van. Jack sat the book down as he examined the shelf. He understood the book would certainly show in the photographs already taken by the forensic people, but felt his breath shorten as he considered a wild, far-flung scenario.

"Maybe I was hasty in blaming the TSA... But how the hell?" Jack said as though talking to Sam next to him on the beat up stool as the two looked through the remaining books. "It does explain how you knew to get out of Dodge, don't it?"

Jack looked away from the fictitious Sam and glanced surreptitiously at the FBI forensic workers as he slid the book into his back pocket and turned toward the door. "Crazy. I need some sleep."

———————————

7

Across Tampa and the coastal waters nearby, the players in the narrative Clayton had set into motion on a quiet evening with scribbled notes across a yellow legal pad and the graphic boosted from a dollar bill were in repose of varying depth.

Jack was dropping his socks in rumpled balls on the floor of his Spartan bedroom and collapsing into his bed, minus his pants, but still wearing his partially unbuttoned shirt. The light on the companion nightstand was aglow and Jack opened his eyes only enough to reach for the switch. His hand came up short and came to rest on the tapered edge of the stand. Just beyond it waited the switch, but beyond that sat the Steinbeck paperback under the padded envelope he had taken from Sam's mailbox. Next to the misappropriated possible evidence was Jack's revolver.

Everything seemed to be dictating a missive. Jack's hand wanted to reach for the light, but was dog-tired and also held back by the last dreamy, disjointed thoughts he allowed to play in his head. The table lamp knew it was hours and hours past its standard usefulness and waited to be put out. The gun was clean, polished, and quiet – showing light signs on the dark metal where the protective bluing had worn away from constant carry – but it was coiled as always, waiting until its balancing action in Jack's mind, hand, and circumstance was needed yet again.

The book was silent and waited for another calm turn at bringing to life the "whores, pimps... angels, saints – that is, everyone..." who inhabited the aged pages compliments of Steinbeck. The girl on the cover continued to hide her face.

Resting across part of the book was the padded envelope. It was screaming about the violation of rights guaranteed under the law, clamoring over illegal search and seizure, evidence tampering, larceny, malfeasance. Then everything was drowned out by a nearly inaudible vibration. It stopped and came again. And another time.

Jack's face pulled into that awkward contortion of concentration as a tired mind tried to focus on a silent sound. His eyes woke. His hand started to reach for the package then stopped. Instead, he threw his feet off the bed and sat up in a rush with the sheet struggling to hold him in the bed as the repeating vibration registered as the silent ringing of a phone. It was more instinct and reaction to the realization that made him lunge for the package, but his grab ended in a grimace when the thought of what the package might contain brought him up short. It wasn't the thought of a ringing phone – he was certain there was a phone in the envelope now – but the probability, however remote, that the package might hold something more. Perhaps a mistake that left a piece of trace evidence – a hair, a fiber – or a latent fingerprint.

The DA kicked at the troublesome sheet as he ripped open a drawer on the busy nightstand and yanked out a stainless steel knife that would have looked more at home in a Rambo movie than the District Attorney's bedroom. He held the wide blade in the palm of his hand and gently sliced the back of the stolen envelop as though the gaudy knife had been a razor blade. To hold the package steady against the pull of the knife, Jack pinched one corner as he had when he took it from the Ciampiano mailbox. The neat cut revealed clear bubble wrap. The knife pried the phone free from the envelope and its cushion as it vibrated for the last time.

Jack stared at the silence and balanced his knife in his hand. The simple digital clock next to *Sweet Thursday* said it was four seventeen in the morning. "Okay. Okay," Jack said as he pried the phone apart with the knife until its spring took over and snapped open on its own. "No one calls anybody at four in the morning unless they're calling a guy who is up at that hour headed to work. Like a guy who peddles newspapers maybe."

The silent phone would win the staring contest. Jack watched it and examined its rudimentary buttons at length. Certain he'd mess up any digital fingerprints in the phone's history, he decided to wait the few hours it would be until he could get this thing in the hands of Hefner Oakes. If Oakes could trace the origin of the call, Jack would have probable cause to–

The phone vibrated again.

Jack let it ring a second time and a third before he felt the knife point gently pressing the green talk button as he leaned over the phone without touching it.

There was no voice, but the timer indicated the call had connected. Jack could wait, listen, breathe – even talk dirty, he mused. None fit him. He was tired. He had already blurred a dozen lines not the least of which was one big one John LaRoy had lectured him on just prior to Jack tossing the paper with Clayton Rand's name on it across LaRoy's desk. Rand's had worked well that day. Today was another. Jack took a breath.

"Good morning, Mr. Rand. You don't know me, but I might be the only friend you've got."

The line went dead.

Across town Clayton Rand was sitting in boxers and a t-shirt on the edge of his bed. He was staring at a basic flip phone in his hand. It was the kind he had sent Raphael and matched the one Jack Aaron had just answered. The timing had thrown him off. As he raced against next moves like a chess champion outguessing his opponent, Clayton's elaborate smart phone rang on the nightstand next to his bed. He heard the set tone and without looking knew it was his brother Carl. Still, the timing of the ringing while Clayton held a phone with an unknown and potentially dangerous voice on the other end made him look twice at both pieces before he set the one meant for Sam aside and took up the other and said hello to his brother.

"Hey, Carl. It's early. You headed to work?"

"Yea. Morning, Clay. You got the news on?"

"No. What's up?" his voice harried from the last call and not the groggy sleepy voice Carl should have expected if his thoughts went that far.

"Lots of stuff. More bombings and shit all over. Somebody shot that shank from the IRS," Carl said with no small measure of excitement. "But check this out – the cops are at Sam's place."

Clayton grabbed the cheap pay-as-you-go phone, bounced off his bed, and jogged down the hallway to his media room still listening to his brother ramble.

"There's cameras and reporters and those big-assed news trucks with the towers and coils of wire on 'em all over the streets in front of Sam's house and Ciampiano's newsstand. Something's messed up."

The trendy huge screen was instantly on and he tuned to a local channel and their early morning news. Carl's reference to Sam had uncharacteristically startled him for several reasons. There was the cheap, but still warm phone that held the echo of the strange voice who purported to be a friend resting where he had dropped it on his couch when he scooped up the remote for the television. There were the words 'cops' and 'Sam' in the same sentence. And most urgently, Clayton knew his phone was tapped. Here was his brother referring to the last man Clayton wanted to be connected to just then.

"What?" was the best he could offer as scenes of flashing lights around streams of flickering yellow police barricade tape played across the wide television.

"The cops are all over Sam's house and the newsstand. Ain't that some shit?"

"What? Who?"

"Sam. Sam. You ditz wad."

"Sam who?"

"For a smart sonofabitch, you can be as dumb as dirt. In fact, if you was dumb as dirt, you'd cover a whole acre, you know that? Ciampiano, moron. Turn your TV on. There's cops at Sam's house and the newsstand."

"Ciampiano? From high school?"

"Yea, no shit from high school. The guy was all-state everything then joined up in the Marine Corps or something. You know him."

"I can't place him," Clayton said with much thought.

"Oh, bullshit! If you'd use your head for something besides video games, you'd remember. We all ran together out of the stand. We both hawked papers for his old man. Old man Ciampiano? Tough as nails sonofabitch? You remember old man Ciampiano, don't you? What are you, still asleep?"

"Yea... Yes, I remember him. He ran a magazine store downtown. I think I might have sold papers there for a short while one summer."

"There you go, Einstein! Every kid in Tampa worked at that paper shack."

Clayton recovered and smiled as he thought to himself, "Oh, very good, Carl. Very good. I hope you heard that, FBI. Every kid worked there."

Carl continued. "Hell, I still do. I cover for Sam once in a while when he can't work or whatever."

"Oh, yea? I didn't know that."

"Just to make a few extra bucks. Sam's had it pretty tough since his old man died and then he pulled out of the Marines to run the shack. I think he got tired of taking orders. I know I'd get tired of being told what to do all the time. Plus all that marching. That's total bullshit."

"That would get old pretty quick."

"Damn right, but I wonder what he did to make the news? Damn. I just thought of something. What if he got killed? Like a robbery at the stand. Oh, that ain't good."

"I hope that's not true. Maybe somebody broke in the business."

"No way. It says 'FBI' on the backs of some of the cops. FBI wouldn't give a shit about no bullshit burglary, asshole."

"I don't know, Carl. I'm wondering out loud, the same as you."

"I hope Sam's alright. What do you think happened?"

"Beats me. Thanks for waking me up though."

"Yea well, I'm sorry about that. I guess I thought you'd remember him. You gotta admit, it's pretty wild seeing the stand surrounded by cops. Maybe they'll want to talk to me."

"If they do, just be honest."

"I will. I got no problem with cops. It's not a big– Hey... I'll bet I know what it is."

Clayton let the pause hang as Carl collected his thought.

"Old man Ciampiano ran numbers out of there," Carl followed himself. "You've got to remember that. I'll bet anything, Sam took over his father's racket and now the Feds are closing him down."

"That could be."

"That's it. Gambling."

"Sounds like it."

"It's the gambling. I'm sure of it."

"Well, let me know if you need bail. Otherwise I'm going back to bed."

"Shit! I don't have nothing to do with that. I just open up and sling papers – just like when we were kids."

"That's good, Carl. Stay away from anything else. If the police want to talk to you about gambling out of the stand, you tell them everything you know about it."

"That'd take about two seconds. I don't know anything."

"Good. Hey, enjoy the news. I'm going back to bed."

"Naw, I'm headed to the docks."

"I've got a couple of hours yet. Good night, Carl. Swing by after your shift and catch me up on your part-time boss's book making business."

"I'll do that. They just said they're looking for him, but ain't found him yet."

"People do all sorts of things. Who knows? I'm going to catch another forty–"

"But still in all, Clay, when you think about Sam he don't impress you as a criminal type. You know?"

"Like I said, you never know about people, Carl."

"But gambling – especially bolita – that's not really a crime. Not really. It's like lotto and lotto's legal. The government is probably pissed that they're not getting their cut. That's all. Sam's dad–"

"Hey, Carl? I'm sorry, but I've got to crash for a little while. I've got a busy day coming up. Can you stop by later? I'll have a cold one waiting for you."

"You got it. I never turn down a free beer."

"Don't I know it."

"Shit... Don't offer then! If I said no, you'd start crying."

"Thanks for your concern. See you after work."

Clayton ended the call and dropped the high tech phone on the couch. The two phones were a stark contrast as Clayton ratcheted up the volume and settled onto the edge of a soft brown leather chair. He was still there several hours later – caught in the repeating cycle of nighttime videos of flashing lights and yellow tape. Sam's house and the newsstand were the backdrop of talking heads trying to scoop each other with equal amounts of nothing. As the sun came up, little information had leaked out. A press conference would be scheduled, but no time was given. By morning, the night time videos were replaced with fresher day light versions of evidence technicians walking in and out of the yellow tape with impunity. The big networks were slowly connecting dots to the recent rash of assaults, bombings, and the killing of the IRS agent. Red banners flashed 'Breaking News' and 'Home–Grown Terror' across the screens as Clayton surfed through channels. One of the few constants across the news outlets was that the property owner had not yet been located. The lead at the eight o'clock hour contained the first tie to The New Illuminati. At that, Clayton pulled his laptop out and went through his virtual backdoor onto the internet and well beyond to see what he could learn from those his firewalls had been placed to protect. Before he could navigate far, the lesser phone of the pair on the couch began to buzz. He recognized the non-descript number that came up as the cheap phone he'd sent Raphael.

"Good morning," Clayton answered quickly.

"Good morning? Have you seen the–"

"I'm watching it now."

"What the hell's going–"

"Breathe," Clayton said though his own was short.

"Breathe? Fuck you! Breathe. Is–"

"Why don't you come by for late lunch? I'm pretty busy right now."

"I'd imagine so."

"Two o'clock?"

"See you then."
There was no goodbye and no peace on either end.

8

The company around the circular table at MacDill included the collection of investigators of various stripes that had convened at Andrews Air Force Base some months before plus talent compliments of the local District Attorney's Office. John LaRoy headed the cast and the meeting as he had done prior. Instead of a pleasant afterthought as at the first conference, Karen sat tight at his right hand. Alyn Nuary had injected herself at his left. Calburn Denti was next. Jason Meyer had purposely arraigned to be as far away from Alyn as possible though he'd slept close to her the short night before. Helfer Oakes was unceremoniously plopped next to Meyer by the DA so, "the eggheads can talk shop," Jack said as he sat next to Cal and Marcus between his boss and the DA's one man forensic unit. The last seat in the circle, completing it back to Karen, and the last to arrive, was held down by Major Doug Caulden, Special Forces.

"Morning, Major," LaRoy said grimly as the others settled and ran their fingers across cell phone screens. "Well," LaRoy burst as he clenched his hands tight with interlaced thick fingers in a combined fist that leaned heavy on the table. He looked at everyone and no one in quick succession as the updates and directions came with an ease that an observer would have thought grew from a rehearsed speech. Under LaRoy's words and behind his eyes however, there churned an indecision that would have disturbed his audience.

When Cal had offered LaRoy the obligatory, "How are you?," LaRoy's countenance flashed dark. The FBI head turned away toward the figurative dais where he would sit at the round table and said, "I'll fill in everybody at once."

True to her word and LaRoy's order, Karen had been in tight lockstep behind him. Now she sat beside him partially numb, as she wrestled with current events in Tampa and the unknown condition and whereabouts of Sam. Others at the table shared at least one of her thoughts – everyone wanted to know where Sam Ciampiano was.

"There's been movement," LaRoy began as he flipped open a disarmingly simple folder. "Helluva lot of movement in this Illuminati thing and I shouldn't have to tell anyone here...," LaRoy looked directly and obviously at Jack. "Anyone who's living in the twenty-first century anyway, that this entire shit storm has been ratcheted up considerably. Whoever's behind this – and we've got some names and faces that are looking good for it – has gotten their asses promoted to the big leagues. Last time we met, we were looking at theft, assault, conspiracy maybe, and a bucket load of cyber-tech crimes. Now they've picked up a body – at least one that we know of. There's been bombings, serious injuries."

"Civilian?" Jack interrupted.

"What?"

"Civilians. Who got bombed?"

"Of course they're civilians, Jack. The Illuminati haven't decided to take on our military, not yet anyway."

"I mean, who got bombed?"

John looked into the pages within the folder. He leafed through a few papers. "Depending on the local definition of 'bombing,' the Bureau is reviewing nine different incidents across the country. On the low end, somebody put a burning paper bag of dog shit on a Congressman's porch in New Jersey, rang the doorbell, and took off." LaRoy stopped and looked again at Jack, adjusted himself in his chair, but didn't smile. "That one sounds like something you'd do, DA."

The table laughed with various enthusiasm. Jack was thoughtful, leaned forward, and put a finger to his lips. "Actually... I think I was in 7th grade. He was my homeroom teacher. Meeker. Jerry Meeker. I still remember. A bunch of us–"

"Mother of God, Cal," LaRoy sputtered as he turned and looked at Cal. "Can you corral this guy?"

Cal leaned on the table toward Jack's longsuffering second. "Marcus? Whose turn is it to watch your boss?"

"I got it," Marcus said, a little uncomfortable with the awkward attention, but Jack, in hidden but full command, eased him off the hook.

"Petey, c'mon... It was funny as hell. That's a helluva gag."

Alyn Nuary turned her palms up as she too leaned forward on the table. "Setting fire to a Congressman's house is funny?"

"No one set fire to the house."

"It was a paper bag–"

"On his porch."

"On the teacher's porch."

"No, the Congressman's."

"I thought this was a bombing?"

"It was dog shit."

"What?"

"The bag's full of shit."

"Somebody's full of shit."

"What?"

"I was twelve years old, for cryin' out loud."

"That'd make a nice campaign ad for whoever they put up against you in the next election, Jack," Cal said smiling.

"Oh, you'd like that, wouldn't you? Then who would solve your cases for you?"

On another day, LaRoy might have relished the banter, but the flight with Karen, and the conversation preceding it, coupled with the short night to wear him down and test his patience. His tired eyes jumped between Cal and the DA. "You girls ready to stop pulling each other's hair?"

Cal sighed and apologized sincerely. "Sorry, John."

"Excuse me?" Nuary objected and looked to Karen for reinforcements.

Karen only smiled, grateful for any distraction.

"Oh. I'm in this alone, I see," Alyn snipped at the JAG officer before LaRoy shut her off.

"Don't get your panties in a wad, Alyn. Jesus. It's a joke. Let's move on—"

"The oldest one in the book."

"Excuse me?" Nuary said again. "We can deal with the inappropriate dialogue another time – and rest assured, we will – but making light of a bombing—"

"No one's doing that. We're back on track as of right now." LaRoy looked to Marcus. "Investigator Pete? Would you do your damnedest to keep your boss's foot out of his mouth?"

Marcus smiled and nodded.

Jack shot Petey a terse glance. "Traitor."

"Are you ready now?" LaRoy asked the DA.

"It was a simple question," Jack said briskly.

"What's that?"

"Were the targets of the bombings civilians? I mean, were they John Q. Public or were they politicians?"

LaRoy looked again into the folder, but didn't need to. He knew where Aaron was headed and had drawn the same conclusion. "The targets weren't all politicians in the strictest form of the word, but before I let the definition dog loose again, I'll say that nine out of nine were elected officials or appointees of elected officials. You're all smart enough to figure out how far you can throw that stone. Levels range from county appraisers who gave their unqualified kids cushy high priced jobs to members of the U.S. Congress. Bombings run the same gamut – from Jack's flaming dog shit to damn elaborate high explosive, the way I read the reports." LaRoy motioned to Meyer. "Jason, in a nutshell, what have you fellas turned up?"

Like everyone who was pulled into a conversation at a table, Meyer leaned forward as he spoke. "The sum is exactly as you said – a range of devices that cover the spectrum from firecracker to shaped charges. Gunpowder to ammonium nitrate and then some. Hard wired triggers and fused ignition to what we think is at least one infrared detonator. Most are generations away from high school pranks on a porch. They're elaborately constructed, technologically well designed, highly effective IEDs. Powerful. And growing."

"Growing?"

"In frequency anyway," Meyer said as his thumb traced over his phone's screen. "There's been another explosion."

Several of the federal phones at the table began to buzz as if on cue. The quiet phones of the locals asked the forensic head to provide a readout as John LaRoy rubbed his eyes.

Meyer was looking at his phone and talking with his free hand as if reluctantly conducting an orchestra. "Details still coming in. Fairfax County. Residence of Congressman Becker. He's DOA."

LaRoy lowered his hand and stretched his neck up and around. "We have an open case on him. Corruption. Bribery. Campaign finance. Misappropriation."

"You can close that one," Jack said to no one particular as he sat back and waited to hear more.

LaRoy came out of his stretch and nearly glared at Jack for the inference. "Yep."

While the others were occupied with their phones, Karen's was still in LaRoy's pocket as far as she knew. She watched John instead and caught the disapproving look he shot the local District Attorney. It seemed to Karen there was something between these two men who, on the surface, were so much alike. But what Karen didn't catch was that as she watched Jack, he was studying her.

"The press will have us for breakfast," Nuary said absently as she flipped through her own phone before she looked across the table at Meyer. "Can we tell if these bombs are the work of one man?"

"Not yet. Early analysis says this one had a mercury switch. That's the first one of those. Others had cell phone ignitors, fused, timers, etc."

Nuary smirked. "This is sounding like terrorism to me."

"It's all terrorism, isn't it?" Helfer Oakes heard himself say.

"All criminal anyway," Marcus answered. "I wouldn't have guessed we had so many bombers coming out of the woodwork though."

"Maybe it's just one group. Just mixing up their techniques."

"Bombers don't do that," Helfer said. "They have a style."

"Style? Please," Nuary snipped. "Let's not glamorize terrorism."

"No, style like they do what they know. What works for them." Helfer motioned to Meyer next to him. "If you're on about those initiators, you're after nine different – ten different – people."

"Ten bombers?"

"Ten bombers."

"And more computer bombers on top of that," Meyer followed. "We've got ongoing investigations flowing in from a mayor's office in Southwest Podunk to the White House regarding hacks. We're drowning."

An uneasy wave rolled around the table.

"Take a deep breath, Jason," LaRoy's voice bellowed. "I get it this thing is getting some footing, but we've got boots on the ground at every site and an army of geeks burning up keyboards. Plus we've got a couple of hot names and faces."

Jack leaned into the mix. "It's like they just had graduation at a bomb making school."

"They sort of did."

"Excuse me?"

It was Major Caulden's turn. "They sort of did. When you think about our guys coming back from the Middle East. Ten years ago no one outside of the military knew what an IED was. Now you can find plans on the internet."

"That's true," Jack smiled. "An IED use to be what kept you from getting pregnant, right?"

That even gave LaRoy pause and Nuary was on him. She motioned to the local DA while looking at her boss. "John? Is this character for real? I'm not comfortable with what I see as national security issues being discussed here between bouts of potty humor."

"You better get comfortable, Agent Nuary," Jack snapped. "If not for us, you'd be in front of a Congressional oversight committee that isn't too happy with their police protection trying to explain what it is you do."

Nuary leaned even further across the table. "Really? Are you pulling my leg?"

Jack couldn't help himself and Cal and Marcus weren't quick enough to stop him. "Not yet, but you do have a nice set of pins there, Agent Nuary. But what say we focus on the case for a while? John, it sounds to me like you federal boys... and girls... have got your hands full with all the IEDs going off. If it's all the same to you, I'd like to make a request that the Lieutenant there go along with my crew." Jack had ignored Alyn's reddening face showing through her heavy make-up and pointed at Karen. "We could use her information, insight, and contacts as we run down this mad dog. I apologize Lieutenant that we are apparently of the lowest sort, but we have good hearts. The Ranger's local. We'll focus on him – find that slippery sonofabitch – then set him down across from Mr. Rand and see who flips first. What do you say, LaRoy?"

LaRoy was tense. It was uncommon territory for him and it showed. Alyn had been partially right. Having local authorities this involved was difficult. They were not accountable to the Bureau, not answerable to LaRoy, beholding to him, or intimidated by him. Jack Aaron fell into that latter category in spades. Though it had never been John's intent to control the DA, he did need to control the investigation and doing one left an imprint on the other.

LaRoy looked at Karen. She knew what he was thinking and answered with her eyes set on the only person to hold her secret. LaRoy, she reasoned, would want to keep her under his thumb.

"I'm available certainly," Karen said to LaRoy primarily and the entire delegation in general. "But you and I have already begun that series of steps concerning Ciampiano. We should finish that background analysis first." Then she looked at Jack and Marcus. "What we uncover may assist you with locating the suspect." Karen involuntarily shot a dagger at Nuary. "And I have no hesitation with sharing what we uncover."

"That works," LaRoy said, wrestling control of the group back to the ground. "Jack, touch base with me. Engage your local resources with ferreting out Ciampiano. You're correct – he's home grown. You know the stomping grounds. Cal will be the conduit between you and the Bureau. Don't cover the same ground twice and stay off each other's toes."

Nuary was edgy and felt the reins slipping away. "John, I'd like to stay involved with the locals."

"Didn't you just say you—"

"This is my region."

John slammed his fist on the table and phones and pens and coffee cups rattled on the other side. "Goddamn prima donnas! Cal will keep you in the loop. Cal, run everything up the flagpole to Alyn."

"That's irregular," Alyn quipped.

"Call J. Edgar. We've got work to do." John's frustration was showing and it confused everyone except Karen. "Anybody! What do we have on this Ciampiano Army reject? Major? Throw some semblance of sanity on the table, will you please?"

"I'll try, but this is going to look like I'm throwing a net over smoke." Caulden replicated LaRoy's moves and flipped through a few pages in front of him. "Ciampiano enlisted out of high school. Rudimentary basic training. Infantry. Nothing special. A grunt. He applied for sniper training. Shows rejected for eyesight and served as a warehouse clerk and truck driver stateside for almost fourteen years then is discharged."

"Discharged?" Jack asked.

"Discharged."

"Honorably?"

"Yes."

"Why's a guy pull his ticket six years short of retirement and a federal pension to run a newsstand?"

"Newsstand?" LaRoy said.

"Yea, John," Cal filled in. "Ciampiano runs a newsstand downtown. His father had it until he passed away."

"Sells papers? I didn't think those things existed outside of New York."

"We're special," Jack cracked.

LaRoy ignored him. "I'm guessing there's another side to this guy, Major."

"Good guess. Remember I said he washed out of sniper school for bad eyesight? When I reviewed his enlistment physical it says he was twenty–twenty. He doesn't show up on any standard documents saying so, but if you understand all the acronyms and codes – his pay and service items – he disappears in sniper training and goes underground in the system. He's Special Forces. Airborne, Rangers, and then some. Was assigned to SOCOM – Joint Special Operations Command for my civilian friends. Right here in Tampa. Served countless classified missions. Has all the unique skills you would expect – weapons, survival, surveillance, close-order-combat. Excelled everywhere we sent him. Decorated a hundred times over."

"And this war hero drops out?" Nuary asked. "To become part of a home-grown terrorist network? John, let's get the CIA's counter terrorist people involved. Somebody recruited one of our most dangerous assists."

Major Caulden wasn't finished. "I'm not certain about that. Karen – Lieutenant Auburn – might be able to pick up the story from there. The last thing I show is JAG involvement."

The revelation caught Karen off guard, but relieved LaRoy of the duty of pulling back the curtain on how Karen met the absent Ranger.

Karen would only tell what little she knew was in the formal record – something Major Caulden likely had in the folder in front of him. Unlike the others, Karen stayed back in her chair. Her posture did not invite questions or further discussion. Through an apparent unconscious and unintended lapse, she even pronounced Sam's name wrong.

"Campano was charged with aggravated assault prior to his discharge. The case likely would have worked its way through the system with little notice but the sergeant evoked a layered code – Blackbird – that dispatched both him and the entire case. I, that is, JAG, was summarily dismissed and rendered no additional representation or investigation."

"What was the nature of the assault?" Marcus questioned.

"A, ah... a confrontation. A fight between the sergeant and another man. An NCO, as I recall."

"That sounds pretty casual to me," Petey continued. "To be discharged from the Special Forces over a fight – a punch in the nose or whatever – after the investment the military put into this man?"

"Coupled with his listed qualifications," Helfer Oakes added. "And his medals."

"It was more than a punch. As I recall... The... the case seemed to... The facts of the case were that Campano nearly ripped a man's arm off with seeming little provocation."

Caulden interjected. "These men can be get wound pretty tight. Even with the very best psychological screening, a soldier who is highly trained will react with that same training if confronted. The correct circumstances may trigger–"

Nuary was making a statement she took for fact. "So you discharged a trained killer – a maniac who can't control his violence – and dropped him in Tampa. Now we're supposed to be shocked he hasn't stopped killing people? How many others like him have you turned loose on us? Little wonder there are nine, ten bombers as Mr. Oakes suggests. Unbelievable."

Karen was bristling. "I don't believe Sergeant Ciampiano is a maniac. He has received training, I grant you–"

"Let's save the Advocate General's 'ass covering' for later," Nuary said. "Can we find this time bomb and his friends before he kills again?"

Jack was looking at Karen, reading every move. LaRoy was doing the same. "Tampa PD locked down every road in and out of the city before we moved yesterday," Marcus said.

Cal added the federal response. "The bus terminals are being monitored. We alerted TSA and the Coast Guard. They, along with our own agents, local sheriff's department, and city PD, are heavily engaged at the airports and the Port of Tampa. His picture was released to the media this morning. If he moves we'll know it."

"He may be underground already."

"Quite possible."

"He's a local product. Certain to have contacts."

"We know he does at that," LaRoy said. "The search warrant last night turned up an interesting photograph. Cal?"

"Well, it was the DA's office really, but–"

"It was pinned to the wall, Agent Denti," Nuary popped. "It didn't take Sherlock Holmes–"

"–we have a very credible photograph that ties two of our potential players together. I've sent each of you a copy of the picture. It's obviously dated, but it establishes a relationship between our ex-Ranger and another individual who we have been monitoring for some time. Clayton Rand. I've forwarded you particulars on both men. I'll defer to our military colleagues to continue addressing Ciampiano, but Rand is a computer wizard. He designs firewalls and handles installations for much of the Fortune 500. He has a long list of government clients as well. If anyone could touch off the type and magnitude of hackings we have seen, as Jason referenced, it'd be Rand."

"What his status?"

"Under twenty-four hour surveillance. Physical and data."

"Anything?"

"Not a hint."

"Even after the raids yesterday?"

"He was home last night and went to work this morning."

"Are we ready to pick him up?"

"For questioning?"

"We certainly don't have basis for an arrest yet."

"Hell, we can question anybody. That'd be easy."

"John?" Jack's voice had less edge. "Just a thought from the cheap seats here, but I'd let Rand float a while longer. I don't know about you

Feds, but I like to ask questions I already know the answers to. Know what I mean?"

"I do indeed." LaRoy overlooked Alyn yet again and turned to Cal. "What do you say, Cal? We're taking a risk leaving him on the streets."

"What do you forensic guys think? Can we keep him under wraps?"

The junior Helfer Oakes gave way to Meyer, but the volley came back. "We've got a tight handle on what he's receiving and sending out, but I don't know what that really accomplishes. Helfer? Thoughts?"

There was no hesitation. "Clayton Rand will only let us see what he wants us to see. This guy is really tremendous. Fantastic."

"I have no argument," Marcus entered. "But that given, I side with Jack – more time, more answers, is our best bet. Once we bring him in we'd better have all our ducks in a row. We won't get a second chance."

LaRoy smiled slightly for the first time since he sat down. "Ducks in a row... I'd guess you didn't use that expression too often until you got under this guy's wing," he said as he threw a thumb at the DA. "So we let Rand have a little more rope and hope he hangs himself? Any other thoughts?"

Karen broke her stance and leaned forward. "If Rand is directing these bombings and assaults, as part of a network of ex-military or, perhaps more likely, home-grown para-military wannabes, do we want him on the streets? If he's as good as Helfer and Jason are saying, he's still directing the movements of the Illuminati regardless of our surveillance of him. We can't afford to have him roaming the virtual world at will."

"Jack?" LaRoy was asking the obvious.

"Well, now, that's true," he said slowly and ran a hand through his messy shock of thick gray hair. "Can we jam him somehow, Oakes? Like radar interference or something?"

"Nothing we have."

"You Feds got anything?" Jack lobbed the question at Meyer.

"We have some toys – Secret Service stuff. We use it to jam frequencies and transmissions around the Presidential motorcade, but we'd knock out every cell phone within several hundred yards of the target."

"Is that worth it?"

LaRoy answered the softball question. "That's not going to happen. Not in a long term investigation anyway. Let's do this though. Jason, tee that contraption up for us. I know some guys on the Protection Detail. You tell me what you need for clearance, approval, whatever. I'll make it happen. Check that. Alyn will make it happen. You've got more contacts than I do."

"Who do I know in the Secret Service?"

"Get out your rolodex and start dialing for dollars. Find someone."

"Rolodex?" Alyn leaned back. "God, I'm in Jurassic Park..."

"Work with Jason and get him the clearance for whatever the black box is he's talking about. When we're ready to pull in Rand, I want him wrapped tighter than a nun's corset. That work for you Jack?"

"Yep."

"Cal?"

"All good."

"JAG?"

Karen nodded.

"Okay."

"Director?" Marcus said as he almost raised his hand.

"Call me John, please, Marcus. Without you guys we're not having this meeting. What's on your mind?"

"I agree with Helfer and Mr. Meyer regarding the value of our PEN registers monitoring Rand's traffic, but how about a bug? Maybe a – I know I'm over my head technically – but what if we had a camera on his keyboard? At his house, in his office? Maybe he can do things we can't see as they've said, but literally, he has to touch a keyboard or a screen somewhere. Am I right, Helf?"

"That is a sustentative truism. He still requires an input device or entry point."

"Do we have probable cause?"

"Probable cause? We barely got the warrants we have."

"Bullshit. If we got the first set we can get these," LaRoy surged, his confidence in and control over the group restored. "Alyn, I'm calling your number again. You've been pretty fond of calling the Illuminati 'terrorism.' Flip through the Patriot Act. Get what we need to have the Major drop a few of his boys down a ventilator shaft or something and install cameras and microphones above Rand's desk. Hell, maybe the sonofabitch talks to himself."

John let a moment pass and the conversation of the last hour resonate with his collection of cops. "What else? Jason, you work with Mr. Oakes on the forensics. Whip our boys into a frenzy. I'm still waiting to get final reports on that pedophile congressman who dropped dead in his driveway. Tell them get the lead out. If they can give us a tie to Rand, we'll tighten the noose quick and I don't mean maybe. The same goes for these hacks. Christ, I've got three dozen members of Congress bitching about discrepancies in their campaign funds when they looked at their books."

"Shit...," Jack murmured. "Isn't it usually you guys who are doing the looking?"

"Maybe so, but there's a helluva lot going on and we're tasked with getting to the bottom of it and putting the binders on. Jason – you get Rand's keystrokes corralled. Take young Mr. Oakes along with you every step. He's a good man. Okay by you, DA?"

"As usual, the government is picking my pocket."

"I'll take that as a yes. Oh, and Oakes? I'd like you to put together a timeline of this shit storm from that first local commissioner who stepped on his dick. Sound about right, Jack?"

"I–"

"That's a yes, Mr. Oakes. Have at it. I'll facilitate the national stuff – the bombings. Cal? You work with Jack and Marcus and find this Ciampiano sonofabitch. Major, you and Karen muster what you can on our AWOL Ranger. Karen, you're the feed to Cal and the District Attorney who'll manage the locals. Major, I'm going to need you to work on these other bombers as well. What you said makes sense with our boys coming home. Might be a few loose cannons in the crowd who saw a lot of IEDs up close and personal. Alyn, you're running with the warrants. I miss anybody?"

There were casual glances around the table to see all had been accounted for. "Good," LaRoy finished. "Cal will be updating the digital portfolios of Rand and Ciampiano if he hasn't already. A lot of the Ciampiano package will be on the afternoon press cycle to flush him out. Clayton Rand stays within this table. There's strong evidence that this started right here in Tampa with Rand. It's going to end right here with Rand."

"And the ten other bombers?"

"If you want to kill a snake you hit him in the head, not the tail. We'll catch up to the others, but we need to take the head off. Everybody got that?" John didn't wait for or require answers. "Ciampiano looks like a strong right arm and a good way to get to Rand. He's running. We can guarantee he knows why. He's more dangerous now than before. This Clayton Rand is sitting still. His confidence gives us more time. Use it wisely. Questions?"

Hearing nothing, LaRoy closed his plain folder and leaned on it with folded hands. "Just like last time, nothing goes on with this caper that doesn't cross my desk. Alyn's right about one thing – this is a national security issue. Highest priority. There's no room for mistakes. There's already more wrinkles in this than a whore's bedsheet."

People began to collect their phones, their few papers and themselves.

"One more thing," LaRoy nearly snorted. "We all get the end of a piece of rope and work toward the middle. Hopefully we end up with a knot around the bad guy's neck and a case that holds water in court. Whatever end of the rope you got, it's vital. You might think otherwise and I'll just say it for the world to hear – there's personalities in this room whose bent is to be cowboys. I've said it before, but nobody pulls that with me. There's already been some jockeying and I'm telling you, it ends here. Right here. Right now. There's a bunch of politicians with their dicks and tits getting caught in a wringer. They want us to shut the wringer off – in the name of truth, justice, and the American way. You might have your own thoughts on some of this, but I take it as a slap in the face. Senators don't get assaulted on my watch – regardless. I might arrest them myself tomorrow, but until tomorrow comes, I'm in the business of protecting people – good or bad."

Jack leaned and whispered discreetly in Marcus's ear. "And you don't send drones to kill civilians either. Horseshit."

Marcus recoiled. John saw it but let it pass. He stood up and half the table with him. "Cal, I wanted to meet here this morning because I'm lazy and I just got up. Arrange for us to have a secure debriefing room at your office at nine tonight. I'll be looking for updates on whichever end of the rope you have and you will have something. We have fifty agents coming to town. Get 'em busy. Class dismissed."

People who shared leads were talking. As Helfer and Marcus tightened around Jack, he continued his silent opinion statement.

"Collateral damage they call it. Biggest crock of horseshit ever invented – collateral damage…"

LaRoy had abandoned Karen to Major Caulden and was sliding up behind the District Attorney. "Problem, DA.?"

"Nope," Jack said as he turned and invited John into the tiny circle of men. "Me and the boys were just thinking out loud of our next move."

"Want to share?"

"Oh, sure. Just like your she-wolf over there shares. You better assign Special Forces to watch your six while that hellcat's around. My guess is she's sharpening her claws for your juggler."

"I can handle Nuary. My question is for Marcus. Can you manage this guy? You're talented Jack, and against the obvious, I like you, but you will tone it down and make sure whatever you turn up goes to Cal and on to me. This is no longer a disgruntled denizen of Tampa who has it out for a local commissioner. My guess is I've got the best part of your investigation already. If you want to watch the rest of the game from the bleachers keep aggravating members of the team – me included. There's no time for it. Savvy?"

Jack saluted.

"Stick around a minute, Jack." LaRoy turned into the conference room. "Not trying to rush you, but I'm trying to rush you. Hit the bricks folks. I need the room. Marcus? Mr. Oakes? Would you excuse us a few minutes?"

In thirty seconds LaRoy and Jack were seated again. This time their knees were inches apart.

"What's on your mind, Jack? You don't like how the Bureau is handling this?"

"No, you're top shelf. Cal has absolute faith in you and I have absolute faith in him. So that's where it ends."

"So what's your beef? You think we're horning in on your case?"

"Nope. You've been more than fair. You're smart enough to listen to good leads and you've got resources I don't. I'm happy as a pig in shit with the investigation. Like everybody, I'd like to run down this Ciampiano. We'll find him."

"Oh yeah?"

"Yep."

"You know something I don't? That's not how I like to play, you know that."

"I do, and I won't lie, I've got a few cards close to the vest."

"Wanna tip them my way?" John asked.

"Not yet."

"What's the hold up?"

Jack leaned back and crossed his legs. His pants were already wrinkled though it was early in the day. He didn't say anything.

"Nuary under your skin?" John poked him.

"Hell no. She's a whore and you know it. I can deal with her. She's gonna try and jack you up before this is over though, but I figure you know that too."

"I do. So what is it?"

Jack paused again. "The other chick on your squad. The lieutenant. She said she handled Ciampiano's case before the boys from Black Ops took over."

LaRoy felt his throat tighten, but his own experience hid everything that was racing through his mind.

"Yea, so?"

"She coughing up everything JAG has? Far as you know?"

"What are you driving at?"

"Nothing. Yet. Just a cop's hunch."

"A hunch?"

"That's it."

"You think JAG and Special Ops are behind this?"

"I hadn't thought that before today, but it's a clever idea," Jack said slowly. "How long have you been leaning that way?"

"I'm not."

"You sure about that? Sort of makes sense – our best military minds and muscle cleaning up after some real assholes in government."

"What you're describing, Jack, is called a coup."

"It is, isn't it? We've never had one. Might be just what the doctor ordered."

"You're wrong on both counts. We don't need a coup and we have one of our own version every four years. It's called an election."

"You got a point. Opposing parties shake hands. One moves in as the other moves out. A bloodless coup. You're right. Score one for your side."

"I'm not keeping score."

"Yea, me neither."

"So," John encouraged slightly. "If you don't think Special Ops is driving the bus, what's on your mind?"

"One of the passengers. Maybe two."

"Rand and Ciampiano?"

"You're half right."

"Cut the shit, Jack. We're both too old for it."

"Ciampiano and Lieutenant Auburn."

LaRoy was choked into silence. He was nowhere near ready to give up what Karen had told him. He stalled. "That makes no sense. Where're you going?"

"Somebody tipped off Ciampiano. That guy lives in his house or that newspaper shack and the sidewalk in between. Period."

"The forensic boys will turn up a connection to JAG, the military, whoever, if there is one."

"Yep," Jack said as he stood up. "I might be full of shit – it's happened before – but this isn't terrorism like that federal slut Nuary thinks. This is well targeted surgery on a cancer, John. I like Rand and Ciampiano for it real well. They're in it up to their ears. And your lieutenant might be greasing the skids for them. I'd be damn careful what gets said around her until we either clear her or take her down."

LaRoy leaned back in his chair, away from Jack and the opposite of the DA's standing to fight. "Do you have anything that might pretend to be a fact?"

"I might, but I need to work it a little. What she said this morning of knowing him while he was still active. Let's say that I find that intriguing and I'm thinking you do too."

"It's a unique situation, I'll grant you that much."

Jack was prepared to let it go for now and leave when he caught a look in LaRoy's eyes that would have passed for borderline sadness on a civilian's face. On LaRoy it reflected disappointment caught between thin layers of confusion and despair. It was faint, but it was surely there and adjusted the cut of his otherwise hard set jaw. None of these emotions were at home on LaRoy's face and stood out as though they were neon colors. Jack had forty plus years of reading the countenance of faces on each side of the law and in every dim side alley that made the map of an investigation.

"You okay there, Chief?" Jack asked, temporarily puzzled himself.

"With you holding out on me? Hell no, but if you think you've got something, I can't stop you."

"You think I'm holding out?"

"Maybe."

"What could I be holding out?"

"Your theory on Lieutenant Auburn and Ciampiano. You must feel you have something or you wouldn't be wasting your time."

"Not any more than you have."

"Then let it go."

"Is that an order? I don't work for you remember."

"I remember, Jack."

"Let me ask you one thing then maybe I do it."

"Shoot."

"You letting it go?"

The hesitation was too long for a mind accustomed to getting to the truth. Jack didn't need to wait any longer for an answer. He ripped his chair back from the table and dropped so hard and close he bumped LaRoy's knee. "Jesus Christ! You already know!"

LaRoy was up before Jack's chair stopped moving. "We're done here."

"No, we ain't done! Talk about holding out. Christ almighty. I gave you Rand and everything else I had and you've got a potential codefendant sitting next to you while you send me to chase shadows. Hell, she might have tipped him off weeks ago. Ciampiano might be out of the country! He could have a month's head start on me and you're going to let me pound the pavement."

Jack was exasperated – exasperated and pissed, but it was tempered by the paperback book and packaged cellphone in the pockets of his crumpled sport coat. Given his own transgressions, he wouldn't go so far out on the limb he couldn't get back to finish the game.

"The local area still needs to be scrutinized," LaRoy reminded. "Just as if we don't know anything, and there's a good chance we don't. Keep that in mind."

Jack played it backwards. "Just as if we don't know what?"

"You said it, I didn't. I've got some good people looking at the connection between Ciampiano and JAG."

"By JAG, you mean the lieutenant, right?"

John ignored the obvious. His own limb beneath him was swaying in the breeze. "The electronic stuff should tell me most of what I need to know. We'll have it pretty quick. I need a little time."

"Okay. I'm in, but you know we don't have a lot of time. If Auburn and JAG, or our military gonzo squad, tipped Ciampiano off, every hour gets him deeper undercover. Especially a guy like him. Finding him will be dicey, even if he had no help. If they helped him, he's got all the cards."

"Right now I'm giving the lieutenant the benefit of the doubt to her face, but racing like hell to get in front of her otherwise. You said, you're in. Well, I need this kept in the deaf, dumb, and blind category for now."

"Done." Jack took a deep breath and got up. "Cal know?"

"No, he doesn't."

"And you want it to stay that way?"

"For now."

"And that loose cannon?"

"Nuary? Of course not."

"And now what?"

"You go after Ciampiano. I'll babysit the lieutenant."

"Yea. Forget what I said about putting her with me – not right away – I've got a few rocks to look under I'd rather she not see."

"Fair enough."

They walked toward the door together.

"You know, John, if any tiny piece of where you thought I was going – with the military involvement thing, maybe JAG, Special Forces – these guys in Tampa, could be just the tip of the iceberg."

"That's exactly right," LaRoy said as though physically hurt. "What I don't know is if the other shit that's going down across the country is directed out of Tampa or if our boys just started the ball rolling."

"You think the nationwide horseshit we've been talking about is going along without them?"

"Why not?" LaRoy said, forming his words carefully. "Like lemmings, some go off the cliff and it triggers something in their pea sized minds and away we go. Christ, instead of rats killing themselves, they could turn into patriotic suicide bombers tomorrow, wrapped in the flag. How's that sit with you, DA?"

"The hell of that picture is that the country's ripe for it. People are sick of the headlines outa Washington or the local county that starts with a fifty cent placard in red, white, and blue, staked in the ground at every intersection in America and ends with an envelope stuffed with cash and the Constitution getting a swift kick in the nuts."

LaRoy stopped at the door and looked hard at the only other person to have the inside track on the latest affront to the Nation's security. In his mind he wondered which side of the fence Jack would come down on if push came to shove.

"It's still breaking the law, Jack – on both sides. And we're saddled with stopping it."

"The corrupt politicians, or The Illuminati who wants to blow them up?"

"Both of them."

"Ain't that a bitch?"

"Yes it is," John sighed and reached for the door. Jack stopped him with a single finger on his sleeve. "You know, John, either way – whether Rand and Ciampiano are the shot callers or this thing has gone off on its own – me, you, the Bureau, CIA, and whatever part of the military we still have on our side we're gonna be hard pressed to stop them."

"Stop them? It might be the other way. We're a threat to them," the FBI Director said as he opened the door for his confidently beleaguered friend. "Hell, we might be next on their list."

Cal surprised both Jack and LaRoy by having waited in the hall.

"See that?" Jack said as he motioned to him. "With no one to hold his hand, he sits on them. Always waiting on me to tell him what to do next. Kinda like a kid really."

"Your guys are out front," Cal said. "Marcus said you were taking us all to lunch."

"Lunch? I never take a lunch. He knows that. Not with work to do." Jack buried his hands in his pockets.

LaRoy looked around for Karen. "Cal? Where's the rest of our unit?"

"Nuary's gone back to my office with Jason. The Major is talking with people on the base – gathering intel on Ciampiano. I thought the lieutenant would go with him, but she said she needed to run some things by you first. I'm not sure where she went though."

Cal wouldn't have noticed the tightening of Jack's face – he was always going in or coming out of one contortion or another – but when LaRoy's brow tightened and his eyes shifted in unison with the peculiarities of the District Attorney, it stood out.

"How long has she been gone?"

As if in answer, a ladies room door opened in the hall near the three men and Karen stepped out.

"About that long," Cal answered the obvious and, like the other two men, kept the secreted wonder to himself.

LaRoy didn't break stride, but Jack and now Cal lingered an awkward moment in front of Karen, or her in front of them.

"Let's go, folks," LaRoy said over his shoulder. "You two can arm wrestle for who gets to hold the door for the Lieutenant."

"Jack's buying."

"Not yet he isn't–"

"Damn right, not yet. Not ever with this mob of gold bricks."

"We're headed back to your office, Cal. You coming, Jack?"

"No, thanks. I've got real police work to do. I'll come over later, but you'll probably all be gone home to take naps. Cal usually takes in his shingle around two or three and is half in the bag by four o'clock. I took it for federal policy."

"That's about right," LaRoy said, beat for beat. "But maybe we can hang in there a while longer since it's you. Maybe you could swing by and put on a clinic about nationwide investigations."

"I'd be happy to. You better put Agent Denti in the front row."

"Would you help him with his name tag? I've read his reports – can't spell worth a damn."

"Don't I know it."

The two were still tossing barbs as they walked out of the building, both oblivious to any offer to hold the door for Karen who came up behind, smiling slightly and shaking her head along with Cal, who was now watching her every move for reasons he didn't know.

The federal and county contingents split up in the parking lot of the Air Base with no fanfare.

"Call me," was all LaRoy said as Jack got in the front passenger side of the county car and left the driving to Petey. Helfer was already in the back seat behind Jack, apparently looking too much like a suspect.

"Slide over, would you Oakes? I don't like people behind me."

"What if I don't like people behind me?" Marcus tried.

"Basically, that'd be too damn bad. I outrank you."

"You hear that, Helfer? Five minutes on a military base and our boss thinks he's an officer."

"No, I don't. I just don't want to end up like Connie's husband."

Marcus was negotiating the numerous turns to the main gate and off the base. He was trailing Cal who was ferrying LaRoy beside him in the passenger seat with Karen in the back.

"Who?"

"Connie. The daughter in *The Godfather*. Her brother, Sonny, had her husband whacked. Clemenza slipped a garrote around his neck from the back seat. You guys don't remember that? I haven't been able to have anyone in the seat behind me since I saw that picture in 1972."

In the car ahead, Jack and Marcus both saw Karen slide across the back seat, from behind LaRoy to behind Cal. Jack pointed out the windshield. "There's a smart man, right there."

Marcus laughed. "Karen is hardly Clemenza."

"You never can tell, Petey. You never can tell."

———————

9

Don T was walking through The Columbia's front dining room headed for the quiet back room he called his office. Strings from the small private room reached Chicago, New York City, New Orleans, and Las Vegas with implausible ease. The maître d' appeared, made from thin air, as was his custom and walked just behind and to the side of his Don.

"Has that package been sent?" Don T asked as though delivering mass.

"It has, Don T."

"And you will tell me when it has been delivered?"

"I will."

"*Niente di più? Niente di meno?*"

"Nothing more. Nothing less, Don T."

"*Bene,*" the old man said as he stopped and touched Mr. Guzimon's forearm with a paternal pat and moved on as smoothly as though he were gliding a fraction of an inch above the polished old wood floor and melted into the quiet back room.

As the plainly adorned county and federal cars left the shadow of the mammoth air force base behind and weaved across town to their respective offices, Jack kept the conversation in his livery light and lively. The federal car was noticeably quiet. Each time Cal referenced the case or an incidental, Karen, playing out a different type of Clemenza threat from the back seat, caused LaRoy to squelch it. After several minutes of flatten conversation starters, Cal gave up, resigned to thinking the Director was busy in thought. Karen had the advantage on Cal. She knew exactly why LaRoy was uncharacteristically quiet.

Marcus turned away from his tagging along with Cal and headed for the District Attorney's office. When he parked he expected to spend some time debriefing while looking at the soles of Jack's shoes up on his desk, but the DA headed instead for Helfer's small lab.

"I've got a couple of things that need your magic touch, Oakes."

"Sure thing, boss. What is it?"

"Fingerprint work. Toss in a fiber analysis or whatever else you got."

"The Feds didn't take it all?" Marcus asked without thinking. Had he been handed over to reconsideration he would have recollected a dozen times or more when Jack had done things his own way. He knew Jack to have been a great street cop and now District Attorney, but that history sometimes brought what Marcus saw as a conflict between the strict legal constraints of the attorney and the street, with its own unique set of rules. When the trio walked in the lab, it was confirmed.

"Give this the once over," Jack said as he pulled the padded envelop out of his jacket pocket. As Helfer reached for it he noticed Jack was holding the bag by a corner.

"Is that an evidence bag or is that the evidence?"

"A little of both. Go over the envelope, but there's a phone inside. That's the money maker. Can you dust it for prints and then download its guts and memory or whatever without messing it up?"

"Messing it up?"

"Yea, I need it to still work. Can you do that?"

"I can do that," Helfer said as he snatched a legitimate evidence bag off a black Formica topped table and held it open for Jack who did as directed and dropped the envelope and phone inside.

"Good. Get right on it. Pronto. Then run it up to my office."

"What is that?" Marcus asked as though his words were creeping out on thin ice.

"A phone. A cell phone. Something new they've invented. No rotary dial. Just buttons."

"I've heard of them. Where'd it come from?"

"China probably. Most of that shit comes from China."

Marcus temporarily abandoned the chase for the truth.

"You said you had a couple of things, Mr. Aaron," Helfer filled in, one step shy of oblivious. "Is the envelope and phone two separate things? I'll need to enter them in the log as—"

"Nope," Jack blurted as he reached into his other coat pocket. "Got something else right here." The Steinbeck paperback came out in his hand, and, like the padded envelope, was clutched by the corner. "Now before you start in with the techy lecture again, this is all you get. I didn't have an evidence bag. I tried not to mess up anything that might be there, but it is what it is."

Helfer already had another evidence bag ready. Jack obliged and in his mind the transfer was complete. He turned toward the door.

"What's the case number?" Helfer almost shouted then checked himself and asked again. "I mean, for the tags and the logbook. What case are they associated with?"

Jack stopped only briefly, as if his nonchalance would carry over to the others. "List them as 'DA numbers one and two.' Something I've got going on an old caper. Probably nothing, but do your damnedest."

"Sure thing."

Jack paused outside the door again. "Oakes, can we do handwriting analysis?"

"No, we send all that to Washington normally, but it takes a while. I do know a guy at Florida State who's been through the FBI's courses. He could give us a preliminary."

"Have him look at the third or fourth page of that book," Jack said as he pointed to the second bag still in Helfer's hand. "There's some scribbling there. See what he makes of it."

Helfer hesitated. "With handwriting, we usually submit samples for cross checking – elimination or possible confirmation. Do we have samples I can send along?"

"You work your other smoke and mirrors on it first. I'll see if I can pull up an old file and get you some samples."

Jack abandoned the doorway and was headed up the hall. Marcus walked casually alongside but turned his head every few steps to examine his boss up and down as though there was a cartoonish transformation taking place in front of him.

Jack caught the third or fourth glance and mirrored it. "What?" he said with the stymied enthusiasm of one who damn well knew.

"Just wondering how you'll look in a federal prison jumpsuit. I think they have other colors besides orange now if you behave."

"What are you going on about? I swear, Petey, sometimes you just beat all, you know that?"

Marcus motioned back to Helfer's lab with his eyes. "What was all that back there?"

"Back where?"

Marcus just stopped – stopped in the hall – stopped playing the straight man – and stopped wanting to know what he already felt was the dangerous commission of a crime. Without a word, he turned away.

"Petey, hold up."

Marcus waved Jack off without looking back.

"C'mon now, Petey," Jack was saying, but Marcus stepped into a stairwell and was gone.

Across town LaRoy, Karen, and Cal had just cleared security at the federal building. They walked to Cal's office in silence. Karen stopped at an empty cube in an open hall. "I've got a couple of calls to make unless you need me right away," she said, giving LaRoy the chance to squash the idea though she had no phone and leaving the door open for any private discussion he may want to have with Agent Denti.

"No problem," LaRoy said. "Where's your office, Cal?"

"At the end of the hall. Last door on the right."

"I'll be down in a few minutes," Karen said as she tried to gauge LaRoy's take. The moment too long locked on LaRoy's countenance was a moment too long for Cal. He saw the same reaching ask he had picked up at MacDill.

LaRoy answered Karen's unasked question by walking away.

"If you need anything, holler," Cal said to Karen as he too left her alone.

She slipped into the empty cube and sat down. There wasn't even an old calendar or a single paper or pen on the pre-formed desk with the cloth covered low walls. She stretched and adjusted her plain bracelet, watch, and twisted a University of Baltimore class ring around her finger as she waited and thought of Sam, the investigation, her revelation to LaRoy, and what the coming hours and days would bring.

"Do you want me to find, Alyn and Jason?" Cal asked as he slipped behind his desk.

LaRoy's closing the door was all the answer that was needed. "What do you think of this mess, Cal?"

"It's complex."

"Understated."

"I think the other incidents we're seeing of late are unrelated — directly — to our New Illuminati caper."

"Where's the cut off?"

"The assault on the senator being in Tampa keeps that one local. Add that to the fact that our ex-Ranger is AWOL and I'd say he's in. The ad in the San Francisco Chronicle could easily be Rand or someone with his background. So that's in, which seems to bring the assault on the mayor along with it and that has all the earmarks of Ciampiano. After that, it's a lot of technical manipulation that could come from Tampa, Dubai, or Korea. I'd say Tampa until proven differently."

"What about your DA, Aaron, and his original theory on this Clayton Rand character?"

"The guy has all the tools, I'll grant you that, but that alone won't convict him."

"Shit, it won't even get us a warrant," LaRoy complained as he sat down.

"You haven't gotten anything else from the surveillance?"

"Not a thing. Which means one of two things; it's not him, or he's damn good."

"Neither one of which helps us."

"No it doesn't. So, rather than wait for Rand to step on his dick, we've got to keep moving. Question is, which direction?"

"I'd say we maintain the lock on Rand, but branch out to his contacts. Maybe a little indirect pressure might prompt a slip."

"Might."

"We work the nationwide cases and look for connections back to Florida. See if we can get your arrest warrant."

"I'll give your buddy, Jack the local leads on Ciampiano, but the national ones go to Nuary. That leaves you the go-between."

"Mediator between Jack Aaron and Alyn Nuary. That's unenviable at best, John."

"Don't I know it. Tell me from the hip, Cal. What do you think of Jack? Do we even keep him looped in on this? I like the hell out of the guy, but Christ he can even make a curmudgeon like me raise an eyebrow. He's the first politician I ever met who damn near openly despises the hand that feeds him."

"Jack is still more cop than politician. Most District Attorneys are prosecutors first, politician seconds. In Jack's case, he's an investigator first, prosecutor second. The politician in him is a way distant third."

"Fair enough, but in any capacity, is he coming down on the right side in this one? This case? He lets some damn sympathetic comments slip. And you remember our meeting in DC? Christ, getting that name out of his pocket would have been easier if he'd been strapped on a water board, for crying out loud."

Cal took a deep breath and tried to relax his mind and categorize the things he was thinking. He knew Jack was painfully honest – above corruption of any kind – and wouldn't tolerate anything less from his staff. And still, there were times when Jack openly discussed cases and evidence where he had suggested – just beneath a cloak that prevented inspection – that the end was justified by the means.

"John, are you a race fan?"

LaRoy chuckled. "You bet – pun intended. I slip off to Pimlico when I can. Usually I go on the big race days. I enjoy the track, but watch the simulcast of the Derby prep races and the Triple Crown."

"No. No. Car racing."

"Car racing? I used to watch some. NASCAR was fun until they put restrictor plates on them to slow them down. Made no sense. It's a race. The idea is to go fast. First guy at the finish line wins. Simple. Open wheel Indy type is fun once in a while. Great drivers. No rubbing like the Winston Cup. They call it something else now. Not PC to name it after a cigarette company, I guess."

"Yea, well, there's a corner, I think they call it the inner loop, on a track in a little town in New York. Watkins Glen. It's designed to slow down the drivers after a long straightaway. Ever hear about it or see it? You know what I'm talking about?"

"Sure I do. They stuck in that little loop piece to slow guys down – a safety thing as I remember. That was back when they used to let them race like hell. Why? What's racing have to do with Jack Aaron or our case?"

"There's wide red and white stripes on the corners of that small loop at Watkins. The rules say you can't drive on them. Of course everyone drives on the stripes nearly every lap, trying for an edge. If the drivers could, pretty soon they'd nearly straighten out that little curve and defeat the purpose."

"Where's this going, or are we just taking a corner here? Pun also intended."

"Jack drives on the paint. A lot. If he was on that track he'd be cutting through the stripes and be in the grass to get around that curve quicker."

"So this entire discourse is to tell me that Aaron cuts corners?"

"Every chance he gets."

"And you're making clear that that's a danger if I let him manage the local investigation."

"Not a danger necessarily. Jack's a straight shooter. I think you know that, but that cutting corners tendency is something to be aware of."

"And what do you make of his other curious trait? That hesitancy with providing information. Maybe even thinking The Illuminati aren't that bad? Just a bunch of do-gooders trying to clean up the country?"

"I wouldn't give it a thought, John. You've been around him enough to know he'll uphold the law. Don't take me wrong. He'd steer a Grand Jury or whisper in a judge's ear if he thought the strict interpretation of the law needed a hand, but–"

"Needed a hand?"

"When it comes to justice – fair, equal, and prompt under the Constitution – there's no one else I'd want prosecuting me."

"Prosecuting you?"

"Yes. He's that fair."

"Okay." LaRoy let it sink in and ease some of the pressure that was on the surface. The rest – the investigation, political pressure, Karen – most of that stayed on his back with its claws sunk in his shoulders. "So, any thoughts on finding Ciampiano? He's the hottest ticket in town at the moment."

"Not too much different than Rand for now. We'll chat up his friends, stir the pot a little and see what floats to the top. I want to touch base with Nuary to let her know where I'm at. I'll let her pace the Bureau's presence. I'm going back to see Jack. He knows every nook, alley, and gin joint in this town and everybody in it."

"That works. You mind if I camp out here?"

Cal stood up and stepped out from behind his desk. "She's all yours."

"Thanks. Hey, do you have an office for the Lieutenant? Something close by, but more private than that cube she's in?"

"I'll find one."

"Keep her away from Nuary, if you can. Unless she can use them, Alyn hates women more than men, if that's possible."

Cal didn't argue one way or the other as he wasn't ready to ask the questions his intuition was whispering in his ear. Somehow the pleasant JAG officer had come afoul of LaRoy which was neither easy to do nor a good place to reside.

As Cal passed through Nuary's temporary office, leaving with no information apart from an admonishment to call her immediately with any info on Ciampiano, John was settling on Cal's phone. He made calls over the course of the next hour that reached all corners of the country, as had the arm of The Illuminati – extending from Tampa or some other kitchen table, basement lab, or living room keyboard. The regional FBI offices already had located cracks in a few of the cases and a couple names were beginning to surface. No tie to Tampa was evident as yet, but the agents' work would continue.

The bulk of Alyn's time was taken up with hounding Jason. She was dependent on what the forensics division might uncover and the pre-emptive reports Meyer would supply in exchange for 'benefits.' With nothing else apart from conniving and rude behavior, along with tight thighs that led some men to temporary paradise at a high price, the appropriated data and analysis was all she had to support her own counterfeit expertise and leads.

Before Cal could make it to the District Attorney's Office, Jack was perched in Marcus's door, leaning so hard as though to support the frame.

"Busy?" Jack said.

"As a matter of–"

"Good." Jack strode in and closed the door.

"Boss, I've got a lot going on with this Ciampiano thing. Plus we still have a pretty full docket of other cases in the outside chance you've forgotten."

"I haven't forgotten, but let's clear the air. We need to be ready to jump when this thing gels and I can't have you feeling left out or whatever else has bound you up. Tell ole Dad what's on your mind." Jack had already sat down and was leaning back heavily. He crossed his hands on his chest and waited for something his demeanor was already dismissing.

Marcus dropped his pen on the desk. "Well, Dad... where'd the evidence come from you gave Helfer?"

Jack leaned forward. "Is that what's put a burr under your saddle? Why didn't you say so?"

"I did, Jack, and you promptly drifted into left field chasing fireflies."

"I'm just looking for some print evidence – hopefully. That's what we do."

"No evidence bags. No tags. No chain of custody. No case number. No–"

"Alright!" Jack shot up from the chair where he'd been so relaxed a minute before. "Christ, you've gotten touchy."

"Where's it from?"

"You could use a drink, you know that?"

"Where?"

"Downtown. That Fed thing."

"The Illuminati case?"

"That's the one."

"Have you lost your mind, Jack?"

"No, it's around here somewhere," Jack toyed as his eyes searched the floor around his chair.

"Don't joke around. If it's evidence, why do we even have it? The Feds are handling the evidence."

"Not all of it. We were here first, Petey. Remember that."

Boss, we don't have near the resources the Bureau has."

"We found Clayton Rand. Not them."

"Yes. Credit Helfer with that, but not latent print work, trace evidence. They're built, and financed, for that. We can't manage the volume let along the complexities of chain of custody. Let them do it."

"I can't."

"Why?"

Jack sat back down and gently tapped the fingertips of his hands together in front of his face. "I haven't got the handle I want on this caper yet."

"Of course not. We can't even find Ciampiano."

Jack snapped forward. "Right! That's exactly right. And how the hell can that be? Huh? How the hell did he get out of town just before us and the whole goddamn FBI comes crashing down on him?"

"He'll turn up."

"No he won't, Petey. And you wanna know why? Because he ain't here."

"So he got the jump on us and skipped town. He's not the first. Guys like that have a way of turning up. You know that."

"Not this guy. Not this time."

"Why not?"

"My guess is that sonofabitch is dead."

Marcus was more accustomed to Jack than anyone, but this froze him. "Dead?" he repeated, just to hear the word from his own mouth for the assurance it was right.

"Dead," Jack said again.

Marcus leaned back in his chair. He'd not seen his boss in this frame of mind. He was not defeated – not by a long shot – but his feet were shuffling beneath him like a nervous quarterback uncertain where to throw or if it was time to run or just get down on the ground.

"Jack? What's going on?"

"Petey, I don't know. I just don't know and it's making me nuts."

"Tell me what you do know then."

"There's three things on my mind, but it'll be pulling you out on thin ice."

"I wouldn't know anything about being on thin ice. The only ice I've ever seen in almost ten years has been in a glass, under the skates of the Lightning, or in pictures. I'll take my chances. What's going on? You can start with that evidence downstairs. Is that number one?"

Jack was up again. There was some renewed assurance in his voice and stride knowing he would have a sounding board in Marcus. "No, that's number two actually. But I can start there. I got the phone from Ciampiano's mailbox."

"Jesus, Jack..."

"Hear me out, will you? Hear me out. The Feds would have missed it or been too slow to see what I saw."

"Missed a phone? I doubt it."

"No, no, no. Not the phone. The return address on the package."

"Where's it from?"

"Here in Tampa."

"So why would they miss that?"

"The return address – it doesn't exist."

"What's that mean?"

"There's no such place. I've been in this town forever. I know every shithole, mansion, shotgun house, and high rise. The address on the package was made up. I noticed it right off. I didn't know at the time what was in it, but I knew it was probably from our boy, Rand. What better way to stay connected than disposable phones? You move around, bounce off different towers or however that works, and chuck them in the bay."

"And you think the phone was sent to Ciampiano from Clayton Rand?"

"I know it."

"How?"

"He called me."

That would stop anyone's breath and Marcus was no exception. "What?"

"He called."

"Clayton Rand called you on that phone downstairs?"

"Well, I can't say exactly it was him. Not like the man introduced himself, but it was him. I called him by name."

Marcus was pulled to the edge of his chair. "And what'd he say?"

"Nothing. He hung up."

Marcus leaned back again. "So you don't know for certain."

"It was him, Petey!" Jack's face was red around grit teeth. "Oh, it was him alright. I could feel him breathing. He's scared as shit, brother. And he doesn't know where Ciampiano is either. Not now. He expected Ciampiano to pick up that phone and when he didn't, Rand's world jumped the track."

Marcus was staggered and Jack saw it. The old cop in him couldn't resist a grin at the stiff hand he'd just laid on his investigator's jaw. "How'd that feel?" he asked through a crooked smile. "You were watching for the jab and a right cross caught you on the button, didn't it?"

Marcus just stared at the words. His own were still forming in his mouth when Jack continued without him.

"While that punch is still soaking in your rattled noggin, here's a haymaker that'll make sure you don't hear the ref count ten." It was

Jack's turn to scoot closer to the edge of his seat. "You saw that book I coughed up to Oakes, right? I know you did. It was in Ciampiano's newspaper palace. Well, there's a note written in it. Not a code or any such horseshit as that, but a quip about the book – blah, blah, whatever. It's signed, 'Karen' and says the girl on the cover looks like her – this Karen. You think of any 'Karens' who know Ciampiano? Maybe, might have represented him when he was bounced out of the Army? Somebody like that?"

Marcus folded his hands on his desk and leaned forward to fill his boss's face. "Jack. A book with the name 'Karen' in it? That's what you're building a bridge to nowhere on?"

"That's just the beginning, Petey. Think it through. Think it through with me. C'mon. I need the extra eyes on this. There's something here. LaRoy knows it too, but he doesn't know about the book."

"Add 'withholding evidence' to the list of charges."

Jack was pacing. "You wanted to know, now you do. So pony up. Mill it over a bit."

The investigator did just that, but the trip was short. "You said LaRoy knows about this?"

"Some."

"Wow... Only you, Jack, I swear. What part of 'some' does he know, or perhaps better put, do you assume him to know?"

"Oh, he knows. He knows plenty. I saw it on his face."

"So... Let me get this straight," Marcus said with no small measure of cynicism. "You listened to nobody on a stolen phone and 'thought' you interpreted a 'look' on an FBI director's face. That's what you're taking me out on your thin ice with?"

"No. You're not listening, Petey. Who trained you anyway? LaRoy says the hottie lieutenant and our bad guy were fooling around. Nothing more, but I can't shed the idea that Ciampiano bails out the back as we're coming in the front. There's something wrong with that timing and LaRoy knows it. And now you know it."

"LaRoy says the JAG officer was having an affair with Ciampiano?"

Jack traced an X with his finger across his chest. "Cross my heart. From his lips to God's ear."

If Marcus had been staggered by a punch before, he was reeling now – almost going to the canvas as he caught the ropes and leaned into the corner post that was the top of his desk. He rubbed his eyes as though it'd help. Jack let him languish.

The DA settled back in his chair, stretched his neck in all directions and took a deep breath as Marcus eked back from the brink.

"And the next move is?" Marcus whispered.

"John's working the electronic angle to connect the two of them. He still wants us to track down Ciampiano, though I told him he's gone and by 'gone,' I mean dead."

"That's twice you said that," Marcus said as though the words pinched his ribs. "Why?"

"The scope of this thing is big, real big. I thought it started here in Tampa, but I'm rethinking that to say that this part of the Illuminati thing started here. There's other parts that were launched from all over the country – probably around the same time. Maybe even before and a hell of a lot since."

"And how's that leave Ciampiano dead?"

"He's expendable. The military turns out machines like him in every class of Special Forces that make the grade. That major this morning confirmed it. As soon as the uninitiated start to get close to one of these supposed rogues of theirs, pop." Jack leaned in quick, put a finger to Marcus's temple, and dropped his thumb as the imaginary hammer. "One right in the melon."

Marcus recoiled and pushed his boss's hand away. "That's not cool, Jack. Jesus Christ... If half of what you think is right, we're not going to be doing anything but–"

"Anything they want us to do. LaRoy says to go find Ciampiano, who's probably already dead, and off we go!" His arm gave a magnificent flourish that pointed to the door. "We, and that peroxide bombshell nitwit, Agent Nuary, run down every bunny hole in town so it looks like there's a helluva investigation going on. Probably put a hundred agents on it. If we get close to anything still breathing or run out of ideas, we get tossed another red herring and back out we go." There was another equally impressive flourish. "Hot on the trail! But guess what, Petey? There ain't no trail. There ain't never going to be a trail. Because all roads lead right back to the same bunch giving the orders."

"And that's our own military?"

"And JAG, looks like. Probably even the Bureau."

"The FBI?"

"Yep. I sure ain't talking about the bureau your grandmother kept her best lacy doilies on, young man."

Marcus said it again to prove to himself he'd heard it right and to give Jack the option of reconsideration. "The FBI?"

"Maybe, but I didn't say everybody was in on it."

"LaRoy?"

"I don't know. I don't think so. I hope not."

"So, who's left? Department of Justice? Attorney General?"

"Don't know."

Marcus was desperate for a diversion. "How many things was that? You said you had three things on your mind. Theft of evidence, an affair, Ciampiano's dead, the military and the FBI are The New Illuminati... That's more than three."

"You ain't heard the funny part yet."

"There's more?"

"This is number three or five or something."

"I'm listening with whatever I have left."

"Clayton Rand," Jack said with the seriousness and purpose of a fresh bull just released into the arena. "Don't it bother you that this guy doesn't make any mistakes? Criminals – check that, people – people make mistakes. With all the science fiction tricks at the disposal of our federal government, you mean to tell me we can't follow an email or some wire back to this guy's house?"

"I don't think there's actual wires any longer, Jack."

"Well, not a wire then, but something. A keystroke or a phone call, a bleep on a computer screen, something. Don't that strike you as a little odd?"

"It's not good. It certainly isn't convenient for us, but it happens. You've seen it in a hundred cases – you're so old, maybe a thousand – cases with no evidence, no clues, no bad guy."

"Remember the dead baby-raping congressman?"

"The kiddie porn guy? Dropped dead in his driveway in front of the world?"

"That's the piece of shit. Recall how the reporters all got a shitload of trash right from the dead ass himself? How the sweet Jesus is that possible? Oakes tells me it ain't. So how'd that happen? And if Rand had a hand in it, and I know damn well he did, how is it that the Feds can't figure it out?"

"I don't know, Jack. It takes time. Maybe they're still working–"

"Horseshit! Horseshit. They don't find anything because they don't want to find anything."

"Come again?"

"Rand's in the mix with them. His company built their goddamn servers or whatever you call them. He doesn't get caught because they probably recruited the sonofabitch!"

The air was gone from the office. Both men were exhausted from the warrants the day before, the long night, and the recent conversation.

Theories hung in the air like a stench. It was hard for either of them to breath.

A motion detector uttered a soft chime and brought a video screen to life near Clayton's front door and displayed his stoop. The regular doorbell rang and someone rattled the heavy knob. It would either be his brother, Carl, or Raphael. He had inadvertently invited them both. It was an unusual miscue for him, but one he knew would resolve itself. The two had known each other for ever so no one would be uncomfortable. That would come later and provide the resolution. Each would take an ice cold beer and each would sit on the leather couch and relax with the feel of a cold bottle in their hands.

After some catch up talk and another beer, Clayton would quietly dismiss his brother without a word or any hurt feelings by teeing up any number of the old films he and Raphael enjoyed. The sight of anything black and white on the big high definition screen would have the identical effect on Carl as a Cross does on Dracula. Then Clayton would spend the next two hours watching a film he knew line for line while trying to talk Raphael off a ledge and himself into believing what he had begun was still right and that he was also right in that he would not be caught. The strange voice on the phone he had sent to Sam placed the last of these scenarios at risk.

Approaching his own door, Clayton saw Carl on the monitor, ringing the bell again. When the door opened, Carl felt the refreshing blast of cool air welcome him. "Why do you lock your door all the time? What are you scared of? The boogey-man?"

It was standard brother banter and the familial reinforcement of Carl's perceived place as the older brother in the family hierarchy. Playing the role, Clayton snatched a cold beer from the massive stainless steel refrigerator, popped the top, and handed it to his brother.

"Yes. The boogey-man. And here I've just let him in. What's up?"

"You been watching the news?"

"Not much," Clayton lied. "What's the latest?"

Carl walked toward the television with the beer up to his lips. The jostling step called his bare arm into action as a napkin and he wiped his mouth as he sat down, beer still in hand.

"The cops are all over Ciampiano's — the house and the stand. There's yellow tape around everything like it's a murder scene. Cop cars up and down the streets. Vans. It looks like they're shooting an episode of CSI. CSI Tampa. That'd be kinda cool."

Carl picked up the remote and tossed it into what he knew to be his brother's chair. "Turn that thing on will you? Too damn many buttons. I can never get just the TV on. Why don't you get something a little more normal? That thing looks like the cockpit of a freakin' airplane."

Clayton touched the remote and the huge screen flashed to life. "Has Sam been arrested?"

Clayton knew there'd been nothing on the news, but plied his brother gently for any missed skinny from the street.

"Arrested? Hell no. More like murdered or something else awful. I've tried to call him all day to see what was up, you know – thinking he got broke into – hoping he's okay, but he don't answer. You think something happened to him? It must have, right?"

"Obviously something's happened. I don't know what it'd be apart from the gambling, like you said earlier."

"I was thinking about that today at work. I never took no numbers when I was working. I never seen Sam take any. I think that died out with his old man."

"But you also said he's had a tough time since his father passed away. Maybe he got back into it – needed the money or whatever."

"Could be, but I think I'd have seen or heard something. I know I'm not book smart – like you – but I can tell if somebody's on the make. Like down at the docks. All kind of shit goes on down there. And I get wind of most of it."

"Well, get wind, but don't get involved. If you're ever a little short, you know you can come and see me. No questions asked."

"Thanks. Good to know. I'll try not to rough you up too much."

"You helped me out of plenty of jams. I'm glad to do it."

Carl took a long, hard drink. "Oh, that's good. Nothing like a cold beer after a long day. I did some OT today. Hot as a bitch too."

"Drink a lot of water."

"Water?" Carl lifted the beer. "I don't drink water. Fish piss in it."

"That's cute. But drink water. You sweat a lot on the docks. You have to stay hydrated."

Carl drained his bottle. "Got another?"

"Sure."

Clayton headed back to the kitchen as the doorbell rang again. It would be Raphael.

"You got a chick coming over? She got a friend?"

"Raphael."

"He counts as a chick."

"You tell him that."

"He try anything, I'll smack him with a ball bat."

"He'd break it off in your ass."

The brothers were smiling as Clayton went to the door.

"Where's my beer?" Carl called out.

"Hold on or get it yourself. I'm getting the door."

"Oh, I see how it is – I'm treated like second class now that your girlfriend's here."

"Keep talking. I'll kick your ass myself."

"Not on your best day, you little shit."

Clayton jerked the door open. It seemed Raphael had been holding tight to the outside knob as Clayton pulled on the door. Raphael seemed to launch from the outside as though propelled, as indeed he was, but it had nothing to do with physics. He exploded into the kitchen and was backing Clayton up against the wall leaving the hot Florida air following him in through the open door. Raphael was almost screaming.

"What the fuck is–"

"Hey, Carl!" Clayton yelled. "He does want to fight. Beat his ass."

Raphael had not expected anyone else to be there. The alert worked and the attention grabbing assault instantly stopped. Still, his intense focus unraveled slowly as Clayton eased out of his grip and slipped off the wall. Carl was up at the first rush and the three of them stood awkward in the open kitchen foyer as the television replayed from beyond them through a clip of waving yellow tape around the Ciampiano newsstand.

"We were just talking about you," Clayton said as he breathed for his friend. He tried to shed the room of tension by pushing it out the door on the toe of a joke as he smiled and closed the heavy steel door. "Carl was asking if I had a girl coming over and said you qualified. Tell him, Carl."

The door closed, but the tension remained.

"It wasn't like that. How you doing, Ralphy?"

"Good. You?"

"I'm alright, but my brother's an asshole. Don't listen to nothing he says."

The latest arrival murmured, hearing Carl, but looking at Clayton. "Too late."

Both brothers were listening. Carl was concerned, as concern was the emotion nearest the surface after a day spent trying to talk to Sam. "You okay, man?" Carl asked as he looked from Raphael to his brother and back again. "You guys really pissed or messing around?"

"No," Raphael answered for both of them. "We had some things at work."

"I'm guessing the quarterlies," Clayton supported, trying to at least temporarily diffuse his friend and give them both a little breathing room from Carl. "The ones you mentioned earlier, didn't look very good."

"Yes. Things are way off."

Carl wasn't instantly not listening. "Shit, Ralphy," he said as he dropped a well creased, but clean hand on the shoulder of Raphael's tailored shirt. "I hate to break it to you, but all that stuff ain't real work. It's okay though." Carl turned away and went into the kitchen as he talked. "You come to the right place." He opened the refrigerator.

Raphael's words were whispered to Clayton and nearly lost in the shadow of a reckless clinking of beer bottles. "Damn it, Clay? I told you. I told you!"

Clayton twitched a silent, "Shhh!" and pointed with his eyes toward the open kitchen.

The two walked over as Carl was finishing his calloused rummaging through the bottles. He was setting four bottles on the granite. "Okay, Ralphy. I don't know exactly what we got here, but the labels are pretty fancy. I got mine already picked out." Carl twisted the cap off a Miller, dropped the top on the counter, and took a swig before the cap could find a place to settle. "That's good. Cold. I know Clay drinks this foreign stuff," he said as he pointed with his drink to a selection of three other bottles. "Pick your poison."

Raphael was slow, but pointed to the Yuengling. "The Yuengling, Carl. Thank you."

"Ying-Ling," Carl said as he picked up the bottle and butchered the name. He held the bottle and looked at the label. "I say that right? Ying-Ling? What is this? Like Chinese beer? Damn, everything we have is made in China." He twisted off the cap. "Buy American, Clay. It's okay for TVs, but not beer? C'mon. Help out the country."

"I'm trying," Clayton said as he pulled an opener from a drawer for his brother, but looked at his friend.

Carl handed the beer to Raphael. "Here you go, Ralphy. This will take the edge off the day. What'll you have, little brother? We got... Sam Adams or Stella Art-ou-s, or whatever?"

"Artois... The green one."

"Oh, that's cute. Don't get snippy or you won't get nothing, smart ass." Carl tried to twist off the cap until Clayton nudged him with the opener.

"Try this, tough guy."

"Open it yourself," Carl said as he poked the bottle at his brother. "Ralphy? If he says anything else wise, open up a can of whoop-ass on him. Knock the fire right out of him."

There was true menace in Raphael's voice. "Glad to."

"Okay," Carl proclaimed as he took another sip then held his bottle up and out to the others. "To the Three Musketeers. Just like when we was kids pitching papers downtown."

The three bottles clinked slightly and each man drank. Raphael uncharacteristically drained a good share of his Yuengling.

Carl picked up the unselected beer to put it back in the fridge. "Aww shit. Look at that." He was pointing to the label with the top of his Miller. "This would be Sam's beer if he was here, right? Like the fourth Musketeer. And it's Sam Adams. Got his name right on it. That's kinda cool. Damn, I hope he's alright. You heard about Sam, Ralphy? They say the FBI is looking for him. Probably jammed up over his old man's gambling. That's what me and Clay figure. What do you think?"

"Gambling?" Raphael said with a rise in his voice before another hard pull on his beer. "That's what you figure, Clay?"

"I don't know what else it'd be. Taxes, maybe?"

Raphael walked away in toward the television, saw a reporter giving an update that was no update at all in front of Sam's house, and turned away. His bottle was nearly empty already. He circled the big room until he was back in the foyer. "I can't remember the last time I saw Sam." He took a drink and drained the beer. "He must have done something to have the FBI kicking his door down." Raphael carried his empty to the foyer passed his friends and opened and closed Clayton's front door then locked it as noisily as he could several times in staccato fashion. "How's your door, Clay? Think the FBI could kick it in?"

Clayton understood, gave up the point, and was as still as the quieted lock. Minus the shared awareness of The Illuminati, Carl had no such restraint.

"Are you shitting me? That bitch is heavy steel, but the FBI has tanks with battering rams and SWAT teams. They'd knock that door against the wall easier than you did Clay. That door won't do shit to stop the freakin' FBI. Ralphy, you can be just like Clay — smart as shit with numbers and computer junk, but dumb as dirt when it comes to anything normal."

Raphael tossed a less than furtive glance across the kitchen floor to where Clayton was at his refrigerator. He had finished his own beer and was replenishing three more for the party. "You're absolutely correct,

Carl," Raphael was saying as he waited on the new round of beer. "I am dumb as dirt."

"And dirt is damn dumb," Carl reiterated as he took a Yuengling from his brother, twisted the top off, and handed the cold beer to Raphael. "Here. Throw this down the pipe. You'll feel better. That work shit – don't let it get to you. It ain't real money anyway, right? I mean, its numbers on a paper. What's that? The only numbers on a paper I care about are on money – real money – the folding green kind. The kind of money you guys mess with ain't even real. Tomorrow they're different numbers because some other geek-a-zoid changed them. Nobody making anything or really working. Nobody moving shit around like at the docks. We work. We move stuff. Ship shit all over the world. That's work. You two just pretend work. It ain't real."

"I don't know, Carl," Raphael said as he reached around his unintended simple therapist's shoulder and left his beer dangling in his hand. "You're probably right, but sometimes it gets real. It gets real, real quick. All those little things add up to something big. And just like that – bang! The FBI kicks in the door."

There was a lengthy gap casually filled by several pulls on the bottles behind the assorted labels. Behind his swig, Clayton was beginning to worry that even Carl might begin to interpret the innuendos Raphael was tossing like confetti.

"I'm with Carl," Clayton said as he literally and symbolically split the two and walked between them to the living room. "Let's put on a movie. I'll order Chinese food."

"How about pizza?" Carl suggested.

"I just had pizza for lunch," Clayton lied. "You like Chinese, don't you, Ralph? You pick the food and I'll pick the movie."

"Chinese works for me, but I don't want to put Carl out."

"Are you kidding? He'll eat anything that doesn't eat him first."

"Can we at least use forks?" Carl was pleading. "I almost put my eye out with chopsticks one time."

"Sure."

"And I get first dibs on the fortune cookies."

"Good," Clayton said as he rubbed the palms of his hands together briskly as though warming them up to crack a safe. "I'll find us a good picture."

Raphael continued prying the top off the situation like Carl working a bottle top. "How about, *The Great Escape*? Steve McQueen. You like Steve McQueen, Carl?"

"Is it black and white?"

"No, this one's in color."

"How old is it?" Carl asked as a palatable skepticism was rising in his voice.

Clayton played the card. "Early 60's. Pretty tame by today's standards. No bad language. No naked women. Piss poor explosions as I recall. Special effects were pretty tame compared to what goes on today."

"That's what I figured," Carl countered. "What else you got?"

"How about *Three Days of the Condor*," Raphael offered. "That's a good film. The government is after our hero. Imagine that? Runs him to a frenzy. Robert Redford. He does a fine job."

"When was that one?"

"70's."

"Don't you two ever watch anything new?"

Raphael smiled for the first time, knowing he was entrenched under Clayton's thinning skin. "History repeats itself. People think they're going to get away with something – a jewel heist, a robbery, starting a cataclysmic natural disaster, an affair – the list is long, but not endless. Every story has already been told, Clay. Why not see the original and get the best version – minus the explosions and wanton sex, of course."

Clayton took a drink and was thumbing through his electronic catalog. He stopped on a Humphrey Bogart classic, touched the play button and watched the big black and white logo of Republic Pictures come on the wide screen.

"Ah, shit, Clay. Black and white?" Carl was downing his beer as he stood up. He took the slightest breath as the heavy orchestral music sounded behind the opening credits. "I'm gone. Thanks for the brew. You girls enjoy your old timers' night."

Clayton feigned an implausibly weak re-do. "Stick around, brother. I'll find something with tits and explosions."

"Naw, I don't want to spoil your fun. I want to see the news anyway and find out what's up with Sam."

"Call us if you hear anything," Raphael said sincerely. "We'll be watching a Raquel Welch classic."

"Now, that's a name I know. Smoking hot back in the day, am I right?"

"Smoking hot still. Gorgeous in *Hannie Caulder*. Clay, find the scene where she's getting out of the washtub. Oh, my God. I still have fantasies about that scene."

"You and every other kid who's seen it, but I don't think I have that movie."

"You have it. You have everything," Raphael was scolding, wanting to prolong his friend's misery, but spare Carl any real knowledge of The Illuminati that might endanger him. "Welch plays a rape victim and goes after an all-star cast of villains. Remember the classic line, "Tell him to meet me at the prison." Something like that. Remember? "Meet me at prison." It has quite a ring to it."

"Is it in color at least?" Carl's steps were baulking.

"Ralph is full of shit, Carl. I don't have it. I'll get it and we'll watch it another night, but we're going with Bogart and *The Enforcer.* It's a classic. You'll love it." Clayton knew he had his brother on the ropes and headed to the door.

The orchestra was easing down and the film was beginning in earnest. Carl gave the screen half a glance and set his empty bottle on the counter. "That's it. I gotta take a piss."

"Give it a chance," Clayton said as a plea with more holes than a screen door. "What do you want – a movie where the opening credits is a sparkly castle and Tinkerbell flying around? Wonderful World stuff?"

Carl wasn't listening as he stomped up the hall to the bathroom.

"You don't have to give him the bum's rush, Clay."

"He's fine. And we need to talk."

"Talk? We need to call lawyers or move to Costa Rica."

"Relax."

"You tell me to relax once more and–"

Carl's emergence from the hall stifled the words. He didn't stop, but went straight to the door. "I'm out. I'll call you if I hear anything on Sam. See you, Ralphy." The door opened and Carl looked at it as he shook his head. "You ain't bolted it already?" he said to Clayton then looked at Raphael. "He locks up everything. Scared the boogeyman is gonna get him. He used to sleep with me half the time. Scared of the dark. Now you've got him worked up about the FBI kicking in this door. He'll probably be showing up at my place wanting to sleep on my couch."

"Goodbye, Carl," Clayton said as he turned up the volume on the TV.

"I wouldn't let him sleep with me any more 'cause he'd wet the bed. He–"

The volume had crept to deafening and a myriad of speakers around the room were vibrating making screaming the only recourse, but even that ineffectual.

"What?" Clayton played the part. "I can't hear you!"

Raphael waved to Carl and shook his head.

Carl brushed them both off with a grin and a flip of his middle finger then disappeared out the door. It closing was his goodbye. Clayton watched the door and the monitor a moment to outlast his brother's short patience before he dropped the volume to normal.

Raphael walked away from the first minutes of a film he knew by heart. His friend was watching the black and white characters as though the picture was all new.

"Why didn't you just throw him out on his ear? You were pretty rough on him. He isn't my brother, but I've been around him long enough to know that getting bounced like that will bother him. Not right now, but tonight, or in the middle of the night, he'll wake up and go, "Hey, that wasn't very nice." You know how he thinks." Raphael opened another beer, but made no offer to his host. He leaned on the black granite counter and drank heavy as he continued. "Carl's got a heart of gold. You can tell by how worried he is about Sam. Are you worried about Sam? Even in the slightest?"

"Of course."

"Or worried about how he might lead back to you?"

"You want me to lie?"

"That's what I figured."

"What else have you figured?"

"Very little, Clay. Very damn little. But I do know you're not as clever as you thought. You said this whole thing was untouchable – untraceable – but they got on to Sam pretty quick. It's a short jump from Sam to that door," Raphael said as he pointed. "And Carl, with all his callous disregard for the wonders of intellect, is spot on about one thing."

"And you're about to share with me what that is."

"I am. The FBI can take that door down with ease. Oh, but they won't use a battering ram like in Carl's action adventure flicks. They'll take that door off its hinges with a single piece of paper. It's called a warrant."

"By God, you are a doomsday-sayer, aren't you?"

"What did I miss? Are the FBI not camped out in Tampa looking for one of your 'untouchables?'"

"That would appear to be the case, but Carl – that sage of wit and wisdom – said it himself. It's as likely to do with gambling as anything else."

"And by 'anything else,' you mean your Illuminati."

"Who knows what Sam could be involved in? He was pretty deep into black operations when he was in the military."

"Black operations?"

"Super-secret stuff. Illegal, most of it. Border jumping. Kidnapping. Clandestine prisoner transport for the CIA. My guess is Sam's foot was on the tilting end of a water board more than once. That's probably why they want him. I always thought it odd he left the Army, didn't you? He was a natural."

"A natural."

"Right. A natural. Physically gifted. Tough as nails."

"And this black operations secret stuff – you think Sam would just talk about doing that? As you portray, Sam doesn't impress me as a man who would kiss and tell."

"He didn't tell me anything. It's all in his record. You just have to look in–"

"Stop! Unreal. You are enamored with dancing with the devil, aren't you? I shudder to think what other curtains you've peeked behind."

Clayton smiled. "I could make the Wizard of Oz blush."

Raphael allowed his friend to relish in his glory for only the time it took him to move from the kitchen back to the living room and drop in a chair. He leaned forward with his elbows on his knees. "Have you stopped? I see a lot of things in the news. Bad things. Explosions. Hacking. That lady from the IRS got shot."

"I'm sure her death is a tragedy for someone, but any soldier killed in war should be more deeply mourned. If you stomp on the Constitution, you will be held accountable. End of story."

"Isn't taking the 5th Amendment guaranteed by that same Constitution?"

"It is. Of course. But what people – people in government service certainly – have forgotten is that the Constitution and the Amendments were put in place to protect the people from the government, not the other way around. The Founding Fathers had in mind something to protect the public." Clayton paused and watched Bogart working across the screen. "You don't need a history lesson from me, Ralph."

"No, I do not."

"But it's very clear we've forgotten what the Constitution was for. Not so much forgotten, but permitted the political class – who's only real purpose is job security through re-election, empire building, and generational perpetuation – to twist and cloud the Constitution into a document Washington, Franklin, and Jefferson wouldn't even recognize in its application."

Raphael was shaking his head. "You should be giving commentary on CNN or Fox."

Clay seemed not to hear. "Executive orders? If the President doesn't get what he wants, he bypasses the entire system? General Washington would have had himself impeached!"

"Clay? Clayton? Listen. Again, please. What you've done, it's gotten out of hand. I get the perversion of the Constitution and yes, something has to be done. The news has another member of Congress under investigation once a month. One of them got blown up just last night. He was under investigation, but not convicted."

"You think the FBI investigates innocent people?"

"Like Sam?"

"That's a cheap shot."

"Clay, how about that IRS lady? She's dead. Shot for taking the 5th? Isn't that extreme – like blatantly, obviously, insanely, criminally extreme?"

"They think they're untouchable, Ralph. Jesus! Somebody has to remind people that despite what we're told, we do control the five hundred men and women we elect to manage us. When they fuck up, they have to be held accountable. That's all I'm saying."

"And by accountable, you mean dead."

"Possibly. How many people have politicians killed in this country?" Clayton didn't wait for an answer. "There was a notice put right under their noses to start flying right. There were subtle manipulations that they chose to ignore."

"But murder? I know this sounds naive, but couldn't you just, I don't know, rig an election instead of kill people?"

"I didn't kill anyone, Ralph. Just to be clear. And what would a rigged election do? Not that it'd be the first. Have you ever looked hard at the slate we get to choose from these days? Millionaires and multi-millionaires. The last gubernatorial election I voted in gave us the choice of two candidates, both of whom had been indicted. Do you think men and women with that moral character really give a shit or have any idea what the people of this country need?"

"But you do?"

"I know what we don't need. Lifetime politicians. Professional thieves. What we do need is a dose of honesty and accountability. The bitch who got whacked is the example those assholes needed. The congressman too."

"And what does Sam need, besides a good attorney? What about him? I don't know what he's done – and I don't want to know – but look at him. Jesus, the FBI is after him. Am I next? You? Who else? They're not stupid."

"No, they're not, but they also don't have much if anything to go on. They'll poke around, maybe find their patsy, but in the meantime the Illuminati will be putting a stop to whatever and whoever we can reach and we have long arms, Ralph. Very long arms."

"And you're okay with letting Sam be their fall guy?"

Clayton leaned back in his chair. The move signaled the end of the conversation.

"Sam's smart. They don't have him. My guess is they won't even find him."

"You're so sure?"

"Yes."

"Anything else?"

"Do you want to know?"

"No, I guess I don't. But when they come to talk to me–"

"If."

"If. When. We've been friends forever. Sam too. I give financial advice and we watch old movies."

"And chase skirts once in a while."

"So this continues?"

"It's just beginning."

"Christ..."

"It's alright. I've got a couple aces in the hole. I think I have a new friend. I need a little more time to figure out how to play him."

"A new friend?"

"Yes, but don't worry. You're still number one. This guy... This guy could be different..."

Raphael's eyes drifted to the television and picked up the middle of a scene he'd watched twenty times. Clayton was settled in his chair and watched Bogart's tough prosecutor rough up a killer.

"Now, look at Bogey. There's a District Attorney I'd vote for," Clayton said. "Yep, there's a DA I could vote for."

10

Carl Rand was moving slowly through the dark early morning streets of downtown Tampa. His hands were buried so deep and hard into his pants pockets that his elbows were locked and forced his shoulders up and forward. His steps were short, almost comical, like Chaplin in an old silent film. Despite the peculiar short steps which seemed a trotter's gait, his progress was purposefully sluggish. He was headed to the Ciampiano newsstand. From the end of the street he could see the lights still glowing a full twenty-four hours plus after the search had been executed. A marked Tampa PD unit was parked in the street in front of the building. The FBI van was gone. Yellow tape still surrounded the stand like a ribbon without a bow on a Christmas box. The generators still whirled beneath the lights and the smell of the burning diesel reached up the street on the humid night air.

Bundled newspapers, neatly tied but haphazardly dropped were on the sidewalk near the yellow ribbon. They were why Carl had come. Since he had learned of the raid on the newsstand he had worried about his friend and also about his place of part-time employment. The money was never much, but Sam always paid even when business was slow. This morning, assuming correctly that Sam wouldn't be opening the stand, Carl was concerned about the newspapers.

"Excuse me. Hey. Excuse me," Carl was almost shouting long before he came up behind the patrol car. He hadn't had any bad experience with the police, but knew better than to walk up unannounced from behind policemen watching a spot for a reason Carl wasn't certain of. When the officers didn't respond over the noise of their cruiser and its air conditioning, Carl fell back, crossed the street and walked away from the newsstand on the opposite side of the road. He didn't go far when he crossed back and came up on the patrolmen from the front. He pulled his hands out of his pockets, showed them empty, and moved up to the driver's window.

"What is it?" the driver said over the dropped edge of his window.

Carl leaned down. He could see the officer in the passenger seat was asleep.

"I work here," Carl said as he motioned to the stand. "It don't look like she'll be open with you guys here and that tape all around, but I was wondering if I could maybe put the newspapers inside or something."

"Not likely. That place has been sealed by the FBI."

"FBI, huh? How come?"

"The owner's part of some terrorist outfit."

"Naww. Not Sam. He's a war hero. He just got out."

"I don't know about any of that, bud, but I do know nobody is going in that shack."

"Damn... People will be stealing the papers or they'll get ruined if it rains. See, in the paper business, Sam gets money back on everyone he doesn't sell, but if they don't get returned, he's got to pay for them. I hate to see him stuck like that."

"Sorry, bud."

"He's been real good to me. And his dad before him."

"That's the way it goes."

Carl was deflated and looked across the hood of the cruiser at the stacks of papers with their tight plastic cordage. "Yea. That's the way it goes." He hesitated as he watched the papers sitting on the sidewalk beneath the impenetrable ribbon.

"Hey, um, Officer? There's a list of phone numbers on the wall just inside the door. It's newspaper wholesalers. Sometimes I have to call them about orders. You suppose I could jot them numbers down and call those guys and tell them to stop bringing papers until this stuff with Sam gets squared away?"

"I can't get in there myself, bud. And even if I could, I couldn't let you in there."

"Damn. Those papers are going to keep coming. It'll make a helluva pile in a couple days."

"Maybe the FBI will release the place in a few days. I hope so. This is the most boring thing I've ever done."

"Yea. I guess it would be."

"I'll watch your papers and make sure no one steals any."

"That'd be good. Thanks."

The cop looked at Carl and waited for him to leave. Though he was grateful for any interruption to the monotony of making sure no one stole the newsstand, and now the stack of newspapers, his boredom had extended to the conversation with Carl.

"Okay. See ya around," Carl said.

The officer nodded and the window slid closed.

Three steps were all Carl managed before he turned back around and went to the window again. It slid down as if on a motion detector. Carl could feel the cool air spill out.

"Hey, sorry to bother you, sir, but you suppose if I gave you my number you could ask whoever's in charge if I could write them numbers down from the wall? I won't touch nothing else. I promise."

"Sure," the cop said as he begrudgingly pulled a small notebook together with a pen from his shirt pocket. Carl watched the notebook and saw the bulge above the notebook and knew it was the policeman's bulletproof vest under his uniform. As he waited for the notebook to open and the pen to be poised, Carl considered that sitting down in an air conditioned car was a pretty good job compared to the lugging he did on the docks, but that vest, he thought, "I wonder if they're heavy? I bet they're be hot."

The cop said he was ready with his eyes.

"Yea, umm. Carl Rand," he said very slowly. "That's Carl with a C. C. A. R—"

The patrolman handed the pad and pen out the window. "You jot down your name and a number where you can be reached and I'll pass it on. How's that sound?"

Carl looked at the pen as if it was magical. A policeman's pen had special powers – the power to write you a traffic ticket, or an appearance ticket. A policeman's pen could land you in trouble or cost you money as easy as his handcuffs. This was heady stuff, but Carl accepted the instrument delicately as though his hand and not the pen, might break.

He printed out his name, stopping once to admire the pen. By the time he had written his phone number, the pen had become quite comfortable and didn't seem to mind Carl at all. He considered that his fear of the pen was misplaced. He was about to hand pad and pen back, in fact the officer was already reaching for it, when Carl held it a second longer and drew a snappy line under his number. It had all gone quite well.

The patrolman tossed the pad on the dash of the car and slipped his pen over the bulge in his shirt back into its place. He didn't look at Carl. "I'll turn it in, but I can't guarantee they'll call."

"Alright. Well, thank you. Thanks for trying. I appreciate it. Sam's a good guy. This'll clear up. I just don't want to see him lose his shirt over them papers, you know?"

"Yep. Have a good one." And the window slid goodbye.

The gray of an early Tampa morning slipped away quickly. A cloudless clear blue sky welcomed a sun that was brilliant even before it cleared the land-bound eastern horizon. In seconds it seemed, the first rays were peeking around the city's tallest buildings and massaging the gray of pre-dawn off the sidewalk in front of the newsstand. The patrolmen looked out their car windows through tired, bleary eyes and searched for their replacements. When a cruiser appeared it was welcomed with a yawn, a stretch, and the eyeing of their watches. Babysitting a newspaper shack was damn boring. The only interruption had been the delivery of the daily papers and the visit by a part-time worker.

"Let's get out of here. My ass hurts."

The rolling police car stopped alongside and the pair of black and whites lowered their windows while the babysitting driver put his car in gear.

"Anything?"

"Hell no," the ass weary passenger said.

"Wait." The driver reached for his note pad and tore off Carl's name and phone number. He stuck the scrap through the open window and handed it to his replacement. "This guy says he works here and wanted to cancel the papers. Give it to the DA or the Feds and see if it's okay."

"You want me to give it to the DA or the Bureau? Which one?"

"I don't give a shit. Throw it in the street. We're out of here. This is a pain in the ass."

"Literally," his partner added.

The driver pulled away quick, as though he'd just received an urgent call for backup. He'd be pulling in the underground garage of the police station in minutes.

Though the new day's foothold was still slight, the District Attorney appeared. Marcus Pete was in tow. Both men exited Jack's county car in front of the newsstand steadying their coffee cups as they did.

"Latté? What the hell is a latté anyway?" Jack said as though he was defending his honor.

Petey's early morning defense was weak. "Coffee."

"Then get a coffee if that's what you want. Latté. Sounds French."

"Italian really. Means, milk."

Jack motioned with his paper cup toward Marcus's. "So you got a cup of milk? What are you, still in diapers? Milk. You need an eye opener? Get a cup of joe."

"It's coffee. Coffee with milk."

"Like creamer? You lightweight." Jack toasted himself with his cup. "Be a man, Petey. Hot and black. God, after all these years and still so much work to do. I dunno..."

Marcus took a sip. The coffee was hot. "I say the same thing. Every day. Trust me."

Jack heard the innuendo and understood it exactly. He smiled slightly within the sense that his work with Petey was yielding fruit and lots of it. Marcus was witty, clever, and a good cop. Jack also knew that within the workings of the District Attorney's office, Marcus was the bubble in the level that reflected when Jack's passion was getting off course. The DA had several thoughts in mind regarding the Illuminati, some of which he had flashed to Cal and John LaRoy to gauge their position, and like as not, Marcus already had an inkling of his boss's sentiments on the group, but Jack had yet to lay any cards on the table for his investigator and friend.

"What are we stopping here for, boss? Need a paper?" Marcus joked between sips. "I doubt they're open."

"More like you doubt I can read. A newspaper is a wonderful thing. Tangible. You hold the news in your hand—"

"And get ink on your fingers."

"Getting dirty is what men do. Your hands ever been dirty?"

Marcus had been watching and listening to Jack from the earliest days of The Illuminati and had been considering his boss's tenor toward the case and considered it was bordering suspect when held up to the light of the oath of the District Attorney's Office. "Often," Marcus said. "I like to mess with my yard, work on my house. That guy stuff. You know that. But I limit the definition of 'dirt' to manual labor, not my day job."

"Yea, well, sometimes dirt just gets on you, you know? Happens to me every day. I get home and there's a stain on my shirt or mud on my pants, and I'll say, "How the hell did that happen?" I really have no idea. Kinda funny. Like a kid, I guess. Show me a little boy who's clean all the time and I'll show you a mamsy-pamsy."

"A what?"

"Mamsy-pamsy."

"I have not heard that used in intelligent conversation my entire life."

"I always thought your education was pretty lacking. This confirms it." Jack elbowed Marcus and jostled his cup. "Don't worry, I know you ain't no mamsy-pamsy, Petey. You're more like Cal with your clothes – neat and pressed. You two probably go to the same dry cleaner. Maybe you could commute together. Save a gallon of gas. Think of the environment once in a while, Petey."

"Wow. How much coffee have you had already? Please don't tell me that's your first and you're already this wound up?"

The pair were at the newsstand and raised their cups as a good morning to the policemen sitting in their cruiser nearby.

"Wound up? Hell, I'm just getting started," Jack chirped. "Ask the uniforms if anything went on last night. I wanna take another look in the shed."

"You never did answer me as to why we're here."

"The 'dawn's early light.' Like the man said in the song. Might see something different. Only be a minute."

Jack's voice trailed as he slipped beneath the yellow tape and through the door of Ciampiano's newsstand. Marcus veered off to the patrol car. The tinted window of the passenger's side came down to greet him.

"Morning," a fresh recruit said.

Behind the wheel, a seasoned officer barely raised a hand from the still steering wheel as a hello.

"Morning," Marcus asked. "Anything happening?"

"Nothing," the young face said. "The eleven to seven said the building never moved all night."

"Fine police work," Marcus smiled as he turned away with his coffee. "See you guys. Keep your heads down and your powder dry."

"You've been working with the DA too long," shot the voice behind the wheel. "You're starting to sound like him."

The reference stopped Marcus as much as a hand on the back of his suit collar. He turned around to the officer in the window.

"You're right. That does sound like the old man, doesn't it? I better schedule some time off." Marcus took another step and was stopped again.

"What's that mean anyway?" the rookie cop asked. "He says that all the time. I mean, 'Keep your head down,' I get. But what's the 'powder' part?"

The older cop took a halfhearted swing at his partner's arm inside the car. "Gunpowder, moron. Keep your gunpowder dry. In case you need it."

"Dry? What are you talking about?"

The driver leaned obtrusively over his partner until he could see Marcus out the passenger window. "I'll explain it to him, Marcus. He's just a kid. Doesn't know shit. The only thing he watches on History Channel are reality shows. He wouldn't know real history if it bit him in the ass."

Marcus laughed as the driver continued to lean hard on his young partner. He stuck the note Carl had written out the window. "Marcus? Night shift said this guy stopped and wanted to see about shutting off the deliveries. Said he works here."

Stopped for the third time, Marcus returned to the car and took the note. Like anyone, he read it, but unlike the policemen or almost anyone else in the world, the name almost glowed neon in his hand. Rand.

"This guy said he works here?" Marcus pointed with the note at the newsstand. "Here?"

"According to him, I guess. It came over from the night shift. They said that guy came by early this morning. They asked me to give it to you or the Bureau. I saw you first. Your lucky day."

"Might be." Marcus read the name again. 'Rand' stilled glowed. "Might be at that."

The early light was filtering in the door of the newsstand. Jack was standing in the near corner to the back just inside the door. His position caught Marcus off guard, but only for the time it took to tap the note in the palm of his hand.

"Find anything new?" he asked.

"Still looking."

"From the corner?"

"Good a place as any. I didn't stand here last night. New perspective."

"Here," Marcus said as he held out the note. "Don't say I never gave you a present."

Jack read the note and Marcus read his face. He could tell the instant his boss saw the name Rand.

"This our Rand?"

"Not our Rand as in Clayton the whiz kid, but there's a Carl Rand in that picture we found," Marcus said as he pointed to the bleached spot on the wall where the clipping had hung. "Looks like he still works here. The night shift said he came by and wanted to stop the newspaper deliveries, but needed to get in here to get some phone numbers." Marcus turned away from Jack and saw a stained and faded list of company names and phone numbers printed out by hand in different colored inks held to the wall inside the door with rusty thumbtacks. "Probably this is what he was after."

Jack's walk to the phone listings was accomplished absently. He was already several steps down the road as his thumb twitched on top of Carl's name. "Yep," he said. "Jot those down, would you, Petey? We'll get a hold of Mr. Rand and see if we can't help him out."

Marcus could smell the smoke from wheels careening wildly in Jack's head. As Jack stared at the numbers but was seeing something else, Marcus pulled out his phone and snapped a picture of the list. "Got it. You want to call him or me?"

"Don't you ever carry a pencil?"

"No one does, Jack. Except maybe carpenters."

"Carpenters. How about a note pad?"

Marcus held up his phone. "All gets typed right here."

"Helluva world," Jack said as he stepped out the door.

"We done here?"

"Yep. Let's run over to Cal's office and see if the FBI is outa bed yet."

"You don't want to swing by Ciampiano's and see it, 'In the dawn's early light,' like you said?"

Jack was moving away. The spur worked on him like a horse and he quickened his step. "No, sir." He waved Carl's note in the air as he walked. "Let's go fry us another fish."

If Jack had really wondered about the state of the FBI he needn't have. John LaRoy and Cal were in the local office already. LaRoy was leering through the phone to the forensic unit in Washington which had been up all night yet again. He was getting answers, but wanted more. Cal was scanning the results on his computer screen while LaRoy continued barking into the phone. Across town, Alyn Nuary came out of the bathroom of her hotel room dressed to the nines in an over elegant business suit whose skirt would have deemed shorter than regulation had such regulations existed or ever been adhered to by her. As per her modus operandi, Nuary liked the attention and, regardless of how the men she worked around felt about her, they never complained about seeing too much of her thigh.

Jason Meyer was still in her bed. He propped himself up and stared.

"Nice," he said as he watched Nuary's skirt slip higher as she raised her heel to pull on her designer pumps. He rubbed his crotch through a tangled sheet. "This is the way to start a day." He laid back on the rumpled pillows and flung his arms out across the bed. "I tell you what, let's keep this arrangement going a while. Tell me what you want, darling, and it's yours."

Alyn was onto her second shoe. "I want you out of my bed. Get me the prelims on the evidence from that dumpy house and that shitbox store."

"Newsstand."

"Whatever. Get up. Forward me everything before I get to Denti's office."

"Yes, ma'am."

"You better get over there too," Alyn said as she collected her computer and Coach purse. "LaRoy will have called you already. You'd better check."

"Like you said, 'Whatever.' I'll call him when I'm up." Jason lifted the sheet and peeked under it. "In fact, I might be getting up right now. Why don't you come over here and let me send you to paradise once more before you go?"

"Don't flatter yourself, Jason." Alyn grabbed the back of a small chair from the desk and dragged it to the hotel door as Jason tossed aside the sheet to display himself proudly in front of his own smile.

"You sure, baby?" he said grinning.

"I'm sure." Alyn propped the door open with the chair. "I've been wetter riding a horse on a merry-go-round." As she walked out, she heard Jason scrambling behind her.

"Close the door, Alyn. Alyn! Close the f–," as he went pell-mell for the chair and the open door with the sheet trailing around and behind him like the tail of a wet kite.

The resounding echo from the slamming door was still subsiding when Jason wadded up the sheet and tossed it on the bed. Though naked – his erection lost in the dash for the door – he touched the on button of his computer and began the security laden login to his federal account. By the time Alyn walked into Cal's office, she would have whatever Jason could access.

Jason waited and lingered over latent fingerprint reports at the hotel as other reports trickled in. He sent them on to Alyn without much consideration until one caught his eye. A match had been made between prints found in the newsstand and a set of fingerprints on file. The report had a red header that said, "Cross Contamination – Federal – Military." Before looking, Jason was ready to write the federal match off as the target's military fingerprints, but five lines lower a name caught his eye. Fingerprints from the Ciampiano newsstand had matched a member of the military, but it wasn't Sam Ciampiano. It was Lieutenant Karen Auburn. Jason scrolled through the access records in the chain of custody attached to the newsstand. JAG Lieutenant Karen Auburn had never been in that building. The fingerprints couldn't be hers. Fifteen blocks away in Hyde Park, Clayton Rand was covertly reading the same report.

Sam was in a different time zone. At night he slipped out of the cell/room to make his way along the deck to the rail. On his first sortie to the rail, he tossed his passport into ten thousand feet of black water. He made certain no one saw him stretch his legs and he was as quiet as a church mouse. He read what was in the room – worn paperback Louis L'Amour stories of the old west – and laid on the plain bunk and let his mind wander through the hours and days as he pondered that he'd been born a century or more too late. He might have fared better as a Texas Ranger in the 1870's. According to L'Amour, the rules were simpler back then. By the last chapter of each book the bad guys had been dispatched to hell and the hero was in his lover's arms. Often the couple literally rode west into the sunset. Based on what the captain had said and confirmed by reading the stars at night from the lower deck, Sam wasn't even headed west and his lover – pushed away months before under his own hand – would never sleep in his arms again. Elbowing aside his selfishness, Sam thought it possible Karen might never even sleep in her own bed again. When the police came for him, they'd find her. Right now, she could be in a prison cell charged with anything and everything – enough to keep her in federal prison for years. And while she sat, he ran.

Sam looked back along the rail the length of the ship as far as he could see into the black wake of rumbling water that stretched out for miles behind the huge stern. He had committed too soon. He should have only run enough to watch out for her. Or ran with her, not away from her. His crimes would be counted as hers. He would not be found due to the code of honor and the memory of his father, but Karen had no such black luck history to ferry her into the void. Her only salvation would be his testimony and even that would likely not be enough. Karen had clouded his vision when she appeared at the newsstand under that silly hat and behind the big glasses. He had lost himself in her arms in the shadow of the counter and took her word that there was no answer but to run. Too many days in, it had come to him. She had planned it and he had been a pawn. Karen knew she could convince him, he thought, and she had.

She had always known she'd be found out. By coming to him a free woman instead of reaching out from a cell, he would go. If she had lingered and been arrested, he would have walked into the nearest police station, arms raised, to free her. The long distance sprint to Florida would save him, but insure she'd be snared. If she had stayed in Virginia, there was a good chance their relationship would have only derailed a promising career, but saved her from prison. Instead, Karen chose to suffer the consequences of triggering his flight. It was her plan and it had worked flawlessly.

"Why?" Sam whispered to the black waves and the hint of the moon through the heavy clouds. He tried to reason it out with the railing. "She stays away, SWAT takes me out. They find her – maybe. Maybe. She tells the truth, probably takes a shot, but stays out of jail." The rail wasn't listening.

Sam's mind was talking now. "A text, an email, a call would have never convinced me. She had to come. I had to see her face when she told me. See her eyes."

He watched the water rushing by fifty feet below as he lowered his head to the quiet rail. The steel was damp and cold on his forehead. It smelled of rust. Sam closed his eyes. She'd played him – played him into saving him. He loved her. It had been an awkward hesitant love of a cold soldier whose empty life meant little, but it was there in the restaurant, the beach, and his bed. Now, already a thousand miles from shore and conditioned like a dog to open his steel door and pick up his food tray, Sam felt his thick throat tighten and a welling come up behind his eyes. He tapped his forehead on the railing slowly and gently. He might have smashed his head against it on another night and slumped away broken and bleeding as punishment, but not tonight. Not knowing now what he didn't know then. Karen loved him. That's why she came. That's why his father made him walk home after a lousy practice and let him drive when he had worked so hard. His father loved him. It had made him a better man. Karen loved him. He was a far better man with her in his life. She centered him, gave him balance, and he loved her for what she'd made of him.

Sam raised his head from the steel and the salt water spray drove the rusty smell from his nose. It was too late to go back. He'd carve out a niche wherever Don T put him ashore then he'd go back for her. Maybe she'd be out by then. If she wasn't, he'd get her out. One way or another, they'd be together. Until then, he hit the pressure release valve that he knew was controlling Karen's life.

Sam went back to his room and waited for the next rap on the door. When it came – signaling feeding time – Sam opened the door, much to the surprise of the captain of the ship.

"I told you, Yankee," the captain said recovering as he bent and set a full tray down and picked up Sam's empty. "No one see you, not even me, until I come for you in Trapani. You not listen?"

"No. That is, yes. I heard you. I'm sorry, but–"

"No sorry," the captain turned his back and hustled down the passageway. "You don't answer door. We don't speak until Trapani."

"Wait. I need you to do something for me."

The man continued hustling away. "I don't work for you."

"It's very important."

"Go away."

Sam jogged down the hall. "Hold up. I need to send a message back to Tampa."

The suggestion stopped the diminutive captain more than the hulking form chasing after him.

"Message?" The captain stared for a moment, truly taken in by a desperation in Sam's voice and eye he would not have expected to find. "No message."

"Just a short one – an email, a tweet, something back to the States."

The captain looked puzzled and turned away slowly as though he was backing away from an animal that might bite. "No message, Yankee. I tell you. No message."

"C'mon," Sam was begging now and it didn't suit him. "A little favor," he said as he walked as unthreatening as possible.

"No favor."

"Okay. I'll pay you. Whatever you want. Just a couple quick notes."

The captain's face was stern and held the answer. Sam was more desperate. "Captain. I need this done badly. Very badly. Someone – a girl," Sam said, trying the weakest ploy to tweak the answer. "A girl is in a lot of trouble. I need to send a line, only one line. To let them know it wasn't her. She had nothing–"

"No!" the captain said as loud as he dared and rapped the empty metal tray against the railing of the stairs at the end of the tight walkway. "No message. Go! Go back to your room. We don't see each other face until Trapani. Go away!"

The captain bounded up the heavy steel grated staircase like a cat. "Damn Yankee trouble..." He was gone.

Sam took a few steps and tested the first stair gently, looking up the well. He wouldn't run the man down. But he wasn't giving up either.

The tray was still waiting where the captain had set it. Sam's cell door was still open. He bent down, picked up the tray, and locked himself inside. There'd be another knock around six AM. When it came, instead of the Pavlovian response, he'd rip through his cage and take his handler by the throat.

Sam was leaning against the wall of his room with one hand on the unlocked door's latch at ten minutes to six. The first of the now expected three knocks came at six-o-four. The second rap hit open air as Sam tore the door open. His hand was a blur from the handle to the captain's neck. The man was ripped inside and put against the wall by his throat as if he were little more than a rag doll. The shock and surprise had scarcely registered when he felt the serious end of a pistol pressing up under his chin. Though his hands shot to his own throat as an unconscious reaction, they relaxed and held themselves up, palms out. The captain's toes stretched to touch the floor.

"Shhh," Sam whispered. "The bridge. Communications. I have a friend in trouble. We're going to send a message. Understand?"

The captain didn't make a sound or try to nod.

"Okay? You with me?" Sam said.

The captain lowered his hands to his side. Sam saw the fear flow out of the man's face and felt the tension slip out of his body. Again, the captain said nothing and made no attempt to move.

"That's good. We all relax." Sam eased up a little on the captain's throat and let his feet rest flatly on the deck. "You've been decent. Don't spoil it. Let's go up to the bridge."

When Sam tried to ease the man off the wall and toward the door, the captain resisted. Sam tightened his grip again. The captain met it force for force and jutted his chin out and down hard on the end of Sam's pistol, creasing his throat.

"Shoot," the captain said plainly through his Filipino accent.

Sam had handled bluffers and drugged mercenaries before. He pulled the man down the wall, collapsing him to his knees with a push of his own knee behind the captain's legs. His gun hand's thumb cocked the hammer on the H & K and pushed it into the captain's cheek until the man's face was pressed against the green steel wall. Sam turned his own face away slightly as though to shield it from the splattering blood and brain that was to come.

As before, the captain resisted the pressure between the pistol and the wall and leaned heavily into the barrel already embedded in his face. Though his mouth was distorted, he began to recite what Sam took to be a prayer in his native language.

Sam's face came back to the man kneeling in front of him. "You ready to move now, Captain?"

The man continued praying.

"I said, let's move!" Sam hoisted him without effort and forced him out the door by the back of his neck, the pistol tucked under the captain's ear. "You don't want to die and I don't want to–"

"No message."

"Oh, now that's where you're wrong, friend. I'm sending a message to Tampa. I have a friend I left in a jam. It was a–"

"No message. I take the bullet now and save my family."

Sam moved like water flowing. He holstered the automatic in the waist of his pants, snatched the captain's wrist, and had him stretching on his toes, dangling from a bent arm that turned his joints white with pressure. Muscles, ligaments, tendons, and bones were fractions of seconds and millimeters from snapping. Sam's free hand covered the captain's mouth to squelch the screaming and felt hot breath and the overflow of tears spewing from the man's nose as loud as a racehorse that just passed under the wire. The captain clenched his eyes as Sam drew up close to his ear.

"There won't be a bullet, but I'll make you wish there was."

Sam eased the pressure and as before, the captain's feet were back on the decking of his ship.

"Ready now?" Sam asked.

The skipper's head faintly moved from side to side under Sam's hand. The pressure came back again and the grimace crept toward fainting.

"What is your malfunction, Captain?" Sam brutally teased with the grip on the man's wrist. "You and I are going to the bridge and send a quick wire off to the States. *Capisci?*"

Again, the captain's head moved in a quick jerk from side to side as much as he could.

Sam had an answer of his own and wheeled his catch from the passageway through the door. "Goddammit!" Though exasperation came from his throat, his arms tossed the captain with considerable force across the room onto the bed. "Don't make me–"

"Everything from boat leaves a wake. Everything. You *capisci*, Yankee?"

The glare in the set of Sam's jaw was already melting under the weight of something he most certainly had always known, but hadn't let himself see.

They watched each other across the span of the small room and the quiet quaking rumble of the ship's engines. The skipper began to massage his elbow and wrist.

Sam's voice was weakening. "I need to send a–"

The skipper's voice was also gentler. "No, Yankee, no."

Sam breathed deep and the captain's chest heaved with his. Both men relaxed a step.

"Do you have a global phone?" Sam asked.

"Of course, but still, answer is no."

The taste of defeat was sour in Sam's mouth. "I could find the phone on my own."

"Maybe. But you kill me in the hunt."

"I'm not going to kill you, Captain. I might knock you out, tie you up, and store you in a locker for a while though."

"Might be so, but you still kill me. All communication is monitored. Everything. Whatever you run from will follow the wake of your message back to this ship," the captain said with some authority as he pointed down at the gray steel floor. "And then me. Tampa will not let it happen."

The shaken man was done rubbing his arm and almost done explaining. He produced a soft pack of foreign filterless cigarettes and shook one from its place. He took it in his mouth and pulled a cheap lighter from within the torn cellophane of the pack and lit up.

"You go find the global phone, Yankee. Go ahead. You big man. I can't stop you." The captain drew on his smoke. "But when you make that call, you kill me and my family as plain as you pull trigger now."

"No one's going to kill your family if I make a call."

The captain drew long and deep against the cigarette. The smoke he blew into the room offended Sam but he only waved his hand at it.

"It is the rule of the game, Yankee." The skipper baulked at his words then waded through. "You must know this thing." He paused. "You would not be on boat otherwise."

Sam stared blankly as though he was looking at the words hanging in the air instead of a man. The captain was right of course. Any and every transmission of any description was susceptible to monitoring, perhaps even more on the heels of the dashing exit through the Port of Tampa. A message would go up as a flare and likely the end result would be ten squads of soldiers waiting at the first port of call to take custody of Sam or kill him outright. The captain, for losing his cargo, would likely suffer a similar fate in time.

The captain field stripped his cigarette on the edge of the bunk and dropped it in his shirt pocket. He got up slowly, still conscious of being bitten by the barrel of Sam's pistol, but with a small measure of confidence reinforced by the new look in Sam's eye. He walked slowly to the door. Sam slid to the side and let him pass.

The skipper bent down outside and picked up the tray. He turned and held it out. "Here, Yankee. Your strength is fine – believe it – but you should still eat."

A thick hand took the tray.

"Drink wine with the food. It will settle your mind. I see you in Trapani, Yankee."

The skipper pulled the door closed behind him and left Sam alone with the annoying smell of the cigarette. The captain's counter punch for his bruised cheek and wrist would begin and end with the smoke.

———————————

11

I t would be two more weeks of muffled thunder as the droning diesels churned deep in the ship before Sam heard them ease. The sound of the ship changed, but the drop in speed was undiscernible from his buried perch in the catacombs of the monster ship. That night he went to the rail and saw the lights on the shore. It was Tunisia.

Tug boats came out and thumped the side of the big ship. Sam stayed hidden but saw the water froth like the base of Niagara at the stern of the powerful tugs. As the dock came closer, Sam retreated to his cabin. Fortunately the wait was brief. New noises clanked and groaned through the vessel as containers and freight exchanged places between the ship's deck, hold, and shore. In efficient order, the tugs returned and muscled the ship back into the deep cobalt water of the Mediterranean Sea.

The next leg of the voyage was quick in comparison to the Atlantic crossing. In this passage, Sam started several letters that attempted to exonerate Karen. Should the landing in Trapani not go as planned, he hoped a letter, even one found on his corpse, might accomplish what he had been unable to do from sea. Each attempt ended in a crumpled piece of paper many of which were thrown against the steel walls. Each scrap was collected and carried to the rail and entrusted to Davy Jones' locker. If Don T's plan held, a document detailing any information regarding who Sam was and his recent history could be fatal – for Sam as well as those that had sought to help him.

The fits and starts of his letter writing continued, but fortunately there were relatively few notifying knocks at his cabin before the engines quieted again and the predictive bump of the tugs came alongside. Port put an end to any foray with pen and paper.

This time Sam watched the shore in daylight. When the dock loomed, he retreated to his cage for the last time and packed his few things. There was disappointment that they had made landfall in the daylight. Darkness had always served as a welcome helpful confederate. As he sat on his bunk he checked his weapons. The H & K went to its place in his pants at the small of his back. The larger guns were locked and loaded in the black bag. The canvas duffle from the maître d' had been relieved of its wine and foodstuffs, but Sam packed his books and surrounded them with some of the cash and identification from the weapons cache except for a small bundle of currency he sat near his pillow. He went over the room and wiped it clean of his fingerprints as a precaution. There had never been much to do in the small room, but now even that was done. All that remained was to wait.

There was no dread, certainly no fear, but also little anticipation of any description. His training told him that the best laid plans could go to hell in a heartbeat. Sam would rely on that training when the knock would come on the cabin door. The passageway would be covered without feeling. It might be the inmate's few short steps to parole and freedom, or a walk to the death chamber. Sam couldn't know, so like a hundred missions before, he steeled himself against either eventuality.

There was a solid rap on the door and the captain's voice. "Yankee?"

Sam was at the door, having pulled the automatic from his back.

The captain heard the tumblers fall and the groan of the steel. The door opened less than an inch. The two men saw only one eye of the other's through the two-way crack.

"Yankee, let's go," and the captain slid away from the crack.

When Sam opened the door further, he instinctively poked his head out, looked up and down the corridor quickly, and retreated inside.

"Come, Yankee. You must go."

Sam rammed the pistol back in his pants and grabbed his bags. He was bounding up the passageway and had nearly caught the skipper as he hit the first steps.

"When we come on deck, say nothing. Follow me to the gangway and go down. No stopping. When you step off the boat, walk fast – don't run – across the trucking lanes. On far side go left and keep walking. A truck will pick you up. They will ask you if you want a ride to 'C' gate. Get in. There is no 'C' gate. You know Italian, Yankee?"

"Yes," Sam said as both men hustled up the stairs two at a time.

"If anyone stops you, tell them you're going to the crew terminal and ask for a ride. They will ignore you and drive on. Understood?"

"Yes."

"*Capisce?*" the captain couldn't avoid the jab.

Sam cringed inside. "I do."

"Good for you, Yankee."

They cleared the final stairwell and were moving deliberately along the length of the deck.

"Hey," Sam said as he looked around and shifted both bags to his left hand, freeing his right to take the gun or toss a punch if necessary. "I'm sorry about your wrist. I was—"

"There," the captain pointed to the gangplank that would free him of the responsibility from Tampa. "Go off my boat now."

Sam looked away and took an unguided step.

"Yankee? Maybe you good man, maybe not so good. I don't know. It good to help a friend, but no good to hurt others, even if they mean nothing to you. Have a good life, Yankee."

There was a short spin that was so graceful it almost appeared not to happen and Sam's hand was sticking out toward his benefactor. The captain shook Sam's hand quickly and discreetly.

"Thank you, Captain. Thank you for everything."

There was the slightest nod of the man's head, but his eyes were looking elsewhere. "Get off my boat, Yankee. And you were never here." The captain had turned away and dropped back into the hold of his ship leaving Sam alone in the Sicilian sun.

He wouldn't dawdle – there was no time and no future in that. His heavy boots made no sound going down the long aluminum ramp. At the end, Sam was met with flat-bed small cabbed tractors lining up to take the trailer sized containers from the ship on their backs. The towering cranes grappled with the tractor-trailer sized containers, slinging them from the ship's deck to the flat beds with the apparent ease of so many Lego blocks. Sam kept his face down, but his eyes up and weaved through nearly twenty lanes of stop and start traffic coming to and away from the dock. When he cleared the last truck he turned left as instructed, but chanced a look at the ship, half thinking – hoping – he'd see the captain. There was only room for the briefest disappointment as he threw his bags over his shoulder and walked on, waiting and wondering how long it'd be before he was picked up as the trucks whizzed by.

With countless missions as complex as this current one in his pocket, Sam understood that innumerable things could and would go wrong. The dock was so long it had a vanishing point on the horizon, but it would eventually end. If Sam was still walking when it did, Plan B likely was jostling in the small of his back. He thought again about the letter that didn't exist in his pocket – the one that would try to exonerate Karen. If he lost in a shootout, the letter might help. If he was captured, it might—

"You need a ride to Gate C?" came a voice in Italian out the window of a truck as it slowed next to him. The cab was about half the size of a regular truck and likely never left the acres and acres of concrete surrounding the waterfront. Its wheels didn't quite stop rolling.

Sam nodded. The driver jerked the door handle as Sam jumped on the running board, pulled the door open, and swung inside with his bags cluttered on his lap. Before he had settled to the seat, the driver gunned the light diesel engine and sped off.

The bench seat was small and the men were close, but neither looked directly at each other. Sam watched both the driver and around the truck as the narrow tractor and empty flatbed wheeled around and through the maze of cargo containers that were piled in neat high rows and seemed to go on endlessly. Despite the scope of the dockage, the truck and its unique cargo pulled up short two minutes after Sam had jumped in. He was at the far edge of the interminable concrete at a small walk-thru gate that held a painted white plywood sign which read, '8-3,' in big blue letters. A tiny guardhouse next to the gate was empty.

The driver didn't speak or look at his passenger. He pointed across Sam's face out the side window to a dark blue four-door Lancia sitting just outside the unattended gate. In response to the stopping truck and the gesture of its driver, the front passenger door of the car popped open slightly. Sam left the tiny cab of the truck without a thank you, didn't look back, but heard the truck roar away.

The short walk to the car felt longer than it was. No one was in sight. The towers of shipping containers – mostly rusty reds, blue, and a few greens were behind him. The pale concrete was hot and reflecting a tireless sun. His bags felt heavy and it occurred to Sam that he should have run the deck of the freighter at night to keep up his strength better. His simple exercises in his cabin perhaps had not been enough. In the adjacent thought he recognized that his breath was short and tight. He didn't know where he was going, only barely knew where he was, and was lost as to what he had left behind. For perhaps the first time in his life Sam's nervousness was getting the better of him.

He adjusted the slings over his shoulder to clear the gate as the door of the Lancia opened further. Inside the car, the driver reached over the seat and stretched to open the back door as well. Then the man leaned across the front. He was smiling when Sam got to the door.

"Toss your luggage on in back, my friend."

As Sam complied, the driver adjusted his rearview mirror and watched. "Those are nice," the driver said in English with a disarming chuckle. "Are they *Versace?*"

With the duffle bags stowed, Sam hopped in the front. The tension and his near ignorance of fashion conspired. "I think they're canvas," Sam said as he looked straight ahead out the windshield.

The driver laughed out loud. "Good one!" he said and hit the steering wheel as he rambled in Italian. "That's funny. American humor. I like it. I like your TV shows too. The jokes are different in the United States. Much different than Europe. But," he continued as he tossed the car in gear and pulled away without any rush. "You will like it here. You'll see."

Sam ventured a look. The driver was still smiling. He was a handsome man, smaller than Sam, but most men were. He looked to be in good shape, just thirty, and his face was lean and tight. He had jet black wavy hair and dark eyes under thick eyebrows.

As Sam was gauging his latest benefactor, the driver looked with a quick jerky motion from the turns of the seaport to Sam and back again. "Do you understand Italian?"

"*Po.*"

"English is better?"

"Yes."

"Not a problem. I speak English. My... um... I don't know the words. My brother's babies. *Come si fa a dire?* How do you say, my brother's children?"

"Nephews and nieces?"

"*Certo! Certo.* Na-few. And nee-says. Good. I have it now," the driver said as he wheeled the car with one hand and pointed to his head with the other. "My na-few and nee-say speak English very good. And write the English the same. The schools now. They start the English first time. English is language of commerce, yes?"

"I suppose."

"My English is good, but my conversion – dollars to euros," he said as he turned quickly again and smiled broadly. "That *perfetto!*" He laughed. "Commerce. That is a good word, yes?"

Sam was quickly growing annoyed with the rattle-trap conversation. He very much liked the sound of quiet. The dialogue was also unnerving in the midst of what he still saw as a mission. He silently nodded agreement and returned his gaze to the road.

"My father teach me this word. Commerce. He teach it to my brothers and me when we were babies. You will meet him. He knows your Don T well. And my grandfather before him." The driver crossed himself. "He is died now, but my grandfather knew your father's people."

That jerked Sam's attention from the road like a rifle shot.

"Oh, yes. I see you did not know. It was years ago, I have heard. It is sad for you that the old ones are some died now. Your *padre*, he go to

America, but my brother says the Perricci family and yours are different limbs on the same tree. I don't– Don't? Is that the word?"

"Yes," Sam said, eager for the driver to continue.

"The American words that are two made one."

"Contractions."

"Hmm?"

"Contractions. When two words are cut down to make one." Sam was teetering on being agitated.

"Cut? *Mozza?*"

"Two words. Do. Not. Don't."

"*Si.* Don't." The driver pointed to his head again. "Don't. I have it here now. I don't know what my brother says, but two limbs of a tree – we share the roots, no? The soil." He pointed out the window. "We share these mountains. My mother and your father are from the same town. This is *importante.*"

It was a bit lofty for someone like Sam, especially given the urgency behind him. At the moment he had no common tie or concern for the driver and it was showing.

"Rest, *mio amico.*" The driver shifted gears on the car and the conversation with equal ease. "Have you been to Sicily before?"

"No," Sam answered with hesitation still bound to hearing the reference to his father. "Who are the Perriccis?"

"Ah, Americans! They go to walk in the Coliseum and ride boats on the sewers of Venice. Everyone goes to see the Pope. Everyone knows Leonardo, but this–" he said as he pointed again out the windshield in a wide slow arc to the mountains and countryside that continued to stretch up as Tripani disappeared behind the Lancia. "This is home, Ciampiano. This is your home."

Sam was suddenly dumbstruck by both the thought of his ancestry and sound of his name. "You know my name?"

"*Certo!* I know many Ciampianos! We go to Ficuzza – home of my mother and your father. There are a few Ciampianos in Ficuzza this day. One more," he said as he motioned to Sam. "One more, no *differenza.* We stay in Ficuzza at my brother's house. Antonio. He is a pain on my ass. You will like him. Everyone likes Antonio. Then, when my father says it is time, we go to Messina to ride the ferry home. Maybe a few days. Maybe a few weeks. No more."

"Ficuzza," Sam's voice echoed the reflection in his head. "My father spoke of Ficuzza."

"*Certo.* That is where he was born, I am told. My mother and her father too. But my own father," the driver smiled, cocked his head and waved his finger as if scolding a child as he ranted in broken English. "He was a sly one, that one. I have heard the stories. He is of the mountains in the heel – Italian, not Sicilian. My grandfather disapproved, but my mother..." His countenance changed to a warm gentle glow. "The love of those two! My father would not say so in a voice, but he lives to my mother. He is— Ah! I talk and talk. Ciampiano, are you hungry? Do you need a drink?"

"No. *Grazie.* I'm good."

"*Bene.* Soon we are to my brother's house. We eat there. An hour maybe. Always food. Lots of food and my family's wine. Great wine. Not like the American wine. Americans would give us all their money for my family's wine, but your government is owned by the big business. The bullshit... Bullshit? That is the good word?"

"Bullshit is a great word."

"Great word. The bullshit big businesses tells your government what to do." He rubbed his thumb and fore finger together. "Dollars. If they let our wine in your country, your California would be broken."

That made Sam smile. "You're right."

"Our cheese too. Americans make a barrel of goo and paint it yellow and say, "Now you are cheese!" They put it in jars and cans. Imagine! Cheese like a can of spraying paint! It is for *pazzia*! Crazy thing. That is more of the bullshit."

The car worked its way further from the port city and began a winding, jutting series of long switchbacks as it crept into a mountain range. The sky ahead was turning grayer with each mile.

"Rain," the driver said, announcing something neither good nor bad.

In a few miles the first drops appeared on the windshield. Sam slipped out of character as he watched the first raindrops collect and under the weight of many, begin sliding along his passenger window. He thought of everything he'd just heard and was surprised and confused by so much new information. He expected the continued tight lipped nature of the ship's captain. This man, who claimed his family knew the Ciampianos – perhaps even his father – talked with an ease that suggested they were old friends on a casual drive.

"Your brother is Antonio," Sam said slowly, already uncomfortable in asking any questions. "What do I call you?"

"Oh, my Gods! My mother will break her broom over my back! I am so sorry. Please. My name is Giuseppe Perricci. My mother is a Colletta. Collettas and Ficuzza. They are the same name. You will see."

"Giuseppe," Sam said and nodded in his companion's direction.

"My brothers call me Joey. You should call me Joey."

"Fair enough. I'm Sam."

"I know. 'The Hammer.'" Joey puffed his chest out, made a tight fist, and flexed. "It is a good name for you."

The banter, though a bit much for Sam's taste, was genuine. It did much to gently displace the weeks of solitary confinement on the ship from Sam's head. When the small town of Ficuzza, cradled in the arms of Mount Sicani, suddenly appeared, Joey's voice eased away from the early excited edge.

"You will like Ficuzza. Maybe our parents went to university together."

"I don't think so."

"*Non e importante*. The stones are the same under their feet. Tomorrow you go to the palace. Everyone wants to see the palace."

Sam didn't answer. He was quiet and looked out each window around the car as they pulled into the small town. Giuseppe recognized the look.

"It is fine, my American friend Sam. This is your town. These are your mountains. Besides, there are only three roads into the Ficuzza. Some tourists come for the palace, but anyone else? My family has many friends. The eyes of the mountains will keep you safe. No one comes to Ficuzza who does not belong."

Joey roughly pulled off the street into an alley so narrow the doors would likely not open fully. Ahead was a rusted sliding gate eight feet high. He laid on the horn until a young man, maybe sixteen, stepped out, unlatched the gate, and began sliding it to the side. Joey put down his window and shook his hand in the air.

"*Spostare*! Move! Move! Tell your lazy father we have a guest." Joey waited on the gate and looked at Sam as he pointed with an open hand out the windshield. "Antonio's baby. *Poco* Tony. Good boy."

Sam listened to the creaking gate and continued letting his eyes survey the old urban terrain. The houses, tightly packed were various shades of terrazzo. Their roofs were mostly tile and every window on the first floors had bars.

Giuseppe reached across the seat and patted Sam's leg.

"It is *bene*, Sam. This is not Corleone, your American *Mafioso* movie town. Ficuzza is a quiet. Most of the time."

Joey shifted the Lancia and pulled through the gate. A wide courtyard awaited around the back of the building. Another man, looking much like Joey and easily his brother, walked down three short steps and held his arms out in a welcome.

"But, Sam. Corleone? The movie town?" He pointed over his shoulder. "It is twelve kilometers that way."

"It's a real place?"

"It is very real. Maybe we go there sometime. We ask my father. Just to visit. It is not a dangerous place. The danger is when Corleone comes here. Ficuzza is for Colletta and Perricci *famiglia*."

Joey winked and got out of the car.

Antonio Perricci waited at the base of the short stone steps. He was a near mirror of Joey. He was almost twenty years older and carried a hint of gray in his hair. Antonio, often called Tony by everyone except his parents, had a different look around his eyes than his younger brother. To Sam, Tony's eyes were tighter, wiser, and guarded.

Behind him stood his house – his grandfather's before him. The lowest level was stone and had been the original clan's center of life through a hundred and fifty years of revolution and invasion. Additions to the old house – some of them nearing a hundred years old themselves – had fresh stucco that had been recently painted a stunning dark burnt sienna. Upper floors were much more recent, but painted to match the rest of the house with a lighter complimentary trim. Holding to the edges of nearly every upper window or glass door was a narrow black wrought iron balcony.

Sam's arrival at what he would come to call the 'Island House' was not like he'd expected. He had anticipated a still confine, closer to the hidden room of The Columbia or the cabin onboard ship. He'd considered that he would likely be tucked away beneath a barn. Instead, Tony hugged and kissed him on both cheeks as Sam held his canvas bags. Sam was casually ushered into the main house where an expansive table, spread with cheeses and breads of assorted shapes, sizes, and varieties, was carefully laid out. The counters nearby were weighed down with pastas, meat, and fish. More than the many dishes, Sam was shocked, almost anxious, with the number of people that were milling around the table and the kitchen. In their boisterous coming and going, all stopped to introduce themselves and kiss both his cheeks. Without touching them, Joey pointed beneath a chair at the end of the table and asked Sam if he would like to place his bags there.

Sam heard names, saw smiles, and lost track of the number of Antonios and Antonias of various pronunciations, and quickly realized his Italian was well beyond merely rusty or lacking. Among native Sicilian speakers, adding the complexity of a unique dialect, Sam was nearly deaf and dumb.

Antonio, true to the backhanded compliment Joey had paid him, saved Sam from the chatter with the same apparent ease he was saving him from pursuit.

"Come, *signore* Ciampiano. Stay," he said in English then turned to the young man who had opened the gate. "Antonio. *Inglese. Si, bene. Bene.*" Then the father spoke to the son. "*Tradurre.* To the English. *Fare nessun errore.* Make no error."

"*Si, Padre.*"

"*Grazie.* Good boy. Here. Stay," Antonio said to Sam as he gently touched his son's face and motioned to the corner of the long table and the chair over Sam's bags. He himself immediately sat at the head of the table.

While their guest was seated, Colletta and Perricci hands and voices flew over and around the table with a noisy reverence. Sam was the first to be served though he tried in vain each time to defer. After weeks aboard ship, each course was more splendid than the first as the lengthy meal, with side dishes of laughter and stories of family and Ficuzza history – seemingly tied at the hip – continued until the sun had long set. Young Antonio grew exasperated trying to both eat and translate until Sam put a thick hand on his arm and pointed to the young man's plate.

"*Mangia. Il piatto,*" he said. "*Mangia.* And thank you. *Grazie.*"

The table was instantly quiet. Sam knew something was wrong. In a country of customs, in a family of traditions, there was a genuine concern he'd offended his hosts.

Antonio pulled every eye off his American guest as he spoke in staccato Sicilian. "Be respectful. It's nothing. No jokes. Just eat."

The table eased back into its steady banter until Sam, eyeing young Tony next to him, asked if he had done something wrong.

"No. It's a little funny," Tony whispered as he picked up his plate, much to the chagrin of his father, and pretended to bite the dish. "You told me to eat my plate."

Sam cringed and looked around the table, straight into every eye. Though embarrassed, an emotion he hadn't felt in recent memory, Sam shrugged his shoulders and smiled broadly. Little Tony's brothers and sisters, all in their teens and twenties, picked up their plates and pretended to chew the edges to an eruption of laughing faces, including Sam's. The laughter was the second emotion in as many minutes which had long atrophied within the ex-Ranger.

The senior Tony reached across the corner of the table and massaged Sam's heavy shoulder.

"Laugh. *Bene. Benvenuti nella casa della Colletta*," he said with a rough but cordial slap and returned to his pasta.

Young Tony pushed aside a mouthful and leaned toward Sam. "Papa says, 'Welcome to the house of Colletta.' We have many, many guests, Mr. Ciampiano, but Father doesn't welcome them to our family like this. He likes you."

"*Grazie. Grazie*," Sam said looking from the father to the son.

Antonio dismissed it with a wave of his hand while little Tony focused again on his plate and dipped fresh bread and buffalo mozzarella in olive oil.

"This is ours," Little Tony said as he pointed with the cheese to the olive oil. "It is the first press. The very finest oil."

"You make olive oil?"

"The best. I will ask Father if I can show you the orchards and the presses. The first press of the olives – you call it virgin, or extra virgin, extra extra virgin. That first oil is *qualità superior. Buon gusto*."

"It's delicious," Sam said around a mouth of silky cheese.

"Perriccis wean babies on this oil."

Sam grinned and dipped another piece of cheese.

Encouraged and relaxing for the first time in over a month, Sam posed a question to his young interpreter. "Your father and uncles are Perricci, but the house is Colletta?"

"Yes. My grandfather is Perricci. My grandmother, Colletta. This was her father's house. Italians and Sicilians – everything stays in one family. It can be crazy. Now, my father and his brothers work for my grandfather. Their cousins too – Collettas. My father runs the businesses of oil and some wine here in Ficuzza. We sell tomatoes, wine, and oil from my grandfather's land in Italy. My uncle, Antonello Jr., is there with my grandfather, who is Antonello the senior. My father manages most of the business here on the island. Uncle Antonello manages other interests of the family."

Sam motioned with his fork down the table to Joey as his mind slid gently around the definition the "other interests" might take. "And your uncle Joey?"

"*Lo zio Giuseppe?*" Tony said as he followed Sam's fork down the table. "He balances both businesses and does what is needed. He likes to talk and he's very good at it. Did he talk all the way here?"

"Almost."

"That's *Zio* Joey. It can be very good for negotiations. My grandfather says to save a single cent in a deal is earning money as though you had gathered the olive with the same hand. My father can negotiate some, but he works best with the inspectors and the workers. He collected fruit from my grandfather's vines for many years and today he will still prune and harvest when he is in the fields. He always carries the pruning knife of his mother's father. I would wager it is in his pocket right now."

Tony leaned across the table and requested in Sicilian. "Papa, can I see your knife?"

Antonio produced a folding four inch knife from his pants' front pocket without breaking away from the conversation he was having. Tony took it, opened the stubby hooked blade, and pointed out the deeply worn steel to Sam.

"See? The metal is worn away from so many years working the vines. If you had the fruit this has trimmed you'd be a rich man." Tony handed the knife to Sam by the blade. "It is an antler handle," he said smiling. "When my brothers and I were small, Father said it was bone, made out of the leg of a Norman killed in the battle for independence."

Sam ran his heavy fingers across the years of working polish on the knife and looked closely at the making of the handle. "Hmm," he said as he examined it closely. "I think it is bone."

"No..." Tony's eyes widened and looked at the knife as if he were seeing it for the first time.

The knife was handed back and a big smirk followed it. While Tony flipped the knife carefully over and over in his hands, Sam's smile grew. Tony looked up to him with a question and met the big grin.

"Do you really– Oh... Okay. I see how you are. Father is right. You fit well here. *Papa?*" Tony said as he leaned back across the table with the knife now folded. "*Grazie.*"

The senior Perricci returned the knife to his pocket without a question. Then broke out of his present conversation and spoke in soft Sicilian to his son. "Tony. Tomorrow take Sam around town. Show him the palace then take him to the fields. Not Corleone. In two or three days, you will take Sam on the train to Messina. Cross the ferry with him. Antonello will meet you there." Antonio continued to speak Sicilian, but directed it to Sam with Tony translating close behind. "Antonello is my oldest brother. He will take you across the mainland. My father will have things in place for you."

"I will meet your father?" Sam asked, continuing to be brought out of character by these people.

"*Certamente,*" Antonio answered without pause. "He has a hand on all family business."

"I am, 'family business?'"

Antonio laughed at the translation and brought his youngest son with him. "You are. It is the family's word to make you safe. My father and my brother touch many men. You have no troubles. You will see."

Sam dipped another piece of fresh bread in oil though he was stuffed. "Your oil is great."

"*Grazie*. The family works hard. Tony will show you. We manage the fields here and in Italy, Antonello watches trucks and imports – petrol, clothing, and insurance, but Papa sees all things."

"Your family is busy. My father was busy." There was an implication that 'busy' was well defined.

"I know," Antonio continued. "Papa spoke of him through our friends in America. He was a good man."

"Sounds like your father is a good man – quite a business man."

"No... Papa is no businessman. He is a cook."

"A cook?"

"*Si*. He is a cook. A simple cook." Antonio winked.

The meal winding down, Antonio's voice rose as he addressed his wife and oldest daughter who it seemed had scarcely stopped serving for the last two hours. "*Limoncello*, Mama. For our guest."

Small ceramic glasses materialize and double shots of the opaque yellow liquor were distributed to everyone. Antonio stood and raised his glass. He spoke in Sicilian while Tony translated each word in Sam's ear.

"We welcome a friend of ours, from America. A friend of our family. We offer a prayer for his continued safe travel – which we will assist God in providing – and hold a place at this table for every meal. *Prosit!*"

A chorus of salutes went up over raised glasses. Sam held his glass and acknowledged them all. The attention was more than he was comfortable with, but the eyes behind the words and smiles carried a familial love he had not felt since he was a boy riding unbuckled in the front seat of his father's car. The supper table that followed their rides home from football practice were quiet and calm compared to this scene, but there was a sentiment at the Ciampiano table in Ybor City, Florida that had never been matched until today.

Over the next several days Sam was handed off from one Perricci or Colletta to another with seamless simplicity. Clothes appeared on his bed when he returned from walks on the few quiet streets of Ficuzza. Young Tony was the mainstay, though others took over from time to time, each capable of conversations in English in varying degrees. There was no rush or concerned air around the house or the town and Sam began to breathe again.

On the third day, he was up early. The house was always alive with people, seemingly indifferent to the time of day. Some twenty-somethings he had not met were coming and going as though their presence was commonplace as Sam filtered through rooms he had not yet quite memorized. Everyone smiled and said, "Good morning," in English, Italian, Sicilian, or a combination, and moved on. Giuseppe and Antonio weren't around, but young Tony was already in the kitchen.

"Good morning," Tony said in English. "Your running shoes fit well?"

"*Perfetto. Grazie.* I thought I'd break them in. Go for a run."

"I don't know that there is time. We are going to Palermo this morning."

There was an instant that suspended Sam's voice and movements. The vacant look was so apparent, even a sixteen year old could see it. "We are to take the train to Messina."

"No problem," Sam said as he wrestled himself out of the peculiar relaxing hold and back to the kitchen. "I'll get ready."

"I'm sorry, Sam. I just learned myself. Sometimes things–"

"Not a big deal, Tony. *Grazie.* I'll get my stuff."

The rush away from the comfortable center of the house back to his room was as much an escape as the gangplank in the Port of Tampa. He had been so taken in by the loyalty and comfort of the family and the protection and anonymity of the hills towering around the small town, he had lost sight of the fact that his race – his escape – was but half over.

Sam had never forgotten what was behind him. He certainly never allowed Karen to be covered by the shadows from either the laughter or the towering rocky escarpments, both of which had surrounded him and strangely sheltered him with a veil of comfort. For weeks, escape and safety had taken his focus and energy. In Ficuzza, protected by the cliffs and the eyes of a family given to observance, Sam was able to slip back to thoughts of Karen and what would come. In his mind she was walking with him under the arms of the olive trees while in reality, the arms that reached for her could soon be placing chains on her wrists.

In his neat room, Sam was busy stuffing new clothes he had tried to both turn down and pay for, into the simple bag that had once held wine, cheeses, and books packed by the maître d' back in The Columbia Restaurant a forever ago. He hesitated over a wad of hundred dollar bills and considered leaving some on the bed to pay for the clothes, but understood doing so would be nestled close to an insult. The money was blue Lancia.

"We will meet again," Antonio offered as he approached Sam and his
son and led them to where Joey waited with the car.

Sam was quiet, retreating back into the unknown that was both
behind him and before. The comfort of Ficuzza was already slipping
away and he had yet to leave.

Antonio looked sharply at his son and spoke in rapid Sicilian.
"Watch the schedule. Don't miss the trains. Antonello will be crazy. I
don't want him calling me screaming. He will have his oldest boy meet
you at the ferry."

"Yes, Father."

Tony opened the trunk for Sam's bags, but had offended his brother
by moving too slowly. As Antonio checked his watch, he launched a
diatribe that escalated to a shouting match in the space of a single
sentence. Tony and Sam worked around the screaming siblings and into
the small car while the faces of the brothers reddened and the words grew
louder.

"*Zio* Joey, let's go," Tony attempted to break off the argument from
the back seat. "Goodbye, Father!"

Joey narrowly missed the gate backing up too fast into the street
before turning to Sam so pleasantly, it was as though a switch had been
flicked. "So, ready for the long train?"

"Sure," Sam answered as he waved beyond the closing gate to
Antonio.

Tony was laughing in the back seat. "I won't translate most of that.
They're terrible to each other."

"I got the gist of it."

Joey shifted the quiet diesel and wheeled down one of the three roads
out of Ficuzza. "What is 'gist?'"

"It's... the general idea. Enough. I got enough to figure it out."

"Oh. 'Gist.' *Parola peculiare*. Strange word. 'Gist.'" Joey looked in
the rearview mirror and adjusted it to see his nephew rather than out the
rear window. "Tony, you have gist what Antonello does you miss the
ferry? He breaks his leg off in your ass. You hope the train is going on
the right schedule." Joey looked at Sam. "It is okay for you. Antonello
wants things to go properly."

"And properly means his way," Tony said from the back seat.

Joey pointed at his nephew in the mirror. "I will tell him you say so!" he quipped and readjusted the mirror. "Be careful you should not fall down his stairs." Joey was suddenly animated, the red long gone from his face, and the shouting match with his brother forgotten.

"Sam. Sam? A joke for you. You reply. Tony, you quiet." There was a slight pause as though for great dramatic effect before Joey continued very slowly. "How many–" Joey chuckled to himself. "How many of Antonello's sons it take to throw inspector down a stairs?"

Joey's eyebrows were up and he was nodding and smiling wildly in anticipation. Sam wouldn't deny him and had nothing besides the obligatory shrug of the shoulders and shaking of his head. "I dunno. Three?"

"None!" Joey was already laughing so hard he struggled to get the punch line out. "None," he said between fits. "No one throw him. The *ispettore*, he fell!"

In the laughing – some genuine and some polite – within the confines of the car, Sam felt his father tap the shoulder of his soul. In this family that would harbor and protect him, was a current that ran against the flow of any commonplace tide. Sam had seen that same reverent irreverence at his father's kitchen table and in voices from the other room as he laid still in his bed as a boy. Later, he had heard the stories and came to understand the unique fraternity his father steadfastly belonged to, yet worked to keep his son from pledging.

Don T had maintained an unwritten ledger and now Sam was collecting from the stores his father had laid up. The Perriccis, for all their genuine concern and forthright protection, existed in a labyrinth that was made gray by the influx of pure allegiance and absolute love for family. The nudge from his father reminded him that this life was never what the elder Ciampiano had wanted for his son. Given Sam's circumstance and present reliance, not to mention his honest like for this family, he would do well, but be hard pressed, to steer clear of the Perricci family business.

"I am to Foggia or Bari one month," served as Joey's goodbye at the bustling train depot. "*Ciao!*" he yelled out the window and waved to no one as he forced the car into a line of traffic that countered for its pathetic pace with the frequency of horns and volume of yelling out drivers' windows.

The ride to Messina would take about three hours. The train was comfortable and quiet. Sam was pleased that young Tony was his escort over the chatty Joey. The teenager had a few questions about Florida and the United States, but they were grounders. Sam dispelled theories that had persisted for decades – everyone was a millionaire, everyone had a mansion, and a garage full of cars.

"United States is a big country." Tony said. "–much larger than Italy. Your government is all over the world. You have *militari* everywhere. You take care of everybody. Here, we take care of our own people and our own families first. We let the government take care of itself. My grandfather says to keep the baby lean, you shut off the tit. He pays few taxes. The government stays skinny. It doesn't have the money to grow fat."

"You're smart," Sam said as he pushed himself deeper in his seat and felt the H & K bite his back. "But sometimes a country has to fight. If it wasn't for American soldiers in World War II, you'd be speaking German instead of Italian."

Tony relaxed and brought Sam with him. "No more politics. One more question though. You answer for me?"

"Sure."

"What did you do in America?"

Sam openly baulked.

"No! No, Mr. Ciampiano! Not to come to my father's house. Many men have passed days with us at different times. I understand that very well. What did you do for money, for a job? As work."

"I sold newspapers."

The look from the young guide was predictable and priceless. "Sold newspapers?"

"Some magazines. A little candy sometimes."

Tony looked at Sam's muscled arms then he unfolded his own, stretched, closed his eyes, smiled, and folded his arms again across his chest. He rested his head to the side as though to take a nap. "And my grandfather is a cook."

———————

12

The rest of the trip east to Messina was a comfortable quiet. Sam tried to brush up on simple Italian and Tony did what he could to coach the newspaper peddler in the hours that remained.

The ferry ride across the strait to the mainland at Villa San Giovanni was quick. The water was beautiful, even for someone who had just become accustomed to land following a month at sea. The boat was a car carrier, but wasn't packed. The deck was open and a small stand sold drinks and snacks. Sam and Tony were leaning over the stern rail watching Sicily slip behind when Tony's phone rang. It was a short call, in Sicilian. When it ended, Tony slapped Sam's broad back.

"We can continue our lessons. Father said my cousin, Uncle Antonello's oldest son – still another Antonello, the 3rd – will not meet us here. I will ride on the train with you."

"Good." Sam was legitimately pleased.

"It's a long trip," Tony said. "Twelve hours," he said as he glanced at his watch.

"Maybe you could see that I get on the right train," Sam suggested. "I could go on alone."

"My father would take my head off. Besides, your Italian is not so good. You may need me."

Tony had been a good traveling companion. He was also a patient teacher. The long trip ahead wouldn't be wasted. They talked in both languages, ate from a rolling cart, and fitfully slept.

A drop in speed woke Sam like a gentle nudge. Training had him immediately wide awake and he scanned the rail car instinctively. It was dark outside. He pushed Tony's arm a few times to bring him around. He looked at the glowing hands on his big black watch. It was after three in the morning.

"Hey, *amico*? I don't know where we are, but we're here."

Tony wrestled and wiggled himself up and awake. He tried to see out the windows, but was greeted by the light of midnight. He looked at his watch and calculated time and distance. "Bari."

The station had some traffic, but was quiet, given over to the dark lit wee hour. Sleepy passengers disembarked orderly carrying their backpacks and luggage. As others filed through and disappeared into waiting cars, buses, or the streets, Tony looked around for his cousin. Sam looked around as well for everything and for nothing.

"He looks like my father," Tony said as he implied help in finding the next leg of escorts. "Younger, of course. I think he's thirty. Bigger. Never smiles."

Sam knew what that meant. "Is he a cook too?"

Tony continued his search, but grinned. "No. He's no cook." He looked around the station platform a moment longer then smiled though he was tired from the trip. "He sells newspapers."

The phone in Tony's back pocket buzzed. There was a short message. Quick typing sent a reply and another came back as an answer.

"My cousin is out front," Tony said. "Another Antonello. Antonello Three. It is an Italian thing. People live forever this way, they say."

Sam understood well. He tossed his bags in the open trunk of a big Mercedes minus an introduction. At the last minute the driver, Sam's age with almost his build, got out of the car.

"You drive," he said to Tony in Italian.

"I don't have a license."

"Then you need the practice. I'm tired." The 3rd Antonello in the family was already settling in the back seat. "Drive. Drive! You know the way. It is an hour or so, American," he said in Italian to Sam without looking at him. "Sleep if you trust this one's driving."

Sam slipped in the front passenger seat as Tony got behind the wheel. "You okay?"

"I drive some – Joey's Lancia, but not this big car. This is huge."

"Just take it slow," Sam said. "Or you want me to drive?"

"You drive, Tony," came a voice in Italian from the back seat. "Don't make our guest drive. Go. Go!"

"I'm going."

"Then go. I have to be up in a few hours."

Tony was trying to familiarize himself with the big car. His cousin was impatient. "Move. Drive!"

"I am!"

"Now! Go. Go!"

"Shut up, Baby'tonello! I never drove this thing."

Antonello reached up to cuff his cousin in the head, but Tony turned in the seat to look for instruction and instead lined up his face to take the brunt of the slap. The smack in the nose stunned them both and drew blood, but Antonello recovered first. "Watch your mouth. Put the car in gear and head south or I'll slap you again."

Sam knew not to interfere.

Antonello disappeared across the back seat and Tony wrestled the car into gear and away from the train station.

The trip south took longer than normal even in the nonexistent traffic of the hour. There was no distraction in conversation of language studies or politics. The entire trip was accomplished in near silence. It afforded Sam the time to weigh the recent past and draw a bead on the near future. In the mesmerizing darkness beyond the headlights beneath Tony's nervous hands, it seemed neither direction held what he truly sought.

At Antonello Junior's house, Tony sighed in both relief and satisfaction as he pulled through an electronic gate which triggered a series of motion lights.

"Nice job," Sam said.

"You weren't scared?"

"A little," Sam chided.

"You're a better man than me, American," came Antonello's voice for the first time since they left Bari. "I said the Rosary thirty-seven times and never shut my eyes for fear. Thanks for nothing, Tony. Now I go to work while you sleep."

The three extracted themselves from the big car. Antonello went to the door with the keys and let themselves in while Sam carried the black bag and Tony, The Columbia's satchel.

Antonello entered the home he shared with his parents and siblings with an authority that ignored the time. But if he considered a ruckus to announce his arrival and delivery, those thoughts vanished when a single dim light, enough to cast a glow across Antonello Junior, the patriarch of the house, but not enough to silhouette him through any window, came on with an attention gathering click.

The heir apparent of the Perricci Family sat deep in a comfortable chair with the weak light a thin blanket over his body. Though it was close to four in the morning, Antonello Jr. was fully dressed in pressed gray slacks, shiny black shoes, and a buttoned down starched white shirt, open at the neck. His legs were crossed at the knee and his fifty-some year old hands were folded on his thigh. He looked as prepared to go out the door to an office as if it were eight AM. His face and manner didn't give notice of being tired if he was. He knew the three men entering had seen and heard the light come on and were now staring at its revelation.

Antonello Jr. raised a barely moving pair of fingers from his leg and motioned the three toward him with the subtle move and his eyes. Tony was unsettled by seeing his uncle waiting up like a father waits for a daughter who's made a poor decision and stayed out late. Sam didn't consider the hour. Instead he knew from the stance of the man in the chair and his companions that Junior held sway over much of what would happen with him and that he'd be very indebted as a result. He moved forward with the same respectful reverence he had always shown Don T.

Antonello the 3rd spoke in Italian. "It's very late, Father. You didn't need to wait."

Junior stretched his neck – more as a sign of annoyance than a necessary exercise of a cramp – and motioned his son closer.

The simple mannerisms of a father – the squint of an eye, the wave of a hand, the tilt of his head – silently displayed his displeasure over something the younger men had missed. The son leaned close to his father and Antonello Jr., in a voice stronger than a whisper and meant to be heard by Sam and Tony and serve as a lesson to his offspring, said, "We have been asked this favor. To not meet the guest of your grandfather in San Giovanni is disrespectful to both men." Then to Tony as he looked around his oldest boy. "Thank you for your escort."

The delay was too long. Tony might have been considering covering for his cousin, but it would have been unwise. A knockout punch from the youngest Antonello would cause pain for a day. Any attempt to fool or mislead the heir apparent Don of the family would generate a slight that could tarnish Tony's reputation and limit his access to the family's interests for years. As it was, Antonello tossed himself on the sword dangling in the hesitation.

"I couldn't get to San Giovanni. I asked Tony to bring our guest."

As the senior stood, he motioned to his nephew, and to Sam, who had understood very little. Tony kissed his uncle on both cheeks then saw his uncle's finger bobbing an inch from his nose. "That was close, nephew. You did well, but next time, do not hesitate to use your voice." The finger fell away. "Introduction, please," he said in English and motioned warmly to Sam.

"*Zio* Antonello, this is a friend of ours from America, Sam Ciampiano. His family is from Ficuzza. Sam, this is my uncle, Antonello Colletta Perricci Jr."

"Ah! Ficuzza," Junior nodded. "*Paisan.*" He had Sam by the shoulders and kissed his cheeks. "*Benvenuto. La mia casa è la tua.*"

"He says 'Welcome.' And that 'his house is yours.'"

Sam smiled and threatened a short bow. "*Grazie. Grazie.*"

"Good," Junior said in English and put one arm over Sam's shoulder and the other over Tony's and began to walk them into the kitchen. "Come to eat. *Mangiare, sì?*"

"Thank– *Grazie*, no," Sam said gently.

"We ate well on the train, *Zio*," Tony continued.

"*Domani*," Junior said as the brighter light of the kitchen exposed the dried blood beneath Tony's nose. He stopped and, beneath a furrowed brow, turned his nephew's chin from side to side and examined the damage. He pointed flippantly among the three men, but saved a harsh glare for his son. "We are all well acquainted now, I see," he said in Italian.

Tony translated.

"Was I going to hear of this from gypsies in the street?" he snapped at his boy.

"No, Father, I was playing and–"

"My reach is like the lights of the house – arms from the windows soak out into the street and into the gutter where you stumble." His voice was rising. "I can see to Ficuzza with no problems. Your grandfather – he has eyes like the sun. He can see to America. And back again!

"So, you will tell me once again. You were playing... I know... But not now."

Junior's countenance changed in an instant and he reached out to take Sam's arm. "Please. Come, *Signore* Ciampiano." Then to Tony in Italian. "Take our friend to one of the back bedrooms." He ignored his son and dropped away at the base of a narrow staircase and invited the three younger men to ascend without him. "*Buona notte, Sig. Ciampiano. E voi*, Tony."

"*Buona notte, Zio.*"

"*Buona notte*, Don Perricci. *E grazie*," Sam said as he followed Tony up the stairs carrying the black bag while Tony shouldered his second. He heard the youngest Antonello stop behind him, but he and Tony continued, each knowing they'd only embarrass themselves and their host if they were to linger.

Tony translated an abridged version in a whisper as the voices downstairs grew louder behind them.

"Playing? And your cousin's face is bloody? He's just a boy. You're a man."

"He was being disrespectful. I had to–"

"In front of a protectorate of your grandfather? That is no good. You make bad decisions. I'll ask your grandfather what is to be done."

"There's no need to tell Papa."

"Now you want me to lie to my own father to cover for you? He is smarter than me, and much kinder – thanks be to God for your sake."

"But–"

"Leave me be! Go to bed!"

"It–"

"If it were up to me I would put you out of the house. This business is my father's. Leave me be, I told you."

"It was an accident."

"I said go to bed. Do I have to put you in your bed like a baby?"

Upstairs, Tony smiled and would have laughed had he not caught it with his own stifling hand. He grabbed Sam and hustled him up the long tight hall and through the last open door and snapped it closed behind him.

"My uncle is about to call him, Baby'tonello," he whispered in a laugh. "If you were not here, they'd be on the floor fighting and my aunt would have to beat them with her broom like dogs in the street. But Junior won't allow it with you under his roof. Another day, sure. Not tonight."

"If that's some kind of comfort, it's not reaching me."

"My cousin does these things to himself."

"Yea, but I owe big-time. Taking me in–"

"Sam," Tony said in a rush, pulling himself up as tall as he could and shedding any of the delight he might have for his cousin's brow beating continuing on below him. "I know you for only short time. I mean no disrespect to your father, but you were not bred on this ground, in a house such as Perricci and Colletta. Sure, you are Sicilian, but if you talk of 'owe' and 'debt' within the family, it is the worst sort of insult. Call me a gypsy, even a bastard, but never speak of 'owing.'

"What takes place between my grandfather and America with men like you – it is an honor to be trusted in such a way. It is... an allegiance. There are few men such as my Papa, Don Perricci."

There was a necessary gap as Sam digested Tony's words and formed his own. "Of course, Tony. *Certo. Mi scuso.* I apologize."

"Forgotten!" Tony brushed his hands together and tossed them in the air. "But you have more questions. I see it in your face. You can ask me. I'm just a kid. What do I know?"

"You know plenty."

"Of course it is so. Then ask."

"No. *Grazie*. No questions."

"If you change your mind, come find me. You bite your tongue with my father and my uncles. I see it. But me? Ask me anything."

"*Grazie*, Tony. *Grazie*."

Tony stood stock still though they were both tired. "So? Anything?"

"I'm good."

"I answer one thing for you then on my own. People wonder how an Italian, my grandfather, has come to manage a Sicilian family. I tell you."

"I'm good, Tony. Really."

"No, it is *importante*. You're Sicilian. You must see. My grandmother was of the House of Colletta before she married my grandfather. There were many wars – some big, some small – while my grandfather was here on the mainland with his bride. Many of her brothers were killed. Others sent to prison or exile. There were cousins – Collettas – but they were too young. When my grandmother's father, Don cha Chrio de Fillamino Colletta, was an old man, he saw there were few to trust with the family. My grandfather had been respectful and a good earner.

"Plus," Tony smiled, "My grandmother is the only one who can control my grandfather. Her father must have seen that even then. He gives control to his son-in-law, who is controlled by his daughter. See it? It is unusual, but there was no one else, and more importantly – this is very, very important, Sam – no one better."

"I got it."

"It is all good now. Ten, fifteen years ago, I heard, some of the oldest Colletta cousins made some noise, but there is a saying, 'A noisy wheel gets the grease.' Do you have that saying in America?"

Now it was Sam's turn to smile. "Yea, we do. Enough said."

"Maybe not so fast. In Ficuzza we have a second line to the saying. A noisy wheel gets the grease, *si*, but if the wheel is too noisy, you know... maybe it is a bad wheel. The wheel gets replaced with another wheel." Tony smiled and the boyish charm that had been held up since they first met slipped away for a moment like the moon slides behind a heavy cloud.

There was no gray area of misunderstanding.

"Yours is a serious family, Tony."

"Loving, respectful, kind, but, *si*, serious is a good word."

"A good word," Sam echoed and thought of Joey in the Lancia.

The cloud cleared the bright moon of Tony's face. "I am across the hall if you need anything, *amico*. I will knock in the morning. Wait for me. My cousins and others who pass through the house will be scared of you."

Tony flexed his arms and back like a bodybuilder in competition before he relaxed. "Let me introduce you at breakfast."

"Will your grandfather be there?"

"No, my uncle will take you to him and make the introduction. It wouldn't be for me to do so."

"Understood. Night, Tony, and thanks again."

"Good night, Sam. See you in the morning."

"Hey. Where does your grandfather live anyway?"

"Right here. Only a few blocks, but in the old town. He and my grandmother live above their *osteria*, the café. It is the center of our business."

"The old town? Where are we anyway?"

"A wonderful town with two freshly scrubbed faces – the old and the new – washed and fed by the Adriatic. Tomorrow you can walk to the shore and sit by the most beautiful water in the world. We are here on the coast of the Province of *Bari*, Region of *Apulia, Italia*. This is your new home, Sam. Welcome to *Monopoli*."

————————————

13

Broaching the waves in the darkness of pre-dawn off the coast of *Monopoli*, watching the eyes of the shore-bound houses blink open as the first lights came to life signaling a fresh day, reminded Sam of home and the newsstand. In Tampa, the opening flap of the newsstand was the first gesture to indicate the stirring of the city. Another hot night spent sleeping amid the distant drone of small lapping tidal waves in the protected waters of Tampa Bay was ending. In the Adriatic Sea, the waves were much bigger – deep cobalt blue under white churning explosions against unprotected rocky shores – and constant. His wooden boat, twenty feet of innumerable layers of bright blue and orange paint, was laid up with thick, heavy plank that reached the gunwale on a high freeboard that rode the coarse surf with a rhythm that over the last few months had become expected and even comfortable. Sam's hands had become rougher, cut and calloused by thick nylon leaders and hand-over-hand pulls on long fishing lines. He wore old loose clothes to hide his bulk. He hadn't shaved close since the morning he had been taken to meet his new benefactor, Don Perricci, but kept his beard trimmed to not cross from soft disguise to a symbol of a wild wayward mind. A short brimmed dark blue Greek fisherman's cap became perched on his head with regularity. For any meandering tourists – their eyes taking in the sight of old narrow streets, their noses the salt of the sea, and their hands the coarse four hundred year old stone walls trailing along beneath their fingertips as they passed – Sam was another life-long local who plied a trade from the sea before dawn and tied his hooks and lines while sitting on the steps of the Castle of Charles the 5th in the quiet afternoon sun.

In the first days there was always a young guide with Sam, their newest 'Zio.' Often it was Isabella, Antonello Jr.'s eldest daughter. Holding both more patience and a more complete mastery of English than most of her relatives, Isabella became Sam's tutor and readily welcomed the teaching-excuse-laden reprieve from working in her grandparents' café. When others noticed Don Perricci's insistence on

Sam's local education and language, without asking, they knew this man, this particular *zio*, was different.   While other men had also come by necessity through the small room above the *Osteria Perricci* Sam presently occupied, the Don had taken an obvious interest in this one.

When weeks became months, the novelty of Sam's sudden appearance wore off.   Coupled with his increasing reliance on the native tongue, he was left alone more often.   Escorts were less in attendance, though Isabella continued her lessons, often sitting next to Sam as he threaded the heavy nylon leaders rapidly and securely through the hooks he'd cast into the sea in the following morning's darkness.   Sam's new life had taken root with those same hooks.

When Sam wandered up to local fishermen and struck up limited, one-sided conversations in the earliest days of his stay, it had been drawn from equal parts boredom and sincere interest.   After he was shown how to tie the hooks of a local, Sam asked to join him on his boat.   The boatman took his next lunch at the *Osteria Perricci* and hat very literally in hand, asked Don Perricci if taking Sam aboard his small boat would be alright.   It was.

Sam fished the next day with his new mentor well before the sun woke.   The work was vigorous.   Being on the water and the small sandy beach where the wooden skiffs were pulled above the reach of the tide and waves reminded Sam of home.   He was waiting the following morning to go out again.   That afternoon, he sat in near silence beside the skipper and tied off hooks and prepped lines.   In the darkness of the next early morning, Sam waited by the boat.   The men who scoured the sea helped each other urge the heavy boats into the surf.   Sam's strength made much of their straining unnecessary.   By the fourth day, it was clear this was not the flinging fancy of a foreigner.   This man, a novice to the long-line fishing they practiced, was accustomed to rising early and hard work.   Before many more days Sam had boats pushed to the open arms of the Adriatic by the time their captains arrived.   And when the blue, red, and orange boats formed up the colorful palette of the short fisherman's cove on their return, Sam was there to heave each to.

Before Sam's first month was out in *Monopoli*, he had acquired an old boat.   He scrapped alongside old calloused hands that spoke around his poor Italian and pointed often.   Isabella attempted to translate a few times, but was gently rebuffed.   Sam would learn refinishing and fishing by mimicking the hands of his new friends.   When the boat was ready to be painted, paint cans and brushes appeared magically overnight tucked neatly in the bow.   When uncovered, Sam looked up and down the beached row of skiffs and caught subtle smiles and abbreviated salutes before the fleet went about their business.

Around the same time the paint on Sam's boat was curing, Antonello Jr. was wandering around his father's kitchen within the *Osteria Perricci*. "So, Papa," Antonello Jr. was saying as he looked in the oven at the café. "What of the American?"

"What of him?" the old man said as he sprinkled flour and folded bread on a hardwood table.

"Where do you want him?"

"Where he is."

Junior tossed a hand toward the coast. "He is fishing! Every day he fishes!"

"He brings me the first of his catch. Such good fish. The things I can do with such fish."

"No, Papa. No. He is strong. Tough. Tougher than any of my men. We can use him. We have collections to be made."

"No collections."

"Fine. He is not known in any region. He would be useful in Palermo or Rome – many places. He's a fighter. He brought his own guns. I have a job for him today. We need to deliver a message to– "

"No." Don Perricci continued to work his dough.

"What?"

"I do not stutter, Antonello."

"But, Papa. We can use–"

"No. I told you."

"Why not?"

The kneading stopped, but the old man's gnarled fingers stayed on his work. "You question me?"

Though in his early fifties, Junior's feet shuffled like a teenager, but boldness and curiosity made a strong team and pulled together in a stout harness and the words came out. "It is a simple question."

The father turned his head slowly and dressed down his son with a glance. "It is the wish of America that he not be involved in business."

"How does this American stay in the House of Perricci and contribute nothing? No. He can drive the petrol trucks. We are bringing a load down in two days from the north. He will drive a truck for his board."

The senior Antonello picked up a small piece of dough and weighed it in his hand. "Have you taken my bread? Is it in your ears? Why do you not hear me? His hands touch nothing. He wants to provide fish? I let him and I thank him. Nothing more."

"So for our risk and our protection, he does nothing?"

"Our friends in America have asked this thing."

The team pulled again in the harness of Junior's throat and would feel the lash. "When did the Perriccis become lap dogs to the Americans?"

The old man was far too quick for his age. When his tough hand slapped Junior's face a puff of flour left an outline of white around the crimson handprint. It was no attention grabbing tap. It was an open handed strike from a viper, intended to hurt and disorient. If Don Perricci had intended, he could have followed with a fist or maybe two before Junior's hands had time to react and protect his face. But it had never been the old man's purpose. And while his own reactions failed him, Junior's protection took the form of his mother, Palma, as she came into the kitchen unknowing until she had come one step too far. She stopped on the single step down into the low ceilinged kitchen before the flour from her husband's hand and her son's face had reached the floor. The argument was instantly ended. The senior Antonello turned back to the wooden counter and gently tossed flour across his dough and began working it as before.

Palma took the last step down and walked without a word to the large bank of sinks. She pulled a well-used towel from her black apron string and ran it under cold water. The ancient handle squeaked under her hand as she shut it off then carried the towel down by her side to her son. She didn't stop or look at him directly as she handed him her towel. "Wipe your face."

Palma stopped alongside her husband, but like her son, she didn't look at him. She was focused on the dough as Antonello carved it with a large wedged knife into chunks for the waiting bread pans. "Do not forget to bless the dough, Papa."

"I won't forget," her husband answered as his hands worked over the table.

"Otherwise it will not rise properly."

"Yes, Mama."

Palma turned slightly and without looking called her son. "Come here." He did and she took the towel from his hand. A hidden glance showed flour he had missed. When Palma dabbed at it, Junior pulled away.

"I'm not a child, Mother."

She slipped her towel neatly under her apron string and brushed it flat. Her hand came up empty – slow and gentle – and gripped her son's chin. She turned his head to the side so the redness and missed flour was away from her. "The Bible says you should turn the other cheek. You have another cheek. This one," she said as she poked him harshly with her finger. "Perhaps you need another slap, huh? You say you are not a child? Then don't act like one."

Palma took her son's hand. "Here," she said as she stretched Junior's hand out over Antonello's bread pans as they received the dough. "You bless the dough."

Junior was slow and fidgeted, but complied. "*Luogo luogo per tutti la luna.* **Rise, rise for all the moon.**" And he traced a cross with his thumb on the soon to be loaves.

"*Grazie*, Antonello. **You are a good son and a fine man.** You are also your father's *consigliere*, but do not question him. Advise only. Now, go teach these things to your son. Go on."

"Yes, Mama."

"Antonello?" his father said as his oldest son's foot touched the single step.

"Yes, Papa?"

"Thank you for blessing the bread. I'm sure it will grow and fill the pans to overflowing. *Grazie.*"

"You're welcome, Papa. *Prego.*"

Palma watched her son leave with some assurance that the short falling out was behind the family. "I told our son to teach his son. You heard me?"

"Of course. I was standing right–"

"But our grandson is not the problem."

"Oh, yes he is. Baby'tonello is always dipping his hand in the pot."

"That's true, but this time – regarding the American – the trouble will come from Isabella."

"What are you saying?" Antonello asked as talk of his princess brought any work on the old counter to a standstill.

"She has been helping him with language – a noble thing."

"Has he taken liberties?" Unconsciously, Antonello's hand tightened around the handle of the squat blade he had been using to cut the dough for the pans. Palma saw his knuckles turn white and eased her hand over his and patted gently as though reassuring a child in the fit of a dream.

"No. No. Not at all. The men at the markets would know, and then we would know. Isabella would have told me herself. She's such a good girl."

"Hard worker," Antonello said and returned to his bread pans. "Where is the trouble?"

"She loves this American."

"Nonsense. She is a baby." The dough was struck a little harder.

"You have only a grandfather's eye, husband. She is a woman, the loveliest in town, most probably the entire region."

"No... She has no boyfriend. No one calls on her."

"Is that a surprise? Don Perricci? Who dares call without your blessing? And who dares ask their Don for such a thing?" Palma walked away from her soft words and pulled her towel from her waist and began wiping down the sinks, counters, and stoves though they were already spotless.

Antonello kneaded slowly. His shoulders swayed and he brought his palms up from the dough as though he was about to speak, but nothing came. Palma came behind him and put away her towel. She patted his shoulders and gave him a hug then retreated to the single step.

"She is old enough?" he choked out in a whisper.

Palma hesitated on the step, turned, and smiled. "When I was her age, we had four children."

There was layers to the pain. The recognition of the inevitable regarding his granddaughter, and the reminder that now there were three children where once there had been four.

"Antonello?"

"Yes?"

"It's time."

The old man nodded, but said nothing.

"Do not tire the dough," Palma said and left her husband alone with his thoughts of the young girls in his life, old and new, taken and given. There had been times – a great many times – when Isabella had been more than a surrogate for a daughter lost. The two girls had become one and had protected him from hurt. Letting go would not be easy.

He stared at the empty doorframe where Palma had passed and where first his daughter and then his granddaughter had jumped over the single step – up and down – a million times that he had not noticed. He wandered to it and stood on it with both feet. Palma was beyond in the entranceway to the café watching the street through the open dark maroon doors.

"My Palma?"

"Yes, Papa?" his wife answered without looking away from the street.

"The American may be gone one day. I don't know yet."

"He is polite."

"Yes, but trouble must be in the dust of his footprints or he would not be here. Go to Ficuzza and talk to your family. Find a good boy."

Now Palma turned enough to see her husband, but folded her arms and raised her eyebrows. "Find a good boy?"

"For Isabella. A young man – her age, a little older – respectful and from a good family."

"And what do I do with this good boy when I find him?"

Antonello motioned with his hands – still covered with flour – as though he were awkwardly juggling. "Put him with Isabella. Talk to the boy's family. Make the arrangement. She will have a dowry, of course. I will talk to her father and decide the amount."

Palma's arms dropped straight down. Her shoulders sagged in exaggeration and her head leaned back as far as it would go.

"What is it?" Antonello asked.

She didn't answer but eased across the room until she closed in front of him. He was still on the single step down into the kitchen so she met him eye to eye.

"Papa. Papa. Papa." She rested her hands, heavy on his shoulders. They were still solid and thick despite the years of carrying the burden for a broad family with interests deemed gray at best, nefarious at worst. "We are not in Ficuzza after the war years," Palma said and kissed his forehead. "I will speak to her and her father. I will let a few know she is approachable – with the blessings of her Papa."

"That is how it is done now?"

"Almost, but it may matter for nothing."

"Then why do you put me through this?"

"It may not matter as she may have already made a choice."

"You think so? Who is the boy? Pray he is not one who needs a firm hand and a job."

"No, no firm hand. The job? I don't know yet."

"Who is this boy?"

"The American. Ciampiano."

"That is twice you connect him to my baby. Why so certain?"

"I see it in her eyes and the lightness of her step. But you say he may go?"

"I said, 'Maybe.' This American is different. He does not touch the business of my friends in America. It was his father's wish I am told, and his father was of the highest respect."

The wheels were instantly churning behind Palma's eyes.

"What is that? What is that look?" her husband asked.

"That could be a good life for her."

"Out of the business? Of course Isabella is not involved. I'd cut off my hands first!"

"No, husband, no. A good life for her if her man was... like I've heard you say, a civilian."

"You want her to starve?"

"A fisherman's wife is never hungry."

Antonello was waving his finger in front of a tender smile for his wife. "You. You are the smart one in the family. You outpace me in every race. Go! Talk to her. See what she says, but not too far. I will make an inquiry back to America and see... you know... just see."

"Thank you, Antonello. You are the wise one and I love you for it." She took one last advantage of him being on the low step and kissed his forehead again.

On another step a half-dozen blocks away – a narrow one atop the stairs above the street leading to the old castle – Isabella was sitting next to Sam watching the Adriatic roll rather quietly and her some-time-student tie off tomorrow's hooks.

She spoke in English often, but seasoned the often one-sided conversation with enough Italian in the hopes that osmosis might do the rest.

"The fishing's good?"

"Yes."

"My grandmother is very pleased with the *pesce* you bring her. She loves fresh. Papa too."

"That's good."

"*L'italiano*, Sam."

He thought a moment and said quite accurately, but hesitantly, "*Ciò che è buono?*"

"*Perfetto!*" She slapped his thigh twice. "You're doing very well."

He smiled, but kept his eyes on the hooks. "*Grazie.*"

"*Prego.*"

The steps were quiet again. The sun was warm. A couple strolled on the wide sidewalk that sat above the retaining wall that kept the Adriatic at bay. Huge boulders, dark and wet from waves, littered the base of the wall along most of the breaker.

"Do you want me to help?" Isabella asked as she motioned to the fistful of lines draped across Sam's lap.

"No, I'm almost done."

She laced her fingers around her knee and thought of another tact. "Since you're finished, we could walk over to the *piazza*. There's a shop I know that makes wonderful pastries."

"I said, almost finished. Not quite."

"I can wait."

"Are you hungry? I hear *Osteria Perricci's* is good."

She smiled politely at the joke. "True, but they don't have the pastries like this place. *Espresso* is good too."

"Your grandmother makes good *espresso*."

"She does, but Sam, the pastries! *Comé una caramella!*"

"*Caramella?*"

"Umm, candy. So sweet!"

"*Caramella.*"

"So, we go?" Isabella was up and brushing the ancient stone dust of the steps off the back of her ankle length skirt.

There was no movement to get up coming from beside her. All that followed was Sam collecting his tied lines, being careful to avoid the razor pointed hooks.

"That was the last one. We can go now," she encouraged.

"I don't think so, but *grazie*. Another time."

She grabbed his empty hand to playfully tug him to his feet. "It would be fun."

Sam's recoil from her touch was too much and too unexpected. He inadvertently yanked her off balance, but sprang up to catch her, scattering his lines and hooks down the old staircase.

"I'm sorry," echoed from him in English and her in Italian. "*Mi dispiace.*"

As soon as she was set aright, Sam let her go. "I'm really, really sorry, Isabella. You've been so nice. Teaching me and helping me out. Your whole family. I... I'm a little keyed up from the trip still, I guess. I'm sorry. I mean it."

Isabella was stunned, and embarrassed. She crouched down on the steps and began collecting the tangled leaders and hooks.

"I'll get them," Sam said.

"No, let me help."

"Stop. You'll hook yourself."

"I made the mess, I can help clean it up."

"It's fine. I dropped them."

Isabella began covering her embarrassment with anger as she fought to straighten out the tangled fishing lines. "I didn't know my hand held such a poison."

"That's not it."

"One time in my life I hold a man's hand and he tries to throw me down a flight of stairs."

"It wasn't like that. I apologize. It was a mistake."

"No mistake. I know your ways. They are American, but they are our ways. It comes from your family. Like mine. You don't like me. Fine. No one does. *Capisco molto bene. Molto bene.* But tell me, what's wrong with me that you can't have a cake and *espresso* with me? Even as a friend?"

"You are my friend. Of course you are my friend." There was a pause that jaded Sam's version of the truth. "Your grandfather told me to stay close to the Café and the docks. Not to go further."

"Is that so?"

"Yes."

"But you have an escort. Me. No. Don't answer. It wasn't my Papa that made you pull away from my hand. It was me."

Isabella had done what she could with the hooks and lines. She had laid them out straight on a step. She stood up and walked down to the street. "*Ciao*, Mr. Ciampiano. Your Italian is going along well. Practice. Go talk to your *pesce*."

Sam stood up, but didn't chase her. "Isabella. Wait. It's not you."

"Not a problem." Isabella looked more mad than hurt as she cleared the stairs. "One time. One time I like a man," she repeated as she stared at her open palm. "What an ugly girl I must be."

"Don't say that. Come on. It's not you. You're beautiful."

"Stop it. There's no need to be kind."

"Are you kidding? You're gorgeous. And sweet." Sam's voice was trailing off badly. "And it's not your grandfather either. It's not even me. It's someone else."

That brought Isabella up short.

"I had to leave someone behind," Sam said as he knelt and began absently collecting the fishing lines from the stone.

"A wife?"

"No, not a wife."

"Girlfriend?"

There was a strange pause that boosted Isabella, but confused Sam all the more.

"I don't know. Once, yes. Now, I mean, before I left, I guess not. There wasn't much time."

"You weren't together when you left?"

"No. But she..." Sam let his voice crawl to a stop – the brakes applied by his own good sense. He picked up the hooks and walked down to the street and Isabella. "I can't say more."

"Because it hurts you?"

"Yes, and it's not good to–"

"I understand. I live in a house where questions often go unasked."

"There's that, yes, but I'm not sure I did the right thing by leaving."

"Will you go back? Will you go back to her?"

"I don't think I can if... I don't think I can."

Isabella put her hands behind her back and began to walk away from the castle toward the beach and the brightly painted fleet of small boats whose bows were nestled in the dry sand like the noses of sleeping children in soft pillows. Sam walked with her. He stopped at his skiff and hung the freshly tied and recently tangled leaders inside.

"In Tampa, these would probably be missing by morning."

"Is that true?"

"I don't know. Maybe not the fishhooks. Probably the whole boat."

Sam's light laugh and smile eased aside some of the tension, questions, and doubts from both their minds, but there was a significant stride between them when they turned their backs on the sea and began heading for *Perricci's*. The sand beneath their feet was mixed with stone and coral pulverized by the waves of ten thousand years. It wasn't the fine white sand of Tampa. Two steps on the old stone street and all traces of the beach were left behind though the awkwardness from the castle steps remained.

"What is America really like?" Isabella asked as she walked, shaking her hair to the side and stretching her neck up and around to loosen a kink or to try and see around the world.

"Compared to *Monopoli*?"

"Compared to anyplace."

"It's big. Things are big. The houses are big. The cars are big. The cities. The roads." Sam laughed. "The people."

"The people are big? Like you?"

He laughed again. "No, not like me. There's a lot of really heavy people. Overweight. I'm trying to be nice."

"What do you mean?"

"They're fat."

Isabella stifled a laugh. "Don't be silly."

"It's true!"

"One time I heard my grandmother say that fat people were rich. They have lots of food and don't have to work. They can hire people to do everything, so they get fat. It is a sign of prosperity."

Sam was smiling. "America is a prosperous country, but that has nothing to do with people not taking care of themselves. It's not everybody – don't take it that way – but lots of people eat junk and don't work."

"They're not rich?"

"They're not rich."

"That's too bad and it doesn't seem smart at all. I thought Americans were smart."

"Not any smarter than anybody else."

They walked along quietly as Isabella formed the next inquiry. "Apart from big, what else is America?"

"What else is it?"

"What do you like about it?"

He thought for just a moment. "I've been in lots of other countries and I'll take the United States over any of them."

"Why?"

"I'd like to say 'Freedom,' but that sounds like an ad for democracy and capitalism."

"Italy is a democracy and we embrace capitalism."

"We're better at it."

"*Così dice lei.*"

"What?"

"*Non capisco l'inglese,*" she countered, shrugged her shoulders, and shook her head no.

"Oh...," Sam had to think. "Umm... *Non capisco, 'Così dice lei.'*"

"So you say. *Così dice lei* is 'So you say.' You think America is better at democracy and capitalism than Italy?"

"I like it. I've never gone hungry–"

"Nor me."

He didn't seem to hear her. His mind drifted back to dozens of long plane rides with weapons and night vision googles as his carry-ons. "People like what they know. I've seen lots of countries, mostly at night. I only saw the worst of them. I guess it's not a fair assessment."

She had not heard him either. Both had been consumed with their preparation of a defense or a wayward rambling. "Being a tourist is never a fair way to judge a country. You have to live as the people live, see the day on day, not the resorts and beaches."

Sam resigned the fight before it began and raised his hands in surrender. "You win. I'm no good at debates. Everybody probably likes their country best. I don't know. But I like my country – a lot. I love it. I fought for it and would again."

Isabella turned toward Sam on the sidewalk and stopped him without a touch.

"You were a soldier?"

Sam stopped for only a heartbeat then pressed ahead up the slope of the sidewalk further away from the sea. "I was."

Isabella caught up. "If you liked to be a soldier for your country, why did you stop?"

"Long story."

Isabella let almost a full minute pass. "Is that story what brought you to *Monopoli*?"

Sam sighed. "That's where it started, I guess. I don't know what happened. I lost my job, my career, now I lost my country. I made a mess out of everything."

"And you lost the girl?"

Sam shoved his hands in his pockets. His shoulders hunched over him like a ravaged umbrella with only the wires remaining to protect him from a downpour. "Yea, I lost the girl."

———————————

14

An ocean away, the lost girl, nauseous and nervous, fidgeted in an empty office. The computer on her desk bounced a lazy screen saving FBI logo. Moving the mouse only helped a little. The computer had no connection to the internet and only a highly filtered portal to the Bureau's internal mainframes. With a simple password, Karen was able to review portions of the working case file of the Illuminati, but that was all. LaRoy had Jason Myer see to it himself – a fact that was quickly relayed to Alyn Nuary in exchange for a ten minute tryst. The old cradled phone on the edge of the desk was wired only to the building. Karen was living and working on an isolated island she had created when she confessed the inevitable to LaRoy.

The months since the FBI's descent on Tampa and Sam's disappearance, had been a whirling dervish that blurred time, space, and good sense. Karen had admitted everything traceable – the initial contact, her first visit on a hot street on a hot day, their trips, emails, texts, and phone calls. Each event easily reconstructed.

While there may have been initial hints in the emails following Sam's indoctrination into the New Illuminati of his change in demeanor, Karen attributed the break-up to the stress of a long distance relationship – both believable and supported by their diminishing then vanishing contact. Though awkward for the Judge Adjutant General's Office and the Bureau, the story was supported by the evidence and timeline of Illuminati activity.

Karen did not admit to her frantic dash to Tampa. Minus any electronic footprints or eye witnesses, that final chapter needn't be put on the laundry line. She would suffer the scrutiny of having an affair with a man who was rapidly ascending to the FBI's Top Ten, but she'd be cleared of any involvement with the Illuminati, and rightfully so. Suspicions may linger of contact following the break-up and prior to Sam's flight, but her legal training told her that unsubstantiated speculation would burn hot, but wither and die on the vine minus proof and there was none. Sam was gone. She would stick to her story and take a career stifling hit for her association, but that would be all that could be legally mounted against her. But all her careful planning, her honesty to a single point in time, her hope for salvaging her career, ended when she woke early in Tampa two months after the pursuit of Sam had begun. In her closely monitored private barracks on MacDill Air Force Base, down the hall from John LaRoy, Karen got up, rushed pell-mell into the bathroom, and threw up.

By nine AM that morning Karen was in Cal Denti's office. LaRoy asked her to recount her relationship on the record. This time Cal would politely join the inquisition. Her story was the same – easy to tell and adhere to as she carefully stuck to the truth – up until she saw Sam's name on the report of resigned Army Rangers. Cal was as convinced as John had been two months before on the tarmac of Andrews Air Force Base.

LaRoy had two reasons to ask Karen to submit to the retelling. The lesser of which was Special Agent Nuary. She had pigeonholed him in a hallway of MacDill regarding the presence of Lieutenant Auburn's fingerprints being in the newsstand when she was really after the reason LaRoy had had Meyer restrict Karen's computer. Jack Aaron, the stronger reason, had done the same, but far less formally, concerning Karen's prints being in the paperback book he had taken to his one man forensic team of Helfer Oaks. Through circuitous routes, Nuary and Jack had each arrived at John LaRoy's door with the same question – How did the JAG officer's prints end up in the Ciampiano newsstand?

Nuary had been calculating until she screened the personnel access record via Jason Meyer, and saw that the lieutenant, who arrived with John LaRoy from Washington, wasn't at the newsstand until the following day – well after the forensic team had checked for prints and bagged evidence. LaRoy dismissed Nuary with contamination, poor scene security, and an inaccurate log though she toyed with Karen's failing to respond to an email in an attempt to elicit more answers. John was convincing regarding the prints as in his own mind he dismissed them – though he knew none of the trifecta pieces of his argument were accurate. John thought Karen's prints were left on her admitted visits and dismissed Nuary's concern out of hand.

LaRoy did however leave a hint on the table when he suggested the print contamination was indicative of shoddy work and asked Nuary to "pal around" with Karen to get the skinny on JAG's military minded approach. LaRoy posed the reason that perhaps JAG might be covering for one of their own. Nuary forgot the wayward fingerprints and leaped at the chance. Jack would not be swayed so easily.

"Whatdaya talking about?" Jack barked. "Cross, what?"

"Cross contamination." LaRoy barked back.

"I heard you."

"So why are you asking me again?"

Jack was snippy. "I was hoping to give you some time to come up with something better than that."

"Excuse me?"

"Your own log says the lieutenant wasn't even in that newsstand."

"Clerical error. And I want that evidence back under federal control."

"I'm calling horseshit," Jack said as he tossed a large envelope on LaRoy's temporary Tampa desk and sat down.

John picked the envelope up by the corner as if it were a dirty rag. "What's this?"

"It's your evidence back. You said you wanted it, you got it. There you go. Happy?"

"Hardly." John peeked in the open end of the envelope and saw the paperback, but checked himself before dumping it on the desk. "The processing complete?"

"Better than your boys would do."

"I think they could find a print," John said as the Steinbeck original spilled out.

"Maybe. But they don't know what I know. More importantly, who I know."

"Do you always talk in riddles, Aaron? Speak plainly, for Christ's sake."

"Would your lab rats know who's working this case?"

"It'd be on the submission reports. We call it 'chain of custody.' Something you obviously never heard of nor practice."

Jack leaned back deep into the chair. "You know, LaRoy. I always said I'd slap the first man I heard use the word 'nor' in a sentence, figuring they must be British – snobby or something. But when you say it, it sounds impressive. Damned impressive. I always figured it'd be Cal. You should use that word more often. It looks good on you."

LaRoy laughed out loud and picked up the book. "You're a jackass. Have you read this book? I'm pretty sure I've read everything Steinbeck ever wrote. I must have read this one, but it's not coming to me."

"Here, let me help you," Jack said as he got up and took the book out of LaRoy's hands.

"What? You underline the dirty parts for me?"

"Better. Read this."

Jack pressed the book down on John's desk, opened to the title page. He was pointing to the handwritten inscription. When Jack began reciting the last line, LaRoy tried to shut him off. "I can read—"

"What 'Karen' does that cover remind you of?" Jack continued anyway.

LaRoy pulled the book out from beneath Jack's paw and looked at the pretty girl's silhouette on the yellow cover. Her shoulder length brown hair had a distinctive cut and her figure showed tight curves in the right places. It was how no imagination at all would picture Lieutenant Karen Auburn in something other than her white Navy JAG uniform.

John set the book down and laced his fingers together and rested his hands on the pretty girl in the snug purple dress. "You got any idea how many 'Karens' there are with brown hair – just in Tampa?"

"Oh..., you're way smarter than that," Jack said as he reached into his coat pocket for a single page report. "And so am I." He dropped the paper on John's folded hands.

"You're a dramatic sonofabitch, aren't you? Now, what's this?"

"I'd tell you to read it, but I can't wait that long. It's a handwriting analysis from the Florida Department of Law Enforcement. We have a pretty good team of geeks too, you know? And us poor local hicks know who's on first while you Feds couldn't find your own ass with both hands. In this game, your lieutenant is throwing spitters and greasers and you're swinging way behind with your foot in the bucket."

LaRoy unfolded the report. "You should have your own TV show, you know that?"

LaRoy looked at photocopies of the inscription in the book and the sign-in ledger from the District Attorney's Office.

Jack pointed to the latter. "See that? That's the sign-in sheet from my office." He stabbed the report too hard and poked it loose from one of LaRoy's hands. "Unlike you guys and—" Jack flashed quotations marks in the air with his fingers, "your 'clerical error' missing the pretty lieutenant from the log of who comes into a crime scene, we like to keep track of such goings on. There's the real match right there. Forget her fingerprints." Jack paused only enough to catch his breath then pointed just above Karen's name from his sign-in sheet. "You can just make out your name right above hers."

It was meant as a sharp stab, but not as deadly as the precursor it was to become.

"Keep talking," LaRoy said as he sat the paperwork aside and picked up the book again. He was looking at the cover as though the girl might move.

"You might get some takers on that print contamination horseshit in Washington, but not in Tampa. That little number in uniform is up to something. Like as not, she's neck deep in this Illuminati thing. No wonder we can't get any traction on it. She knows what we know, and's been relaying it along to her Ranger boyfriend Ciampiano, Rand, and who the hell knows who else. And you gave her the keys to the asylum!"

There was little LaRoy could do. "I know."

"And while we're spinning our wheels... What'd you say?"

"I said, I know."

"You know what?"

"That Lieutenant Auburn was involved with Ciampiano."

There was a crack in the conversation. Jack dropped down hard in his chair and stared at LaRoy as though he was trying to decipher a Dali painting at the museum on the other end of the Tampa skyline. His brow wrinkled and his head tilted like an inquisitive dog. With his cadence broken, Jack reverted to pointing back and forth across the office as though the persons were in opposite corners.

"The lieutenant, and Ciampiano?"

"Correct."

"You knew about them?"

"Correct again."

"Wh– I mean, how the hell?"

"They got together after she represented him prior to his resignation. She went over it briefly when we first met at MacDill. Remember that?"

"Yea, yea," Jack said in complete absentia. "I mean, how do you know?"

"She told me."

"You shittin' me?"

"Nope," John said as he slipped the copy of the handwriting report into the folds of the paperback and then the book back into the evidence envelope. He held it up, but not to hand it over to Jack. "You mind if I have my guys take a look at this?"

"Naww... Sure. Sure." Some clarity came back across Jack's face and into his voice. "It ever occur to you to mention this to the rest of the team?"

"Team? Did you say, 'team?' You?" Now John did hold the envelope out to Jack, but only to rattle it in his face. "The sonofabitch who lifts evidence and runs your own little sidebar investigation?"

"It was a hunch. And a damn good one."

"Damn illegal one," LaRoy cracked back as he tossed the envelope to the corner of his desk. "If this meant anything, you could have jeopardized the entire case. But she told me all about her and Ciampiano before we ever left Washington. Your hunch – though fun to watch – doesn't help us."

"But you kept her? Why isn't she locked up?"

"For what? Fornication?"

"You have nothing to tie her to Ciampiano?"

"We have plenty tying her to him, but it only supports exactly what she told me. They met. They banged each other's brains out and split up. It happens."

"And you believe it?"

"Until I find something to prove otherwise, I do. She's a good attorney. A good person. I asked for her myself specifically for this Illuminati deal."

"It ever occur to you that she's only giving up what she knows we'd find anyway?"

"Oh, it's back to 'we' now? Of course I've thought about that. What do you suggest? Kick her to the curb? How'd you say it a minute ago? 'You're smarter than that.' Well, me too. Keep your enemies closer. Ever hear that one, Mr. DA?"

"Once or twice."

Both men sighed more than breathed. Jack broke the respite. "Cal know about this?"

"I should be asking you the same thing," LaRoy said as he pointed to the envelope again.

"Oh, hell no. Cal wouldn't do anything like that," Jack spit as though the question was contemptuous.

"Good."

Now Jack laughed. "Does he know about the lieutenant?"

"Yep."

"Little sonofabitch. Never let on a thing. I give him credit for that. Good cop, but don't tell him I said that."

LaRoy pinched his fingers together and pulled a zipper across his lips. "What's your next move, John?"

"For Karen? I'm going to have Nuary babysit her for now," LaRoy said and sighed as he said it.

Another sigh met his. "She's a bitch that one is."

"Just the person for the job," LaRoy said with a resignation that didn't match the words.

Another moment slipped by quietly as the two seasoned cops looked at each other and inward at the same time. True to form Jack moved first, slapped his knees and stood up. "Well, that's a kick in the head."

"What's that?"

"I thought I had just found the button to start the whole whacky thing spinning and you take the wind right out of it. I'm back to square one."

"Nothing on Rand from your end?"

"That guy might not even be breathing he's so quiet."

"We've got nothing either."

"He's tucked in the long grass," Jack muttered as he went to the door and leaned on the knob.

John's big hands slapped down on his temporary desk. "Well then, it's time to beat the bushes and see if we flush anything out. Let's start with that picture from the newsstand. It's a perfect lead into Rand. We're just looking for Ciampiano. Period. Never know. It might spark a move. You and Cal interview those guys – the Rand brothers and the third one."

"Bordaine."

"Yep. Work with Cal, but leave Nuary out. I'll take care of her."

"Works for me," Jack said as he opened the door.

"Hey, Jack? Anything else in your pocket? Books? Reports? Anything else you forgot to mention or walked off with?"

"Nothing. You?"

"Nothing."

Both men smiled potential lies. They snorted nearly identical laughs, Jack let himself out, and LaRoy reached for the phone. In seconds Cal Denti was on the other end of the secure land line in a one-sided conversation.

"Hey, Cal. Just so you know the lay of the land. I'm attaching Nuary to the lieutenant. I'm telling her we're a little concerned with Auburn's contamination of the newsstand, etc... Yeah, that's what we're going with for now. I'll tell her it was sloppy and I want to make sure JAG isn't missing something else... Right. Alyn's a goddamn expert at playing people. I don't expect anything new, but it'll keep them both tied up. Know what I mean?

"Thanks, Cal. Oh, Cal? Still there? Jack's coming to see you. Let's interview those newsboys."

Cal looked up from the phone as Jack opened his door without knocking.

"With the District Attorney?" Cal said into the receiver in front of Jack.

"He there already?"

"Sure is."

Jack made a megaphone of his hands and shouted, "Relax, LaRoy. We got it from here."

He was easily heard on the other end of the line. "Damn pain in the ass, isn't he?"

"He is quite a bother," Cal said as he watched Jack make himself comfortable.

"But what a set of street eyes. Glad he's on our side," John whispered. "Start with Clayton Rand's brother. Get to him before his brother can coach him. Have the others teed up so we avoid any cross talk."

Cal smiled. "Like the man said, we got it from here."

"Thanks, Cal. Keep me in the loop."

LaRoy and Cal hung up.

"Okay, partner," Jack grinned and rubbed the palms of his hands together rapidly. "Let's get after it."

———————

15

Straight forward background work gave the Bureau the family, education, and work history on Clayton, Carl, and Raphael. A few more steps offered up the harsh distinction between Carl's challenges and Clayton's gifts. Data mining exposed the contact between Clayton and Raphael and the lack of a technical landscape for Carl. The flags that went up when Jack had first looked into Clayton's company were still flying as high. His obvious expertise and government work on security was more than a concern.

When Jack and Cal set out to pick up Carl from the streets of Tampa when he got off work at four AM, they were led by a marked Tampa police cruiser. Having an unmarked car and two guys in suits approach anybody on the street at that hour would likely not end well. The patrolmen would take the lead with Jack and Cal stepping in to manage the conversation.

Cal was pacing the slow rolling marked car.

"This will put him off his feed," Jack said.

"What?"

"Us grabbing him like this. It'll knock him off his feed."

"Off his feet?"

"Off his feed. Feed! You stop understanding English there, my friend?"

"Off his feed?"

"Jesus... You and Petey. You need to get out more?"

"On this planet, yes. I don't know where you're from. 'Off his feed?' I think you just make stuff up in that cavernous brain of yours."

"If you do something to a horse or a cow — change their routine. Animals like routine, you know. No surprises. It raises hell with their eating. Knocks them off their food or grain or whatever for a little while. Throws them a curve. Us talking to Rand in the middle of the night like this will mess him up. Catch him off guard. I hope."

"It would me if you stopped me on the street at four AM."

Jack spoke to the window and looked again at the sleeping houses. "It's like working alone. I swear. Gotta explain everything. Worse than a kid."

Cal was on the verge of laughing, but shook his head and the rough camaraderie away to concentrate on the police car ahead and the neighborhood around.

"What do you think of big brother Carl?" Jack asked.

"From what we've gathered thus far, he's either not involved, or so far on the fringe he doesn't know he's involved. Did you see the notes in his profile? Looks like he had a hard time in school. No college. String of jobs until he hit the docks. Manual labor kind of guy."

"Saw that. He rode the short bus in school."

"Not married. No kids. Shows up for work every day. Probably an okay guy."

"With a genius for a baby brother. Must have been a bitch growing up."

"That's hard to call. Surveillance indicates he stops by his brother's place at least once a week. He doesn't stay long, but they must maintain some sort of relationship."

"Ain't that sweet. It's that Clayton I want to chat with."

"What would you say? We don't have much if anything."

"It's him. Has to be."

"Do you need the umpteenth reminder that he can't be guilty just because everyone else is innocent? Ability to commit a crime does not equate to guilt."

"Keep talking. I need the sleep," Jack said as he looked out the side window at the dark houses still settled in the pre-dawn darkness.

The cars cruised around the block and stopped up the street from the simple row house where Carl lived. Their previous surveillance served them well. In less than ten minutes Carl came around the corner at the opposite end of the block walking toward them, headed home.

Both cars crept down the street unintentionally looking like stalking cats. The police car bumped its blue and red flashing roof lights on and off and the street erupted in momentary color. It had the desired effect and Carl stopped on the sidewalk as the patrol car stopped nearby.

"Mr. Rand? Carl Rand?" a patrolman was saying as he stepped out of his car into the street as Jack and Cal did the same behind him.

"Yea?"

"Good morning, Mr. Rand," the patrolman continued as Jack and Cal walked up beside him. "This is Jack Aaron of the District Attorney's Office—"

"Oh, yea. I seen you on the news."

"—and this is Special Agent Cal Denti from the Federal Bureau of Investigation. They'd like to talk to you for a few minutes."

"What about?"

"Sam Ciampiano," Cal said gently. "I understand you work for him?"

Jack stuck his hand out. "Jack Aaron, Mr. Rand. We spoke briefly on the phone a few months ago. You had stopped to look in on the newsstand. I'm sorry it's been so long getting to say hello."

"Yeah, yeah. The papers was getting ruined. I couldn't get nobody to let me in."

"That was me who got you the wholesaler's phone numbers."

"Yeah, I remember. I didn't know you was the DA. Thanks for calling me like that. That was real nice. You saved Sam some money right there."

"No, you saved him money – looking after his place like you did."

"Well, he's a good guy. If he's in a jam I'd want to help him out, you know? But I haven't seen him in months now."

"I was wondering," Jack said slowly. "As we haven't seen him either, if you'd come to the office and help me out with some questions I have. You might be able to help us find him – make sure he's alright."

Carl looked up the street to his house. "Yea, I could do that I guess."

"Good. Thank you. Thank you very much," Jack was saying as he led the way to Cal's car. "Thanks, fellas," Jack said by way of dismissing the officers. "You can ride in the back with me," Jack rambled as he held the rear door then slid in beside what would have been taken as his new best friend.

"You're with the FBI, huh?" Carl asked Cal.

"Yes." Cal was getting behind the wheel.

"Don't hold that against him, Carl. You mind if I call you Carl? You call me Jack."

"I don't hold nothing against nobody. It's cool. I met FBI before."

"When was that, Carl?" Cal asked as he crept the car quietly through Tampa, a couple of dozen blocks toward the heart of downtown.

"That day the cops were all over the newsstand. I heard about it and went over, you know? Thinking maybe Sam got robbed or something. Though nobody in this town would try that."

"Why's that?"

"We talking about the same Sam?" Carl acted like he was holding his upper arm as if the arm was as big as his leg. "You see the guns on that guy? He could throw the three of us in a dumpster with one hand. Plus his dad's thing." Carl brought himself back awkwardly. "Anyways, the FBI guys were around the stand talking to people about Sam that day. I talked to them a while. Tampa PD guys too. I don't mind cops. They got a job to do. I talk to them, you know, once in a while. They're okay."

"You never had any trouble with the police, Carl?"

"Never."

"How about Sam? He ever in any trouble?"

"Kid stuff. A long time ago. Somebody'd pitch an egg and then we'd run up the alley. Wasn't me, but some guys around town. I think he got in trouble once for stealing some candy from the little league snack bar, but worked it off. Nobody got arrested or anything."

"Nothing else?"

"No. We was pretty good kids."

"You have any kids, Carl?"

"Not that I know about," he grinned.

"Someday?"

"I hope so. Just hasn't happened yet."

"Any other family, Carl?"

"Just a brother."

Cal was parking the car under the county and city offices next to the Tampa police station. As the three men got out and made their way through the quiet of early morning, Jack kept the easy flow going.

"Yea? He around?"

"He lives here in Tampa. Same as me."

"You close?"

"I guess so. He's a good guy. Smart as hell."

"Smart, huh? What's he do?"

"Computers. He's got a TV remote that looks like something from the cockpit of a fighter jet."

"You see him much?"

"Oh, yea. I stop over every once in a while. He's pretty busy. Runs his own company doing computer shit. I don't know much about it."

They were meandering through the elevator and hallways to an interrogation room.

"Your brother, what's his name?"

"Clay. I call him Clay. Clayton, really. Clayton Rand. Same as me."

"Does he know Sam Ciampiano?"

"Sure he does. We all went to school together. We were in the same grade. I'm the oldest, but got held back a year, maybe two. I hate to read. That's why. If I had to read a big book, I'd probably pass out, know what

I mean? I hate reading. I like movies. Clay too. We're movie guys. Same as Ralph."

"Ralph? Who's Ralph?"

"His real name is Raphael – like the Ninja turtle. Bordaine. He went to school with us. Me, Clay, and Sam. Ralph's another movie guy, but they like old shit – black and white. I can't stand a black and white movie. I mean, what's the point of watching, you know what I mean?"

"Me too. I can't stand them," Jack agreed and encouraged.

"Right? They're slow and the actors suck. And special effects? Are you shittin' me? Total bullshit. But Clay and Ralph, they go ape shit over them. If they fire one of those oldies up, I jet."

"So, this Ralph, he knows Sam too?"

"Yep. We grew up together. We all worked at Ciampiano's newsstand, downtown. I still do sometimes. I cover for Sam if he's gotta do something else."

"Like what? I mean, what's Sam like to do? Where's he go?"

"Shit. I have no idea. He don't talk much. Real quiet."

"Do you remember when you covered for him last?"

Carl rubbed his face, squinted hard, and stared at the ceiling. To the side, Cal was shaking his head no.

"No... Not really. I mean, not dates or nothing. He calls me once in a while and asks if I can open for him. It's only a few hours. It's right when I'm on my way home from work, so it's no big deal."

Cal made a note and underlined it.

"He calls you when he needs a hand?" Cal asked.

"Usually. Once in a while I stop and shoot the shit at the stand on the way home. He opens up about the time I get off work. If he needs somebody he asks me right there sometimes. He don't strictly call every time."

"You help him out often?" Cal continued.

"No. He keeps it under control, I guess."

"You don't remember the last time you helped out?"

"Not really. He just lets me know and I stop in if I can. It's four in the morning, you know? What else am I going to do anyways? Go home and go to bed? I open the stand and Sam throws me a few bucks. Why not, right?"

"He ever say where he was going? Why he needed you to cover the stand?"

"Nope."

"No vacations? Ever tell you about where he's been?"

"Nope."

"He ever mention San Francisco?"

"Nope."

Cal leaned in unnoticeably. "When was the last time you saw him?"

"Boy, you guys don't get tired of asking me that one, do you?"

"How so?"

"That's the third time, at least, you FBI guys have asked me that same question. Oh, wait, once was an FBI girl. A real good looking girl too. Real good looking. Blonde. Smoking hot." Carl smiled.

Cal's face tightened. "Was that the day you went to the newsstand? That first day? You mentioned talking to someone in the FBI that day."

"No, this was a couple days later. After you called me with the phone numbers," Carl said as he pointed to Jack. "This smoking hot chick shows up at my door asking me about Sam. I think she was a reporter. She said she was with the FBI and flashed a tiny bullshit badge, but there's no FBI agent that looks that hot, I'm just sayin.' It ain't like the movies."

"And she asked you about Ciampiano?"

"Yea. Same as you. 'When'd you see him last? Where's he at?' Same as you."

The veteran cops exchanged a glance that wordlessly moved the revelation to a list of topics to be discussed later.

Cal and Jack exchanged places as Cal eased back and Jack forward. "Say, Carl?" Jack said as he looked at his watch. "It's morning. How about a cup of coffee?"

"No, thanks. Keeps me awake. I got to get some sleep. I go to bed when I get home." Carl looked at his watch now. "We going to be much longer?"

"No," Cal said. "Just a couple more questions."

"Can you give me a ride home?"

"Happy to. We appreciate you coming in. Carl? Are Sam and Clayton close?"

"I wouldn't say so. They weren't even close in school. Sam was a jock. Clay was, you know, like a brainiac?"

"Do they get together?"

"I don't think so."

"When was the last time you saw Sam with your brother?"

"Recently?"

"In the last year or so."

"Never."

"You ever hear them talking... about anything?"

"I haven't seen or heard them together or talk or nothing since high school. Why?"

"Carl, this is important. Clayton ever ask you for help on anything?"

"Sure. That's what brothers are for. That ain't a crime. What's going on?"

"We're just trying to find Sam, Carl."

"Then why you keep asking about Clay? Go ask him yourself. I don't know shit about what he does. Look, I gotta go get some sleep. Can I go now?"

The inquisitors let the tension die away for a moment.

"Sam have a girlfriend?"

Carl looked again at the ceiling for answers. "I don't think so. I never saw him with no one. If he did, he didn't tell me about her. But that don't mean he didn't have one. Or two. I dunno. He's not a talker, like I said."

"Can I ask you one more thing, Carl?"

"Sure."

"You ever hear Clayton or Sam mention The Illuminati?"

"You mean that gang on the news?"

"Yes. The gang on the news."

Carl shook his head. "Nope. Never."

"Everybody's talking about them, Carl. They're in the news every day. One of them must have said something."

"Not to me. I never heard either of them say shit about it. And that's the truth."

The barrage ended. The room was quiet. There were other things to inquire about, but they'd wait. Carl was being as helpful as he could. Both Cal and Jack sensed it. There was no blood to get from this stone.

"I wish I could help you more," Carl said sheepishly. "I'd give anything to help Sam out. It'd be good to know he's okay, you know?"

"Anything make you think he wouldn't be okay, Carl?" Jack said, leading as much as possible. "Like what you said before when you said..." Jack looked at his notes. "You said, 'His dad's thing.' What's that mean? 'His dad's thing?'"

Jack already knew the answer, but let the mixture stew in Carl's head and apparently on the ceiling again – Carl's repeated go-to spot for solutions.

"I don't know what I meant..." Carl labored. "I was just talking, you know?"

Time slipped by as Jack looked gently, but intently into Carl's eyes. "I'm just trying to help your friend here, Carl. He could be in a jam, like you said." Almost a minute passed. "Sometimes, when money's changing hands, people do funny things, you know, Carl? Maybe something's happened – might have had nothing to do with Sam, but he got caught up in it. You know how those guys work."

Cal was lost, but for Carl – a kid who grew up working under the tutelage of Sam Ciampiano Sr. – 'those guys' made a lot of sense. He had also gone to his old boss's funeral and seen the long line of black cars and gruff looking men behind dark glasses who seemed to use the reverent tone of their funeral voice whisper every day.

Carl spoke very slowly. "I don't think Sam was doing none of that stuff."

"You're sure?"

"I mean, I never seen nothing. Not like when the old man was around." Carl was picking up speed in his voice and his story. "I'm pretty sure Old Man Sam ran a full book when we was kids. There was always somebody coming up with a slip. Not a lot of money maybe, but yea, he had a little side business going, but not Sam. Sam didn't even take numbers after his dad died. It just went away. I know I never took a number. Never. Nothing. None of us kids did. The old man wouldn't allow it. If we was watching the stand, people knew not to give us numbers, you know? Mr. Ciampiano would have knocked the hell out of them if they did. People had to go to him. Not us kids. Not Sam neither. Not even now."

Jack let him wind down and relax before he prodded just a little. "It might be, you know, Carl, an old debt or vendetta – something left over from Sam's father. They might have it in for him."

Carl was quiet but shook his head no.

"If Sam was in trouble where would he go?" Cal asked and got no answer.

Jack leaned in very close. "Carl. Sam's in real trouble. Where would he go?"

Carl looked at the ceiling then at Cal and back to the ceiling before he settled on Jack. "Probably to those same guys you think have it in for him."

———————

16

The morning rush hour had just begun as Jack's car stopped in front of Carl's house to let him out. Downtown, Cal's was easing up in front of Raphael Bordaine's high-rise building. Marcus Pete was with him. The two discussed their approach, the ground they hoped to cover, and any leverage they thought they could bring to bear as a result of their surveillance and the interview with Carl. The chance of seeing anything pertinent in Raphael's apartment was remote, but possible. Criminals often made foolhardy errors.

"Do you know a Sam Ciampiano?" Petey said plainly following introductions at Raphael's threshold.

Raphael was nervous the minute he saw the badges. "I used to. He was in my high school class."

"When did you see him last?"

"It's been years."

Cal was soft, but direct. "May we come in, Mr. Bordaine? We have some questions you might be able to help us with."

"About Sam Ciampiano?"

"Yes."

Raphael was equally as soft and direct. "High school was almost twenty years ago and, as I said, I haven't seen him in several years. I don't believe there is any more to add."

The standoff was increasing in tension as seconds ticked.

"Sometimes," Petey tried. "We don't realize how much we can help until—"

"But I haven't seen him in years and years."

"Any idea who he might be hanging around with? Who his friends are?"

"None."

"Where he might hang out?"

"Gentleman, I'm reasonably assured you are doing what you think is best, but I've answered your question – more than once. I don't wish to be rude, but I'm afraid I have to leave for my office."

The game was nearly up. Raphael was gathering what chips he had and was going to disappear toward the payout window. Cal played his ace and pulled out a copy of the newsboys' picture from the Ciampiano newsstand.

"I understand, Mr. Bordaine, but could you tell me, is that you in this picture with Ciampiano?"

Raphael looked hurriedly. "It is. At least twenty or twenty-five years ago."

Cal continued. "And these other men. Do you know them?"

To Raphael, this was going too far. He chose his words carefully. "I do. We were all in school together."

"Could you tell me the last time you met or spoke with Clayton Rand?"

"You referenced that this was regarding Sam Ciampiano. Clearly that's not entirely the case. Unaccustomed as I am to fielding questions from the police, I will have to defer to my counsel for his legal perspective on how to proceed. Good day, gentlemen. You'll have to excuse me. I don't wish to be late for work."

Raphael retreated and closed the door. He instantly fell back against it. He was exasperated and exhausted from holding himself together. Outside the door, Marcus and Cal had shared a disappointed look then turned and walked up the hallway.

"That went well," Cal said.

"Jack will never let me hear the end of it."

"No worries, Marcus. We should have expected that. From his profile, Bordaine is a smart man. Likely a different type of smart than Rand – a pragmatic smart. Lawyering up was the right move for him. Our knocking on his door still has good potential."

"A stir of the pot?"

"Exactly."

"Let's see if he calls Rand before we get there," Marcus said. "Any guesses?"

"See, you haven't been totally corrupted by Jack yet. He'd have positioned that same question as a bet – loser buys lunch. So there's still time to save you."

Marcus laughed a little. "True, that would be Jack."

"But to answer the question, I don't think Bordaine will call. He's too nervous to risk being recorded. He'll go talk to Rand."

"Right now?"

"If he does, he'll see our car parked out front. That will stir that pot of yours even more."

As Cal and Marcus were parking the car just as they had said, Alyn Nuary was weaving hers through security onto MacDill. She would take her first stab at babysitting Karen and backtracking with her over Ciampiano's military career and JAG's involvement. Alyn remained unaware of Karen's confession to John and Cal regarding her relationship with one of the FBI's Top Ten. She took LaRoy's direction to team up with Lieutenant Auburn as a challenge to find something that, as was her custom, she could use to leverage herself into a better position. Her knocking caused Karen to glance at her watch over her steps to the door. She flung the door open and turned away without looking, all in the same motion. "Let me grab my purse."

"No rush," Alyn said as she stepped in and looked around.

Nuary's voice brought Karen back around. "Good morning. I thought you were John."

Alyn looked up and down at herself. "Wow. No wonder LaRoy wants me to review the JAG file. Your eyesight is dreadful, Lieutenant."

"How's that?"

"If you think this," Alyn said as she motioned with both hands down the sides of her form fitting blouse and skirt. "This is LaRoy's body–"

"No, I'm sorry, I didn't even look. I'm so accustomed to John picking me up. What did you say about reviewing the JAG file?"

"A 'second set of eyes' he called it. He wants me to peruse Ciampiano's military records and anything else you may have on him."

"What else would I have?" Karen said in a too anxious voice anyone else would have picked up on. Alyn had diverted to the open bathroom and was lost in checking her hair and makeup.

"I have no idea, Lieutenant. I suppose we'll know when we find it – hence the double checking." Alyn's voice rang as she emerged from the bathroom and crossed the room for the door. "Ready?"

To Karen, the spring in her escort's step and voice sounded like they were headed out on the town for the night instead of going to the office to pursue some of the most wanted people in the country.

They were getting in their car as Cal and Marcus were ringing the doorbell of Clayton's expansive, rolling home. The men could hear chimes play a delicate series inside.

"Wave Good morning," Marcus said as he pointed to a camera perched in the high corner of the entry.

Cal glanced up. "There's likely to be audio surveillance as well."

On cue, Clayton's voice came through an invisible speaker. "Can I help you?"

Cal pulled out his identification and held it up to the camera. "My name is Calburn Denti. Special Agent in Charge of the Federal Bureau of Investigation's Tampa office. This is Marcus Pete. Investigator with the Hillsborough County District Attorney's Office. Is Mr. Clayton Rand available?"

"This is he."

"Mr. Rand, we have a couple of questions regarding Sam Ciampiano."

Without missing a beat Clayton came back. "Certainly. Go right ahead."

Cal and Marcus looked quickly at each other, the door, and back up at the camera. "Might we speak in person, Mr. Rand?" Cal asked.

Again there were no qualms preceding the response. "I'm afraid I'm indisposed at the moment. I can hear you quite well. Please continue."

All the hesitation was captured outside the door.

"Thank you, Mr. Rand, but I'm afraid I need to verify who I'm speaking with."

"That makes perfect sense," Clayton said. "But, as I said, I'm unable to meet with you now. Perhaps another time."

"I'm going to have to insist, Mr. Rand," Marcus said suddenly, not hiding his frustration as he stepped around Cal and closer to the camera.

"You seem upset, Investigator Pete. I apologize, but you've caught me unaware. Perhaps you might have made an inquiry prior—"

"Would you come to the door, Mr. Rand?"

"I told you, I am—"

"Yes, 'indisposed.' I heard you quite well," Petey mimicked. "We're going to need to see who we're speaking with. Would you open the door, sir?"

"Do you have a warrant?"

"No, Mr. Rand. What we have are a few questions we'd like answered in order to possibly help a friend of yours who's been missing for some time. Are you interested in helping find your friend?"

"I never said the man you're inquiring about is my friend. Those are your words, Investigator Pete. Please chose them more wisely. They could be misconstrued."

"Do you know, Sam Ciampiano?" Marcus persisted.

"I know of him. We went to school together twenty years ago. I once worked for his father selling newspapers. They ran a bit of a landmark downtown."

Cal gently spoke to the camera. "When was the last time you saw Mr. Ciampiano?"

"To the best of my recollection, it's been years. Will there be anything else?"

"Yes," Cal continued in his disarming manner. "We have additional questions we believe you may be able to help us with. When might you be available to meet with us?"

"As you've heard, I know almost nothing about Ciampiano. I don't see—"

"When, Mr. Rand?" Marcus blurted.

"I don't care for your tone, Mr. Pete. This conversation is over. Enjoy the sunshine, gentlemen."

"Mr. Rand?" Cal offered again. "I will leave my card on the door here," he said as he did exactly that. "I would like to have you call and make arrangements to meet with me. It can be here or at my office. Wherever you are most comfortable."

"Again, I don't see the—"

"As Mr. Pete suggested, I'm afraid we're going to have to insist. A man is missing, sir. We're trying to locate him and you may be able to help whether you know it or not. If you'd prefer a warrant, one can be obtained. That would be your choice. You may be a material witness in Mr. Ciampiano's disappearance. I'll expect to hear from you by tomorrow afternoon. If not, we'll be back with that warrant. Thank you, Mr. Rand."

Cal stepped away as he uttered his ultimatum. Though Marcus followed, he glared back at the camera and caught it pan to follow them.

The investigators didn't speak until they were in the car.

"I take back what I said," Cal grinned. "You have been working with Jack."

Marcus shifted in his seat. Uncomfortable. "Arrogant prick."

"Yes, Jack has rubbed off on you."

"Indisposed? Who says, I'm indisposed? Can't federal agents issue warrants under the provisions of the Patriot Act?"

Cal was smiling now. "We can."

"Draw one up and we'll go back right now."

"Settle down, Jack Junior," Cal patted the air between them in the car as he drove back across the city. "We'll go over this with LaRoy. Rand likes cameras? Good. He's been on one for weeks. My guess is John will move the surveillance out into the open and turn up the heat. You stirred the pot up very well. Jack will be proud. Bordaine and the Rand brothers will be talking and we'll be around to put the pieces together."

Neither reached for their phones. Their respective bosses weren't the type of men who required news with the juvenile imperative made possible by the availability of modern communication and seemingly warranted by its sickly cousin, the brevity of the common attention span. John LaRoy and Jack would sit and listen to the verbal results of the curtailed interviews with Bordaine and Clayton Rand. The senior investigators would alternately lean on their fists and back in their chairs. They'd season the conversation with nods, brief clarifying questions, and occasional grunts that hinted at neither understanding or confusion, approval or dismay. When Cal and Marcus set their digital notepads aside, John and Jack would drop their antiquated ball-point pens on their lined pads, stretch, and rub their faces until they were able to smooth the tension into the corners of their eyes then out and make it vanish under their palms as they combed their hair coarsely with their fingers.

Jack gave way to LaRoy who was technically in charge. For his part, John looked around the office and rubbed his back against his chair like a bear might scratch his back on a tree.

"I'm glad we got that out of the way," LaRoy said through a deep breath. "These guys are consistent and that's good."

Marcus was thinking out loud. "You mean, consistently clever. How's that a good thing?"

"Lawyering up was the smart move. These guys are smart. And they're smart all the time. That's consistent. And consistent also means what?"

Marcus and Cal were locked on LaRoy. Jack had slumped slightly in his chair and was looking at the two returned interrogators as though, like John, he was waiting on an answer. None was coming.

"I'm not following, John," Cal said. "I get 'consistent,' but I'm with Marcus. How's that a plus?"

LaRoy looked to Jack. "DA?"

"If they're consistent, which they are," Jack said as he folded his hands on his lap. "That also makes them predictable." Jack grinned. "Why do you think we sent the 'B' team to interview them?"

Cal shook his head and smiled. His partner was incredulous.

"I knew it. Here it comes," Marcus said as he looked at Cal and the others.

"Admit it, Petey. I interview the first Rand brother and he blabbers on for two hours in the middle of the night. You say, 'Hello' to your guys and they clam up in two minutes. Nice going. Who trained you?"

"You."

"Cal, you want to reconsider recruiting this guy?" Jack said as he pointed to Marcus. "His interview technique seems suspect. Maybe it's me. What do you think, John?"

"I think we're done. We're ratcheting up the pressure on Rand. Bordaine and the other brother—"

"Carl. My buddy," Jack winked.

"Yea, Carl. Carl and the other guy are of little or no consequence at the moment. Rand, however has our undivided attention. And tomorrow, we'll have his."

"How about Ciampiano?" Cal said as he got up, went to the window, and leaned against the wall. "He's still wandering around out there somewhere."

"That he is. Jack's been marshalling that piece. Anything?"

"Zero."

"Anything on the horizon?"

"Nope."

"Next steps?"

"Backward, most likely. I'm having Oakes and your geeks go back further into his spending history. Looking for anything – something. The guy went to work and went home. We can almost account for every day – every hour – of this guy's life since he got out of the Army."

LaRoy closed his notes and got up. "Stop screwing around and get rid of the 'almost' then, Jack.

Karen was sitting in her cloistered office at the Federal Building, strategically placed between Cal's regular office and LaRoy's temporary one. Through the limited access of the computer in front of her, it was clear she might be getting left off some updates, but through the meetings she'd attended, it was apparent Clayton Rand was outpacing any attempt to corral him. There was nothing to indicate the brother and the last boy in the old newspaper photograph were involved. Nothing yet anyway and it might stay that way, if it all ended now.

She reviewed the synopsis of each interview as they were entered in the case file. With no revelations, no confessions, and nothing new on The Illuminati or the missing Ciampiano, the rapidly stalling investigation in Tampa could have ended there. She wanted it to end right here, right now. She would return to Washington with the inevitable black mark on her name and her personnel file. She would continue her work, be denied promotion, but eventually take her pension. Hopefully, she would meet someone along the way. Have a family. Live a quiet and blessed life while Sam, The New Illuminati, and the current memory making process faded from her mind and the news.

Sam was safe, wherever he was. He might be lost to her, but he would use his talents – as many, varied, and complex as they were – to land on his feet.

Land on his feet...

Karen thought of Sam's boots hitting the ground then rolling out beneath the wings of his collapsing parachute. He'd be in another country to execute both a mission and likely, a person.

Her mind, starving for work and striving to distance itself from the recent past, began to wander through the dogma FBI profilers had assembled on The Illuminati and its likely members. Sam was the good guy, wasn't he? "We're the good country," she thought as a reminder or reinforcement. "Fighting for freedom and democracy the world over. Fighting for the oppressed. Fighting for those who couldn't. Right?"

If that much was so, The Illuminati's mantra was bringing the same standard home. "For the practicality of it all," Karen thought, "What were the tea tossing colonial Americans, dressed as Indians?" She scrolled through another page in the profile on the screen. "They were seen as Freedom Fighters from the North American continent and terrorists from the European shore." It was a perspective veiling that lay over right and wrong.

She was adrift badly.

"But that was taxation without representation. That was wrong. We were right. History has proven us right."

"But what about the laborer who was supposed to unload that tea? No work – no pay – no food on the table." Now she was arguing with herself. "He just wanted to do his job. Like most people in countries all around the globe. Apolitical. Stop it!"

Karen shook her head to clear the cobwebs and mist of a history of errors that included her own submissions. She felt queasy and put her hand on her stomach. It passed and the political history lesson with it.

Sam would make out. He was too resourceful to not physically manage. His happiness however, was far from certain, as it had been when they spent that first afternoon together in Tampa. Yes, she loved him and missed him, but knew she could never see him again. Karen was likely to be monitored ad-infinitum by the Feds in the hopes of reaching Sam one day. Any contact or attempt would increase her risk and guarantee Sam a prison cell or a bullet. That couldn't happen. Wouldn't happen. If it ended now.

Karen let herself linger over the photograph of the newsboys in her case file. The police and prosecutors, like herself, were trying to tighten a digital noose around the neck of the young boy next to Sam in the picture,

Clayton Rand. The young boys in the old picture contrasted sharply with the crimes and the pursuit. Sam didn't have much of a smile in the picture and you couldn't yet see the thick shoulders under his father's hands or the soldier who would parachute into open oceans, kill, and be extracted before the echoes of flying bullets faded away.

Clayton and Raphael were about the same height as Sam in the picture – all of them standard twelve year old boy size. Clayton was smiling a pleasant smile with no indication of genius apart from perhaps the single pencil sticking out of his shirt pocket in front of a small spiral bound notepad. Raphael was next to him and though forcing a smile, looked like he wanted to be somewhere else. The brother, Carl Rand, was at the far right, a little taller, smiling broadly. His thin chest almost appeared puffed up with the thrill of having his picture taken. There wasn't a criminal in the bunch, Karen thought, except maybe the lone figure in the back row.

Sam Ciampiano Sr. was stiff and resting both hands on his son's shoulders. There was enough of a smile to appeal to the camera and the media interests of employing vintage news criers on the modern streets of Tampa. Still, behind the small story pleasing smile, Mr. Ciampiano had the look of a 1920's gangster. His neck was thick, his hands and arms muscular and hard. Even in the grainy newspaper print, his knuckles looked large, as if they'd been abused, maybe broken or poorly set. His hair was plastered straight back over his head, but most revealing to Karen was the set of his eyes. They were tight, hard, dark, and piercing – in spite of the seemingly friendly smile beneath them and the little boys nearby.

Mr. Ciampiano was spared by his death from anything that might eventually befall Karen and the newsboys. Sam had told her of his funeral in response to questions about the few pictures of the elder Ciampiano around Sam's simple house. That was the only time Sam had referred to his mother, as Karen recalled, saying when his dad died he had become totally an orphan as opposed to just being motherless. She had consoled him with her own story of having buried both parents and of their shared lack of siblings. At that same time he had showed her a poorly framed photo – maybe a Polaroid, with its out of balance contrast and dark colors – of a beautiful, but frazzled and sweaty very young woman holding a new baby in a hospital bed. In the white border of the picture someone had written, "Marian (mommy) + Sam (baby)."

That day seemed years ago. Her time with Sam ended too quickly and she realized too late what had supplanted her – this Illuminati thing. The same thing that tore them apart, brought her back to him and now left her dangerously close. Karen thought again of the fruitless interviews from earlier in the day. She hoped it would end now. Wanted it to end. At least in Tampa.

She felt sick again.

While Karen convulsed over a toilet and the investigation around her stalled further, the digging continued elsewhere. In two dozen states, agencies were working assaults, shootings, and bombings thrown up against corrupt and indicted politicians at every level of government. Exposed businessmen and women were taking heat as well for their own misdeeds or perverse greed gilded under the heading of business expense and the like. Lobbyists who connected the first two groups who found themselves in the crosshairs of The New Illuminati also began to topple.

Simpler to access, the money changers were easy targets for Illuminati marksmen and while Sam had been interrupted before he was pressed by severity of offense to watch through a far ranging rifle scope as blood pooled around a motionless body, other self-appointed members handily pulled the triggers on an increasing list of miscreants.

While improbable that a death sentence would have waited at the end of a trial, the chilling effect of repeated gruesome headlines was working. Deals were being squashed, turned down, or not even offered. Flights across country at taxpayers' expense were cancelled as influence peddling posing as political fundraisers went unattended, compelling members of Congress to stay in Washington and focus on issues rather than their coffers for the next run up to a re-election bid. Some weighed the increasing boldness and severity of the Illuminati mark on letters and graffiti warnings prior to attacks, and made the choice not to seek another term. Others, brazen in their greed, pushed forward to fill the vacuum being left by their heretofore power and money-hungry peers to pick up the fat being left unattended at the corruption table. But their gorging would end badly as more and more citizens took up both visible and clandestine arms against defendants any commission or committee chose to brush quietly beneath the rug of the ethics office.

Deaths were mounting and straining the resources of those sworn to protect and serve – resources who may have been card carrying members of The New Illuminati if such things existed. And while the police were stretched and sympathetic, the internal sources and leaks throughout the halls of the powerful were turned loose. There was a wave of recruited righteousness that held itself in check only until indictments from secret or public grand juries, listed enough evidence to levy charges.

The New Illuminati however, did not harbor the same inclination or confidence to wait on trials. Money to fund and support was trickling into splinter groups operating under different banners with the same intent. More than one report surfaced of destitute, lifer inmates who horrifically assaulted or killed imprisoned bankers who had inflated books and their own pockets through pump-and-dump schemes until systems collapsed and took innocent lives with them – main street Americans pressed to suicidal despair by the loss of their life's savings. Congressmen and governors who smiled on video tape as aluminum briefcases of cash changed hands in hotel rooms were suddenly sprawled on shower room floors in the protected wings of state and federal prisons as their blood swirled around and around the drain and down to the sewers.

Clayton had lobbed the first volley. It was his invisible voice that shouted from his keyboard and in doing so dislodged the first crystals of snow from a precarious peak, long posed for collapse. From the onset, the snow collected more of its own then slapped ice and now rock into the crushing escape from the mountaintop. Clayton's Illuminati triangle and eye, and the Bible verse Sam had painted on the wall in San Francisco, had been replicated hundreds of times since in anonymous letterheads and crime scene graffiti. Street art took up the cause and decorated government buildings with the new eye of the people and the now ominous, "To those whom much is given, much is expected." Clayton had started the avalanche. But he couldn't stop it. No one could.

"Hey," John LaRoy said as he drummed the back of his fingers on Karen's open door. "Let's hit the road."

The day had slipped by almost unnoticed. Karen had read the painfully thin regurgitations of the newsboy interviews and done little else. LaRoy had startled her when he stopped.

"I thought I was riding with Alyn."

"Not tonight. She's giving a statement."

"Giving one?"

"Yes, as opposed to taking one. She got herself on my shit list today and a plane for Atlanta tomorrow. By morning I'll have forty emails asking why I was mean to her. Probably one will be from that socialist sonofabitch President of ours. Forget I said that. I'll deny it. Let's go."

Karen had nothing to collect apart from her purse and was up before LaRoy could pull his hand from her door. "What happened?" she asked.

LaRoy was already walking up the hall with Karen hustling up alongside. "It's a need to know," John said. "And you don't need to know, not the particulars anyway. But I'll give you this as a clue for your own self. She stepped out-of-bounds talking to people she shouldn't have been talking to. This ringing any bells for you? I'm pulling her off the investigation."

The move more than the tone came as a shock. Clearly, LaRoy had not had a good day and it might get worse.

As they pulled out from the parking lot beneath the secure building and pointed the car toward MacDill, Karen asked if they could stop at a store and pick up some personal items for the continued stay.

"They sell those pre-paid phones there, don't they?" LaRoy said through frayed nerves, a feeling he was not used to entertaining.

"Likely."

"Having any ideas?"

"Not one."

"Give me a list" LaRoy said dismissively. "I'll pick up whatever you need after I get you back on the base. I'm going back to meet with Denti and Nuary–"

"Sanitary napkins, John."

LaRoy cringed, unable to mask the shrinking virility of the male gender after a thousand years.

"Hypo-allergenic. No scent and the adhesive can't contain–"

"Alright. Christ. I'll stop, but I'm going with you."

"Fine. Come with."

"Listen, Karen. Don't get pissy with me. I'm the only friend you've got. You're out on a narrow limb and I'm out there a step or two myself. If everything pans out, I'll do what I can. I told you that."

"I'm in a cage, John. I barely go to the bathroom alone."

"I'm trying to trust you. You can still access the case file, right?"

"My email didn't work today. Shock of shocks."

"I'll talk to the IT guys."

"Let me do something. Let me help. I know Sam. Maybe I can help find him."

"Maybe. I'll talk to Cal."

"Give me something. Even if it's a dead end. It's starting to look sort of silly, don't you think? Me sitting in an empty office all day? I don't even have my phone. How's that look? Who doesn't carry their phone constantly?"

LaRoy pointed out the windshield at a chain pharmacy. "That work?"

"Yes."

The store was banks of bright fluorescent lights buried in a suspended ceiling. Rows of items, most disposable by design and intent if not packaging and price, called out from colorful dangling signs that described that aisle's contents. The end caps were chock full of impulse items that had no relation whatsoever to the guts of the row.

LaRoy watched Karen hastily pick a new toothbrush, toothpaste, body scrub, and deodorant.

"You can get all that at the commissary on base. You're military. I should have you go there to get my stuff. Cheaper."

"They don't have what I really need." Karen took a few steps toward the competing stacks of toilet paper and the confusing array of feminine products facing the shelves just beyond. "You want to help pick something out?"

He held out his hands. "Give me that stuff. Hurry up."

LaRoy took what Karen had collected so far and walked toward the front of the store and the checkout line. There was no one in line beneath the express line light, but John looked in his hands and counted the items and back to the light which read, Ten Items or Less.

"It's alright," a waif figured young girl with a silver earring stud in her nose said with a bored, tired smile. "There's nobody else here. You're good."

The cashier was right about there being no one else in the store. Apart from a single pharmacist tucked behind a wall of glass in the far corner of the store there was no one in the aisles – clerk or customer. It made Karen's move easier physically but brought about a testing strain otherwise. In her walk away from LaRoy she glanced around as though searching for an item, which she was, but was more keen on LaRoy and who else might be watching her. There might be clandestine security, but she'd risk it. Not a thrill thief, but desperate nonetheless, and seeing no one seeing her, Karen passed the three tight shelves of home pregnancy test kits, took the easiest one to grab and went to the stacks and stacks of colorful, but sedate feminine hygiene displays. She knelt and pulled three competing brands down around her, effectively blocking her next move. The directions on the box were simple, short, easy to read, and memorize. The test kit was opened, the contents stuffed in her sock under her pants leg, and the empty carton jammed behind the display on the bottom row all in a neat flash.

Karen stood abruptly and looked at the bundles in her hands as she picked each up from the floor, though she needed none of them under what she thought to be her current condition. Taking the one that said, "Hypoallergenic" on the label, she hustled toward the front of the store while the contents of the test kit jostled against her ankle like an unruly horse in a starting gate, reminding her that she had never stolen anything in her life.

She came out near the express lane and saw what she took to be her items on the conveyor belt. John LaRoy was not there. Suddenly anxious, she looked around and caught him coming from the corner from the aisle opposite her theft. Her heart was pounding and she felt the package slip in her sock. She held the soft pouch of napkins out in front of her as if they might provide protection.

John said nothing as he tossed a pay-as-you-go smart phone knock off on the conveyor belt.

"This all together?" the teenaged clerk asked.

"Yes." "No." came spontaneous answers from Karen and LaRoy.

"Get your stuff. I got the phone," LaRoy clarified as he examined what Karen was putting on the counter. Seeing only the things she had handed him in the aisle and the napkins, he slid the phone back up the belt and dropped a store advertising stick ahead of it. "Business expense," he muttered and reached for his old billfold.

Karen's items were totaled and bagged. She swiped a card and took the receipt along with the perfunctory, "Thank you for shopping with us today."

After John had paid for the phone, the clerk asked him if he wanted the pre-paid cards that generally were purchased with it.

"No thanks, but do you have some scissors? These packages are hell to open."

The girl sliced the package, thanked him and he her, and the customers went on their way. Outside, John stopped at a garbage can and Karen involuntarily with him. She watched as LaRoy tossed out the packaging, instruction book, and charger. Then he tried in vain to pop off the back of the phone.

"I don't think they use sim cards or removable batteries any longer," Karen said as she caught on.

"No?"

"You can check with IT."

"I will. Here," he said as he handed over the dead phone. "Don't try to charge it, fire it up, or whatever. Just carry it."

"Thanks."

The couple walked across the parking lot. "You can show it off," John said unpleasantly as he pulled out his keys. "It's about appearances, isn't it? But you'd know all about that."

"And perspective."

"Perspective? That'll bite you in the ass every time if you're not careful."

Karen felt the test kit biting her much lower as she slid into the car. "I suppose it can."

After several minutes and miles they were working their way silently through the security layers of MacDill. In the hall of the barracks, LaRoy reminded her. "Don't leave. Don't try to leave. Don't think of leaving. I'll pick you up tomorrow morning. Eight o'clock. No calls, no—"

"I got it, John."

"Hey," he said and took her arm, firm and fleeting, but not rough. "I want this to work out for you, Karen. I really do. I've watched your career. You're a good officer. A good cop. And, I think, a good person. But for this to work, you have to stay straight with me."

"I know."

"You've seen the reports coming in. You know the deal with your prints. I can dance around a bit, but my ass is too old to get caught in a wringer. Follow?"

"I do."

"K," is all he said. He truncated the 'O' in an attempt to distance himself from the conversation and Karen herself. He didn't offer a goodnight, but turned and headed up the hall.

For her part, Karen watched him go only long enough to insure he kept going. She let herself in her Spartan quarters and locked the door behind her. When she sat on the bed her pant leg came up and showed the tip of the bulge in her sock. The test kit gave up its place and was set with near reverence on the nightstand to wait until morning. Karen stared at it for a time before getting ready for bed. When she laid down, she looked again at the pregnancy test kit. Hours later, she was still staring.

She moved the kit into the bathroom and went back to bed to try again. Eventually she found some fitful sleep to the drone of midnight television. In the morning, the pregnancy test would still be waiting.

17

As Karen fought with the future beyond a restless night, Raphael's concerns couldn't wait even another hour. He'd struggled through his day doing little but stare at a plodding clock. He didn't trust the phone. Instead he relied on his regular practice of stopping by Clayton's house after work. When he was certain he'd given Clayton enough time to see him on the security monitors, Raphael flipped his friend the finger. The electronic lock tripped open as a response.

Inside, Clayton emerged from behind the refrigerator door holding two beers. "That's a helluva way to say hello. I should have let you bake in the heat."

Raphael took the beer and walked on into the house, away from Clayton's raised bottle. There would be no standard clink of glass and salute.

"Was that a pun? 'The heat?' Because I'm feeling the heat alright. The FBI was at my house this morning."

"Here too, so don't feel special."

"Jesus, Clay. It's exactly like I said would happen. And you remain still so cavalier."

"Because it is also exactly like I said it would be. They ask a few questions – totally fishing in hopes we stay true to the form of a Hollywood script and start crying and confessing our sins and doing their job for them. They have nothing, Ralph. Absolutely nothing. I know what they have and it is zero."

Clayton took a drink and walked by his friend. "Relax, Ralph. Sit down. I've got the perfect movie for tonight."

"Relax? That's all I get? You telling me to relax?"

"Yes. That's all you get, plus the pleasure of my company and indomitable charm."

"Unreal." Raphael headed for the door and set his unfinished beer on the counter as he passed.

"Hold up. Wait a second, Ralph." Raphael's hand was on the heavy doorknob. "Com' on. Wait."

Raphael turned away from the door, but left his hand in place. "Why do you play with me like this?"

"I'm sorry. Stick around."

"Doesn't the fact that the FBI wants to talk to you bother you? At all?"

"Ralph, if you knew what I knew, you wouldn't worry."

"So help me not worry."

"I can't. Telling you that would be telling you too much. It's better the way it is. I get it that it's painful and I am sorry – I mean it – but everything is alright. You don't know anything and that's the best position to be in. Can you stick with me a little longer?"

The doorbell chimes rang. Clayton looked at the monitor by the door. It was Carl.

Raphael stepped back into the kitchen and picked up his beer. "They probably talked to him too. You want me to go? You might have to talk him down from the ledge."

"No, he called already. He's fine."

Clayton open the door. By appearances one might have thought Carl had been flung through the door rather than walked in voluntarily.

"I could barely sleep! Wow. The FBI," Carl said as he held the index finger of one hand down with the index finger of the other hand as though counting the tally of a tremendous event. "And! And the District Attorney." The District Attorney was assigned a second finger. "The DA and FBI. Both of them. Ain't that some shit? Ain't it?"

"That's some shit, Carl."

"That is indeed some shit," Raphael echoed Clayton and took a drink.

"Let me get you a brew, brother. You've had quite a day."

"You can say that again." As Carl relaxed he zeroed in on Raphael, who had yet to hear his tale. "Ralph. I was walking up my street, see? Right in front of my house. And 5-O flashes their lights. I don't know what's going on, you know?" Carl's moves acted out his version of the memory. "I'm thinking I should get spread eagle on the sidewalk maybe. Or raise my hands. Something. But bang! They're on me!"

Clayton touched his brother's still raised arm with the cold Miller. "Easy, Carl. It's all over. You're safe."

"Whoa. Thanks, Clay," Carl said, distracted by the beer.

"Tell Ralph what happened at the station. You know, lots of questions about Sam and me, and then they took you home. Right?"

"Yeah, that's exactly how it was. Lots of questions about Sam, then about you, then they took me home. Aww, you're playing with me. He's playing with me, Ralph. I told him about it on the phone."

"He likes playing with people, Carl. Keep your eye on him."

"Let's get something to eat!" Clayton said as he popped the top on a Stella. "Pizza and wings. Pony up. We'll all watch a good picture and have pizza and beer. Just like back in the day. And I know the perfect film."

"I'm not gonna stay if it ain't in color," Carl said as he planted himself in Clayton's recliner.

"*Master & Commander*. It's in color."

Raphael was musing. "Interesting choice. The hunter becomes the hunted and so on and so forth."

"That's not it, but there is a character you have to pay strict attention to tonight."

"Who's that?"

"The old salt with the words tattooed on his fingers."

"The recipient of the rudimentary brain surgery," Raphael declared.

"That's the guy. Tell me what his tattoos say and I'll spring for the pizza."

Raphael waited on Carl, but try as he might to search his recollection of the movie he came up short. "I dunno. You got anything, Ralph?"

"I believe I have it."

"Good! Make him pay, Ralph."

Raphael hesitated for effect. "Hold Fast."

"Ding ding ding!" Clay shouted as he set his beer aside and clapped slowly. "We have a winner. Thanks for playing our game. 'Hold Fast.' That is exactly what we do. Hold Fast." Clayton said smiling. "Our word of the day."

"That's two words," Carl corrected.

"Clay is not one to trifle over minor details, Carl. There is but one captain on a ship, as Mr. Crowe is setting forth to remind us. Lead on, 'O Captain, My Captain.' Lead on."

Carl smirked and saluted his brother half-heartedly from his chair. "Fire up the TV, Captain, and you're buying."

Meanwhile, Carl hadn't notice his brother freeze both in movement and expression. A pallor flashed over Clayton that Raphael took notice of and followed with his own reference to a classic film.

"Why, Johnny Ringo," Raphael quoted from the movie *Tombstone*, replete with western accent. "You look like somebody just walked over your grave."

Clayton, still temporarily mindless, responded robotically. "Val Kilmer. Doc Holiday in *Tombstone*... Great scene... Tremendous writing..."

When Clayton stayed in his fog, Raphael eased forward with an out. "Right you are. As always. I'll go halves on dinner. You alright, Clay?"

"Huh? Yeah. Yes. That piece you mentioned. The poem. Who wrote that?"

"Walt Whitman."

"Right. Right," Clayton answered. "About the assassination of Abraham Lincoln. 'My captain is fallen, cold, and dead,' something like that."

Raphael wanted the words back. Despite his many grievances, he wanted his friend confident, but not reckless. "No, not that at all. I was thinking *Dead Poets Society*. Robin Williams. Leadership. Molder of minds and men. That's you."

Clayton had to ease back to clearer thought from the lapse that had given a foothold to the events of the day. There was doubt in his mind surrounding the tenuous grip he held on the founding of The Illuminati that he labored so hard to make appear so easy to escape.

"Are we eating sometime tonight?" Carl blurted before a long draft of his quickly draining Miller.

"Of course. I'll make the call."

Master & Commander slipped the mooring of the monstrous screen and flooded the room. The pizza, wings, and beer disappeared until boxes, cartons, and bottles littered the exquisite tables. Little was said apart from a few mimicking lines and Carl noting he liked certain refrains of the classically themed music. By morning, the big screen was quiet, the room was empty, and the boxes and bottles vanquished to the trash.

Deep inside the Air Force base, Karen was knelt down at her bathroom vanity. Her hands barely held the edge of the sink above her and her head was resting uncomfortably in total collapse against the cabinet door. In one hand was the test strip that had kept her awake most of the night. On the tester were two distinct lines – the indication of a positive result. Karen was pregnant.

The result in her hand crippled her. She was unable to stand or hold her head. She stayed near the floor, leaning into the vanity until her hands and feet tingled from numbness. As the numbness began to border pain, she eased up and sat on the edge of the tub. She emptied her hand of the offending plastic wand and rested her face deep in her hands. More time passed until she eased her head and a hand up to check the number of lines for the twentieth time. They were still there.

The small military bathroom was no haven. As she waited for the known shock to ease, she knew she would find no protection anywhere. It would be pointless to try to hide the pregnancy to full term. She could bear any stigma that might be visited on her for being unwed, but without a fiancé or even a boyfriend, she'd have to tap dance around the inevitable questions. The countless whispered ones would be comparatively harmless. The ones from within JAG, the FBI, and specifically, John LaRoy, despite privacy laws being on her side, would be much more difficult. The fact that her last known boyfriend was on the FBI's Most Wanted List would not go unnoticed.

She had another problem besides the baby inside her. A simple comparison of her statements made to LaRoy and Cal Denti indicated she had not seen Sam for months prior to the net closing around him and his immaculately timed Houdini act. If a good cop had any doubt, he would be waiting for the baby with a subpoena for a blood test. The results would be an indictment of her honesty. Her perjury and the baby that came from that unplanned passion in the newsstand the day of her mad flight to Tampa and Sam's disappearance, would be delivered on the same day.

Karen wept until there were no more tears. As the tears dried, their names evaporated with them. Most were for the initial despair that followed the renting of the veil that had provided a shield of protection against the worst that might happen. A few ran down her cheeks for a lost career she loved. But the bulk of the cascade were for the loss of a family.

For a lifetime she had dreamed of this moment – a high pitched scream coming from the bathroom as her husband ran in only to discover her grinning from ear to ear waving the test stick like a magic wand. She'd throw her arms around Sam's neck and leap on him. He'd support her effortlessly and she would show him the result again and again until he joined the celebration. Laughing, scheming, and screaming they would fall on a bed still warm from the night before and make love. Sam would hesitate. "What about the baby?" he'd say genuinely concerned, until reassurances and her passion persuaded him. Even so, he'd be gentler until the birth of their child and the true beginnings of their family. There'd be baby shopping and maternity clothes, changes in diet and doctor visits. They would...

Karen threw up violently. When it passed, the blissful vision vanished with it and she was back in the sterile bathroom of MacDill, alone with the mocking test kit.

She stood, dizzy, and moved to the sink where she rinsed her mouth and face. The reflection in the mirror was all swollen red eyes and shattered dreams. A washcloth was bathed in the coldest water the faucet would produce. Karen didn't pick up the test kit again, but brushed it off the vanity counter with the back of her hand into the white plastic bag that protected the waste basket from its intended, took the cold washcloth, and retreated to bed. The compress went over her eyes as she laid back and tried to reason out her next steps.

By eight o'clock Karen had struggled to find both the strength and the will to get dressed. Her white JAG uniform skirt was tight – a fact she had noticed nearly a month ago but summarily dismissed. It took extra care and make-up to shield the state of her eyes from others who would be able to see something was amiss with the lieutenant's countenance. With just minutes to spare, a knock came to the door.

"Good morning," Karen said with decent enthusiasm as she opened the door.

"At least you got the face right this time." It was Alyn Nuary, still fulfilling her babysitting/spy function for John LaRoy.

When Karen turned to collect her fake phone and purse, Alyn whisked by into the bathroom. "I'll just be a second." The door closed on any conversation leaving Karen with the instant realization that her greatest secret and the greatest self-promoter of hidden secrets were sharing the same small room.

It was an eternity and a moment before the semi-industrial toilet flushed loudly. Karen heard the water run in the sink. She tried to busy herself with the unpowered phone as though checking messages when the bathroom door opened. She didn't look up completely until the obvious reached across the room and slapped her face. Alyn was leaning against the door casing holding the tester with two fingers as if she dangled a dead rat by the tail.

"Congratulations, Lieutenant."

It was a moment too long in the recovery. "Thank you," Karen said through an inescapable phony smile. She motioned with her phone. "I'm still sending out the news. I just found out. But you can see that."

"I can indeed. Do you know how these things work?" Without waiting for the answer that was stuck in Karen's throat, Alyn continued. "They measure a hormone in your pee. I can't recall the exact name just now, but it doubles in strength each day after conception. These gizmos almost never give a false positive, but they can give false negatives if you test too early. You see, the hormone hasn't had time to replicate itself enough. Wait a week or two and test again is my motto. But this one," Alyn said as she looked at the results again. "These are jumping-off-the-page bright." She turned back into the bathroom and dropped the tester into the trash then washed her hands while she chatted. "My educated guess – from personal experience – is you're twelve weeks, give or take." She emerged fully from the bathroom. "And now that I take a closer look, you might want to have the waist in that skirt let out. It looks a little... constricting. I'm surprised you needed that test kit at all. Why haven't you been to the Base doctor? Or was this just a last ditch Hail Mary?"

Karen was struggling mightily against a master of subterfuge on untested ground. "It was... unexpected."

"I think that's mild compared to the look on your face. Here. Come here," Alyn said, but met Karen halfway and put her arms around her in a sincere hug.

Karen could smell the expensive perfume and feel the tightly woven fine silk of Alyn's designer blouse.

The hug broke but Alyn held Karen at arms' length. "Here it comes. I don't do this often so make a note of it in your date book. I know who and what I am and also, have a pretty good idea what you think of me. But–"

"No, don't be–"

"Hush." Alyn put her finger to Karen's lips. "But even a bitch is a female. Am I right? Of course I am. I'm always right and I'm still a woman. That hug is a congratulations if that's what's in order or, if not, that hug means I can help. Without naming names – especially my own – I've been in your position. I know a very good doctor, and by very good, I mean very discreet."

"No... I mean, thank you, but no." Karen slipped out of the hold and picked up her purse. "It has been a lot to take in, but I'm fine. I just have been so busy with this case I haven't been able to get to the doctor. I feel good and I'm very happy about it."

Alyn held up her hands and headed to the door. "I believe you're trying to believe that, but you'd better keep working on convincing yourself."

"What do you mean?"

Alyn stopped and stood in the open doorway. "That last sentence. There wasn't one 'we' in the entire thing. Does Mr. Wonderful even know?"

"As I said, I was just sending out the news."

The pair moved down the hall and the heavy door closed behind them. "Yes, about the blessed event." Alyn held up in the hallway and Karen stopped with her. "We've been in Florida at least three months, Karen. It must have been a helluva goodbye kiss." Alyn took a step and jerked to a stop again. "Or have you been banging the bell boy? No shortage of men here. After all, you are living on an Air Force Base – something that I find distasteful. I mean, look at your accommodations? Really, Karen." The women began walking again. "Let's talk to John about getting you moved to my hotel, for goodness sake. It's the least he can do."

They stopped for the third time. "Oh, wait... Are you going to tell him? I'm sorry," Alyn said and waved herself off and back to walking. "You decide what you're going to do and let me know after. As I said, congratulations, or call me and I'll connect you with an old friend to make this go away. I'm here to help either way."

Within the federal building that housed Cal Denti, the rest of the local FBI, and the out-of-town squatters, John LaRoy was convening a meeting. Jack Aaron and Marcus Pete were there along with their complete forensic unit in the sole person of Helfer Oakes. Regional Director Alyn Nuary and JAG Lieutenant Karen Auburn were the last to arrive. Major Doug Caulden pushed a chair out with his foot for Karen when he saw the uniform. Alyn went to the head table next to LaRoy.

"Good to see you, Lieutenant," the major whispered. "How you getting on with the civilians?"

"Very well," she whispered.

"If you've tamed that one," Caulden motioned with his eyes toward Nuary, "You're one up on most of the Bureau. They say she's hell on wheels."

"She's tough, but she has a good side."

"You're the first to see it."

LaRoy stood and called the murmuring to order.

"Here's the skinny, folks. Oh, before I forget, don't say anything bad about Agent Meyer. He's on speaker. You there, Jason?" LaRoy said louder than his usual loud voice in the direction of a speaker module on the big conference table.

"I'm here, John."

"Good. Alright. We worked our asses off to get our ducks in a row through surveillance. We thought our boy would have left us something or tripped up somewhere. The geek squad has been combing through everything again and again for the last three months and are still coming up empty. Naturally, we wanted some answers before we took our first big swing at the target. But... that hasn't happened.

"Well, the truth is, we took a half-assed swing yesterday and we struck out. Sticking with the baseball thing, Rand is pitching a perfect game and we can't even tell what color the other team's jerseys are. It's no better with Ciampiano. We can tell you what he ate for breakfast the day he fell off the earth, but don't have clue one as to where he fell to. We're on the verge of going house to house in Tampa, but I will remind you – all of us – Ciampiano came to us as a name on a list of maybes. He fits the bill in a dozen ways, but the fact that he's gone over the hill and was a school chum of Rand's doesn't convict him. We're going to be taking a lot of second looks.

"Meanwhile, this Illuminati thing is growing. We have incidents almost daily. You name it. Bombings, shootings, assaults, threats – runs the gamut. Police departments are overrun if any local shit bird or businessman makes the paper for dipping into the till or tripping over a political favor or some such bullshit.

"Thank the good Lord for the competence of several state police agencies. They've been picking up the slack on both ends – for small town police departments without manpower and where the Bureau is stretched to the limit. They've made a number of good arrests, but the dike is crumbling, ladies and gentlemen. For every arrest, some asshole politician redoes his kitchen out of his campaign funds or drops his pants for his web girlfriend. Then it's off to the races again. It's open season on assholes."

LaRoy looked directly at Jack.

"I know some people – even some people in this room – don't find that too unsettling. But beyond breaking the law – which we have all sworn to uphold – there a risk here that this business gets such a head of steam it takes a bad turn – a real bad turn."

LaRoy waxed vacant as he and his eyes drifted to another time for a moment. He shifted his hefty bulk between his feet. "I remember telling my daughters when they were sprouts, 'Trouble always starts out as fun.' I forget who said that first, but I stole it. I made a sign and put it up on the wall of their room to remind them. Sometimes it worked. Most times it didn't.

"Christ, I walked in their room one day and they were playing 'Camp Out.' They had made tents out of their blankets and had stuffed animals in a circle on the floor singing camping songs and pretending to roast marshmallows. Damned if they hadn't started a camp fire – a real fire –

right in their garbage can! The room was filling up with smoke. Could have burnt the house down and killed us all." He was serious, but couldn't hide a smile at the remembrance if not the danger.

LaRoy came back from twenty-five years earlier and the set of his jaw returned even tighter. "That's how this is going, folks." LaRoy sat down slowly, resigned. "In a perverted way, it may have had some good intentions, but it's going to come off the rails." LaRoy paused, looking tired. "I think the DA called this right. It started here in Tampa. Rand led with the two of clubs and Ciampiano followed suit. Now half the country is on the bandwagon. Can we prove it? No. So, after more than three months of intense work, we're pulling the plug.

"It's not quite 'tail between our legs' full blown retreat, but we have cases coming from all over. Hell, our Washington office is literally under siege by members of Congress begging for round the clock protection." LaRoy flipped through a stack of tattered paper held on a ratty clipboard. "We've got requests from six governors, eleven big city mayors, attorney generals from a half dozen states, CEOs from fistfuls of the fortune five hundred, even judges. None of which will say *why* they want us, they just want us.

"We can't justify so many agents here. Cal and his team will keep at it. The DA has been instrumental from the beginning and I know he'll keep beating the bushes. The rest of us are headed north unless somebody can toss something out on the table to convince me otherwise."

Empty silence filled the room.

LaRoy stood up and flipped the papers on his antiquated clipboard back into place. "It's not fancy, but there's a flight out of MacDill for Andrews at 0600 tomorrow. Let me know if you're interested. Thank you, everyone."

Sound filtered back through the room in low measured tones. There was no shock, no disagreement, no encouragement or thanks beyond what LaRoy had offered. The principals talked briefly and drifted away. Jack asked LaRoy if Helfer Oakes could fly to Washington to review in sum the evidence related to Tampa. LaRoy saw no hope in the move, but couldn't say no. Karen had gone to the front of the room and was the last to leave with LaRoy after Jack's request.

"John?" Karen asked.

LaRoy looked up rather absently and continued collecting his papers. He didn't answer directly, but offered a glance of recognition instead.

"I'm guessing there's a seat with my name on it for that flight to Andrews."

John breathed deeply through his nose. He was relaxed. "Did you want to stay here?"

"No, I guess what I'm really asking–"

"I know what you're asking, Lieutenant."

They looked at each other for a few moments that would have passed several camera cuts back and forth if they had been characters in a charged drama.

"I know. Cal knows. And you know. That's where it ends. Take the plane back to Washington. Back to JAG. Damn it, we need a break in this mess. That work for you?"

"It does."

"Good enough then."

"Thanks, John.

"Sure thing."

Karen was walking away. "Hey," John called. "Your phone is in Washington in the Forensic Unit. I'll have it released. You get downtown often?"

"I live downtown."

"You'll have to sign, but go pick it up."

Karen shook her head yes.

"Karen, I'm sorry for the rough time. You're a good cop, and a good sport."

"I've always understood."

"Fair enough. See you in the morning."

LaRoy left the conference room and headed up the hall toward a stairwell.

"You sure you don't want to take the elevator?" Jack called from down the hall. "You're moving a little slow there."

John turned around and walked the length of the hall. "What are you doing still here? You stalking me?"

"Yea, you're a real starlet," Jack teased, but was tense. "I was wondering if I could get your autograph. Because you're gonna be famous when we crack this thing. We just need one break – just one break."

"It's no different than any other. We always need that one piece."

"It'll happen."

"Maybe. Maybe not. We'll clean up the mess he's made, but Rand is the coolest customer I think I've ever seen. He's playing it exactly right. Quiet as a church mouse. It's like he is always a half step ahead."

"It's still early, John. A few months is nothing in a caper like this. Time is on our side. You got to go, I know it. But I'm not going anywhere. He'll step on his dick some day and I'll be right there with my hammer."

John stuck his hand out. "In case they ever get wise and throw your ass out of office, let me know where you're at. Keep Cal in the loop. If you need anything I can help with, holler."

"You bet," Jack said as he firmly shook LaRoy's hand. "It's been a barrel of laughs. Take care of yourself."

"You do the same. You ever get to Washington, give me a call. I'll show you around so you can stare up at the big tall buildings."

Both men smiled as they shook hands and went in opposite directions.

Upstairs Alyn was hastily packing her temporary office. LaRoy stopped in the doorway.

"When you get back to your office, I'd leave your stuff packed."

"How's that?"

"Don't bother stowing your gear in Atlanta. I'm transferring you. I'm leaning toward the Canadian Office. Maybe Iceland. I'll have to see if we have an igloo, I mean, an office there."

"I'm not following any of this."

"You're being transferred, Agent Nuary. It'll all be laid out in the disciplinary hearing you're entitled to have."

"Disciplinary hearing?"

"You tried to interview our targets regarding the investigation into The Illuminati in advance of the official investigation."

"I was looking for Ciampiano." Nuary's voice was rising.

"Not hardly. You were asking about Rand. Looking for another notch in your gun or some goddamn headline."

"That's not true."

"You asked the wrong set of questions if you were trying to find Ciampiano. Plus you and your little friend in the Forensic Unit have been sharing lab and data results prior to their release to the field. I don't care what else you share, but nobody can see findings until they clear Washington. That's protocol, Alyn. There'll be an internal review, but I thought I'd just tell you now. Don't bother unpacking."

John stepped out of the frame of the door and was walking up the hall to his own temporary office. Nuary filled his place in the door. She skipped any clarifying questions and went right to shouting.

"It'll never happen, John. Don't trouble yourself!"

"It's no trouble," John said as he kept walking. "No trouble at all."

Nuary was fuming. Inside her office, behind the closed door, she quickly called Jason Meyer. He was shaking when he hung up the phone.

Alyn was not. She made several more calls – some venting, some pleading her case on few facts. The calls released any anxious energy. By eleven she had run through her early damage control and wandered down the hall. Thankfully, LaRoy's office door was closed. She passed Karen's office without looking in only to discover Cal's empty. She stopped at Karen's door as she retraced her steps.

"Do you have a minute?" Alyn asked from the open door, but didn't wait for an answer. "There's a meeting of the boy's club down the hall," Alyn advised. "I think the girl's club should go to lunch. It's been quite a morning. My treat." The saccharine texture of Alyn's voice sounded equally awkward to both women, but Karen picked up her purse.

In fifteen minutes they were parking on 7th Avenue, up the street from The Columbia Restaurant. "The locals say this place is absolutely exquisite," Alyn said as the beep from the locking security on her car chimed, followed by the rhythmic click-click-click of her tall heels on the occasionally uneven old paver stone sidewalk. The classic path led to ornate tiled walls rising from the sidewalk. The wall, in turn, cradled the main door to the landmark restaurant like the broad gold-leafed frame of a painting.

It was early for the lunch crowd and the expansive many roomed restaurant was empty and quiet. The wait staff was reviewing the day's menus in the kitchen. The stately but diminutive maître d' showed the ladies to a premium table himself.

"Here we are," Mr. Guzimon said as he helped each with their chairs. "It may be early in some parts of the world, but in others, we are far behind. With that in mind, merely as a suggestion," he said apologetically. "Might I interest you in a complimentary splash of our world renowned sangria?"

Alyn touched Karen's arm. "I love sangria."

The maître d' seemed to pull menus from thin air and handed them with a balanced practiced professional delivery. "You are The Columbia's first guests and then, mine as well. The sangria is on the house, as they say."

"No–" Karen was cut off.

"*Certamente.* Or is it, *ciertamente?*" Alyn asked. "I can't quite tell if I should speak Italian or Spanish here. Which is most suited to the cuisine?"

"Here, we speak the universal language of good food and fine wine," Mr. Guzimon answered with a flourish.

In less than a minute a young man was at their table peeling, cutting, and mixing the fresh fruit and wine of the sangria. His gentle banter was distracting and disarming. Karen relied on his entertainment and pushed back from the table.

"I'll be right back," she said to Alyn, then to the server. "Where's the ladies' room please?"

He smiled a pleasant smile and pointed with a broad carving knife.

As Karen walked away any sense of relief at being unattended for the first time in months was quickly overcome with dread. She went into the narrow confines of the hallway pointed out with the knife, looked back casually to Alyn and found her smiling and flirting. Karen passed the restroom and made for the front door. There she would find Sam's maître d.'

The unlikely couple saw each other at the same moment. When Mr. Guzimon stepped to help his patron, Karen rushed to keep him in the lobby, away from Alyn's temporarily diverted eyes.

"What is it, my dear? Is there a problem?"

"Yes. No. Not here. Everything is fine. I'm hoping you can help me. I am a friend of Sam Ciampiano's. We had dinner here a couple of times. You seated us."

The maître d' ignored the name. "Miss, I seat everyone. We have thousands of guests a week. I'm sorry, but I—"

"Pretorian."

"Pardon me, Miss?"

"Pretorian. Sam said to tell you, 'Pretorian.' They protect the king."

"Caesar."

"Yes! Caesar. And... I'm sorry, this may sound even crazier, but I had half of a driver's license. Sam's license. But I don't have it with me. I wouldn't dare."

"What is your name?"

"Karen."

Mr. Guzimon had her arm and was shuffling her quickly into an ante room off the main foyer. "That is three correct things to say, Miss Karen. I may not be able to help you," he said as he closed the door behind them both and leaned against it. "But I shall try."

"I'm in trouble," Karen said as she grimaced and dropped her head.

"Then you should go to the police. That is their job to—"

"No. Not that kind of trouble. I'm a girl in trouble." She put her hand on the slight baby bump of her stomach. "Sam's girl."

An instinctual comradery between males brought out a pronounced pucker in the man's lower lip as he shook his head no. "That is not good." He would tread no further. Men had left unattended pregnancies in their wake since the beginning of time, most by design and scheduled escape. Sam had plenty of trouble already. He didn't need anything more.

"Maybe you should find a good doctor," the maître d' said, providing the cloak of abortion as a way out for this girl and his *amico* he had help spirit away.

"I will," Karen said too quickly, nervous about being away from the table, before the implication came to her. "No, I won't do that. Listen to me. I don't want anything from Sam except for him to know. I think he deserves to know, would want to know."

Mr. Guzimon looked at her closely and measured the sincerity in her voice and the desperation in her eyes. Both were intense, full of concerned passion, and true. He would relent – to a point.

"Miss Karen. I suspect you should return to your table, but I tell something from the heart of my heart," he said as he pressed both his palms over his chest. "Think of the future this will bring to this boy, Sam, who you speak of and of whom I do not know. If there was such a boy and he was to learn of such news, what would become of it?"

"I don't want anything."

"What would such a boy do for his child?"

"I–"

"He would come. He would come to you. To you and the *bambino*. To do less would make him not the man he is, or if he was a person I knew, the man I would think such a man would be."

The realization hit her in the face like a scalding slap and her stomach as if she had just been kicked. She was sick. Perhaps it was the baby, but more likely the sudden understanding that Sam could not learn about the baby. He mustn't know. If he did, he'd certainly come back. In the arrival he'd be met not by a woman and child who loved him, but by armed federal officers who would likely kill him.

Sam couldn't rush to save her. Perhaps that is what she had secretly longed for though her words pretended to lead elsewhere. He could not rescue her and their child – be a knight on a prancing white horse. He mustn't. It would be a waste of a life. It shouldn't happen. Couldn't happen. Wouldn't happen.

The maître d' had summed up Karen's future with Sam in an instance of brutal clarity with the benefit of distance. Her love for Sam and now their baby had held her too close to the request she had been ready to make. She hadn't seen the true inevitability until this very moment. Karen held her stomach, felt the bump, and nodded. Her eyes were welling anguish.

"You should return to your companion," Mr. Guzimon offered as a first step toward her uncertain future.

Karen's throat was tight and parched. She couldn't answer, but nodded again which dislodged the tears. She hit them with the heel of her palms and drove them from her cheeks and spilled back through the lobby leaving the maître d' alone with too much information.

The bottom of Alyn's wine glass was pointed at the ceiling when Karen emerged from the ladies room in earnest having washed her face and dried her eyes. She was rattled, but loathed to show it.

To Alyn it seemed as though it was a magic trick in that as she lowered her empty glass and looked over its lip, Karen had reappeared in her seat. "Oh," she said, genuinely startled, before she noticed Karen's still puffy eyes. "Are you alright?"

"It's just the morning thing, I guess. I'm fine now."

"The sangria is amazing," Alyn said as she jumped topics with an air of nonchalant ease. "Have you thought about what you'll do? I can make that call as soon as you're ready."

Karen was still reeling beneath the surface, but was as honest as her current state would allow. "I can't do that."

The maître d' appeared. "Are you ready to order, ladies?" He discreetly placed a glass of ice water with a delicately carved lemon twist balanced inside, on the edge of the table near Karen.

The unlikely couple ordered from the lunch menus and handed them to their host. As if he were perpetuating a magician's trick of misdirection, the maître d' fanned the leather bound menus, thanked his patrons, and slipped Karen's sangria to the most distant corner of the colorful multi-table-clothed layered table. The sangria server reappeared with fresh warm bread and placed it in the center of the table between Karen and her wine.

"You are in very capable hands," Mr. Guzimon said as he rested a hand on the young man's shoulder. "Thank you for the pleasure of meeting you. Enjoy your meal. Good day, ladies."

The diners took turns reaching into the basket and tore off pieces of the soft bread. Karen's thoughts were her own and she moved absently. Alyn however, found her attention pulled toward the water glass and the banished sangria meant for Karen. The sleight of hand had been imperfect.

"So," Alyn said between nibbles at the bread. "You're going to have the baby."

"Yes. After that, I don't know."

"What don't you know?"

"Oh... nothing. It's just a lot to take in, you know? Having a baby. It wasn't exactly planned, as you might have gathered."

Alyn reached across the table and took Karen's glass of sangria. She raised it in toast. "Well, you won't want this then. Here's to you." She took a sip. "I couldn't do it – be a mother. Wow. I'm sure it was a shock for your beau. How'd he take it?" Alyn sipped the wine again and looked over the rim for an answer.

"He... I... I haven't told him yet. I'd like to do it face to face." Karen wasn't lying.

"I suppose that's best in a delicate situation such as this." Alyn took another healthy sip. "My, that's delicious. These people are wizards." She caught herself as she saw Karen pick up her water. "I'm sorry. I'm rubbing it in. I'll stop."

"No, no. Enjoy it. You deserve it. It's been tough going down here. You're probably glad to be headed home."

"It hasn't been easy. But that's true of all of us." Alyn changed gears quickly. "You know, I understand some people aren't comfortable with the notion of an abortion, but there are other things, like adoption."

Karen baulked for only a breath. She was still distracted by the echoing words of the maître d' in her head. "I grew up in foster care. It wasn't that nice." The recollection crossed the table and momentarily cooled Alyn's focus on the movement of the glasses. "My father was killed somewhere in Kuwait before I was born, but he was a contractor, not in the military. They hadn't even gotten married yet. My mother died when I was thirteen. Cancer, so you don't have to wonder. It bothers me a lot, but what can you do? I wasn't planning to start my family in such a haphazardly similar way."

Alyn reached over and covered Karen's hand. "It's not the same," Alyn said as her shot fell further from the mark than she could know. "You have someone. Your mother didn't." She smiled a genuine smile. "Your baby has a father."

She squeezed Karen's fingers and let go, returning to her sangria. "You don't mention him though. We've been here over three months and you haven't told him? I can scarcely believe it. Not even a hint? I'll stop talking. It's none of my affair. If there's something I can do, let me know." Alyn produced her business card and quickly jotted down her cell number on the back. "Call me."

Karen took the card and rested it on the edge of the table tucked beneath the leading edge of the top table cloth. She breathed deep and tried to clear her head. Across the table, Alyn's was spinning. She covertly watched the maître d' as he passed through the dining room with new guests. When the luncheon was complete, she beckoned their waiter.

"Excuse me," Alyn said when Karen had slipped off to the restroom again in earnest. "The maître d' was a delight. What's his name?"

18

John LaRoy closed his eyes and rested his head back against the rumbling wall of the C-130 as it lifted off. Karen had her head between her knees. She was certain she'd vomit the water she'd sipped for breakfast onto the wide floor. Helfer Oakes was sitting next to her, shaking with the plane, but rubbing her back, trying to help. When the cargo carrier leveled off, so did Karen's stomach.

The noise of the impromptu passenger compartment made conversation difficult. Karen's green gills made it impossible. After an hour in the air she managed a slight smile and thanked Helfer for his encouragement if nothing else. LaRoy had yet to open his eyes though he was a long weary road removed from any restful sleep.

When they touched down, there were stout handshakes and an exchange of business cards, but no long goodbyes. LaRoy took Oakes to FBI headquarters with him, and left Karen to search for her car – parked in a distant, nearly empty lot over three months before. She made two stops on the way home – one at the grocery store and the other to pick up a new phone. At home, she tucked away the food, plugged in the phone, showered, laid down, and cried.

Helfer Oakes was comfortably overwhelmed nestled in the unending labyrinth that was the FBI's labs. LaRoy had provided him with a miniscule cube and limited credentials. He passed a full body scanner going in and leaving the building. His phone and wallet were locked in a storage bin at the reception area. It was tight security, but expected and it was a small inconvenience for the thrill of working at FBI HQ. Jack had arranged it as a bone for the work Helfer had done, but also hoping against hope his guy could scare up a wild break like he did with first finding Clayton Rand.

After his initial check-in, Helfer was handed over to the watchful wandering eye of Jason Meyer who curtailed his access further by channeling everything Oakes reviewed through his office. Meyer countered the DA's intent by providing stacks of paper reports and not direct hands-on access to evidence. Two weeks later, frustrated and numb from reviewing neatly typed accounts of examinations, Helfer asked to see the hard drive found on the Congressman who had succumbed in his own driveway after his sins had been revealed. He was rewarded when Meyer walked into his cube along with a technician. Each carried at least six reams of paper. The twin stacks – each over a foot tall – were unceremoniously plopped on Helfer's small desk.

The technician abruptly left while Helfer stared at the piles and at Jason. "What is–"

"The Congressman's hard drive," Meyer said smiling.

"Wouldn't the physical drive been easier to carry? You've sacrificed an entire redwood."

"The drive is still being examined. This will have to suffice. Enjoy." Meyer stepped away and returned as quickly. "Remember – no copies. Nothing leaves the building. Any concerns, come to me." He vanished down the maze of halls.

Helfer ran his finger up the stack, sighed, and sat back. It wasn't long and he was trying to call Tampa on a phone that had a label taped to the handset. It read, 'This is a recorded line.' In another moment he had been patched through the FBI switchboard to Jack's office.

"How you making out up there, Oakes? They treating you okee-doe-key?"

"They're fine."

"You find me a smoking gun yet?"

"Not yet, but I wanted to ask you," Helfer said as he looked again at the mountain of paper. "How long do you want me to stay here? I mean, how much time have I got?"

Jack eased back in his chair. "I dunno. How much time you need? Another week or so?"

"There's a lot of evidence. It's a big case."

"Yea, well, keep it confined to Rand. Work up something on him."

"Got it. I don't think I can finish in a week though."

"Give it a shot. Call me next week some time. Take a big swing, Oakes, but don't kill yourself. The Feds have probably squeezed everything out of it already. I thought it might be good for you to see how the other half lives. Keep us in the loop."

Helfer exchanged his phone for the top inch of paper from the first stack and began leafing through code.

As Jack hung up on his end, across town, Mr. Guzimon had the restaurant's phone to his ear and was listening to the line ring. A woman glanced at her caller ID and answered. "*Zio?*"

"Yes, it's me," he said in a half whisper.

"What's happening down there?"

"No news from the papers."

"I understand."

"But there is something more." He hesitated.

"Go on."

The maître d' hesitated. "I have called few times only. When he died. I knew you would want to know."

"I did. And now this latest business. Thank you."

"There is something more now."

"More trouble for him?"

"Ah, if he were to know, yes, but he will not know."

"What is it, *Zio*?"

"He had a friend here. A good friend. A close friend. Very pretty."

"A girlfriend? Are you certain?"

"Of course! I am old, but not so old to not know when lovers are at my table. I see a couple and can tell you how many times they have been out or how long they have been married or the depth of *amore*. Ah, these two. Such *affetto profondo*." He baulked again. "Do you still know *la lingua Italiana* or do you keep your back to your country as you do your family?"

It was her turn at silence. "That was thirty years ago. Don't start."

"Yes, and in those years I have called you two times – to tell you when a boy comes to trouble, when there was a death, and now I call to tell you there will be a life."

"What are you talking about?"

"The girl. The girl will have a baby."

"Why call to tell me that? What do you expect me to do?"

"I am not angry. I know why you left. Ah, but now. But now there is another chance. It is redemption, Marian. It is God's chance at redemption."

"I need no redemption, old man. Thank you, but you needn't call again."

"I don't trust the phones. It is an old habit. Mind the post. The particulars will arrive."

"You needn't bother, *Zio*–"

"Ah, it is no bother."

"Please–"

Guzimon shouted for the first time in memory. "This is your blood, Marian!"

"It was blood that drove me away! You forget. You forget what I saw him do to people. I wasn't going to live with him. He was a monster."

"He never harmed you."

"Only a matter of time."

"Or anyone else who did not need it or expect the same. He was no monster. And he raised a fine son. The boy has no tie to the business."

"I doubt that. I sincerely doubt that. If not, he wouldn't be in trouble now."

They were both listening to quiet phones.

"Ah, I have made the call my heart told me I should make. There is my blood in that child the same, but I am an old man. Ah, I will send a name and what I can know. If you walk away again, it stays with me. I will do what I can. *Ciao*, Marian. *Ciao*."

Another call was happening at almost the same time and was centered on the same topic but from a vastly different perspective. It was Karen's first from her new phone, though she'd managed to transfer her old number. She had an appointment with her OB-GYN in a week. It would show her tired, but healthy. The baby was fine though the doctor admonished her for waiting so long to come in. Karen explained the minimum via the entire first trimester spent in Tampa working. The endeavor was the provided reason she was worn down and beat up, but the work aspect revealed less than half the true root cause. The emotional toll only showed on her pillow, left damp each night.

With Sam gone and Clayton digitally underground, Tampa's role in The New Illuminati continued to wane. Other parts of the country flourished with activity. Indicted attorney generals fell into Illuminati snares that had real teeth, unlike the manicured criminal court circuses they had thought to dance through. Mayors of cities with populations from three thousand to three million found themselves bankrupted by other hackers who operated from the minor leagues of Clayton's realm. Their skills were enough though, and the money taken to feather nests and for hookers and junkets with no purpose, was drained with the click of a mouse.

Super PACs were being fleeced. Lobbyists and their bed fellows were being sent The New Illuminati symbol then summarily shot. Snipers of assorted skills exhibited their best efforts — some deadly, others inaccurate, but all leaving wounds or whistling whispers that cut equal scars which spoke of a landscape that had changed.

Grown men and women gnashed their teeth, cried in the dark over their losses and in public for justice that had already been dealt out by a public that celebrated The Illuminati's symbols as the months passed under fresh headlines, tracked by nervous politicians. One of the guiltiest of the innumerable members of Congress under covert investigation – by the FBI or their own ethics committee – put an end to the stress when the anxiety poured out through a bullet hole in the side of his head. As liberal and conservative media jousted with their patented and timed cycle of responses related to the killing, the coup de grâce for the wicked came when Illuminati concussion explosions with no physical projectiles, detonated at the funeral of the corrupted corpse. Like minded members of Congress in attendance ran over the dead man's widow to save themselves from nothing but loud noise in a televised display of their selfishness.

While the body count trickled upward, the message that The Illuminati could reach into their midst was compelling and crushing. Phones in the offices of the FBI were ringing madly from Congress while the ones in the hands and pockets of influence and money toting lobbyists went quiet. The tide had turned.

Helfer had returned to Tampa to the more rudimentary work that waited in his small lab. His debriefing with Jack had lasted all of three minutes. He had reviewed what he could in the time allotted and found nothing. When he suggested a complete analysis would require another month, Jack laughed it off as if the case were not the encompassing national pastime. Jack may have meant to say, "Let it go," but whether it was a simple mistake or something more Freudian, it came out as, "Let them go." The reaction left Helfer confused. Not long after touchdown at Tampa International, he sought out Marcus as a sounding board.

"Jack wanted you to have the exposure – get experience," Marcus explained as the two walked up the hall of the civic building. "Look at the trip as a reward of sorts. You were able to go to Washington. Did you take in the sights? I could wander the monuments and museums of the mall for days."

"No, there was a lot to go through. I didn't get finished. Think he'd let me go back?"

"You want to?"

"Yes. Reports from new cases keep coming in. I wonder about a connection we might be missing. These guys will trip sooner or later."

"They will, but we have two problems, at least two problems. Number one is the volume. Cases are streaming in from what Cal shares with me. And second, we're not after one person any longer, like Clayton Rand. Probably not even one group. From what Cal suggests, there are hundreds, maybe thousands of individuals or small cells executing their own plans. They share the framework of a common agenda somewhere in the philosophical tree and the symbols and motto, but as far as a real connection? That's doubtful. It makes unraveling the massive ball of knots almost impossible."

"If I could get a couple of more weeks, maybe I could get through the Congressman's hard drive at least. That's a Florida case. Do you think the boss would let me go back to DC for that?"

"It's a Florida case, but even it isn't one of ours."

"But if there's a wrinkle somewhere, it's probably there."

"You have a hunch on something?"

"Not really. I don't do hunches that well, but the masses and masses of data that moved in that case offer the widest array for potential errors. I have some time off coming. I could go on vacation – see the museums between reviewing the data."

"There's no need to go that far. I'll get you a couple more weeks after you clean up the cases on your desk. I think the locals criminals heard you were out of town and have been taking advantage. Catch up and I'll get you back to DC. How's that sound?"

"Perfect. Thanks, Marcus, but can I ask one more thing?"

"Always."

"Is the boss still hot for these guys? He seems to have cooled off a little in the chase."

"He's getting his second wind. Toss him a bone from Washington and he'll run with it."

A week after Helfer had fulfilled his commitment to Marcus, he was in a coach seat bound for Reagan International Airport. The flight was quicker and quieter than his last ride up on the C-130 and was also minus Karen doubled over next to him. The recollection caused him to make a note to look her up when he landed.

The week before Helfer landed in DC, Karen had slipped into her first maternity uniform. There were whispers, but nothing serious. The law protected her rights. For now.

A friendly reunion would have to wait as the second stack of printed data from the dead Congressman's hard drive took precedence. Helfer had left Jason with the notion his return was imminent, though that was hardly the case as he turned in his temporary ID. When Helfer took up his old temporary post, calls were still pouring in from government officials wanting answers in front of the press, but protection behind closed doors.

The pages of the hardcopy computer drive turned with a slow rhythm that picked up momentum as Helfer became more familiar with the computer language behind his very physical scan. He gave his eyes breaks and looked at evidence examination results and log entries on a temporary computer setup. He scrutinized so many screens, his eyes jumped straight to the boxes that carried the vital information. Throughout his days to weeks-long scouring, he fluctuated from marvel at the volumes of work to disgust at the waste of paper and disappointment in what he began to recognize as his limited access. His second go-round would expire before he could wade through it all. He understood there would be no third attempt. He worked longer days and increased his efficiency until his jotted notes became almost indecipherable. He was running out of time. Upstairs in the FBI building, John LaRoy was running out of manpower. He was also dealing with a major side effect.

"Of course, I understand that," John was speaking intently into his phone in a one sided conversation that his expression demonstrated was clearly not going his way. "My phone rings every five minutes. We're pulling in people from foreign posts – Puerto Rico, Canada... I know... Yes, sir, but it's even more important than ever to maintain tight security. We can't have her running roughshod... Yes, sir, but she may have tipped our hand by forcing the issue with our targets. That exposes... Yes, sir, I'm well aware... No, I don't agree... She's coming to DC to assist with the concussion bombing. Would you consider a review at the minimum? I'd like it in her record... Of course it's not personal. This is maintaining the dignity and professionalism of... Very good. I'll see to it. Thank you, sir."

The handset of the internal hard-wired phone hit the cradle too hard and jumped out onto the desk. LaRoy replaced it with an absolute certainty of measured force.

In Atlanta, Alyn had retreated and regrouped to battle LaRoy's charge of violating protocol by conducting a private investigation of Ciampiano and Rand. She was quite certain recent events and her many favors would stymie LaRoy entirely. Now she was waiting at a Delta terminal gate to board a plane for DC. She sent a brief text. "Leaving for Dulles flight 1195 eta 332 Dinner?"

In less than twenty seconds she had her answer. "I'll pick you up."

The top of Helfer's temporary desk was coated with classified documents of mixed ilk. The bulk was the still cumbersome, but diminishing pile of hardcopy printouts of the digitize coding that made up the contents of the congressman's computer drive. Helfer continued to spell his brain by thumbing through the simple evidence logs. He began to piece together actions from across the country. While each event was ominous and interesting, he confined himself to the Florida activities attributed to The New Illuminati. He knew he'd run out of time before he ran out of places to look. The volume was too immense.

In the master logs he read late entries from John LaRoy. Helfer saw a lot of his boss in LaRoy and liked him for the same reasons, but was also intimidated by the gruff no-nonsense approach that was also reminiscent of his District Attorney chief. Their tenor was oddly refreshing yet seemingly so out of step in the politically correct charged workplace of the present day.

The final two lines on the sheet were both from LaRoy. The first listed a phone with the name "Lt. K. Auburn" next to it. The second entry was "paperback book, Lt. K. Auburn." Neither had a request for any analysis, in fact, the phone had a note, "to be released to Lt. K. Auburn JAG" accompanied by LaRoy's initials and the resolved/release box had been checked.

"I wondered what happen to that stuff," Helfer said aloud as he ran his finger up and down the list rechecking. Other items carried a reference to 'TPD continuity,' demonstrating that the Tampa Police Department had made the initial recovery, but nothing suggested the origination of the phone and the book. "Huh," he muttered to no one.

Helfer's continued leafing vacillated from intense concentration to superfluous scans of mundane machine language as he returned to the congressman's hard drive printout. A germ of an idea had been forming since Marcus had suggested he go to Washington. When Clayton Rand first came to light, Helfer recalled someone saying that Rand couldn't be guilty merely because everyone else was innocent. It had hung with him. He began to apply it from the moment he touched the first evidence at this desk within FBI headquarters. Helfer looked for the absent pieces as much as the standout sore thumbs. He did a hardcopy scan looking for the gap or probability – much like his original leap for the DA when he did the comparison of televised coverage of the burning cypress trees that had ignited The New Illuminati. Only a limited set could have seen that newscast. Cross referenced with abilities, the set narrowed itself to Clayton Rand. The FBI would have skillfully torn into the multitude and myriad of evidence linked – in truth or speculation – to The New Illuminati. Helfer wouldn't retrace the forensics of one of the finest and best equipped labs in the world. Instead, he would look at the comparison of closed sets of information and let the overlay expose the invisible.

In point of fact, the process had taken days, weeks, but when the worm began to turn, a vibration became a spin then a dashing tornado of crushing, crumbling, unstoppable, but motionless momentum. And there it was – the clue, the answer – laid bare on the temporary desk surrounded by reams of computer gobbledygook, yet to Helfer, it was suddenly crystal clear.

Peering up from the desk was the hard drive's system log file. It was a snapshot of activity meant to be retained – for an instant or forever. As with most systems and programs, a backup log file existed alongside. What Helfer had stumbled across was not what was there, it was what was missing. In the backup file, several lines of code occurred that were absent in the original system log. The language indicated a massive data dump was happening. He thought it must be videos or photographs to be so large and recalled the Everest sized heaps of kiddie porn sent to the press from the dead congressman's computer. The volume was so great it had gone into a buffer overflow as the processor pushed the wide load to a third party server timed to release to the media. The smoking gun rested in the hands above the keyboard at the other end of those missing lines of code. In the backup log file, the gun was still smoldering. He stared, thought, and replayed what he knew of the timing of that day. Then he smelled the smoking powder from the gun.

Oakes was up and almost running down the hall to Jason Meyer's office. Twin sheets of code – twins, but not identical – waved from his hand like luffing sails in high wind. He hit Jason's open door almost breathless.

"Got a sec?" he pleaded between gasps.

"Sure," Jason answered interrupted and bemused.

"Here it is." Helfer waved the pages as he came in and spread the simple sheets in front of Jason with two hands and pressed them flat several times as though ironing a shirt. "It was in the system log file backup. Look at this." His finger skated and danced ahead of the instruction making him difficult to follow. "Everything matches up. Fine. Fine. Fine. Until you hit up against this monstrous dump. This has to be the photographs of all those children. It's so big it rolls into the buffer overflow. Whoever triggered this was a wizard, so I couldn't see how he missed this."

"Where's this from again?"

"The hard drive of the congressman. I remember they found it in his briefcase. Well, that's why the backup log file doesn't match the original system log file. The congressman literally pulled the drive out of his machine – physically yanked it out! Even powered down, it would have been connected to the hacker, but once it got pulled out of the machine, everything, and I mean everything, stopped. Right then. Pop. Done. That instant! A dump that big would have taken a few seconds at least, maybe longer. It's a safe bet the hacker's processor outpaced the congressman's. So, while the hacker is mopping up his tracks like the genius he is, the congressman disconnects his hard drive from the world and turns it into a paperweight. The tracks never get completely wiped away. The hacker doesn't even know it. He backs out wiping his prints as he does, but the drive is gone – physically gone – before he can finish. Wow! A few seconds more and he'd have done it. Maybe milliseconds. I need the product and model numbers off the hard drive to calculate–"

"Slow down a minute." Jason held up one of the pages. "This is the backup systems log?"

"Sure thing. Half blind luck, I know. There might be more on the drive. If we run a scan for–"

"You think this ping would lead to an IP address? That'd be a sloppy hack, wouldn't it?"

"Normally, yes. But Rand, that is, the hacker, wouldn't expect the mark to pull the hard drive out. Lots of people can get in systems. The real pros can get out and not let you know they were there. This guy is incredibly good, but he couldn't anticipate the timing of the congressman pulling that drive." Helfer pointed to the pages. "This is probable cause."

"Maybe."

Helfer finally did slow. In fact he stopped. "Why not?"

"Is there something that makes you think we haven't seen this?"

"Well, I hadn't heard anything."

"There's likely a reason for that too."

"So, you have this already?"

Jason motioned to a chair. "Sit down a minute, Helfer. Oh, would you close the door first please?"

The clicking of the door closing was the starting pistol in Jason's race to lie. "Nothing, and that means nothing, I am about to share with you leaves this room. You good with that?"

"Naturally, but why all the cloak and–"

"Even if it hits close to home?"

"What do you mean?"

"Tampa. The District Attorney's Office."

"I don't get it."

Jason leaned forward perpetuating the illusion of taking Helfer into a great confidence. "You did an outstanding job coming up with Clayton Rand. I really don't think anyone else could have done that – had that insight. I've already talked to some people about you. We think you'd make a fine addition to our lab."

"No fooling?"

"No fooling. That is, if you'd be interested."

"Sure I am. What an opportunity. Wow."

"But there's a few catches and this is where it's unsettling. It's also where I must require your strictest confidence. Nothing I say in the next few minutes can go back to Tampa. If it should, that 'opportunity' you just referenced, disappears because we'll know you can't be trusted with sensitive information. More plainly said, there could likely be criminal charges levied. Even more specifically, make that 'more' criminal charges."

"Against who?"

"Do I have your word, Helfer? Your solemn word nothing I tell you gets repeated to Tampa?"

Helfer straightened a little in his chair. "You have my word."

Jason took a deep breath and bought himself the time and leverage he would need to extend his fringe benefits with Alyn indefinitely. By the time Helfer walked out of Jason's office almost an hour later, he'd been convinced of Jack's ghosted involvement in The Illuminati and his imminent federal indictment on obstruction charges. The FBI already had the information from the backup systems log, but weren't prepared to share it with Tampa for security reasons. In the coming half-staggered walk back to his tiny office, Helfer forced the last pieces of the confounding puzzle into places they never would have fit otherwise. There was Jack's off handed comments about The Illuminati cleaning up politics which Helfer shared with Meyer who greedily built on it with a fictitious foundation of evidence that was struck from thin air. When Helfer thought out loud and mentioned the phone and Steinbeck book Jack had asked him to examine minus any evidence log or case numbers, Jason suppressed his interest, but made an anxious note. He underscored it when Helfer indicated what he assumed Jason to already know that both pieces had now been delinquently entered into FBI evidence.

For his guarantee of silence, Jason granted Helfer a look at the hard drive to gather make, model, and system capability only. "I'll send the evidence room a memo. Go ahead." Any further results would continue to come to Jason directly. "This is strictly federal business," Jason reminded as he walked Helfer to the door. "There is no local involvement or jurisdiction. Can I make that any clearer?"

"I've got it. Strictly federal."

"Thanks, Helfer. You're going to come through this in a wonderful position. You just don't know about people. There's hidden agendas everywhere, you know what I mean?"

Helfer did know. He had found Jason rude and stuffy from the beginning. Now he found him confusing and watched and listened as Jason stepped on his own lies, stubbing his toes on contrivances as soon as he told them.

Helfer had his own share of confusion and needed some time and a new sounding board to straighten it all out. He would have dismissed nearly all of what Jason said had it not been for the echo of Jack's own words and actions. The DA had lent a thread of truth to concerns over trust, integrity, and allegiance to law. Helfer couldn't use Marcus or even Cal Denti in Tampa to voice a hesitant, likely unfathomable question because of their relationship with Jack.

Meanwhile Jason was on the phone to the evidence locker. He requested an immediate download of everything from Karen's phone and wanted the paperback book sent up to his office. When the download arrived, he leafed through pages of numbers, location, and coordinates attached to every call Karen had made or received. When the Steinbeck book arrived, Jason found the handwriting analysis from the Florida Department of Law Enforcement still folded inside the front cover.

Helfer had settled back in at his desk and had dropped his smoking gun back on the pile of papers and looked at the evidence log referring to the same pieces Jason was now working. Next to the phone entry it read, 'To be released. Lt. K. Auburn JAG.'

"This is strictly federal business," Jason had said. Karen was federal, friendly, and in the know. She would be a congenial ally and a sure filter.

Helfer orchestrated his own agenda right then and there. He took the copy of the evidence log, along with the knowledge that Meyer had sent a message that Helfer could handle, but not remove, the congressman's hard drive, and took an elevator to the lab's vaults.

The evidence room was heavily secured. Nothing moved without the scan of a bar code and more. Meyer had called and followed with a trackable email to allow Helfer access to the hard drive. When he produced the evidence log and referenced the phone he thought he'd gotten from Jack in Tampa, the technician, speaking through thick glass, brought it up in their system and saw it was released. He made a call via an intercom and in less than a minute another worker brought Karen's phone and the hard drive up. Given Helfer's temporary identification and the release by Director LaRoy, a plastic bag with an imprinted bar code, holding Karen's cell phone, was scanned and slid through a slot like a secure bank teller's. A receipt accompanied it. "Sign your life away."

Helfer signed without thinking, but then picked up the bag and looked at the phone. "Are you sure this is the one? I remember it was a cheapo flip style."

The tech looked at his screen again. "No. That's the one that's been released. If you're looking for something else, you're shit outa luck. Where're you from?"

"Tampa."

"I mean, what agency?"

"District Attorney's Office."

"Local DA? We don't get many of them. How long will you need the other piece, Tampa? It says here it can't leave the locker." An electronic lock buzzed and the tech pushed open a steel mesh gate next to the glass. "Come on in."

"Just a few minutes," Helfer said as he took Karen's phone, looked at the printed case number on the plastic bag and put it in his pocket. He stepped through the gate holding the evidence log with LaRoy's signature in his hand as he took the palm sized hard drive. "I need to see the system on it. Do you have a replica docking station I can plug it into?"

The one man lab from Tampa soon found himself at a work table surrounded by an assortment of cords and cables that would have made Medusa's hairdresser proud. He sat the device and his paperwork on the table and plugged a flat webbed pin connector into the hard drive and saw a remote monitor come to life. He tried a few corded and remote mini keypads until he was on the correct one and typed away until he found the numbers he wanted, the system, and its capabilities. A few notes later, he was finished.

Other lab techs were coming and going. The talk alternated from absent, to light, to loud, boring, and harsh in equal measures around him. Helfer looked over the monitor and kept typing. No one was paying him any mind. He commanded the hard drive to whirl and was looking at the recent tracking to see what had been done to the drive by the keepers of the lab. Several more coded commands and the drive whizzed its way to a blur of a scrolling screen that was the digitized version of the stacks of logs on his desk that had yielded the tracks on the buffer overflow and the backup log.

"If I only had more time with this thing," he thought as the language flashed by too quick to read. With the searches and scans, he'd never get anything beyond the front gate. Ready to give up, he reached for the drive and LaRoy's signature caught his eye. Helfer nudged the still whirling box aside and saw the reference to Karen's phone – not the simple flip he'd expected, but a high tech device with capabilities most users only scratched the surface of.

The monitor kept scrolling and dancing while Helfer looked around the snake pit until he found a length of innocuous gray cord. He typed a few commands and surreptitiously pulled the phone from his pocket. He opened the plastic bag and slid the phone beneath its receipt. Glancing around while appearing to stretch his neck, he saw he was momentarily alone. The gray cord crawled beneath the paperwork and docked with the phone. The other end found a panel of ports that ran to the monitor.

The hesitation was fleeting. He clicked the keys and the phone lit up. Helfer grabbed it so fast he jerked the cables and cords and yanked the hard drive from its temporary port. The clunk, Helfer's abysmal fake coughing, and his hands suffocating Karen's phone against his leg muffled the powering up salute of the cell. Just as quick, he shoved it back under his papers and was back at the keyboard.

The evidence tech stuck his head around a corner from his station at the front of the cage. "You okay there, Tampa?"

"I'm good. Good. Swallowed funny or something."

"Don't hurt yourself on my watch. I don't want to have to fill out any paperwork."

They shared weak grins and Helfer returned to the keyboard, focused and typing with abandon. He erased nearly everything on Karen's phone in a few strokes. A few more and he had opened every crevice it had for data. In less than a minute he had the hard drive humming again as it regurgitated the system log file into Karen's phone. A bar on the monitor screen began turning and ticking off the download.

Helfer's eyes were making rapid rounds from the monitor's timing of the download, the cell, and the hard drive.

"You done with that, bud?"

Helfer literally jerked his eyes up and saw the tech looking at him over the monitor. "Two minutes."

"I can get you the model, system, and all the guts in less than that. Here, let me show you."

The tech took a step to come around the table.

Helfer reached up and switched the monitor off. "Not necessary, but thanks. I'm done," he said as the download continued without the benefit of being able to see when it was finished. "Hey, I was going to ask though. We've been seeing some new languages come across," he stalled. "Not just simple stuff like PHP, C&C++, Assembly, but some real exotics. You guys probably get them all the time."

"We get it all. It depends on the target. Finance is the big deal for newbies – they think they'll get paid, but they use pretty simple stuff."

"What are the hot targets?"

"Info – same as always."

"Knowledge is power. I guess that never changes."

"Mostly military egress. Political. Some Fortune 500 stuff, but the hot item is pharmaceuticals."

"We get a bunch of drug cases every week in Tampa."

The tech laughed. "Not that level. Ours are hacks to see who's taking what. Legit dope. Lists and email addresses make pre-screened targets for marketing. It's a big issue right now."

"That's way above my speed limit," Helfer smiled. "I still work bounced checks."

The tech lab chuckled with him, but beneath the laugh, Helfer heard the whizzing hard drive spin to quiet. The download was complete.

"You're close to MacDill, if you ever get any military spillage, give us a call. Maybe you can tweak me a trip to help out the local office. But do it in February... please."

"I'm on it."

The tech reached for the hard drive. "All set?"

"Done," Helfer said as he asked about the Washington Redskins versus his Tampa Bay Buccaneers to misdirect while he unplugged cords and shoved them back into winding messes of cables, webs, and power cords. He was ready, but Karen's phone was still beneath the paperwork. The hard drive was handed over. "I'd bet this is nickels and dimes to what's behind door number three over there," Helfer said as he mimicked *Let's Make a Deal* and pointed across the room to a heavy steel door with a combination lock so large it resembled a bank vault.

The tech turned his head and Helfer picked up his evidence log and the phone and shoved them all in his pocket as he stepped around the work station and fell in behind his guide.

"You'd win that bet. There's things in there that haven't seen the light of day in decades. Climate controlled. Beaucoup security. If a cockroach walked across the floor in there, we'd know."

Helfer wanted out. "Wild." He was working steadily toward the steel gate, the main door, and out. "After I get a few more years under my belt, I'm applying. I'd like to work here."

"We're always searching for talent."

"Jason Meyer said he'd give me a good review." Almost out. The phone in his pocket was heavy and felt like a bulge awkwardly sticking out.

"That might help," the tech said fishing. "You know him very good?"

"Just from working this Illuminati case." The paperwork rustled loudly as if screaming from his pocket as he heard the mesh gate close and latch behind him.

"It won't hurt, but you'd do better if you wore a skirt and heels. He loves the ladies, but don't we all."

"No argument from me." He was almost to the door. "Hey, thanks for your help. I appreciate it."

"Nothing to it."

Helfer reached for the heavy latch of the door that could withstand a thermal blast.

"Hey!" The tech yelled and Helfer's hand jerked. He was a breath from running, throwing the phone in a trash bin like an idiot, and crumpling under the weight of a half dozen Marine guards. "You have to go through debrief and be scanned. Just in case you pocketed the President's old Blackberry or picked up the Magic Bullet and slipped it in your pocket. It only takes a few minutes."

"Oh?" Helfer turned around slowly, the blood draining from his face.

"Go on, get outa here. I'm playing. See you around and stop down if they ever swear you in."

"I will." Helfer was barely breathing as he slipped from the lab and truly stumbled his way back to his desk.

The call across town to another federal agency went through without a hitch. Karen answered sounding strong.

"Lieutenant? Karen? This is Helfer Oakes from Tampa."

"Hi, Helfer. How are you?"

"I'm good. How about you? The last time I saw you, you had a bug or something."

"I've never been a good flyer," Karen said and stood up at her desk and stretched an ache out of her back. Her pregnancy had advanced well along. Her body had stopped revolting and was accustomed to the idea. "What's up with you?"

"Well, I went back to Tampa for a while after our flight, but they let me come back to DC to do some more poking around on The Illuminati. I'm at FBI headquarters right now."

Karen felt herself tense and sat down. "Anything new?"

"Yes, there's some stuff. I think I could fill you in – you're federal."

"I am at that, but is that important?"

"It is to some people. That's part of what I'd like to talk to you about." Helfer picked up Karen's heavily burdened cell phone. "Plus there's a phone here that says it's to be released to you. John LaRoy entered the release himself. I thought I had examined it in Tampa, but it turns out yours is a different one. Mine came from my boss. I don't know how the phone he had is related. It was really clean. I did some triangulation off it, but didn't get far. I won't ask about it as I'm seeing you federal agencies keep your secrets, but it was a pretty cheap phone for whatever you were trying to do with it. I wasn't even sure they still made flip phones any more. I would have figured you'd have the latest high tech smart phone." Helfer caught himself. "Not that you'd be showy about it, just that it would suit you perfect." He was stumbling.

Karen was confused and cautious. "Mine's a smart, not a flip. I'm not sure how high tech it is, but I don't need it. I'm sure they've downloaded everything they could find on it and then some. I just as soon not have it back," Karen said, concealing the sad memory of lost conversations with Sam. "Just throw it away."

"I can't do that. I don't think these people can either unless you came in and signed that it was alright. But you're wrong about them downloading everything. They didn't do any analysis per LaRoy."

Karen perked up, still confused. "Nothing?"

Helfer looked through his papers for the evidence log. "Nothing."

The thought of either an oversight or LaRoy's cover brought Karen's attention in tight. "You're right. Maybe I should pick it up."

"I have it. I could meet you at the front entrance. You'd still have to sign a receipt."

Karen wasn't certain how far Alyn had spread the news of her pregnancy if at all and was content to limit it though the news would come eventually as surely as the baby. As she held the line and framed her next thought, Karen ran through the list of lies in her head. First she concealed the dash to Sam. Then the pregnancy. Now she had to hide the father. All to protect the first failing. It was a fragile triangle.

"I don't want to put you out, Helfer. I never know when my schedule will have me downtown. If you could get it to the front, that'd save me some time." She had no intention of letting the Tampa prosecutors know she was pregnant if she could help it.

"It's not a problem. Call me from the front desk and I'll come up and say hi at least. This may not be the best place to talk about the case anyway. Maybe we could meet some other time before I go back south."

Karen couldn't fight the intrigue. "Have they found Sergeant Ciampiano?"

"Not that I know of, but like I said, federal agencies play their cards close to the vest, as my boss would say."

"They do do that," Karen said lamely as she drifted to thoughts of Sam as she had done each time she felt the growing weight of the baby in her belly.

"You remember my boss, Jack Aaron? What do you think of him?"

Karen was getting used to being torn from feelings of Sam and was quick. "I like him. He reminds me a great deal of LaRoy. I like those old school types. They're usually not the most politically correct people in the room, but you know where you stand with them. I'd like to be thought of that way."

"You're right – you do know where they stand. I just wonder if they ever changed that stance, how you tell?"

This was a confounding call. "I think you could just ask them," Karen said through a hesitation caused by a direction she didn't follow. "They're pretty straight forward."

"I think they're a little intimidating, for me anyways. You know? For me to just ask."

"They bark, but don't bite. You could tell LaRoy anything and know right where you stood and where he stood. Believe me," Karen said as she recalled the pre-flight confession on the tarmac.

Helfer picked up the printout of the backup log and the original system log and found himself staring at the extra lines of code. "Listen. Could we get together for a minute? I'd like you to know about something I've uncovered. I'm only here a couple more days. Do you think you could make it in today?"

"I'm not sure," then she thought of her phone – protected thus far by LaRoy – and an inside track on the investigation and Helfer's new revelation versus the reveal of her baby. It was another tempt of providence she'd have to take. "Yes, I think so. I'll have the desk get in touch with you when I get there."

"Cool. Alright. I'll let you go. Talk to you later.

"Thanks for the call, Helfer. I really appreciate it."

The instant he hung up, his eyes settled again on the oft handled evidence log. Content with his conversation with Karen, he noticed again the reference to the Steinbeck book. He thought about his local handwriting analysis and began to study the simple one line of the record as if it might clear up a sudden question. What was Karen's dedication doing in the newsstand? The early fingerprints were dismissed as careless contamination, but the book was another level of recklessness, if that was what it was.

Now his calling Karen was not so settling. If she were so reckless as to leave a personal book at a potential crime scene, could she be trusted with the contents of the congressman's hard drive? The plan would be amended. Karen immediately became a conduit. She'd have to know some things, but not all. He'd hold back until the clock and the calendar conspired to reveal the truth bound up in the future.

Until then, he'd troll the waters back down the hall in Jason's office. If Jason knew about the handwriting comparison and Karen remained the free woman she was, the book had to have been her ignorance. If the FBI wasn't aware, perhaps she was even complicit. The book was entered into evidence by LaRoy. Yet, unlike the phone, the novel wasn't to be released and to add another perplexing layer, it had no notes for analysis.

"Maybe they're content to use the Florida comparison," Helfer whispered to himself. Or maybe, just maybe, the sanctity of knowledge about a case traversed deeper than the walls of agencies. Perhaps there were walls within walls. Perhaps some in the Bureau knew what others did not.

Helfer was nearly swimming in his self-generated quandary. He'd like to sit and talk it out with Marcus, but first he'd fish.

"Thanks for getting me access to that drive," Helfer was saying from Jason's open doorway.

"No problem. Get what you needed?"

"Yep," he said as he waved a familiar page from the evidence log. "Hey, on this sheet it lists the paperback book from the news stand. It doesn't list the examination. Did you guys do your own or did you go with ours?"

"Hell, I don't know, Helfer. There must be ten thousand pieces of evidence on cases with probable ties to the Illuminati. Let's see."

As Jason held out his hand, Helfer carried the single page around his desk and laid it down. He pointed to the line.

"This one. It's a paperback book. Old one. First edition, I think."

"You examined it?"

"Me and the Florida Department of Law Enforcement."

Jason had turned to his computer and was bringing up the soft copy. "Anything good?"

"Yea. I read it in high school or college. I can't remember. Everyone has to read *Of Mice and Men*. I thought that was really good so I found another Steinbeck. *Sweet Thursday* is the sequel to *Cannery Row*. Everyone knows that one from the movie, but the movie was really a combination of the two novels." Helfer had been so engrossed in his reading history he hadn't realized Jason had stopped and was staring at him impatiently.

"Oakes?"

"Yea?"

"Anything good in the examination of the evidence?"

"Oh. I'm sorry. I thought you were—"

"I know. My fault for not being more specific. What'd you find?" Jason plied the young man while the book at the heart of the discussion sat on his desk beneath Karen's phone records.

The embarrassing misstep threw Helfer from his well-balanced seat and he spilled his ace. "We did a handwriting compare. It was the JAG Lieutenant's. Karen Auburn."

Jason didn't twitch. "She contaminated several pieces. Sloppy... Very sloppy," he said as he zeroed in on the digital evidence entries. "Find a lesson in that somewhere. Don't ever let that happen to you. Especially if you want to get in this place. Those screw ups will follow you forever." Jason turned quickly from his monitor. "Any other tidbits from Tampa?"

"That's it," Helfer said, now anxious to leave.

"Let me know if you run across anything more from those hard drive specs."

Helfer hustled to the door, but Jason's voice stopped him. "How much longer are you in town?"

"Just a couple of more days. I have to get back to my, you know, whatever, other cases."

"Let's have lunch or dinner or something before you go. You're a good man, Oakes. I hope it works out for you here."

"Thanks, Jason."

As Helfer wandered back to his hole in the wall, he cursed himself for his miscue and the subsequent tossing out of the handwriting report. Still, Jason had taken it in stride. The lack of reaction and Karen's freedom meant she had made yet another mistake, just as Jason had railed against. Helfer would use her to ferry out the hard drive data and tease her with enough evidence to get her to share anything she had. This game of politics and the commodity of information was a new field for him and, despite his obvious fumble in Meyer's office, he was loathe to admit he was no good at it.

Back in Meyer's office, people with much more experience and far less scruples were plying the trade with a professional ease found somewhere in the shaded world between a corner lot car salesman and a hedge fund manager. Horse traders and Florida swamp land developers would have been the analogy in the years before Helfer Oakes was born and equally applicable.

"He's the young guy from Tampa," Jason was reminding the person on the other end of his phone. "He's good, I'll grant him that... Good enough to find the needle we couldn't. And he did it in a blizzard of paper that would have blinded anyone else... He's got the proverbial smoking gun, that's what... How about an IP address that points right to Clayton Rand?... No, I'm not kidding. It's in a collateral history log from one of the first cases. I've been checking and rechecking it since this morning. A direct link to Rand's computer. That smoking enough for you? And there's more... Don't worry about what just yet. I'll fill you in, but it's going to cost – big time. Real big... No, I've kept him under wraps here – no phone, lots of searches and scans – nothing in or out. No calls outside the network... Give me some credit. I've had his phone tapped since he came up the last time. His hotel too. Plus I've planted just enough to shake his faith in Tampa. He's not talking. Not yet... That's your department... Are you at your hotel? Short day... I'm coming over... Bullshit, 'not now.' This is huge! I need to get paid... Well, when? How about... That's a long time to wait... One more thing. Clear your calendar for tomorrow night. We better take the kid to dinner and lock him in tight if you want the credit for this... He wants to join the Bureau, so promise him the moon. Hell, if this plays like I know you want it too, you might be able to appoint him to the Academy yourself... Sure, sure. That's still a long time to wait. I suppose I have no choice... See you at eight."

Jason hung up, leaned back, and looked at his watch. "Shit..." He fidgeted for ten seconds then got up in a heated rush and headed to the door. "Washing her hair, my ass. This will make her career. She can wash her hair after I mess it up."

———————

19

A lyn Nuary set her silver and gold encased phone – her perpetual lifeline to the generally jaded facets of her hedonistic world – on the nightstand of her high end hotel room with surprising care for the level of excitement she was feeling. She stayed laying on her side, propped up on one elbow, totally naked with a twisted and damp nine hundred count sheet loosely covering her hips and thighs and a napping man, facing away beside her. She smiled and her eyes, though still locked on the phone, were captivated by a cinematic view in her head of what the future would hold. Cracking The New Illuminati case – which sounded so corny her smiled flashed wider for a moment – would be her crowning achievement. This, and her hips, would ride her well beyond the next rung of the ladder in the Bureau. This would be a position of visible power. It would grant her access to the electoral elite she aspired to join. She'd make the rounds on Sunday morning through the litany of news programs. Within days she'd be quoted and profiled. Her face and body would secure invites long after the initial luster waned and her runaway notoriety would have her booked on every daily talk show. This would be pivotal. From her new perch – high above – she'd hire the obligatory best seller of politico fire brands and she'd transition to the finite realm of the elected power broker elite. It was heady stuff and she was poised.

Alyn spun on her bed and the sheet unwound exposing her ass. Like the rest of her, its proportions would delight any artist who attempted to capture it on canvas and raise the desire of any man whose view prompted fantasies of capturing it against Egyptian cotton. That is how the man currently half-asleep next to her had been reeled in. That butt – crafted, toned, and carved, carefully tanned beneath the nearly invisible and constantly adjusted bikini string to avoid any line – had been the bait, her lips set the hook. What the macho obliviousness of the man wouldn't let him see was that it was *he* who'd been the conquest. Alyn's time on her back was fleeting and what she traded away, she still had when her men were zipping up their pants.

Alyn slid the sheet down only enough to expose the relaxed sinews of her lover's muscular shoulder. While a kiss and a cuddle would have been the call between most couples, Alyn bared her perfect teeth and bit the fleshy part of the shoulder hard enough to rudely wake her mate then piled from the bed, taking the sheet with her leaving the man stunned, smarting, and naked, thrashing for the sheet and its thin protection.

"Hey!" Major Doug Caulden yelled mid-lurch in a misguided swipe to save the sheet.

"Ought oh, too slow." Alyn teased.

The major rubbed his shoulder and tried to see around it as though he expected to find a gash oozing blood. "That hurt!"

"Poor baby... Here," Alyn cooed as she wadded up the sheet and began to crawl back onto the foot of the bed. "Let mommy kiss it and make it all better."

Caulden retreated. "You're not getting near me with those fangs. I thought the stories about you being a pit bull were only urban legend."

"Stop it. That was a love nibble. It wouldn't even make a hickie you could be proud of."

The major lunged for her, but was slapped in the face with the scrunched up sheet. A more playful chase ensued that ended with the two flinging themselves on the bed. The major's shoulder made a miraculous recovery as he ran his own teeth across Alyn's throat and down to her enhanced perfect and perky breasts. Alyn moved as to join the next romp, but took the sheet instead and flung it out wide. She eased Doug away slightly and let the covering float down over them both.

"Easy, soldier. I've got news from the front lines."

"What front line?"

"The Illuminati. It's perfect. Perfect!"

"What is? You're pretty excited whatever it is. I like it." He pushed into her from head to toe.

"Wait. Wait a minute!" Nuary pushed back hard and bounced up to her knees and wrapped herself in the sheet. "I've got him. I've got the little shit."

"Got who?"

"Rand. Clayton Rand. I've got him by the balls."

"What are you taking about? We haven't got anything on him."

"We didn't, that was true. But it's not true any longer, the little prick. He's been making me look bad. Tampering with my career."

"Can't have that, can we?"

"We? There's no 'we' in my future. Just to be clear."

"Relax, Alyn. Tell me what you think you've got on Rand that's going to get you made Director of the FBI."

"His computer IP address."

"No chance."

"Meyer didn't give me all the details, but he's checked and rechecked. That nerd from the Tampa DA's Office stumbled on it in a 'collateral history,' I think he called it."

Caulden was suddenly more attentive. "How?"

"I just told you. Meyer didn't tell me much, but if he said it's there, it's there. I know what makes that freak tick. He wouldn't play with me. I'd wreck him."

"He found it, or the kid from Tampa? Oakes."

"Oakes, but Jason's got him under glass. I'll get it out before Tampa does. We'll crucify Rand and I," Alyn paused, leaned down, and kissed Caulden hard and pulled his hands over her breasts. "I am riding this winner all the way," she kissed him again and reached beneath the sheet into his crotch. "Riding all the way to the payout window."

The major let her bite his lower lip slightly, but didn't respond. His eyes were open. His own hand reached down, took her wrist and pulled her gently but firmly away. "Hold on, Alyn. There hasn't been anything on Rand from day one, now he folds in the middle of the game? When he's ahead? Makes no sense."

"He's not folding. I'm collapsing his fantasy computer world down on his head. He screwed up. This wasn't yesterday, Douglas. It was something Rand did hacking a computer almost a year ago. We just didn't look in the right place until the DA's whiz kid started poking around. You saw him. Jesus, he should have a pocket protector and taped up glasses."

Caulden was getting out of bed. "You have that much confidence in Meyer?"

"He said he's been rechecking it since this morning. He wouldn't bring it to me if he wasn't over the top certain."

"It doesn't fit Rand's profile." There was an odd anxiousness dangling from the major's words. He picked up his shirt and held it with one hand against his hip, partially covering himself and began to pace.

"So be happy about it," Alyn said as she flopped over on the bed. "The bad guy blew it. That's what they do. That's how they get caught. Stress out if you want, but I'll take it." She fluffed the pillows behind her and held her arms out. "Come celebrate," she smiled.

For all her manicured curves, Nuary had disappeared from Caulden's designs. He saw only the mechanics of the investigation. "No, something's not right..."

There was a harsh knock at the hotel room door.

The reoccurring ships-at-night-couple stared at one another as though the other had the answer.

"I have no idea," Nuary said. "Make love to me. They'll go away."

The knock returned as a pounding. The major went to his clothes and slipped a small automatic pistol from an ankle holster that rested beneath his quickly discarded pants. "Are you expecting someone?"

Alyn was clamoring out of the bed. "Put that away. Why are you so touchy all of a sudden?" She draped herself in the sheet and stormed toward the door. "I told them not to disturb me."

Without looking through the peep hole, she ripped open the door. Jason shot inside before any of the three could realize.

The trio stared. Only Alyn was unembarrassed.

"Cute, Jason. What are we now, in high school? I told you eight o'clock."

"You did, and now I know why."

"Is this where you pretend to be shocked? Or I'm supposed to pretend you're shocked? Next time, do as you're told, like the good boy I know you are."

"You bitch."

"Get over yourself. Damn it, Doug, put that gun away. And put your pants on! Jesus. Bunch of babies." The bathroom door slammed behind her leaving the two men at a total loss.

"Sorry about this, sport," the major said as he set his pistol aside and began turning his pants right side out.

Meyer opened the door and held it open, hoping someone would walk by and see Caulden, but then wondered who would look the more foolish.

"Tell the cunt I'll be in the hall when she's ready," Jason said then stepped into the hall and let the door close behind him.

With the room to himself, Caulden struggled with righting his clothes and getting dressed. Alyn emerged in minutes from the bathroom, fully dressed minus shoes and brushing the tangles from her shimmering blonde hair.

"Did he leave?" she spit as she glanced around the room. "Why that little shit."

"He's in the hall." The major was buttoning his shirt.

Alyn threw the door open exactly as she had done just a few minutes before. "Jason! What a pleasant surprise." She stepped back and Meyer fell away from the door casing into the room without a word or expression. "I believe you know the major."

"We've met."

"Good." She slammed the door so hard the wall shook. "There." Any good humor evaporated. "Now that the pleasantries are aside, tell me about Rand."

Jason leaned against the wall, watched the major slip into his shoes, and looked at the floor. "Who?"

The pout pissed off the loosely defined lady in the room. "Don't," Alyn said as she raised her hand and walked away. "Just don't."

She pitched the brush wickedly against the wall. It ricocheted and carried a clatter into a corner before it settled. Relieved of the brush and a degree of frustration, Alyn sat on the bed and crossed her legs. Her hands folded delicately across her lap. "Let's start again. Tell me about Rand."

Jason's frustration hadn't burned off. He wanted to make Alyn suffer for her blatant whoring, but knew he didn't have the stomach for a fight. "There's some additional lines of code in a backup memory. It points to Rand."

Major Caulden waded in as though they were at a conference table instead of a hotel bedroom. "How's that possible?"

"The dead congressman literally pulled his hard drive. It was probably seconds into a massive data dump. Things were still in a buffer." Jason was condescending. "It's technical. But the trail's there."

The twisted expression on Caulden's face seemed exaggerated to Alyn. "Why is that not good news, Douglas?"

"I didn't say it wasn't. I just find it incomprehensible that the FBI missed what a techy kid from Tampa finds. Even more unbelievable is that Rand would make such a mistake."

"Is it there, Jason? You're sure?" Alyn asked begrudgingly.

"It's there."

The tenor of the major's voice changed as quickly as Alyn changed partners. "Who knows about this?"

"Us three and Oakes."

"Can he be contained?"

"He's under close wraps, but I can't put him in jail."

"Alyn can."

"Why would she?" Jason asked, then her directly. "Why would you?"

"So the Bureau makes the announcement and not some hillbilly by the beach."

"And by Bureau, you mean you," Jason smiled.

Alyn waved off the foregone conclusion.

Doug was still grim. "I wouldn't schedule the victory dance just yet, kids."

"What is your problem with this?"

"Just wait on it." The major was collecting his things.

"For what?"

"Um... Confirmation."

"It's there. I saw it, but there's more."

"What more?"

"Lieutenant Auburn. From JAG. She fits into this somewhere – neck deep – but she doesn't show up on the radar. There's a secret somewhere or she's got special handling."

"Special handling?" Alyn asked Jason, but the major answered.

"CIA."

Alyn's eyebrows went up – no easy task under the anesthetizing Botox. "You think so?"

"I don't know. What makes you throw her name out, Meyer?"

"She's got a guardian angel somewhere. She shows up in Tampa, with LaRoy, but contributes nothing. LaRoy even had me limit her access. Made no sense then, makes less now. Oakes flashes an evidence log in my face today, fishing. I know it. Because I've done it. There was a book in that rickety newspaper shack in downtown Tampa inscribed by our Lieutenant. Someone ordered a handwriting analysis done, but it wasn't us – it was Florida Department of Law Enforcement."

"There was a book with her signature in it *inside* the newsstand?"

"Yes, and it gets better. Remember when her fingerprints showed up on the counter? Who told us it was just contamination?"

"LaRoy."

"And one guess as to who entered the mysterious book into evidence."

"LaRoy?"

"Our illustrious leader is keeping something to himself. And in case you're not convinced yet, here's another newsflash. Lieutenant Auburn's phone was entered into evidence, by...?"

"Are you kidding, Jason?"

"Never. LaRoy."

"What's going on here?"

Major Caulden had stopped preparing to leave. He was listening more intently than Nuary.

Jason continued. "I just now took a look at her phone traffic. Who do you think she was talking to almost every day before The Illuminati started making headlines?"

Alyn was hooked. "LaRoy?"

Jason smiled. "No. Ciampiano."

"Sgt. Sam Ciampiano? The missing ex-Ranger Ciampiano?"

"Yes."

"The one in Tampa?" Alyn asked in a seeming blind confusion.

"I don't think he's in Tampa now, but that's the one."

Major Caulden sat on the bed, some distance from Alyn. Jason pulled up a chair and very relaxed, put his feet up on the hotel desk. "There's something going on between LaRoy and Auburn. He wanted her computer access limited when she was in Tampa, but kept her around. You were tailing her, right, Alyn?"

"For a short while."

"Learn anything?"

"Matter of fact, I did. She's pregnant. She was pregnant when we were all in Tampa."

"LaRoy?" Jason raised his own eyebrows much easier. "Is that why he's been covering for her?"

"No way. Never happen."

"Then who? According to her phone and email accounts, she wasn't seeing anyone else."

The major let a few breaths pass. "Except Ciampiano."

Jason tried to nip it. "According to the data logs, her contact with him ended long before we hit town. It looks like when The Illuminati starting getting active, Auburn, or maybe Ciampiano, cut it off. It would appear they hadn't seen each other in several months."

"*Would appear?*" Alyn said as a possibility she'd kicked around began taking shape beneath her peroxide blond.

"How far along is she, Alyn?" Doug asked very slowly, a scenario of his own coming together.

"When I found out, I'd guess three months or more."

"When would that have put her getting pregnant?"

"Right when we all flew south."

Everyone was thinking, but the ice beneath their feet was thin.

"But when we got here, Ciampiano was already AWOL," Jason offered.

The major ignored him. "How did we learn of Ciampiano?"

"Simple cross check of recent discharges with special ops background."

"When did Ciampiano's name surface?"

Alyn looked at Jason. She could see he didn't want to be revealed as the leak.

"The day before we came to Tampa," she said, leaving out the source.

"Who else knew about the sergeant?"

"LaRoy," Alyn said.

"And JAG," Jason added as a hush stole into the hotel room.

It was another moment before Doug pressed ahead – diverting all attention from the electronic fingerprint Clayton had left behind.

"Can you track where Auburn was that day?"

Jason had a palm sized monitor open and was skating over the screen. "I can track for phone use. Tap the GPS in it. It might give us something. Do either of you remember the date?"

Alyn was checking her old email. "I made a flight reservation out of Atlanta."

It was only a few moments and Jason was scrolling through Karen's cell records and location. "No calls to Tampa." He baulked. "Point of fact, no calls to anywhere."

"She was probably working."

"No... There's no signal history."

"She turned it off?"

"More like pulled the battery."

"That sounds innocent enough," Nuary said sarcastically as she began to fidget with her own phone. "This is leading in a most interesting direction. How long was she off the grid?"

Jason scrambled over the small screen. "Almost twenty-four hours to the minute."

"How long does it take to drive from DC to Tampa?"

"Twelve hours. Thirteen, fourteen. Depends on time of day, I-95, if you're hauling ass."

"If you were going to warn someone – someone you're in love with that they were about to be pulled in for questioning – likely arrested and sent to prison forever and a day – I think you could make it from DC to Tampa and back in twenty-four hours. Douglas? What do you think?"

"Doable."

"I think so too."

"That's a weak legal case, Alyn. A shutdown phone? C'mon. Maybe there's witnesses here to corroborate she was in DC–"

"And maybe there's witnesses that put her in Tampa. If only for a half hour..." Alyn's voice disappeared in the quiet of the room. "Oh, my God..." She was whispering. "I think I know the witness."

"Who? The waiter guy?" Jason guessed.

Alyn seemed almost startled. "The waiter. I almost forgot about him. So?" she began with the subtlety of diving in a pool. "What have you got on the waiter?"

Jason was used to her and didn't miss a stroke as he consulted his hand held computer. "Last name, Guzimon. Sicilian by birth. Seventy eight years old–"

"Citizen?"

"Naturalized. Minor crimes, but I can't get a mugshot. The arrests were forty, fifty years ago plus."

"Forget them."

"He's clean, but his place of employment isn't, or wasn't anyway. That restaurant came up in several cross-referenced organized crime cases, but they're pretty dated. It seemed to have been a focal point twenty, thirty years ago, but I don't see that anything came of them."

"Interesting."

"That's nothing. Here's the interesting part. The ex-Ranger you've been looking for – Ciampiano?"

"Yes. Yes. Get to the point."

"Guess his mother's maiden name."

"Guzimon?"

"Nope, but you're close. Testiani." Jason was scrolling through his notes.

"How is that *close*?"

"On Ciampiano's birth certificate from Tampa it has the mother's name and DOB. Maiden name, Testiani. Would have been seventeen and lists her place of birth as Ficuzza, Sicily. We looked for her through Interpol in Sicily when Ciampiano went on the lamb. Haven't found her yet, but in the process, the Guzimon name came up. Next thing happens is you call me to check out a waiter named Guzimon. You reading the tea leaves here yet?"

"Guzimon and Testiani are family?"

"Not much doubt. Testiani married a Samiste Ciampiano, divorced, and disappeared the same year."

"Can't find her?"

"Not yet. Not sure we will. We don't know how long she was in the country. I doubt she was even a citizen when she got married. Maybe that was supposed to be her ticket. She probably went back to Italy, I mean, Sicily, after she knocked out the kid. We knew most of this when we were looking for Ciampiano, but not the relationship to your waiter. That credit goes to you. Might be coincidence."

Alyn was thinking slowly and half out loud. "I don't think so."

"Could be family somehow. He brings her over for a new life and she thanks him by getting pregnant. He sends her back. I don't know. Anyway. There it is."

The major was feeling left out. "Where's this going? Who's the waiter?"

"Why not send the baby back too?" Alyn wondered aloud.

"Beats me. Probably would have shamed the girl and the family forever back in the old country. Who knows with these people."

"You know what?" Alyn continued in a rabble. "I think she told the waiter she was pregnant. Even that day, I thought he knew. That's why he gave her water."

"What?"

"I couldn't figure out why he did that or why she would have told him. Jesus, he's family. She would trust him," Alyn said aloud to herself as excitement grew in her voice that she couldn't hide.

Jason couldn't keep up his end of the conversation, but, unbeknown to him, he was traveling a parallel road with the wrong pregnant girl. "Naturally she told him, Alyn. Why wouldn't she? She was banging Ciampiano and got pregnant. Got married, but likely blew town after that first four AM feeding. She was seventeen. Who knows? My guess is your waiter – father, uncle, relative of some sort – had her sent back to the old country after the kid popped out."

"I don't know. It's too much. Don't you think?"

"I don't care, Alyn. Cute family story. Whatever."

Major Caulden reeled the wandering diatribe back in. "So who's your witness in Tampa? This mysterious waiter who might be related to Ciampiano?"

"No," Alyn said through a twisted smile. "Ciampiano himself."

The men were confused by the winding street of logic. "Come again?" Doug asked.

"Oh, you'd like that, wouldn't you?" Aylin was up, pacing and smiling as she filled in the holes of her scenario. "Listen to me. Try to follow along. I'll help you with the big words. We know Ciampiano opened his newsstand the day before we got to town. He's in Tampa. We know that. He's seen by countless people. Our JAG lieutenant? Karen Auburn? Anyone see her that day? I'm guessing not so much. But, she drops off the grid and quite purposely kills the GPS of her phone. She's invisible for an entire day – an entire day. Who does that? And coincidentally, that's how long it takes a love struck JAG lieutenant – jacked up on five hour energy drinks and coffee – to race to Florida and back.

"The next thing that happens is we hit town to find our ex-Ranger has pulled a disappearing act Houdini would be proud of. Any of this starting to gel with you two?"

"That's an interesting theory," the major tried.

"Not a theory, Douglas. It's fact and I'm going to prove it. It and then some." Alyn grabbed her purse. She looked around the room for discarded jewelry and slipped her watch on.

"You don't have proof, Alyn."

"Yes I do. I have my witness."

"Ciampiano's still missing."

"But his baby's here."

Jason was genuinely shocked. "What?"

"That baby's Ciampiano's."

"You've lost it," Jason said as he opened the small room refrigerator. "I thought they stocked these with booze?"

Alyn's voice went up an octave. "Auburn screams to Tampa to warn her lover when she sees him on the data pull. A little warm, fuzzy, passionate, and tear stained goodbye then he goes underground while she hops back on I-95 north at a hundred miles an hour.

"She knows we'll find all the electronic stuff – the phone calls, emails, texts – so she tells LaRoy about the affair. That's why he brings her south – friends close, enemies closer – but has you, Jason, restrict her access. That's telling enough right there. She passes it off as email problems. What bullshit. And I fell for it."

Alyn set her purse aside, struggled with a dangling earring in front of a full length mirror, and combed her hair with her fingers. "But she didn't plan on getting pregnant. LaRoy might have played along with the early affair, but no way he doesn't throw her in jail if she tells him she warned Ciampiano the day before." Alyn took a breath. "It was all working. She nearly pulled it off." She stopped and lost her look in the mirror. "Damn it. She was coming in the Tampa office queasy almost every morning. I missed it. That changed everything. She got morning sickness and barfed in the toilet. Well, bitch, it's all in the toilet now and my hand's on the lever. I'm flushing her and LaRoy right down the drain." Alyn stretched her hands together high over her head. Her skirt came midway up her perfect thighs. "Oh, it feels sooo good," she cooed.

Jason turned away instead of on. "Not me, Alyn. You do what you want, but I'm out. I'm done."

She lowered her arms and tugged at her skirt. "No you're not, Jason. This is just starting."

"Not for me, it isn't. I got you the Rand lead you need to make Director or whatever you want next, but we're finished. You're going after LaRoy? He's an icon. I'm just a lab supervisor. They'll run me out on a rail."

Alyn slid between Jason and the door like oil. "Not after I've got LaRoy's job. No one will be able to touch you." She dropped her hand to his crotch. "Except me."

Jason pushed her aside and opened the door. "Pass. I'm not a part of anything like this. I don't know anything."

What Alyn couldn't do with her body, Major Caulden did with words. "Hey, Meyer? You came here to get fucked, right? If you really want to get fucked, walk out that door."

"Excuse me?"

"You heard what I said. If what Alyn thinks is accurate, welcome to the Wild West. There's a fistful of information – that kid from Tampa, Rand's screw up, a JAG officer getting banged by one of the FBI's Ten Most Wanted, an FBI cover-up of an affair. Christ, it sounds like a cheap movie when you toss in your wop gangster waiter. You couldn't make up this shit. The press will go wild. And who's the common denominator in all this information gathering, my friend? You. Someone's going to have their head cut off and shoved up their ass while it's still twitching."

"Why Douglas," Alyn said as she stepped away from one lover toward another. "You paint such a charming picture." She collected her purse for the second time and went back to the door, this time easing Jason aside. "Excuse me, dear."

Meyer obliged, but the major objected. "Where are you going?"

"To sink the battleship USS LaRoy. Straight to the bottom. That goddamn dinosaur. Oh, and to pick up an arrest warrant for one Lieutenant Karen Auburn."

"What's the charge? Fornication?"

"Obstruction for now. There'll be more after I get the test results back."

This was Jason's forte. "What test?"

"That little bastard of hers. If DNA shows Ciampiano's the father, it'll confirm that bitch was in Tampa right before us and right before her Ranger went over the hill. That's conspiracy, aiding and abetting, etcetera. I'll bury her."

"That's a tough sell, Alyn."

"Watch me. Ever hear of The Patriot Act? I'll sign the warrant myself. Jason, send me the lieutenant's phone data, texts, blah, blah, blah. I'll need it for the warrant. Oh, and I'll need a deposition later on what LaRoy had you do with her computer. Listen..." Alyn opened the door and put her hand to her ear. "Hear that?"

The men looked at each other, puzzled. "No."

Alyn smiled. "That's the changing of the guard."

The major stood up from the edge of the bed. "What about Rand? I think you should hold off on—"

"I don't have time for Rand right now. The timing's not right. We wait until I take over for LaRoy. My first official act will be to break The New Illuminati case over Clayton Rand's back. Every member of Congress will be sending me flowers and trying to thank me. I'll have enough favors stacked up to take over as Director of the entire Bureau." She hesitated in the open door. "I think I'll wear that new azure suit to my confirmation hearing. Strong, but not overpowering. Jason, send me that data. Doug, I'll be in touch."

Alyn left the door open, but could be heard whistling as she nearly danced down the hotel hall.

"Is she whistling?" Jason asked his part-time rival.

"I believe she is."

"Wow."

"Oh, it's not that remarkable," Doug said as he picked up his few things and went to the open door. "She's been having to flash those legs of hers to get where she wants to be. Now, you just gave it all to her. I suspect she is somewhere near her version of Elysium."

"Heaven?"

"For her. Hell for anyone in the way."

20

Karen was at the front screening station of the FBI building. She was scanned, signed in, and made to wait with two uniformed Capital Security Officers. Karen's face was full with the weight of her baby. Her hair was slightly longer than it had been when she'd first heard of The New Illuminati. Beneath the baby weight, her eyes were still pretty though tired. The security officers who wandered nearby and all around the area looked at her in her distorted uniform. One brought her a chair she politely refused.

Helfer made her wait only the two minutes it took him to dash up from his little makeshift office. He had her phone in one hand, receipts in the other. He couldn't avoid his locking stare and the surprised look on his face at Karen's pregnancy. Knowing she wasn't married and having zero experience in the matter, he fumbled through a hello while still staring.

"Hi, Lieutenant. It's good to see you. Hey!" Helfer held the phone and receipt out as though he were about to pat her protruding stomach. "Congratulations."

Karen dismissed his attention by reaching for the phone. "Thanks. And thanks for this."

"I'm sorry, Lieutenant," one of the officers at the table said as he intercepted the phone. "I have to scan the bar code first."

"Of course."

The officer did just that and watched the phone's description and pending terminus come up on his screen. "May I see your ID, Lieutenant?" he asked though Karen's photo ID was clipped to a lanyard around her neck.

She slipped the ID over her head and also produced her driver's license.

"Thank you. We're nearly done."

"There's a hard copy receipt," Helfer said as he pushed his papers in front of Karen. "The top one's yours. The bottom one's ours. You have to sign."

Karen glanced at the simple documents and signed the top copy. When she flipped it over to the side, she noticed the back was printed solid with an indiscernible mish-mash of letters and symbols. The odd look brought her pause and both she and the officer looked from the paper to Helfer.

"Recycling make sense," he shrugged.

Karen signed the second receipt and the officer handed her the phone.

"You saved me waiting, Helfer. I appreciate it."

Karen smiled and turned back to the scanner. She set the phone, receipt, and her purse in a tray.

"Glad to help. You need to stay off your feet."

Karen turned back and extended her hand. "Well, thank you again."

Helfer ignored the hand and leaned over her stomach and hugged her. Karen's eyes widened as Helfer said goodbye. "Take care of that little one," he said before whispering in her ear. "Save that receipt and phone. I'll call."

She was stunned. "I will," she said in answer to both statements then stepped through the scanner, collected her things and left the building without looking back.

Once she slid behind the wheel of her car, she opened the folded receipt and quickly flipped it to the back. Under examination she recognized it as computer code. Her hands, holding the receipt, sank to her lap on her distended belly. She sighed. She already was too near the flame as far as the FBI was concerned. The baby presented its own complications for an unwed mother with no family. She did not need this.

The day was nearly spent. Wheels churned and plans that ranged from searches for the truth to horrific schemes with nightmarish consequences were underway across the Capital. Helfer's day finished with the pile of paper and sweating the transfer he had done from the hard drive to Karen's phone. He needed to talk to her before she messed with the phone too much and innocently tampered with its misappropriated contents.

He tried her office after giving her time to get back. There was no answer. Subsequent tries didn't change the result. At the end of the day he passed through the scanners and retrieved his phone and documents. Helfer was dialing Karen's number as he cleared the FBI block and walked to his hotel. She didn't answer and he left no message. He tried again as he walked in his room. Still no answer.

There was also the introductory data on the receipt. When he collapsed on the bed his head was spinning. If he decided she wasn't to be trusted, he wouldn't tell her what was in her phone and the receipt data was really little proof. As a hard copy, it could have been typed by hand on any word processing program. The confusion and the chance he'd taken, along with the doubts Jason had planted about his boss, and Helfer's own concerns about Jason, conspired to make him nearly frantic. He closed his eyes, trying to ease the tension. He breathed deep, exhaled slowly through his nose and listened to the sound of his attempt at relaxation.

His phone rang and he jumped. The number wasn't recognized.

"Hello?... Yes it is... Sure, I remember. How's it going?..." He looked at his watch. "I guess so. Yea. That sounds good. Hold on..." Helfer snatched the cheap hotel pen off the nightstand and scribbled notes as he recited directions. "The Metro Green line... I can catch it nearby?... Cool... I don't mind... Across river... Branch Ave station... Three blocks southwest... Frangipani's Restaurant. Can't miss it. Sounds Italian... Hawaiian? Really? Okay. I'll leave in an hour... No, I'm sure. I need a break. It's been a long day... I'll take you up on that. Second round is on me though... Great. Thanks. See you there."

Helfer touched 'end call' on his phone and immediately felt better. The distraction would serve him well after the day he'd projected on himself. There was still a decision to make regarding how far he could take Lieutenant Auburn so, with his refreshed spirit driving, he dialed her again, but this time on her cell. The number of rings told him the messaging system was about to kick in. When it did, he hung up.

Karen watched his name fade from her screen. She made Helfer's decision for him. She wanted nothing to do with anything. As far as she was concerned, she picked up released evidence and the receipt was just a receipt. Both would go in the trash. If she was ever asked, she didn't notice the drivel on the back of the paper. Oakes had said it was recycling in front of the security guard. He'd go back to Tampa and pursue his career as a crime fighter without her help while she shadowed a new vocation – motherhood.

The phone rang again in her hand. 'Helfer Oakes' glowed on the screen. This time the caller let it ring through and left a message from the side of his hotel bed as Karen set the phone down and walked away.

"Hey, Karen. Um... This is Helfer. I, ah, I wanted to talk to you about what I said before you left. Um... A bunch of people from the office here and some of your military buddies are getting together later. Near the Metro Branch Ave terminal. The Green Line, they said. Oh, you're probably driving. There's a place called Frangipani's. It's a couple blocks south. Can't miss it. Maybe you know it. It sounds Italian, but it's Hawaiian. Kinda different, huh? But should be cool. Anyway, stop by if you can. We're meeting around eight or so. Hey... Just so you know, I'm not trying to get you into anything, it's just a receipt, you know? But I can't take anything out of the building. I know it's... Well, whatever, but that was sort of a scrap I put that receipt on. But it's also part of a backup log from a hard drive that ties things together in Tampa with Rand. There's a marker for an IP address. It might not make sense, but there was buffer overflow. The congressman pulled the drive before it finished. I need to go over it with Marcus or FLDE. These guys here are really touchy. Um... Maybe you could bring it? And your phone... Could I borrow it for a little while? Hey, um... I'm sorry about the cloak and dagger stuff. It's all silly. I'm probably over reacting. Maybe I'll see you later. Or just throw everything away. I don't know. I shouldn't even be talking, huh? I'm sorry. Bye."

The old phone and its receipt were put in the trash. The message went unlistened to.

When the Green Line train crossed the Anacostia River headed to the southeast, the sun was setting quickly. In the last vestiges of vanishing light, Helfer saw a rapid transformation taking place out the window. The famous museums and monuments were behind him in minutes. The countless governmental support entities vanished. Neighborhood row houses turned into low-rise tenements and trash danced like wisps of darting ghosts unbridled in the breezy wake of the train.

There were fewer riders with each stop and those that remained fell into two distinct categories – older, tired, downtrodden – clutching their simple plastic bags close to their bodies, and loud, raucous young men and women with showy red bandanas draped from their pockets or tightly wrapped around their heads. There seemed to be no middle group and it was clear to Helfer that he didn't fit in with either.

Any hints of day diminished with each controlled stop to pick up or discharge passengers. Helfer was looking forward to Branch Ave, his departure, and the security of familiar faces.

When he saw the bent station sign for Branch, he was relieved, but it was fleeting.

"Frangipani's?" he asked an older man getting off with him.

"English, mother fucker! I told you before."

"I'm sorry. Do you know where Frangipani's Restaurant is?"

"Do I look like a mother fuckin' tour guide? Hell no, I don't know."

The rough treatment wasn't expected. "I'm sorry," Helfer said as he bolted out the sliders onto the platform. "Thank you."

"Yo!" the man stopped him. "You don't know where you goin?'"

"Branch Avenue on the Green Line of the Metro. Is this Branch?

"That what the sign say, but it don't make it right."

"I was told three blocks southwest. Can't miss it. Which way is southwest? Judging from the sunset I'd say–"

"The sun? What are you? Mother fuckin' Columbus crossing the Gulf of Mexico? Shit... You in Southy DC already, boy. Southwest? Southwest is right down that street," the man pointed with an old permanently crooked finger. "You know what's southwest a here, boy?"

"Frangipani's Restaurant I hope," Helfer let a smile escape that was genuine, wrought on by the abortion of history and language taking place.

"Shit... You go that way, you be headed to the Highlands. Three blocks?"

"Yes, sir."

"Listen to me, boy." The old man came closer. Helfer could smell old sweat and sour booze. "If you get to Oxon Run and ain't found your spot? Turn your lily white ass right around and get back to this stop. Another train be by 'fore long. You feelin' me?"

"Yes, sir, and thank you again."

"Ah-right then. Ah-right. You have a blessed day."

"Thank you. You too."

Helfer didn't watch the train rattle off into the growing night toward its next stop. Instead he turned southwest per the hesitant guide and stepped away from the weak streetlight that feared leaving its bent and dirty pole. He wasn't alone.

The first block passed quick enough, but with each step the night strengthened its early grip. By the end of the second block darkness had clearly won the daily battle. With no signs of Frangipani's up the intersecting streets, Helfer stepped across the litter filled gutter toward the last block. He knew he'd test the old man's limit – he'd written down the directions from his phone call and they were so clear and easy. Still, there were no signs of a Hawaiian restaurant or any restaurant or any business along streets that were rushing to close in under broken street lamps.

"Helfer. Is that you?"

If there had been any light it would have shown the relief crest and fall across his face and convey through his body. The hunched shoulders he didn't even realize he carried relaxed and he stood straighter.

"It's me," Helfer said toward the voice and figure that half emerged behind him on the corner he'd just left.

"It's gets dark quick, doesn't it?"

"Sure does. It doesn't help that most of the street lights are out," Helfer said as he dodged discarded plastic soda bottles in a hurried attempt to re-cross the street that was empty of everything except Helfer, his host, and garbage.

"Public works. What are you gonna do? This way," the voice called. "I meant to be waiting at the terminal. Sorry about that."

"It's cool. I'm just glad I'm in the right place. Talk about the end of the line. After the speech I got at the train, I didn't think I'd heard you right. Pretty desolate."

"It's right around the corner."

The sidewalk was ensconced in the night. Helfer could just make out his feet as he reached his guide. "Cool."

They were at the mouth of an alley. "This way. There's a back door."

Helfer took a half dozen steps down the alley's throat before he pulled out his phone and tripped a flashlight app. "Damn dark," he said as he peered into the alley behind his present day lantern. "You come to this place much?" he chuckled until he turned slightly and his light caught the unmistakable shadowed shape of a revolver in his companion's hand.

Helfer took the sight right and wrong. "Whoa!" he lurched in a half-choked whisper with a voice instantly tightened by fear. "What is it?" His steps froze, but his hand flashed the light back and forth and behind them in the alley, searching frantically to find the threat. It wasn't out there menacing from the darkness and shadows. His bathing light found nobody – no danger, no target. The pace of the light slowed. "What's the gun fo–"

The report of the pistol masked Helfer's words and rang in his ears as the bullet slammed through his stomach and burnt into his spine. The impact and the deadening of his legs took him backward such that he sat down with astonishing force. His tailbone snapped deep inside, but the severed spinal cord blocked the pain. Momentarily almost blind from the muzzle flash, Helfer looked around more amazed than mortally wounded. "Call an ambulance," he said plainly.

The second bullet exploded into Helfer's face just above the hairline of his left eyebrow. He saw the muzzle blast in that instant and felt a sudden spray of super-heated air slap his face. A black curtain came down over his eyes from inside just as if he were falling asleep. He was dead before his torso fell back and cracked his head on the filthy concrete of the alley floor.

Though Helfer's ears were dead and the ringing of the shots had temporarily immobilized the shooter's, the gunfire did nothing to impede the hands that stowed the revolver and rifled the dead man's pockets. Helfer yielded his wallet, watch, and phone in rapid succession. Quick hands yanked his shoes off and dropped them as soon as they came free. One sock was torn away while the other was left haphazardly dangling from Helfer's lifeless toes.

The killer pocketed the trivial bounty and hustled away, head down, but looking all around and clutching the revolver. Less than a minute had passed since entering the alley. No sirens screamed in the distance. Nothing moved on the deserted block except rats who emerged from their warrens in trash heaps, holes, cracks, and shadows. They raised their noses and tested the scent wafting across the dirty concrete from the obscenity in the alley.

Warm blood seeped silently down into Helfer's still eyes and congealed there. When his body was discovered, the curious potential rollers of a drunk or a dead man fled, crying out as they ran. The dried pits of blood gave the appearance that the corpse's eyes had been torn out and replaced by haunting black holes. Given more time, the nighttime nightmares might have chewed the perception into reality. Instead, local coroners used the minor gnawing and negligible infestation of bugs and flies, along with rigor and lividity, to determine the time of death of an unknown white male, twenty-five to thirty-five, five foot six, a hundred thirty four pounds – their second John Doe bagged and tagged so far that morning.

Elsewhere across the city, thousands of federal workers, residing in a litany of G ratings, and tens of thousands in supporting industries, were watching their computer screens leap between minimal responsibilities, personal and professional email, surfing, and shopping like an equal number of bowling pins twirling above the head and hands of a juggler. No one missed Helfer Oakes. Jason passed the empty temporary office at ten after eight with a cup of coffee and saw the room empty, but didn't stop. By nine, Major Caulden was going through the FBI's screening process at the main entrance. When he signed in, he saw Karen's name a few rows above his own from the day prior. Several lines above hers was Helfer Oakes. He had been the first arrival yesterday, but had not signed in today.

Caulden returned salutes from a few visiting military personnel on his way to Jason's office. He reached through the open door and rapped his knuckles on the wall. "Morning, Jason."

"Good morning, Major." Jason looked up and down at the starched uniform complete with a chest full of decorations. "I almost didn't recognize–"

"I don't wear it all the time. Helps me get in here easier."

"–you with your pants on."

The major smiled slightly. "You ever make it back to her room last night? Sloppy seconds?"

Jason shuffled papers that needed none. "What do you want, Doug?"

"That hard drive."

"For what?"

"The military wants to conduct its own examination in light of what the Bureau missed."

"Not today."

"Go get the drive, Jason."

"Never happen. We're reviewing it again. It could take weeks. I'll let you know when it's available."

"Are you sure you want to play hardball with me? You might find this a different league. Fewer rules."

Meyer slapped his papers and stood up in a huff. He was no match for Caulden in any respect, but was driven by the sight of the major in Alyn's bed. "You're nothing, Major. I'm the goddamn FBI. Generals come to us. The fucking President comes to us! You don't tell me what to do. Ever! Maybe I'll ask one of those General to have you detached from this investigation."

Doug just smiled. "Maybe you'll try."

"Get out."

"Do you want to call security?"

Jason reached for his phone. "No bother at all."

"Forget it, Meyer. I'll go. I was hoping you were a little smarter, that's all. Never mind." Doug took a half step and turned back. "I saw the infamous Lieutenant Auburn's name on the sign-in sheet out front. What was she doing at FBI Headquarters?"

"When?"

Doug grinned again. "See that, Jason? That's the difference between us. Besides the obvious. You don't even know who's coming in your own building and why. I know what my side is doing. And, given a little time, I know what the other side is doing too. You should rethink your position, Meyer. Play for the winners instead."

"Leave."

"Be careful. Jason."

"Are you threatening me?"

The major raised his hands and ducked his head slightly. "No. Of course not. Never. I'm just saying we have shared tastes – at least in one area. I thought there might be others."

That served as their goodbye.

Within moments, Jason had dogged Karen's tracks and found the release of her phone, signed by LaRoy initially and consummated by Oakes. He stormed to Helfer's temporary office fueled by his anger at Caulden. With no one in the dark room to vent against, he tried Helfer's phone, left a curt message, and then called Nuary. He didn't say hello.

"Rein in your pet K-9."

"And good morning to you, Jason. Whatever it is, I'm sure I could care less, but make it quick. I'm busy severing heads."

"Add your boyfriend, Major, to the list. He just left here and wanted that congressman's hard drive."

"Did you give it to him?"

"No, and I'm not going to. He thinks–"

"Good boy. Keep that for us. Now, tell me what's really wrong."

"Lieutenant Auburn. You're keen on her, right?"

"She's next up for the guillotine. Why?"

"She was here yesterday."

"What'd she want?"

"She met with that kid from Tampa and picked up her phone."

"Was there anything on it we don't have?"

"No. I got it all, but he hasn't come to the office yet."

"Who hasn't?"

"Oakes! The forensic guy out of the DA's Office in Tampa. Are you listening?"

"Forget him. Just hold on that hard drive."

"He made me look bad – missing that backup log file."

"It's all taken care of. It will look like LaRoy squelched it by the time we get done."

"What do you mean, 'we?' Who's 'we?' I told you I want no part of this."

"You already have a part, Jason. Doug explained it to–"

"Figures. I want nothing to do with that psycho piece of–"

"It's too late, lover. You're in, so fight nice with the major. Listen to me. I have a warrant for Auburn's blood."

Jason hesitated and laughed nervously. "Out for blood."

"We're going to do a prenatal paternity test. You're a lab guy. You probably know all about this."

"We don't get much call for 'baby daddy tests' in the Bureau, Alyn. Besides, with Ciampiano AWOL, how are you going to get a reliable sample from him? Go back to Tampa and subpoena his toothbrush?"

"It's not necessary. His DNA is on file. Special Forces protocol. If he got killed, blown up, or whatever, they already have his DNA to make a match to whatever's left of him. Our friend, the major, is getting it for us."

There was a hesitation from Jason's side. "So, you're going through with it?"

"That is the understatement of the year. I'm right about this. The DNA test will put that little bitch in Ciampiano's bed just before we would have had him. And LaRoy covered for her."

"He didn't know, Alyn. You said so yourself."

"It won't matter. He's toast and she's going to have that bastard baby of hers in a prison ward."

"You don't have to sound so happy about it."

"Happy? I'm thrilled! Her being pregnant is the best thing to happen to my career since getting my boobs done."

"Damn, Alyn..."

She laughed. "I've got to go."

"Are you serving the warrant?"

"Heaven's no. I'm going to play 'good cop' with her after the fact. We're sending a medical team right to her office at JAG. We'll hit her hard and fast."

"When?"

"We just picked up her doctor. We're taking him along to demonstrate how compassionate we are."

"You think of everything, don't you?"

"That's how you win the game. Oh, and when you learn of LaRoy's resignation and Auburn's arrest, act surprised." Alyn hung up.

———————————

21

The scenario played out as Nuary had planned. Others were the bad guys. Karen was caught totally unaware. As an attorney, she knew her rights and the protection afforded her by the law, but she also knew the limits. The warrant was legit. There may have been a remote chance of avoidance – very remote – but it was likely a delay at best. Physical confrontation was never considered. Strictly speaking, the FBI could tie her down and draw the sample by force though that would not play well anywhere. Her doctor swung the balance when he advised her that his records and her latest samples had also been subpoenaed. They would have what they wanted with or without her compliance. As she rolled up her sleeve for the phlebotomist, Karen was thinking more of her immediate liberty and the next steps. Trying to plan those from a holding cell would be difficult. Her present questions as to what the warrant was in relation to went unanswered as she knew they'd be before she asked. She felt the burning sting of innumerable stabs through her heart as the thin needle poked her vein.

The pain lingered. Karen packed her office and took the rest of the day off. She was dialing before she was clear of her building. The first call was to John LaRoy. He didn't answer and wouldn't answer the next six attempts. She finally left the briefest of messages that yielded nothing of what had happened and only asked for a return call. She did the same with Nuary, who watched each call come up, but didn't answer by design. Alyn would return Karen's simple message eventually – with feigned ignorance and promises to learn what she could – thereby laying the cornerstone that would keep the two close. Alyn might even toss Karen a lifeline to keep her within arm's reach, but it would amount to nothing.

Karen's phone list was dwindling by the time she walked in the door of her apartment. Not wanting a fool for a client, she had called and retained legal counsel rather than rely on herself. She had also reached out to the Department of the Navy and JAG. Now, inside her door, she was down to backup reserves. Major Caulden's phone was ringing. He picked up on her first try, but was ignorant of anything. To Karen – still focused on the poke in the arm and not anticipating the stab in the back – she was now venting thoughts as much as seeking answers. She finally caught herself after hearing the word 'Tampa' come out of her mouth three times in fairly close succession. Only between the aperture of her hesitation did she hear Doug had crossed over some minutes ago from ignorance to inquisition.

"I don't know, Karen, maybe there's a tie. What happened in Tampa?" he asked.

That word again. She baulked, said nothing, and stared into an apartment that was never so lonely.

"Still there?" Doug asked his fifth question in a row.

She felt the baby move. The emptiness escaped the apartment and enveloped her building, the streets, DC, and the world. Somewhere out there was Sam.

The major's voice tried to interfere. "Did I lose you?"

Karen let her hand slide down over her belly and felt for the tiny foot stretching out into her side. Doug's voice brought her attention back to the phone. "Yes," she heard herself say. "You're breaking up. I'll call you later," she said and ended the call.

The phone in her hand held her attention a moment longer than it might have. She watched its screen go black then carried it to the trash.

"Tampa. Tampa," she said to herself over and over.

She opened the kitchen garbage and saw her old phone and Helfer's receipt. Her new phone held the lid as she took the old one and the paper from the trash. Everything went with her to the living room.

The drapes were pulled back ever so slightly as she looked into the parking lot and street adjacent to her building. It was likely she was being watched. She looked at the two phones. They were likely being monitored as well.

A reflex made her power up the old phone John LaRoy had relieved her of. The backlit screen came to life, but was dark blue and anonymously blinked a single slow curser.

"Blue screen of death," she said out loud to the phone and set it aside to look at the backside of the receipt.

It made no more sense than when she'd first seen it, but the replay of constant markers pointing to Tampa, Major Caulden's questions, and mostly, the white tape across the vein in her elbow made her look at it closely. It was nothing she'd ever comprehend. She'd have to ask Helfer. Only now did the frenzied phone calls from earlier abate enough to let her check her messages. There was Helfer, waiting, while she was preparing to call him.

Karen listened to his message and after the day she'd had, regretted instantly leaving him hanging the day before. She'd like to have someone to call who would just listen and help her sound out what was happening. Clearly, Helfer had wanted her to be that same person for him and, so far, she'd let him down. Karen rang his phone. It went immediately to voicemail. Karen left a short note.

"Hey, Helfer. It's Karen. Thanks again for helping me out the other day. I'm sorry I missed your call. Call me back as soon as you can, would you please? Thanks. Bye."

She remembered him saying he couldn't have his personal phone in the building so she searched her phone for his recent call from the FBI building, but he had called her office, not her cell. She didn't have the number.

Karen was still holding the receipt and examined the backside and the extensive coding. While she looked, she replayed Helfer's message.

"It's also part of a backup log from a hard drive that ties things together in Tampa and Rand..."

Tampa. Always Tampa.

"I need to go over it with Marcus... Um... Maybe you could bring it? And your phone... Could I borrow it for a little while?"

"My phone?" Karen thought. "Why do you want to borrow my phone?" Then her eyes went from the phone in her hand to the old one and its blue screen. "Not that one. You already had it. You gave it to me. Why would you..." The curser went from subtle blinking to overt winking. "Helfer... What did you do?"

Karen traded phones. She cautiously touched the screen. A folder appeared. Her hand moved slow gingerly touched the folder. The screen flashed black and immediately began to rapidly scroll computer text. She was reminded of a near ancient DOS screen, but this one was on steroids and flailing by with blurring speed. There was no way to type in a command to stop the screen or close the folder. Mesmerized, she took the phone to her laptop and was searching for a cord to attach the two.

She stopped. Flustered. "They'll tear this thing apart..." she reasoned with herself. The white tape bandage itched on her arm. She tugged it off in one quick jerk and looked at the pink skin left behind and the tiny pinprick healing over. "Three days. Maybe five before they know," she said as she looked from her arm to the still scrolling phone and beyond to a small calendar on her desk. "Three to five days."

A stack of business cards were collected in a small gray stone saucer on the corner of the desk. She flipped through them until she found the card of Marcus Pete, Sr. Investigator, Hillsborough County District Attorney's Office, Tampa, Florida. His email address ran along the bottom.

Karen struggled with her weight, belly, and balance back to her feet. The phone was still in her hand crushing Helfer's receipt and the business card. Everything went with her to the kitchen and took up residence on the counter as she began rummaging until she found a small padded shipping envelope.

The phone was still flashing data while Karen addressed the envelope to Marcus, but stopped scrolling just as she stopped writing. Karen powered the phone down and sealed it in the envelope. She took it and the receipt out into the hallway of her building and knocked on her neighbor's door. A bent gray-haired man yelled something intelligible from the other side as several locks slid and jangled.

"Hey there, kiddo. How's the Navy treating you? Damn good outfit. I should know. Petty Officer 3rd class. Korea '50 to '54. I was on a destroyer. Fletcher class. See, I made PO3. Got busted back down to Seaman, the dirty dogs. We was–"

"Mr. Garnett? How are you?"

"Oh, as good as a body can be at my age. Helluva lot better than the alternative." He folded his hands across his chest, leaned back a little, and closed his eyes. "Get the picture, sailor?"

"I do. I'm glad you're well. If I could ask, I don't think you have a computer, but I've seen you with an iPad."

"Oh, hell yes, I have an iPad. Damnedest thing ever. I'm good on her too. I get most of my best jokes from it. The grandkids set me up and showed me how to work her. Nothing to it. If an old Tin Can Sailor can do it, any damn fool can. You got one?"

"I do actually, but it's not working properly and I need to send something to a friend."

"On the fritz, is she?"

"Seems so."

Mr. Garnett leaned closer, increasing the bend of his back and whispered. "It's the Chinese. They build them, you know? They make them work just long enough to get us used to the idea then they fall apart so you have to buy another. They do the same with parts. You ever try to put together a fan or a shelf or maybe a table? You're always one screw short. Them Chinese do that a purpose to drive us nuts. It's some kinda psycho-propaganda I think. That's who we were really fighting in Korea.

Chinese. They come over the hill by the thousands. Cold as hell. Fighting the Chinese and the cold."

"You've told me. It must have been awful."

"Awful ain't the word. Hell. That's a better one. But enough of that. We'll catch up another time. How's the baby coming along?" The old man laid both his gnarled hands on Karen's stomach.

"Very well. The doctor says everything is normal."

"I think it's a boy," Garnett's eyes twinkled. "What do you think?"

"Maybe. Fifty-fifty chance."

"Ha! Fifty-fifty!" Mr. Garnett turned somewhat awkwardly and pointed across the room. "She's in my chair there. I was just checking my email. I don't get much, but I poke around in the internet pretty fair. I got a couple Scrabble games goin,' but you won't mess 'em up. I cheat like hell anyway. Help yourself. You want a coffee, Lieutenant?"

"No, thank you."

"I keep a pot on most all day. Keeps me sharp."

Karen had the iPad perched over the back of the receipt. She had a clear picture in an instant as Mr. Garnett continued.

"Real coffee too. Not instant. I think we drank chicory aboard ship. We called it coffee, but it weren't really. Watered down dirt really, but we made her through."

Karen forwarded the picture of the computer language along with a brief note to Marcus.

"I saw that they have a Starbucks on an aircraft carrier now," the old sailor said as he poured stale coffee into a stained cup. "Suppose that's true?"

"I had not heard that yet. Anything's possible, these days. Are you registered for your reunion this year?"

"Oh, I don't know. It's up near Philly. Long way to go. Long way."

"You know I'll take you. We've had good times at your reunions."

Mr. Garnett pointed at her stomach. "I think you might have your hands full this go 'round."

"That's a fair assumption, but we'll figure it out. I'd like you to go if you want to."

"I'll keep a lookout." He sipped his old coffee. "Sure you don't want a cup of joe?"

"I'm all set, but you could do me one more favor." Karen pulled the packaged phone from under her arm. "This is a birthday present – a special one, but it's too early to mail. If I go into labor in the next few days, I might not be around to mail it."

"Give her here, LT. I'll get 'er down to the mail room and in a sack for shore. When you want I mail it?"

Karen thought. "A week. If I don't come for it in a week, please mail it for me. And keep it between us. That is, if anyone should ask if you have anything of mine. I want it to be a surprise." Her face tightened involuntarily. "It's very important."

Mr. Garnett picked up the seriousness, but kept it to himself. He saluted. "Aye aye, Sir, er... Ma'am. Top secret communiqué. They won't get it outa me. Oh, I better scratch that down on the calendar." He did just that. "A week from today. I'll have her posted."

Karen went close to him and leaned over her belly, hugged him, and kissed his cheek. "You've always been a wonderful neighbor. Thanks so much."

The old salt blushed and looked away. "Can't say I was ever kissed by no officer before. Been given hell more than I can recall and was twice before the captain's mast, but never kissed. I believe I'd remember that."

Karen couldn't suppress a smile despite the day she'd had as she watched Mr. Garnett touch his cheek.

She offered her own salute. "Carry on, Petty Officer Garnett."

He returned the salute, felt a sense of pride in having a lieutenant as a neighbor – having been kissed by one – and wished he could do more for the unwed mother-to-be. Unknown to him, he'd done more than enough.

Marcus Pete was at his desk when a notice popped up in the lower right hand corner that he had mail from TinCanDDPO3.

He read the note.

"You could find me if you tracked this IP far enough, but before you do, know the FBI will track you as they are me and HO doesn't trust them. H is a friend and got this to me and I have to hand it off. I think he has concerns about your boss's stance in this investigation. Something's going on and is about to break. HO thinks this is a part of it. The attachment is a backup log that ties together CR and FL. There's a marker for an IP address. A buffer overflow and the timing of the congressman's pulled hard drive? Talk to HO. He's not answering my calls and I don't know if I'll be able to try him much longer. He's got more. It's coming. Pls protect the owner of this IP – he knows nothing. Be careful. Few things are as they seem."

Marcus re-read the note at least three times more before he opened the attached photo. Enlarged, he could see it clearly. Three clicks of his mouse and it was printing – one page – nearly solid with commands and coding. He also printed the email as he dialed Helfer's phone. Like Karen's call, it went immediately to voicemail. Marcus left the now standard message and tried the number Helfer had provided as his temporary office. No answer. Marcus headed to Jack's office.

Jack was as confused as Marcus, but also shared his investigator's desire to talk with Helfer ASAP. He tried and met the same result. Marcus was fumbling through the coding and the email as Jack called Cal Denti.

"Cal? Need a favor."

"What else is new?"

"Call that snake pit they call FBI Headquarters in Washington and track down my lab boy, Helfer Oakes. He's up there checking your work for me. Your guys might have eaten him or have him doing coffee runs. I can't find him and he doesn't answer."

"They probably make him check his personal phone at the door."

"Well, he don't answer at his Fed desk either. Are you going to try or do I have to call your girlfriend, oops. I mean, your boss, Nuary?"

"You're a real dip shit. I'll call you when I know something."

"I don't have that long. I need this kid pronto. And what are you doing now?"

"Looking for lost employees of yours."

"Cal. Make a few calls on Helfer for me, would you? Then come over to the office. I want you to see something."

"What?"

"I'm not sure yet. Might be a smoking gun on Clayton Rand. Computer stuff."

"Are you joking, Aaron?"

"Stone cold serious."

"Where'd it come from?"

"My wonder boy, Oakes. He's supposed to be at your place in DC, but I can't raise him. I need to have him explain what me and Petey are looking at. You usually aren't worth a shit, but you'd better come over and throw in your two cents. I don't want you whining about it later."

"Thanks. I'll make some calls then be there."

"Hey, and keep the smoking gun thing under your hat until we have a chance to talk it through. I might be full of shit. You know how I am."

"I do at that. See you shortly."

Jack was talking before the receiver was in the cradle. "What do you make of it, Petey?"

"Obviously, we need to talk to Helfer, but it must be legit. Only Helfer would be thinking to find something like this and get it down to us."

"So who's the Tin Can character?"

"Like he says, we could find out, but I'm more concerned with this veiled threat." Marcus followed Karen's note with his finger. *"HO doesn't trust them... Something's going on... Be careful..."* He looked back at Jack and shrugged. "What's all that mean?"

"We'll run it by Cal. Maybe he can shed some light on what's going on. How about this backup log buffer thingamajig? There's the big question for Oakes. I got no idea what he's talking about. You?"

"A little. I could reach out to FDLE if we don't connect with Helfer pretty soon."

"Cal will sick the dogs on him in DC. Those Fed dickheads probably took him to some strip club and got him shitfaced." Jack looked at his watch. "Oakes is probably just waking up wrapped around some hooker. Dumb kid."

"I hope you're right. You think the Bureau is watching him so close as to make him nervous? Sneaking something out of FBI Headquarters is pretty gutsy. That doesn't sound like Helfer unless he was really pressed. Am I right? Does that sound like our Helfer to you?"

Jack picked up the paper, looked at it again – lost – and leaned back in his chair. "Nope. It sure don't." Jack thought a second. "Petey? Oakes have any family in the military? Tin Can. That's what sailors call ships. Destroyers, I think."

"He's local. I think his family is too. I can check."

"Naww. Not yet. Something else though. This thing says, *'H is a friend...'* Who does Oakes know in DC? Hell, I didn't think he had any friends in Tampa, let alone DC."

"Jack... He's a good guy."

"I ain't saying he ain't a good guy, just boring. Boring don't make friends. Especially in the big city."

"I don't know. I suppose we could track the IP address."

"Let's call FDLE and see if they can make heads or tails out of this gibberish," Jack said as he tossed the paper back on his desk as his phone rang.

"Aaron... You find my boy?... I knew it. I just told Petey, I bet those sonsabitches got him drunk as hell in some whore house. Goddamnit!... Okay." Jack hung up. "Cal's on Kennedy Boulevard. He'll be here in a sec. He can't find Oakes. HQ said he didn't sign in. He's not in the office."

Marcus was ahead of his boss. "It occurs to me that he knows the Bureau people that were down here. I don't know if they would call themselves friends."

"They're probably the assholes who got him drunk!"

"How about Cal's boss? Nuary. She'd like to get her hooks in a kid that clever. He might think she was being friendly."

"Jesus, he'd cum in his britches if she ever got close to him. What a shark that bitch is. Cal's got horror stories by the hundreds on her. Be careful she don't try to be 'friendly' with you."

"Thanks for worrying about me, Dad."

"Somebody has to. You can't take care of yourself. But it's not Nuary. She's works in Atlanta, not DC. It's probably some other nerd he met from their lab."

"I don't think so. It didn't sound too flattering of the Bureau."

"That don't mean shit. I can't imagine what you say about me when I'm not around. 'Jack's dumber than a box of rocks. Grew up in the Green Swamp eatin' snakes and frogs. Changes his socks once a month.' God knows what you say."

"Once a week. I say you change your socks once a week. It was your underwear you change once a month."

"You're a jackass."

Cal appeared in Jack's door as if following a script. "Thanks, Jack. I was just leaving."

Jack was up, protesting as he came around his desk and took Cal's arm. "Not you, Cal. Petey's the jackass." Jack ushered his friend in and closed the door. Once captured, he produced the inevitable. "Well, you can be a jackass, now that I think about it. But you're not now. Sit down and have a gander at that," he pointed to the paper copies of the email and its attachment. "Petey, show Cal the email you got."

As Cal read, Jack sat down, fidgeted, and fought to keep quiet. He tried two phone numbers for Helfer to distract himself and got no answer at either. Marcus imperceptibly studied Cal's face knowing the FBI agent was reading disparaging suggestions about his place of employment regarding the most pressing case in the country.

Cal read the email three times and looked almost line by line through the rambling code before he looked up at the bearers of gifts. "A couple of questions – the answers of which will do nothing to advance or retard our conversation." Cal held up the papers. "Legit? A prankster maybe?

Your email is listed on the website. This Tin Can character could be across the hall or in Pyongyang."

"We can run down the address, but there's too much there. Few people even know Helfer's in Washington. What's the second question?"

"Who's Helfer's friend?"

Jack interrupted any hypotenuse Marcus was preparing.

"How about I ask you one first? Maybe something that's relevant. Like, what the hell's going on up there that Oakes has to smuggle out evidence? Or how about this one? My money's on Oakes, see. After he came up with Rand out of thin air and good police work, he gets my vote. But your outfit has that hard drive for what? Six months? With nothing? And my guy's in town for a week and blows the lid off."

"If this is accurate."

"It's there. If Oakes says it there, it's there."

"This is just a piece of paper, Jack."

"It's computers talking! Tell him, Petey."

"No, he's right, boss. Anybody could type that page and make it appear as if – to your point – the computer said or did a certain thing."

"We need the drive," Cal said as he floated the paper onto Jack's desk.

"Jesus H. Christ... Am I working alone in this thing? We've got the damn driver gizmo, or you've got it. We've got to find Oakes and figure out what's what before your crew mucks it up. Can you get somebody to run over to the kid's hotel or something? Find out who got him drunk, or who went to dinner with him last night. And why he has to raise his hand to take a piss? That how things run up there, Cal?"

"Security is pretty tight."

"Tight? This ain't tight, Cal. This is something wrong. When Oakes found this he'd be on the phone calling his home-girl here to tell him. Oakes is like Petey's kid. C'mon, Cal, you know this doesn't sound right."

"There could be a hundred reasons—"

"But there ain't."

"—why he's taken things the way he has. Helfer's young."

"So why didn't the Bureau find this backup log thingamajig?"

"Because maybe it's not there."

"Or maybe they couldn't find their own ass with both hands!"

"Are we really going there again?"

"Or they've got their own scam going on the inside. I wouldn't put a damn thing past that boss of yours. I say we call LaRoy and pitch it to him. He'll play it straight."

Cal's agreement was in his standing up. "Can I use your phone? I'll put him on speaker."

Less than two minutes was the lifespan of the confidence and hope the trio had understandably placed in John LaRoy.

A man's voice answered and identified himself as Special Agent So-and-So. Cal ID'd himself and his shield number. Director LaRoy was not in that office. When would he return? He was no longer assigned to that office. How's that? He's been reassigned. Where? I don't have that information. Cal asked for another Director he knew to be close to LaRoy. And this is who again? Special Agent-in-Charge of the Tampa Office, Calburn Denti. Tampa? Yes. He's unavailable. He tried a second. Unavailable. A third. Out. Cal left messages to be called at their earliest convenience. He disconnected the speaker phone in slow motion as a pallor came over his face and his gray eyes drifted somewhere well beyond Jack's office. He wilted into a chair.

Marcus and Jack had been witness to it all. True to form, Jack broke the fresh ice that threatened to gouge out the underpinnings of the investigation, but even he was tepid.

"I heard it... but what was that?"

"I... ah... I don't know what that was." Cal had his cell out and had already dialed.

Jack was astonishingly quiet. Marcus waited on Cal's call as he slid the copy of the email and computer log from the desk.

"John? It's Cal. What's going–" The pause caused by the one-sided conversation spawned a tension that grew exponentially from the increasing stillness of the office. Cal's intent focus on listening left a gapping crevasse that even repelled Jack's normal wit and disregard. Marcus was looking at the email, but his eyes as well as his ears were listening for any hint. Cal's slightest acknowledgment – a moan, a breath, a groan – seemed like an explosion of sound as the waiting malingered and droned on silently.

"What can I do, John?" A short gap, but the words shook the room from its quiet stalemate. "I will... Yes, I'll talk to him," Cal said as he suddenly looked in Jack's direction before refocusing on nothing but the conversation. "No, I understand. No need to apologize, John... I understand. Another day... Alright... Take care."

Cal ended the call and tossed his phone into the stacks of files and papers that cluttered Jack's desk. He slumped back in the chair.

"I've never seen you slouch in a chair, Cal," Jack said slowly. "You'll wrinkle your trousers. That's a bad sign."

Cal sighed. "I'm not certain what to tell you... I'll probably get my turn in the barrel soon enough."

Marcus volunteered. "Do you want me to step out for a few minutes?"

Jack looked at Cal for the answer. "I don't think— No. There's no need." Cal sat up straighter and tightened the pressed seam of his pants. "John's been temporarily relieved. Lieutenant Karen Auburn – JAG – had an affair with Ciampiano. Sgt. Sam Ciampiano."

"There can't be many sergeants with that name."

"There isn't."

"That's not a total secret though, Cal. Am I right?" Jack said as he flashed the palms of his hands and shrugged his shoulders.

"No. But there's a rub. Auburn told John about it, but said it was long over. He kept her on the case. Now it looks like she forgot a little part. She's pregnant. We issued warrants for her medical records yesterday or a few days ago, I don't know," Cal said, clearly flustered. "And executed a warrant for a blood draw on her this morning. Her medical file says she's been pregnant from about the time we started looking for Ciampiano – months later than when she told John she'd broken it off. The early reports – maybe its speculation – whatever, are that the baby's his. That's what they're telling John anyway... That puts the Lieutenant with the most wanted man in America while she's supposed to be helping find him. And John didn't write up any of it." Cal rubbed his face hard with his hands as he stood up. The paleness disappeared under a near bruising flush of red. "He's getting crucified."

"He told me," Jack said quickly. "He wasn't hiding it. Tell them to come talk to me."

"They will. He told me as well. They're on their way to talk to both of us. You too, Marcus. They'll interview everyone associated with Auburn or John."

"So that clears him, doesn't it?" Marcus said as though he didn't quite believe it himself. "It must help anyway."

"Some, but there's no trail, no documentation. Nothing went out to the team or up the chain. Even what he told Jack and I was just across the desk. He made a decision to believe her. In hindsight, he should have at least documented that decision, but there's nothing."

"So, the lieutenant is in on this mess?" Jack thought out loud. "No wonder we can't get Rand to make a mistake. She's been feeding him all along."

"John doesn't think so and neither does the Bureau from what he can tell. There's no communication between Auburn and Rand. Just Ciampiano, and even that's old – long before she got pregnant."

"But she's pregnant by him?"

"That's the consensus. They're probably using that blood to confirm."

"Holy shit, Cal. Ho-ly shit... I didn't see that one coming."

"Neither did John."

"So, what now?"

"A major investigation. He's sitting with agents right now. They're monitoring his calls. He mentioned retirement."

"No shit? Because he believed that bitch?"

"Because he didn't make it official."

"Christ... Official. I hope they break it off up her ass."

"They're going to pick her up now. John said they were listening to see who she called after they rattled her with that blood draw. Guess who her first call was to?"

"Honest?"

"John LaRoy. That didn't help his case."

"Unreal."

"She's going to get hard time."

"She should!"

Marcus leaned forward and rested his elbows on his knees as he held the printed papers from the email. "The lieutenant. JAG. That's Navy, right?" He flipped the email. "Tin Can. Sailors. You think she's Helfer's friend?"

Cal was up again. "I didn't hear that. You don't want anything associated with her. If Helfer went through her, he'll be tainted too. Speaking of which, I'll see if I have any friends left that can find him."

"Hold on," Jack said as he followed Cal up and pointed at the papers in Marcus's hand. "What do you think of the computer geek-speak?"

"It doesn't mean much without the hard drive."

"Can you get it?"

"I'll try. Like I said, my friend ratio may have shifted considerably in the last twelve hours. Show it to FDLE and see if it looks right to them."

Marcus was the last to stand. "I know who can tell us."

"Who's that?"

Marcus smiled and held up the paper. "Clayton Rand."

"Oh, Petey, you dirty dog," Jack smirked. "Now you're thinking. What do you say, Cal? Want to take a little ride to the other side of the tracks and see how the rich folk live? Been a helluva day."

"Jack—"

"Oh, the whole damn thing is about to blow up anyway. Let's go rattle his cage and see what jumps out." Jack took the single page from Marcus and looked it up and down. "I hear old Clayton's a fair hand with computers and what-not. Maybe he can tell us what this is."

"Okay. I'm in," Cal said quicker than Jack thought he would. "But we have to make a quick stop at the federal building first."

"Done. You in, Petey?"

"Three's a crowd," Marcus said. "We didn't see eye to eye at our last meeting."

"Suit yourself. Might be missing out on the fun though."

"Not likely. I'd be more of a wet blanket. You kids go on ahead."

———————————

22

otion detectors had long since given up the men's approach when Jack touched the doorbell. "Marcus will be disappointed he didn't get to see behind the curtain. I hear him and Rand really hit it off last visit." Jack smiled, first at his joke then up at the camera. "Hello, Mr. Rand. Jack Aaron. District Attorney. You know Agent Denti here. Got a minute?"

"I'm afraid not. Perhaps another time," Clayton said into the intercom then added. "And extend my regards to Mr. Pete. Perhaps he didn't come due to the fragile frivolity of requesting an audience without benefit of a warrant."

"Fragile frivolity. That's good. Real good. You mind if I use that?"

"Be my guest though both the circumstance and recollection will likely elude you."

"You're probably right on both counts, Mr. Rand, but I was hoping you might review a document for the District Attorney's Office. Perhaps as a bit of a public service. I have this computer printout that is really over my head. I hear you're handy with such things. Was hoping you'd take a look for me. What do you say there, Mr. Rand?"

"Not today. Some other time perhaps."

"Mr. Rand? Cal Denti with the FBI," Cal said as he held up his identification.

"I remember. Good afternoon, Agent Denti."

Cal took the paper from Jack and held it up to the camera. "Mr. Rand, there is coding here that contains some very strong indicators. I think you would find it interesting. Can you read it?"

"I'm very busy Agent Denti. As I said."

"If you don't like that paper, try this one." Cal unfolded a warrant and held it up to the camera. "This is a warrant, Mr. Rand. We believe you are in possession of information regarding a criminal investigation. We'll have that discussion now. Right now."

"I'll be speaking with my lawyer first."

"This is informational, Mr. Rand. Not criminal. Your immediate failure to comply with the contents of this duly presented warrant constitutes–"

The electronic locks of the heavy entryway whirled. Clayton opened the door. "Good afternoon, gentlemen. May I?" he said as he held his hand out for the warrant.

After he read it, he stepped aside. "I am not willingly permitting your entry nor am I willingly discussing any matter with you. I am merely complying with the presented warrant to the best of my ability."

"That's all a body could ask," Jack said cordially as he stepped into the cool expansive kitchen. "Nice place, Rand."

"State your business," Clayton said as he held the big door open. "My attorney is in route. I would like to forego questions–"

"I'm afraid that won't be possible. There are exigent circumstances applied to the line of questioning." Cal handed over the copy of the additional lines from the backup log. "Please examine this document."

"Mind if we sit down?" Jack asked as he took a step deeper into the house.

"I do. This won't take long."

Clayton meant to scan the page quickly, but the contents revealed themselves to him and his eyes went back to the top to start again several times. Cal and Jack both saw the restart and the veteran cops understood why. They were patient and let Clayton draw his own singular conclusion. When he'd recovered significantly he handed the paper back to Cal.

"There you are, Agent Denti. I've examined the requested document in full compliance. I'm afraid however, I have nothing that will either assist or detract from its application in any setting. The language is rudimentary and is a series of commands relating to everyday functions. My apologies. I'm sorry I couldn't be of further assistance." Clayton motioned to the door. "Good day, gentlemen."

Cal reached for the coding, but Jack beat him to it. He was enough of a gambler to bet the pot, especially in light of the recent run of bad cards. He didn't feel there was much to lose. If Oakes' work was proven accurate and backed by the hard drive, he'd just come back to it. If it all turned to shit, he'd walk away. Maybe far, far away.

"I was wondering, Mr. Rand, if you'd indulge me a little longer. Maybe if I gave you what I know, it might help prime the pump."

"I sincerely doubt that. I truly do."

"Humor me."

"Suit yourself."

"See this here?" Jack pointed quickly at no particular line. "Now, they tell me this is something called a 'data dump,' but she's a big sonofabitch. Probably a bunch of pictures. They take up a lot of room on a computer, see. But you'd know that, wouldn't you?"

Clayton didn't answer.

"Anyway," Jack continued, pointing again in a flash at no particular line of code. "This is so big it takes a while. Not an hour or nothing like that – these things are quick. But all these pictures go into something called a... shit. What's that thing called, Agent Denti?"

"Buffer overflow," Cal offered with a stern set to his voice.

"That's it. A 'buffer overflow.' While all this is going on – right in the middle of 'dumps' and 'overflows' and 'buffers' – wouldn't you know it," Jack slapped the paper with his hand in a loud crack that made Clayton jump visibly. He'd been listening and the hook was set deep.

Jack tugged the line. "Some crazy sonofabitch pulled the goddamn hard drive right out of the machine. Can you beat that? Took it right out of the computer. So now, if you compare what the computer's doing, with what someone thinks it already did, you get these couple of extra lines here. Ain't that a helluva thing? To me it's all gobbley goop, but it means something to you and guys like you. You're not the only one, you must know that much."

Clayton tried to casually take the page back. Jack gave it up easily and watched Clayton's eyes. "That is very interesting, Mr. Aaron."

"Ain't it though? Who'd expect something like that?"

Clayton regained his form and handed the paper back. When Jack didn't take it, Clayton shoved it toward Cal, who was more obliging.

"The problem with that scenario, DA, is that I don't see anything like that in this coding. And if I did, it would be very easy to replicate. After all, these are letters typed on a page. You could string together anything via a simple word processing platform. Someone could make it say whatever you wish."

"You know what?" Jack paused and smiled. "You're absolutely right. I could have done that. Well, I couldn't, hell I can barely type," Jack laughed. "But someone could."

"Yes they could."

"Here's the thing though, Rand. They didn't. We have the hard drive. And that's just what it says and then some. Like an IP address. Am I saying that right, Cal? IP address?"

"That's correct."

Jack didn't give Clayton any more time. "I appreciate you looking this over," Jack said as he slipped the page from Cal, folded it, took a long step forward, and slipped it onto the black granite countertop of the kitchen. Jack ran his fingers over the stone. "Now that's nice. Cal, isn't that great looking stone work?"

"Very nice."

Jack didn't offer to shake Clayton's hand. He was out the door with Cal falling in behind. "Well, I got to get back," Jack said over his shoulder. "And see what else the lab has pulled off that hard drive. We'll be in touch, Mr. Rand."

Jack waited until they were in the car. "You see that face, Cal?"

"A guilty countenance, it's called."

"We've got him. Remind me to give Oakes a raise."

Clayton locked the door and drifted to his counter where the single folded page waited. He rested both elbows on the cool stone. His hands covered his mouth in some odd Freudian maneuver that the wild haired professor might have suggested showed Clayton's lacking desire to speak about what had just confronted him. There was a painful tightness in the back of his neck. It was creeping up into his head on sharp iron claws. In his stretching to fight the constriction in his neck, his hands went to the counter and found themselves resting on the folded backup log. When Clayton stretched his neck down, he met the paper eye-to-eye. He unfolded it cautiously as though seeing it for the first time.

The talent had betrayed him earlier. He knew right away what he had seen in the lines of code. It was exactly as Helfer had said – the data dump, the buffer overflow, the backup log. Clayton closed his eyes. His shoulders sagged. The tension strengthened in his neck.

He carried the log in one hand at the length of his arm as though it were heavy. The pain evoking page was dropped next to his keyboard as he slid into his finely tuned mesh chair. Freed of the burden of the paper, his hands perched over the keyboard and waited for a signal. They were in their relaxed natural bend and resembled the curved talons of a raptor on a limb. Reluctantly, Clayton turned them loose.

The typing and clicking was near silent. In a few moments a digitized phone pad appeared. He dialed with touches to the screen and waited for the computer's speakers to come to life. A resounding click preceded a woman's voice.

"Central Intelligence Agency. Office of Public Affairs. How may I direct your call?"

"Ext 91728," Clayton said with marked hesitation and an uncommon softness in his voice.

"Thank you. One moment."

Another click and another operator. "Good afternoon. How may I direct your call?"

"Emory Lyle Duncan please."

"One moment."

And again.

"Emory Lyle Duncan please."

"Stand by."

And yet again.

"Clayton Rand for Emory Lyle Duncan please."

"Very good, sir."

"Thank you," Clayton said and promptly hung up the phone.

Within a minute the computerized phone rang. Clayton answered without a word.

A male voice asked simply, "Verify coding please."

"John Frank William 899," Clayton answered.

"Thank you. Third level access code please."

Clayton cleared the anxiousness from his throat and spoke in a slow clear voice. "It is far stronger to walk above the course."

"Thank you, Mr. Rand. How can we help?"

"The dominos are falling," he said plainly.

"Stand by. We're conferencing in your team."

_____

23

By morning, several plans, some well-conceived and executed, and others – forced hands yielding low payouts or merely attempts at minimized losses – were unfolding like flowers unwinding their petals to a new sun. Karen hadn't anticipated that her freedom had been designed only to track her. When she stepped off the elevator on her floor for work, a man moved hurriedly into the elevator behind her and pushed the 'Stop' button. She looked past the approaching uniformed Capital Police – a man and a woman – and saw a full team of FBI forensic investigators through the glass wall of her office. They were examining and collecting most everything in sight. Her computer had already been removed from her desk and sat in a box sealed with tamperproof red tape.

"Karen Auburn?"

"Yes?" she said only loud enough to fulfil her portion of the scene.

"We have a warrant for your arrest. You have the right to remain silent. If you give up the right to remain silent, anything you say can and will be used against you in a court of law. You have the right to an attorney and have that attorney present during questioning. Do you understand each of these rights as I've explained them to you?"

"Yes. What am I being charged with?"

The woman uniformed officer handed her a copy of the warrant. "Obstruction of Justice, Lieutenant."

"Thank you." Karen was reading.

"With these rights in mind," one of the officers was saying. "Would you be willing to talk to us now?"

"No, thank you. No."

Two agents from the Bureau stepped up. One produced a set of handcuffs. "May I have your purse, Lieutenant?"

Karen handed it over.

"Do you have any weapons on you?"

"No," Karen said as she held up her hands. "Go ahead. I understand."

"Just cursory," the agent said to the female officer.

Using mostly the back of her hand, the officer searched Karen, being very gentle and scarcely touching her swollen stomach. When she was finished the woman merely nodded.

The agent held out the cuffs. "Strictly pro–"

"Procedure," Karen finished. "I understand, but may I use the rest room first?" She put one hand in the small of her back and the other on her baby. "I think there's a foot on my bladder. I'm sorry."

"Go with her," the agent instructed the female uniform. To other agents he said, "One wait just inside, another at the door."

"Thank you," Karen said as the agent began searching her purse.

When Karen emerged from the bathroom, the handcuffs were still waiting. The agent holding them was ending a phone call. "We're on our way down now."

Karen went to him slowly so as to not outpace her guards, as if she could. "Thank you again," she offered as she also offered her wrists. She had thoughts of protesting or even suggesting having her cuffed would perhaps be construed as a poor reflection of the Bureau, but gave up quickly. Her mind and body ached. Either one seemed equally measured at the cusp of collapse. Far too drained to burst into full-blown tears, a few did struggle to life in the wells of her exhausted eyes. She captured them with her hands despite the restraints and exited the elevator in the lobby as dry-eyed and composed as she had been riding up a few minutes prior. The wide foyer – covering most of the ground floor – had, however, changed markedly.

Several members of the Capital Police force were inside and encouraged other federal workers – both in and out of uniform – to continue on their way. At the main doors, security had temporarily halted entrance to the building. On the short bank of steps, a massive network of reporters pressed for position – like maneuvering jockeys – with their cameramen in close tow. Behind them were their white logo emblazoned satellite trucks with their dishes and antennae stretched skyward.

Karen's feet involuntarily braced against being paraded into the floor of The Coliseum to face the lions for others' entertainment. Her handlers, one under each arm, felt the change.

"Are you alright, Lieutenant?" Karen's eyes reported the obvious and also the silliness of the question. "Lean on me, if you need to. I'll get you to the car as best I can."

"Are we going to local or federal holding?" Karen said as she encouraged her swollen feet to move toward the circus beyond the doors.

"Federal courthouse first."

Karen knew better, even in this situation and circumstance, than to waste energy quizzing the officer. Whatever or whoever waited, waited. Nothing would change now. She was thinking ahead of the 2nd warrant in as many days, the handcuffs loosely ensnaring her wrists, and beyond the crush of reporters outside JAG Headquarters, to the bond hearing where she would have to rely on her counsel to arrange for her release. She had the money to leverage a normal, reasonable bail, but at the base of the steps outside, between the gaggle of reporters and their trucks, a separate crowd of perhaps thirty people, many with loud placards and crudely fashioned signs, suggested that nothing would be normal again. The first shouts from the collected throng guaranteed it.

"Are you a member of ISIS?" "How long have you been selling military secrets?" "Lieutenant! What number wife are you?" "Do you gain status by having babies?" "Do you want your son to be a suicide bomber?" "How much were you paid?" "How does it feel to kill American soldiers wearing the same uniform as you?" "When did you convert to Islam?"

Karen was stunned to fumbling idiocy. "What? Of course not. I haven't sold anything. I wasn't paid. I have no idea. What?"

The reporters leaned in and professional shoving and crowding matches began between the media and the police. Nearer the street and the caravan waiting to ferry Karen to her next stop, the signs shook in the air and at the very pregnant Lieutenant.

"Traitor!" "They'd stone you in Kabul, bitch!" "Whore!" "Get her out of that uniform!" "Enjoy prison!" "ISIS slut!"

Karen was trembling under the onslaught. The police were trying – some more diligently than others – to stem the small crowd. Occasionally the surge reached her and Karen was shoved back and forth between the men and women sworn to protect the public from people like her and protect her from the public. It was an awkward balancing act that waited on one group or the other to cross a vacillating gray line.

It took several police officers to press back from the car enough to open the door fully in order to accommodate Karen's belly. When she clamored inside an agent went with her and all but finished on top of her. As they rearranged themselves someone struggled at length to close the door. Locked inside, but abandoned, the car's windows became the focal point of rage. People spit and barked obscenities at Karen through the thin glass. She was lost in a crumbling shock.

"What are they talking about?"

The answer came as pounding on the car's roof above her head. The noise was outlandish. Karen held her cuffed hands up to shield her eyes and face from the madness.

"Quite a welcoming isn't it, Lieutenant?"

"Something's very wrong." She was stopped by a sharp pain in her side.

"You better get used to it. You're front page news all over the country. You've seen those red 'Breaking News' banners dragging along the bottom of the news channels? Starting about fifteen minutes ago, every show is about you. There's no other news today. Just you, Lieutenant."

She wasn't so much asking as speaking a repetitive lost thought. "Why all the ISIS and traitor references? All this for conspira—" Another stab severed the thought and the voice at the same time.

The agent had a short limit over his concern. "How are you holding up there, Benedict?"

"What? What'd you call me?"

"Nothing, Lieutenant. Nothing."

"You said 'Benedict' and I didn't hear anything about a Pope. Where's that coming from? And all the references to the Middle East?"

They were questions born in the crazed desperation of the gauntlet she crossed getting to the car. As before, questions of transport officers and agents would be fruitless, but there were words in questions she needed to hear herself say in order to carve out a respectable answer. Nothing was coming easy.

The agent looked away from Karen for the first time. "Beats me. I'm just a foot soldier, but according to CNN you've been supplying terrorists with lots of useful intelligence. That'll get you spit on in this country pretty quick."

Karen moved from shaken through excited and on to angry in the space of a few charged heartbeats. "That's absurd!"

"That's why there's trials, Lieutenant. You get to tell your version of the truth."

"This is obscene."

"You have peculiar definitions, Lieutenant. Let's just leave it at that before one of us says something that might look good in a court stenographer's record."

Better prepared this time, Karen waded through a similar crowd in front of the Federal Building. "They got here quick," she said to the agent who now held her arm as they weaved and bumped through the throng.

"How's that go? 'Good news travels fast?'"

"Yes, and bad news faster. Who's the lead agent on this case?"

"No idea."

"Can you find out? Someone's leaking to the media. I have a few questions for him."

"Oh, not to worry. There's a lot of people who want to run some questions of their own by you. You've become pretty popular, Benedict. I think you'll meet everyone soon enough."

Karen soon found herself oddly enjoying the stillness of a small conference room after enduring the abusive crowds. The room was hers except for two painfully silent and equally burly FBI agents. She had been whisked here to undergo an interrogation and more. The trail of Sam Ciampiano had been nonexistent from the first day and the ties to Clayton Rand still tenuous. To many, the only lead in the origination of The New Illuminati was Lt. Karen Auburn and she herself, through her pregnancy, had forced John LaRoy's hand against her. Down the hall, a not-so-secret federal grand jury had been convened. John LaRoy would be fortunate to escape indictment. Karen was still in her handcuffs and effectively Mirandized for the Obstruction charge – substantiated by LaRoy and others, not the least of whom was the baby inside her.

Though no indictment had yet been handed down. There was a remote – very remote – possibility there would be a no bill finding when the jury was dismissed, but as the hackneyed saying went, "a grand jury can indict a ham sandwich," and Karen had provided enough admissions and omissions to insure that she – as the ham sandwich – would be dropped in a meat grinder.

So she sat with her silent guards in the uncomfortable handcuffs and waited. Though the sudden timing of her arrest had thrown her off, the accusations by the media and the rapid assembling of outfitted protesters ratcheted the intensity and stress up several notches. She understood the Bureau would use her as the pointer of a compass toward The New Illuminati. What she didn't understand was the vilification in the street. Unless clarification reached the press in short order, bail for a supposed terrorist aiding traitor, would be unlikely, if not unaffordable.

Alyn Nuary walked into her new spacious office in Washington looking dazed. The office would be redecorated and outfitted for her in time, but for now she would have to be content with the knowledge of what was coming – a new title, more power, prestige, access to the kings and controllers – LaRoy's job. She would recover quickly, but for now found herself sitting in a very kind, soft, leather covered chair that was older and less stylish than her tastes, but for the moment, very comfortable and compassionate. She touched the dated leather with a perfect fingernail. She could scratch the chair's skin easily, but resisted. Perhaps this chair would stay.

The meeting had been strangely brief given the heft of the topic and far reaching affects. It was in the Director's cavernous office, a short walk up the wide hallway. The Director had been there with his immediate staff, of which Nuary was introduced as the newest member. LaRoy's removal was not discussed and the sideways glances Alyn expected were absent. Perhaps she'd be an afterthought – tolerated – but her sense was more that she had shown her mettle and mirrored the means those in attendance had used and would use again. In this way, she had unintentionally earned their respect and was taken in as either a worthy adversary or ally. Her plan had come together in such a rush it was near overwhelming. The power in the room was palatable and quickened her pulse as she felt it vibrate over her. She perspired.

The Director made rapid introductions of the Bureau's command of which Alyn was suddenly listed. Their guest was the head of the CIA. Next to him sat an older member of the intelligence agency who persisted by necessity through many changes of administrations. The Director of the CIA might serve at the discretion of the President, but those who ran operations held strings that could not be cut by two-term whimsical changes in political parties. Still, it was heady for Alyn to be called to meet with men bearing such strong ties to the White House. But the fog of fresh power parted with the subtleness of a train wreck when Major Caulden walked in and sat very close to the CIA Operations Chief – so close, they shared a glance inside a simple cheap folder.

She fought the desire to stare and instead felt all eyes turn to her following the short CIA Operation Chief's mandate that the target of a recent investigation was not to be touched. The Bureau's Director turned to Alyn.

"Make it happen, Director Nuary."

"Yes, sir," she heard herself say which also served as the school bell sounding, "Class dismissed!" as everyone stood and left the office. Some shook hands and chatted for a moment, but all vanished to give the two appointees of the FBI and CIA a few minutes to discuss positioning, appointments, prices, and their boss.

Moments later Alyn was deep in the chair of her new office when Major Caulden walked in without knocking. She was still staring as he closed the door, walked to her desk, leaned over, and kissed her. "Hello, darling. How's life at the top?"

It was a hesitant fleeting glance, but it was there. Alyn looked back through the door and time toward the Director's office and the recent meeting. She didn't have a flurry of questions, but they all rode on the wings of that glance and Doug had seen it. The questions would go unasked, but covertly answered in the guise of events and attitudes.

"I'd like to say I'm sorry for not letting you know Clark Kent was Superman, but I'm not, so what's the point?"

"Bruce Wayne maybe. And it's a big maybe," Alyn said demonstrating the recovery skills she had mastered in her climb.

Caulden laughed. "Touché! Point made and taken. Glad you haven't lost your sense of humor."

"What I've lost is my arrest warrant for Clayton Rand. He works for the CIA?"

Caulden spun a light chair around in front of her and sat on it backwards, legs straddling the seat and leaning on the backrest. "Lesson one. That's not a question to ever ask or expect an answer to. You're new, so I'll give you a pass. Plus you have the hottest ass in the building."

"Thank you. I think." Alyn was trying to come up with another way to phrase it, but Doug relieved the pressure.

"Rand is in the security business," he said as though explaining a basic rule. "Same as us. Same as you. Doesn't it stand to reason our paths would cross?" He held up his hand. "No answers please. That's lesson two. No answers. No questions. No answers. One and two. Remember just those and you'll go far." Doug smiled and stood up, swirling the chair from under him as he did. "Or, as far as we want you to go. Kind of like this office. Enjoy, darling. I'll be in touch."

He leaned forward and kissed her cheek.

Alyn was slow to react, but reached for footing. "No you don't," she said as she pointed around the room. "This was me." She was up and in Doug's face. "This is mine. I got this!"

He snatched her by the throat and shoved her back down into the soft leather chair. The shock and pressure on her throat stole her voice. Her face reddened as his grip tightened under his weight. "You did nothing. Nothing! You have what we allow you to have. The moment you forget that, you'll be shopping in Wal-Mart instead of online at Neiman Marcus. Yes, we know that too." He released her throat.

Alyn gasped and put her own hands to her neck. "You piece of—"

"Be careful, Alyn."

She massaged her throat. "I'm the Director of Criminal—"

"You are what we say you are. No more. No less."

Alyn pushed by him and stumbled to her new desk. "I'll have you arrested." She picked up her phone.

The major took her place in the leather chair, crossed his legs, and folded his hands in his lap. "No, Alyn. You'll be arrested. By this time tomorrow, you will have been the shortest serving Director of Criminal Investigation in FBI history. How would you like to be remembered? Narcotics possession? Insider trading? Ties to a Mexican cartel? How about something with uranium? That'd be different. Have a preference?" Doug pointed to the phone. "You're not dialing, Alyn. It's 001. Security is 001. Ask for Peter. He's the head of security for the building."

She withdrew her hand, but Doug continued. "Oh, you know what would be colorful? Prostitution. Involved in a high priced call girl ring. That wouldn't even be much of a reach, would it?"

Alyn turned and faced him, one hand still on her throat.

"I thought you'd come around," the major smiled and stood. "But do use the phone. Get that investigation into Rand stopped like a good girl." He crossed the room and opened the door. "Oh, your boyfriend in the lab is doing a shitty job. Somehow that information from the hard drive got to Tampa. We'll find out how and plug that leak too, but get that hard drive scrubbed. Sooner the better.

"And go ahead and do what you want with the JAG lieutenant. LaRoy's history. He was getting difficult to manage anyway. We've set the lieutenant up pretty well for you already. The terror connection always appeases people. Get whatever mileage you can get out of it for yourself, but there's no connection between her, Ciampiano, Rand, The Illuminati – nothing."

"You bastard..."

"If you make her out as the star crossed pregnant lover of a vigilante who's fighting to rid the country of bad guys, they'll crucify you in the press. Our way is better. She's been calling me. I think I owe her a visit, but congratulations, you caught a terrorist infiltrating our federal government on your first day. Good job, Director Nuary. Well played. Keep it up. We know you can."

The major walked out.

———————————

24

In Tampa, Cal's phone was ringing, but it wasn't Nuary. His contacts in DC hadn't found Helfer Oakes, but they had located a dead John Doe that matched his description. Cal pointed them to the fingerprints Helfer would have provided when he went to work for the county. Cal gave them the go ahead to do the comparison and waited. When they called back, their question was who would handle the homicide case? FBI or DC? They'd found Helfer Oakes.

Cal drove to the District Attorney's Office with Nuary in his ear. By the time he arrived, the interview Cal and Jack had conducted with Clayton Rand was as dead as Helfer Oakes. Jack saw things differently and Marcus – stunned and shaken – was on the next plane for Washington.

True to his word, but back in his military role, Major Caulden was escorted to Karen's room inside the infirmary at the Joint Naval Base at Anacostia on the south bank of the Potomac River. Two Marine guards sat in chairs outside the room. A third sat just inside.

"Has the lieutenant had other visitors?" the major said as he briefly handed the guard his identification.

"No, sir. There's restricted access. Medical and family. Everyone else has to be cleared by the FBI. We received your clearance a short while ago, sir."

The major signed an entry log. His was the first and only name. He wrote a phone number at the bottom of the sheet. "If anyone shows up to see her, call that number forthwith. Understood?"

"Yes, sir."

"Provide that number to your superiors for dissemination to the watch."

"Yes, sir."

The major walked in Karen's hospital room unattended and passed the third Marine.

"Hello, Lieutenant."

Karen saluted weakly, barely raising her arm off the bed. "Hello, Major. How'd you find me?"

"It wasn't easy," Doug smiled. "After your last call, I thought I should look you up. You sounded a little frayed around the edges. I guess now I know why."

"You don't know the half of it."

"What's going on?"

"I wish I knew."

"You must know why you're here."

Karen held her ballooning stomach with both hands. "Because they couldn't fit me in the brig."

The major ignored the feeble humor. "What are the charges?"

Karen was reminded of his many questions on the phone. It seemed as though they were picking up where they left off.

"Obstruction."

"Is that it?"

"That's enough."

"What's this all about, Karen? The news is full of pictures of you over a red label that says, 'Military Terrorist.'"

"I have no idea where that's coming from."

"Can you tell me anything? Anything I can use to help you?"

She was still. The major was being measured when he thought he was the one gathering intel. "Nothing," Karen said. "But you can tell me something."

"What's that?"

"Where's Helfer Oakes?"

"Who?"

Karen smiled. "Who? You're kidding. Major, you don't forget a name or a face. You told me that a long time ago. Remember that?"

"No, I'm afraid I don't. And I don't know this Oakes either."

"He's from Tampa. He works with the District Attorney. Helfer Oakes is the one who found Clayton Rand and got us all to Tampa. I know you remember Tampa. Helfer's been in DC working with the Bureau on evidence in The Illuminati cases. He found some interesting things."

"Good. More than good. That's excellent. But what does that have to do with you being arrested?"

"Everything. Nothing. You haven't seen him? I talked to him the other night and–"

"Are you interrogating me, Prosecutor?" Caulden interrupted.

"Should I be?"

The major spun on his heels. "This is going nowhere. I thought maybe I could help you."

"If you want to help me, get a message to John LaRoy or Alyn Nuary at the FBI. Helfer Oakes has more evidence on Rand. They need to talk to him. Something's going on. Just tell them to find Oakes. He has hard copy files. The data files they'll need."

"I'll tell them."

"And so do I."

"Excuse me? You have files?"

Karen grimaced. It was a moment before she recovered. "Oww... That was a hard one."

"You said you had files. Evidence? JAG?"

"No. Helfer's evidence. He's worried about someone covering up the truth. Maybe it's you, Major. He was quite clear when I talked to him."

Caulden had long since turned back toward the bed. "Karen, are you medicated? You're not making any sense. I think you should be more worried about yourself and whatever's gotten you in here than a fanciful idea from some FBI wannabe lab rat. Don't you agree?"

"I'll manage. Marine?" Karen called around Caulden to the soldier in the chair by the door. "Would you call the doctor please?"

"Yes, ma'am."

"I believe I'm in labor."

Karen was right, but it wasn't quite time. The real pains didn't start for another five hours and it would be five more before Samiste Auburn Ciampiano was born into the brig on the banks of the Potomac River. Karen was nearly delirious with exhaustion and overcome with fear when the nurses started to slip him off her chest.

"Don't take him. Don't take him."

"We're just going to clean him up."

"Please. Don't take him."

"He's going to have a quick fit-for-duty and he'll be right back."

"I'm his mother," she began to cry, certain they were taking him away. "Don't take him."

"It's alright, Lieutenant."

"I'm his mother," Karen was sobbing now.

"We'll bring him right back."

"I'm his mother... Don't take him..."

"It's okay, Lieutenant."

"Bring in the other bed."

"Please don't take him..."

"He's going to stow his gear right here, Lieutenant."

"I'm his mother..."

"He's going to do his tour right beside you for now, Mom. We're setting up his rack next to yours."

"He's my baby..."

"Yes, ma'am, and here he is. Right here."

Baby Sam's gear – a single hospital blanket cut into quarters and a package of newborn disposable diapers – was stowed at the foot of the second bed. It would suffice as his locker until the FBI decided what to do with his mother. Unknown to her, and unrecognized by him outside of anything but the need to suckle, his own fate was waiting at a gate in Reagan International Airport for a flight due in from Tampa, Florida.

Marcus Pete had landed before the birth, but had been busy with the identification and investigation surrounding Helfer Oakes. All things – his missing items, the shoes stripped looking for the cheap and modern equivalent of a hidden money belt, the first gut shot – supported robbery as motive in the killing. Why Helfer was three blocks from the last station leading to one of the roughest areas of South DC, was not so clear. Capital Police had already chalked the homicide up to the commercially destructive wayward tourist scenario. There was nothing to indicate otherwise. Interviews yielded nothing – no witnesses, no sounds, and little evidence apart from the two common .38 caliber bullets, disfigured from hitting heavy bone following the lethal paths that stole Helfer's life.

Marcus called Jack almost on the hour with updates. The District Attorney was wrought. Marcus only slightly less so, given the proximity of the body and investigation that commanded a clear head. It was Jack however who put one piece of an impossible puzzle on the table.

"A .38? That's a little different. Damn little, but it's different."

"Different?" Marcus said, obviously still reeling from his young friend's death. "How so?"

"Think about what we see here, Petey. People shoot their cheating lover or business partner with .22 caliber thinking they'll drop in a heap like in the movies. Robbers and gang bangers like the automatics they see in the videos – fools holding their pistols sideways and firing ten shots into space – shell casings bouncing all over the road. A .38? Hell, that's what I still carry."

"I follow. Old school."

"Maybe. No shell casings to be gathered, fingerprinted, and tied to a pistol. Less evidence. More professional."

"Or that's all the thug could get his hands on?"

"Yep," Jack confessed the hole in his theory to nowhere. "Goddamn, Petey. We lost our boy, didn't we?"

There was a gap that assigned no blame, but acknowledged it none the less. "Yes, we did..."

"Who would hurt that kid?"

"Any crackhead, boss."

"Yep." The silence hurt them both. "What's next?"

"I'm going to see the FBI. They're not investigating, but he was at their building."

"Okay. Keep me in the loop. Thanks, Petey. Hey, Petey! Still there?"

"Still here."

"Let's keep that email under your hat for a bit."

"Agreed."

"Thank you for finding me some time," Marcus was saying to Jason Meyer as the two men walked up the hall of FBI HQ.

"No issue whatsoever. He was very diligent while he was here. Very pleasant. The last time we spoke, he was thinking of applying to the Bureau. He wanted to work in our labs. I can scarcely believe what's happened."

"It's been horrible."

Jason stopped in the hall and motioned into an open dark office. "This is where he was working the last day he was here."

Marcus stepped into the dim of the room. He didn't turn the light on instead stood staring at the shadowed desk and simple chair.

Jason reached in and flicked the switch.

The click echoed too loudly and the harsh fluorescent light hurt Marcus's eyes. Through his squinting, he saw the desk was empty. "Do you know what he was working on?" Marcus asked while staring at the chair. "What he was looking at? Anyone he might have been assisting?"

"Oh, um... not specifically. The evidence associated with Tampa primarily."

"Primarily?"

"There's a huge number of cases."

"Do you have a record of what he examined?"

"We don't... We were told to give him access to whatever he wanted."

"But no record? Is that normal?"

"Please don't take this the wrong way. I thought he was very talented, but him coming here was pretty redundant given our manpower and facilities. I took it that it was just a benefit for him – more or less. There were no expectations placed on him certainly."

"So he didn't find anything?"

"I'm sorry? 'Find anything?' Do you mean, like find the magic bullet in the files, kind of thing?"

Marcus turned the light off with that same resounding click, but lingered in the room. "Sort of. You said yourself, he was very talented. He found things in Tampa no one ever thought of."

Jason stepped away and in doing so, pulled Marcus with him. "This isn't Tampa, Mr. Pete. Is there anything else?"

"So, he didn't find the magic bullet?"

"Not that I'm aware."

"Would anyone else 'be aware,' with the unique record keeping, I mean."

"I would know. We spoke several times a day. There's nothing. I liked him very much and he could have been quite good given time. It is a tragedy. As difficult as that is to accept. He likely took the wrong train – certainly the wrong stop. It's happened before unfortunately."

They had effectively walked back to the entrance. Marcus was being shown the way out.

"I was told Special Agent Nuary has been reassigned to the building. I'd like to say hello. We worked together when she was in Florida."

"She's a Director now. The transition is–"

"Could you point me toward her office, or do I need an escort?"

They were at the screening station.

"I don't believe you could see her without an appointment."

"Let's make one," Marcus said, sounding for the world like his boss. He then spoke to a member of the building security. "Would you try Director Nuary's office and tell her Inv. Marcus Pete from Tampa is in the lobby and would like to say hello?"

In a matter of minutes Nuary stepped through the still opening doors of an elevator. She wore a fitted cream skirt, heels, and a matching jacket with wide jet black lapels. Her hair, makeup, and accessories were immaculate. She looked as though she were walking down a runway under popping camera flashes rather than beneath the harsh lights of the windowless first floor of Hoover's decaying fortress.

"Investigator Pete," she said extending her hand. "Thank you for reaching out to me. I am so very sorry about your colleague. Absolutely horrific. I'm certain Jason has already offered any help we can render."

"Thank you. He was just telling me about Helfer's work."

"He was an impressive young man, I understand. Such a terrible loss."

Jason stayed close to steer the conversation and prevent any contradictions.

"Did he reference anything to you he might have found interesting?" Marcus said, ignoring Jason entirely.

Alyn was quick. "I never saw him. I just arrived a few days ago myself. Why? Is something wrong?"

"Not that I'm aware."

"Surely, Investigator, you can't ask leading questions like that to people in our line of work and not expect a retort. What's on your mind?"

"Nothing. Not a thing."

"Really?"

"Not a thing. I'm just trying to piece together Helfer's last day. That's all."

"I understand. I'm afraid I have to run back upstairs, but Jason will help you with whatever it is you require. Good to see you again, Marcus."

They shook hands again. Alyn was turning away before she left the clasp. Marcus released her hand, but stopped her with a question. "Alyn, may I walk with you at the cost of another question?"

"Of course."

They stepped toward the elevator bank with Jason trailing.

"Helfer's death didn't even make the local news here as far as I can tell, but another member of the team we put together in Tampa certainly has."

"You mean Lieutenant Auburn."

"What's that story?"

"It's an ongoing investigation, Marcus. You know that's the polite way to say it."

"I do. But Helfer knew her from Tampa. I'd like to ask her if he looked her up while he was in town. Again, just putting together a timeline."

"I'm sure the Capital Police will do that for you. In fairness, you may be too close to be objective."

"That's fair," Marcus said. "But I'd still like to ask her. Where's she being held?"

"I believe she's in the infirmary at the Anacostia Joint Naval and Air Force Base across the river, but—"

"Which base?" Marcus said as he spun his head like it was on a swivel. "I don't know the city and there seems to be bases everywhere."

"But she can't be seen just yet. She's undergoing a very exhaustive debriefing."

"Which river?" and the Jack imitation came back out and was nicely done.

"The Potomac," Jason said without thinking.

"As I said, she can't be interviewed at the present time," Nuary said as she planted a dagger in Jason's heart with her eyes.

"I can't speak to her about Helfer?"

"Even if she's a suspect," Alyn said. "We'll contact you when she's available. I apologize. I do have to run. Best of luck, Marcus."

Alyn darted away, passing the closed doors on the bank of elevators for some other egress out of sight and sound.

Marcus was outside inside a minute, calling Jack from the sidewalk of the monstrous monolithic square of a building. Something made him look up at the windows of the higher floors, but saw nothing, just as he expected. When he relayed the tale of Karen's incommunicado sequestration, Jack ranted only briefly then sent him off with a new plan.

The Marine guards had grown bored with talking about their football teams, conquests of various sorts, and the next post they hoped for. They were out of their chairs and wandering the hall. They took turns visiting with the new baby which meant watching him sleep. When Marcus, with an escort, appeared at the end of the long hall, he was a welcome relief from the ennui.

Marcus and the escort were met at Karen's open door.

"Visits are restricted, sir," the Marine corporal said.

"He's a process server," the escort said. "He's got a subpoena."

The corporal looked at the sign-in log and at his buddies. "That fall under legal?"

"It does," Marcus said with a disarming smile as he held up a document. "A subpoena has to be served."

"Let's have a look."

Marcus handed over the subpoena for the baneful inspection. The Marines knew enough, read the lawful order, saw the seal of the court, and the space for the required signature of the server.

"I'll give it to her," the corporal said.

Marcus already had his pen and pad out. "Your name, rank, address, a phone number you can be reached at?"

"For what?"

"Without a doubt, you'll be called to testify that you served the order to appear." Marcus looked blatantly at the soldier's name tag and began to copy it down as painstaking as he could. "R. Standish. What's the 'R' for, Standish?"

"Hold up," the corporal said as tried to hand off the subpoena to one of his friends. "You give it to her."

"Not a chance."

"No way."

The Marine handed the subpoena back to Marcus. "Sign the log. Make it quick."

"Hi, Lieutenant. Mind if I come in?"

Karen was sitting up in her bed. Baby Sam was in her lap, swaddled and sleeping. The Marine corporal behind Marcus tapped his shoulder with a hard sharp finger then moved that same finger to his own lips.

"Shhhh. You wake that baby and the only thing that gets to the hospital before you is the lights of the ambulance you're riding in. Roger that?"

"Got it," Marcus whispered and he tip-toed toward the bed.

"It's okay," Karen smiled. "He sleeps like a stone. Good to see you, Marcus. Come see who I've got," said the proud mother, seemingly oblivious to everything around her.

"You know this guy, Lieutenant?"

"Yes, thank you, Corporal Standish. He's fine."

"He has a subpoena, ma'am."

"That's alright. They can't do much more than they have."

Corporal Standish went back to the hall as Karen introduced little Sam to his first official visitor.

"Wow...," Marcus smiled the placid admiring smile of anyone introduced to a baby for the first time. "He's a big boy."

"Nine pounds, eleven ounces. Twenty-four inches long. The nurses kept coming in. They couldn't believe the size of him."

"I don't doubt it. Are you doing alright? Everyone's fine?"

"We're fine. Just tired."

"Good, Karen. How about the rest of this?" Marcus said as he looked around to remind Karen of the place Baby Sam called home.

"I... I expected this. Eventually. I was wrong, but it was my call. It would have worked, but," she raised Sam up ever so slightly in her arms and glanced down at him. "Surprise."

"Karen, they may pull me out of here any minute. I need to ask you a couple of questions about Helfer."

"Oh! Me too. He found something."

"I know."

"You got an email?"

Marcus hesitated only a breath. "I did."

"Okay. There's more coming. Helfer's a genius. He's got the connection back to Rand."

"I saw the printout, but we need the hard drive. And my faith in the FBI has taken a big hit."

Karen's eyes sagged and sighed. "Yours? Look at me? I did this to myself, but there's something else going on over there. Don't trust them. Someone leaked that nonsense about me being in league with terrorists. They issued the warrants. It had to be somebody there."

"I was at their offices yesterday. They're not too helpful, but I can't see the FBI going to all this trouble to discredit – no offense – but to discredit a JAG officer who has already incriminated herself. What's the point?"

"I don't know. I truly don't. But it's tied to Tampa. There's something tied to The Illuminati. That email starts to unravel it."

"But we need the hard drive and the Bureau has it. As we've been reminded, anyone could type–"

"Helfer has it. Or he did. I've seen it. Talk to him. I'm sure there's more. He'll know what–"

"Karen? Karen. You don't know?"

It was her turn to pause.

"Know what?"

There was no gentle way. "Helfer's dead."

She visibly shuddered. It rippled through her baby and he was stirred enough to involuntarily suck on his lowered lip for a short count then returned to his dreams.

"W–What happened?"

"He was shot. Murdered in an alley. Only a few miles from here."

"Near Branch Avenue Station... The Green Line..."

Marcus felt his eyes widen. "How did you know that?"

Karen searched for a breath as her eyes paused over Baby Sam before finding Marcus. "He called me. After he gave me the page I sent you. He was nervous about smuggling things out of the FBI building. He apologized for using me..."

"Using you?"

"The backup log I sent you. He put it on the reverse of a receipt for me to take when I picked up my phone."

"Your phone?" Marcus turned away from the bed. "Why do I suddenly feel like everyone knows something I don't? Nuary and Meyer are coy as hell, and you suddenly have, had, Helfer's total confidence, and he doesn't call me? Something's going on."

"You're right, Marcus. And it killed him. He said he was meeting people from the office, military, was the word he used, I think. He invited me to meet him. I didn't go because I had all this trouble of my own."

"When was that?" Marcus said a little too harsh.

Karen tried to arrange the days in her mind. "I met him at the FBI building. We barely talked, but I took the receipt and my phone. He called that evening. The message should still be in my phone."

"Where's your phone?"

"The FBI has it."

"Shit."

"How about Helfer's?"

"Gone. Stolen."

The return to the young man brought no clearer focus to what was happening around them. It did however stay the flow of other concerns – most reaching, all dangerous. Beneath the confusion, Sam Ciampiano the 3rd was sleeping.

"Marcus?" Karen said through a tight dry throat, barely above a whisper. "I am so sorry. I know he was your friend." She held out her hand away from her baby. "I'm sorry... I don't know what else to say..."

Her hand hung in the air. It didn't flail – hardly moved, but ached to be picked up, but Marcus left it suspended there by strings and wires he couldn't track to places he didn't even know to look. He knew Karen had risked the investigation to save her lover. She had cost John LaRoy his career. Could she have cost Helfer his life? Yet she had played a role in getting the backup log out and to Marcus in Tampa. Where did she come down in this whole mess? This woman holding a newborn baby in front of him, was she a 'military terrorist?' Why the FBI's reluctance? Playing their own cards close to the vest to protect what? From whom? What reason? And why?

"Who's Tin Can DD?" This was as much of a test as he could muster.

Karen lowered her empty hand. "My neighbor. He won't verify it, but the IP would."

"We thought of that. I'm trying to think of a reason to trust you. Some way to tell who's on 1st, as Jack would say."

"I sent you the email. And the hard drive's on its way."

"What?"

"I'm not sure how he did it, but I think Helfer got the hard drive on my old phone. Mr. Garnett, my neighbor – Tin Can – has it. He's going to mail it to you if I don't come home. I told him it was a present and I might be in the hospital. I was thinking I might be here. At least I was right about one thing."

"Would he have sent it yet?"

"It's close. I don't think so."

"Would he give it to me?"

"Never."

"What if you spoke to him? Called him?" Marcus reached for his phone.

"I doubt it. He won't pick up a number he doesn't know. Go back to Tampa. When the phone comes, tell the world what Helfer found and that you're going to shove it right up Rand's ass. Whoever tells you to stop is the one to be afraid of."

"It's too late for that. We already talked to Rand. Next thing we know, Cal Denti, the local Agent-in-Charge, reins us in for reasons even he doesn't know. There's some powerful people behind this."

Karen's voice froze. She looked down at her baby then back to Marcus. "Helfer said he was meeting people from the office or military. The only people he knows in Washington are the people that were in Tampa. The only ones in uniform, 'military,' were me and Major Doug Caulden. Caulden is in this somewhere, Marcus. He's the 'military' Helfer was talking about in his message. Helfer was going to meet Caulden. Now he's dead. Helfer gave the backup file to me, and suddenly I'm a terrorist." Tears were coming into Karen's eyes from a nearly innumerable number of starters. "Someone doesn't want that backup log out there. Go wait for my phone. Do what you can with it, but be careful."

"You're telling me to be careful? Karen, I'm sorry, but you're headed to prison. Forget the terrorism nonsense. Even if that all goes away, you did what you did. They can prove it." Marcus didn't point, but waved his hand ever so gently at the baby. "Right here's the proof." The tears cascaded freely now. "And I can't help you. No one can. Thank you for what you've done for Helfer, and what he uncovered, but what you did..."

"I know..." She ran her hand over the baby's sleeping head.

"There's nothing anyone's going to be able to do."

"I know that. I'm not looking for a bargain."

"Not just you, Karen. There's nothing anyone can do for your baby either."

A woman's strong voice rang into the room from the door. "I wasn't trying to eavesdrop, but what you just said, young man, that isn't strictly true. Point of fact, it isn't true at all. The baby is going to be fine. Just fine."

Marcus eased away from the bed. "This is a privileged conversation. Are you on staff here?"

The woman walked closer to the bed. "No."

"Are you counsel?"

"I'm an attorney, yes."

"For the prosecution or defense?"

"You ask a lot of questions, young man. I'm not sure how to take that."

The woman was attractive and impeccably dressed. She looked maybe forty-five tops, with jewelry carrying stones that would carve plate glass windows by simply walking by. Karen noticed the woman intently staring at little Sam and very consciously pulled him closer to her. "Who are you?"

"I'm Marian Ciampiano. I'm Sam's mother."

The air went out of the room.

25

T he Ciampiano name evoked recognition and recoil in both Marcus and Karen.

"Marcus? Help me," Karen was pleading and pulling her baby closer. "Corporal Standish? Corporal Standish! Help me. Help!" Baby Sam was shaken awake and began to echo his mother's cries with his own.

Standish crushed into the room and headed for Marcus. "What's going on?" The other two Marines were one and two strides behind him.

Karen was pointing through tears. "I don't know this woman. She's trying to take my baby. Get her out of here."

"Lieutenant, she said she's the little guy's grand–"

"She's a liar!" Karen was hysterical. "She's an imposter trying to take my baby!"

The woman took a step back from the bed and turned to the door.

"Keep going!" Karen screeched. "Get out!"

"Lieutenant, I think–"

"Get her away from me!"

"*Zio?*" the woman said toward the door and around the Marine uniforms. "*Zio*, I need you please."

The tenor of the room changed in the drawn out second it would take an old man to step into the perfect focusing frame of the doorway. Only little Sam and the Marines continued their course – one crying, the others poised. Literally hat in hand, the maître d' from The Columbia Restaurant walked slowly into the room and stood with a combination of confidence in his eyes and a firm set to his jaw, but an uncomfortable awkwardness in his body. He clearly did not like the quasi-police uniforms of the Marines or an environment he could not control. He was recognized by both Karen and Marcus immediately.

"How about this character, Lieutenant?" Standish asked over the baby's continued protests. "He says this lady and him are related to you and the little guy. You say the word and I'll chuck them both out the window."

Before the words could work through the filter of Karen's mind and form a conclusion, Mr. Guzimon waved a boney hand at Corporal Standish. "Ah, this one. He's a good man," he continued while stepping to Karen's bed. Their eyes were locked. "It is a wise choice to have him serve as your guard – as your, Pretorian." The old man was alongside the bed, looked down, and stroked the baby's chubby red face. "Shhh. Shhh. You are okay, Tiny Hammer." He coaxed the crooked first joint of his little finger against the baby's mouth until Little Sam began a calming attempt to suckle. "Ah, see? You are fine now. Shhh." The maître d' returned his attention to Karen and touched her face with his free hand. "You are fine now as well."

Air rushed into Karen's chest and it swelled. As she exhaled with a stillness just audible in the quiet room, baby Sam quivered and relaxed anew. Mr. Guzimon let his hands fall away and then held one out to Marian and invited her closer.

"Miss Karen? My niece, Marian Testiani Ciampiano. She has another name," he smiled. "But it is not Italian. I don't work to remember it well. She is my niece and is, *certamente*, your Sam's mama. You should talk." He turned to the staring Marines and Marcus with a dismissing wave of one hand. "You may go."

"Lieutenant?" Standish asked.

"Y–Yes. I'm okay. Thank you."

"Let's go, process server," Standish motioned to Marcus. "You're done. Two visitors at a time is the limit. Out."

"Marcus?" Karen said as she reached out again. This time Marcus took her hand, but held it only a moment. "Go back to Tampa. Wait. Do what you can. And again, I am so very sorry."

"I know. You take care." Marcus looked at the maître d' then back to Karen and the baby. "I think you'll be alright. Both of you."

There was no hug. Just a look and the slightest wave from the door as the Marines escorted Marcus out and removed themselves in the process.

"He is a Tampa man?" Mr. Guzimon said as he looked at the empty door.

"Yes. He works in the District Attorney's Office. Marcus Pete. I should have introduced you."

"Ah, no, you shouldn't. He causes you and the *piccolo* troubles?"

"No. No. Not at all."

"Ah, that is good for him. Tampa man or no.

"Ah, here, Marian, you talk now. I will go mind the soldiers. Speak free." He looked again at the baby then to Marian. "He is the mirror of your Sam, no? A rugged boy baby. Like his papa." Mr. Guzimon motioned the two women together with his hands. "Talk. Talk. I wait outside," he said then walked out of the room with his hands clasped behind his back.

The chasm left by the absence of the connecting link was wide. Karen stepped into it first.

"I had no idea. I don't know what to say."

"How could you know?" Marian came closer and stood at the foot of the bed. "I'd have been sorely disappointed if you hadn't tried to throw me out," Marian smiled. "I may not have been one, but I recognize a good mother when I see one."

There was much to discuss, but Karen couldn't resist starting with the elephant in the room.

"What happened?"

Marian moved slowly, but closer until she sat on the bed and touched the baby's face for the first time. There was a slight tremble in her fingers.

"I was young – way too young. I was from a small town south of Palermo. Naturally, I thought I had outgrown it. Outgrown a town at sixteen. My family sent me to my uncle – who you know," she said as she took her turn referring to the door and the hallway beyond. "He put me to work in the restaurant where I met Sam's father. He was older, much older, but I was impressed with the money, the cars, the power. Until it was too late. I was seventeen when I had Sam. The pregnancy was difficult. Sam's father was a good man, but not much help to a pregnant teenager. I saw him – Sam's father – do things. That's what he did. It was his job in his eyes. It scared me. Really scared me. I wanted out." She got up from the bed and walked on tailor made shoes. "When Sam was born, I swore I'd never live like that. I never wanted to get pregnant again, never wanted to see people hurt, men cry like children. I didn't want the money or any part of it. I had my tubes tied the day after Sam was born while I was still in the hospital. I walked out of there a day later, packed my clothes, and left. I never looked back. I had no regrets... at first. Years later, when I tried to go back, Sam's father wouldn't hear of it. He wouldn't allow presents or money and he stopped any news before long. I know what he'd do if I pushed it.

"That's the short story, Karen. I'm not proud of any of it, but that's the way it happened. There's usually a few sides to every story – not just two – but that's my side and it's as straightforward as I can make it. I'm not really sure what Sam's father told him or what he believes about me, but what I just said is the truth. Warts and all."

"He never said much. He's not big on talking anyway."

"His father was that way."

"He has a picture though. He kept it on his father's dresser."

Marian rummaged through a designer clutch and pulled out a ragged and faded Polaroid. "Is it one like this?"

Karen took it. In the paper margin was hand printed in faded block letters, 'Mommy (Marian) & baby (Sam).' She looked up. "It's exactly like that. Exactly."

"Sam took two that day. It's the only thing I took, besides my clothes. It was just a whim at the time. I didn't care. I just wanted to run. I don't want to run anymore.

"When *Zio* told me about you, I had some reservations. Then I saw you on the news with your belly. I knew I had to do something. I've seen on the news, you're an attorney. That should help. I don't know if you caught it when I came in, but I am as well. I've had a very good private practice for a long time now. My husband and I work together in Chicago. We, obviously, never had children.

"I've been doing some poking around about your case, but it hasn't been easy."

"I haven't even been formally charged."

"Yet, it must be extremely serious."

"Conspiracy. But I haven't even seen my counsel. I feel like I'm in Gitmo."

"Conspiracy is serious enough, but I won't lie to you, I've been pursuing another angle." Marian patted the swaddled bundle. "This little man's immediate future. I'll arrange for the most qualified legal staff I can assemble for your defense, but I'd like to insure your baby – did you name him Sam?"

"Yes."

Marian smiled. "I thought you might. I'd like to make certain he doesn't get tossed into the federal system somewhere."

Karen's arms tightened and Marian saw it.

"I understand and I'll do whatever can be done to keep him right next to you as long as we can possibly do it, but the harsh reality is, whatever is taking hold of you is major. The government can almost do what they will – the military even more so. I'm not trying to frighten you. You know it already. Karen, the cold, hard truth is they could walk in here in the next five minutes and ship you to the women's military prison in San Diego and Sammy would assuredly be bound for foster care."

Tears had nearly run dry, but a few more from the deepest corner of her darkest well where her own remembrances of foster care stayed hidden, squeezed out a few more. Marian stroked her arm and hugged her. Baby Sam was locked between them.

"Come along now," Marian rubbed Karen's back. "We'll beat this thing. Somehow. Some way. But I'd like you to consider something." The embrace melted enough for Marian to cradle Karen's tired face. "I can petition for temporary custody as Sammy's grandmother. Then, should you be moved, he can stay with me." She gave her forsaken son's forsaken lover as much time as she could spare, glanced over her shoulder, and came back to Karen. "Take some time, but consider–"

"Yes. Yes, please."

There was more talk, more plans, realities and expectations. Marian took a picture of Karen and the baby with her phone and had Mr. Guzimon take some of the not quite related three generations. With promises to return the following morning with more news and necessary paperwork, Marian and the maître d' left mother and baby to the once again quiet, boring, but well-guarded care of the Marines.

———————

26

Offices, tied together by the thread of The New Illuminati, were in an assorted array of affairs. Apart from the cause and the case, the only other common denominator was that the doors to each were closed. Pulses were far ranging. Emotions crossed the gamut. Jack Aaron's was perhaps hardest hit and deepest ranging. He was angry – violently so – then moved to the brush of a tear from frustration and loss. He had sent Helfer to Washington, unaware he was sending him into a snake pit. Cal Denti's office was a low hum of attempted phone calls and subsequent slaps on an increasingly sore wrist until he sat back, dismayed and disillusioned.

Across the city, Raphael worked at a frenzied pace trying to lose himself and speed time along so as to outdistance his attachment. He would not see or speak to Clayton. For his part, Clayton Rand had barricaded himself in his home office fortress. He watched the monitors anxiously and took rare calls from clandestine handlers he had long outgrown.

For John LaRoy, also in a home office, but a simple room in comparison to Clayton's high-tech bubble, the air was vastly different. LaRoy was relaxed as he leafed through pages of old notes and files, long since declassified. He had already passed over any ill will toward Lieutenant Auburn. She had duped him, yes, but it had been his decision. The burden was his to bear and he took it. Maybe it was a strange blessing, he mused to himself. Perhaps now he would write about his career or maybe just go snipe hunting.

Only one office held more than its owner. Alyn Nuary was behind her desk. Jason Meyer sat in the soft leather chair while Major Caulden strutted.

"Meyer, you're the one who should clean this mess up. You let that little geek make you look like an idiot. How the hell does he find a backup log file the finest lab in the world missed?"

"It wasn't missed."

"Bullshit."

"The analysis was not complete."

"And then he sneaks it out? Right in front of you? What kind of shit security is that? I'm goddamn glad you're not protecting the country!"

"That's rich" Jason poked him. "I wish I had your track record. Fourteen hijackers walked in the front door on your watch, asshole."

"You little f–"

"Hey!" Alyn screamed to keep the two men apart. "You're worse than eighth grade girls. Listen to me. To paraphrase Rumsfeld, there's 1 – what we know, 2 – what we don't know, 3 – what we know we don't know, and my favorite, number 4 – what we don't know we don't know, or something like that. Where's she fit in a grid like that, Doug?"

"She came to this building," the major emphasized, "And picked up her phone from Oakes. He called her later."

"We know that for certain?"

"We do. It's on both their phones."

"We have his phone?" Jason questioned. "How'd we get his phone?"

"Shut up a minute, Jason," Alyn scolded. "Keep going, Doug."

"His message is still in her phone. We took it off her when she was arrested. He referenced a receipt and her old phone. That connects the existence of data he likely loaded on the old phone." Caulden glared at Jason. "Right downstairs in your lab. So she's got the hard drive."

"And that old phone? Where is it?"

"Not in her apartment," Jason volunteered. "We gutted it."

Caulden stabbed back. "Which means it's probably laying on the kitchen table."

"Do we need it?" Alyn asked anyone.

Doug answered with a question of his own. "Has the hard drive been fully compromised?"

Alyn looked at Jason.

"It's done. I told you," he shouted. "Irretrievable."

"I take no comfort in your say so, Meyer. You're incompetent."

"Fuck off, Major. Sir." Jason saluted with his middle finger to his brow.

The major leaned against Nuary's desk and pointed at the door. "Either walk out that door, you little lab rat, or I'm going to put your head through it."

"Give me a break, Rambo. You goddamn Nazi."

"You're done, Meyer. Toast! Get him out of here, Alyn. Hurry up."

She brushed Jason out the door with her hand, but he baulked halfway. "If anyone ever starts listening to the lieutenant, you'll lose what you've gained, Alyn. And you'll be able to thank this psycho." He left without another word, grateful to be relieved of any more culpability.

Alyn pushed her chair back and gave herself room to cross her legs. Caulden was not distracted.

"Doug? What's the matter? You're terribly tense." It was the old game and the only one she really knew. "It's unlike you. Why don't we take the rest of the day? I'm apartment hunting. Come with me. It'd be fun."

He stared at her with loathing. "Meyer's right, you know?"

"About what?"

"The lieutenant. Talking one day. Producing that hard drive data."

"No one has access to her."

"You have no idea, do you?"

"About what? You talk in riddles lately. I like my niche. I want to keep it. I want more. Tell me what I need to do. Tell me what's so important about that hard drive."

"You are so damn dumb. Honest to Christ."

"Don't you dare insult me. I know where a few skeletons are buried too, you know. And if you ever touch me again, I'll shoot you myself."

"Oh, that's right. You're the top marksman, aren't you?"

"Remember it."

The major laughed. "You don't know shit, Alyn. You never have."

"Then enlighten me, oh, wise one. Why's that drive so vital?"

The major crossed the room, momentarily less tense with Jason gone. He sat in the leather chair, slumped, and pointed to the computer on Alyn's desk. "See your computer, darling? Guess what's between that computer – that one right there – and a computer on the other side of the world?"

"You make no sense."

"What's between the two computers – the actual machines? What's between them?"

Alyn shook her head and shrugged. "I don't know – eight thousand miles? A trillion feet of wire? Firewalls? I don't know. Nothing. Nothing connects them."

"That's the closest answer, right there. Nothing. What separates that computer from one eight thousand miles from here is nothing. Air. Everything's wireless before it's done. We can hard wire this building and call it a closed loop, but everything will hit a satellite sooner or later and what goes up," Doug pointed to the ceiling then turned his hand over and crashed it into the arm of the chair. "Must come down."

"Another riddle."

"The only thing that separates your computer from the computer of the biggest, baddest, craziest sonofabitch in the world is software. Invisible data. Ones and twos doing gymnastics to keep your computer from figuring out what my computer is doing. 'Why's that important?' the silly blonde asks again. Because, darling, if someone sees you planning the President's day, they're going to be waiting, and put a bullet in his head and that's bad for this experiment called democracy. It's bad for business. Bad for capitalism. Bad for the American Way. We better keep him alive, don't you agree?"

"Give me a break."

"So we try to keep your online shopping and your investigations from being seen by the Koreans, the Chinese, hell, even the Germans, or each other for that matter. And guess who keeps us all tucked in at night? Go ahead, guess."

"No idea."

"See? See, Alyn? That's why we wanted you here. You shop, catch a headline now and again, maybe do an interview on TV, and write a book. While we protect the world from itself."

"Okay! Some super satellite. NASA. The FBI and the CIA's top secret lab buried beneath a mountain in Colorado. How about Area 51?"

"How about Clayton Rand?"

Alyn stopped her rambling and began to follow. "Rand?"

"Clayton Rand. In quiet little Tampa, Florida."

"Are you playing with me?"

"You have no idea. Perfect, isn't it? Smart guy running a nice little multi-million dollar business. Seriously, they're a dime a dozen. No one looks twice. Successful. Nice guy. Not some whack job in a cabin on a mountainside or, as you suggest, some dick in a lab coat with a pocket protector and thick glasses beneath Area 51." Caulden was up from the soft chair. "He's brilliant! He's written codes the Chinese will be scratching their heads over for the next five years. And the hits just keep coming. He's a goddamn wizard. It's perfect. The fact that MacDill Air Force base – home of Special Operations Command – is five miles from his house is pure coincidence. Pure coincidence."

"Alright, I'm tagging along. But if he does all this miraculous stuff, what happened? What went wrong?"

"Who knows? He got bored. I don't know, and more importantly, I don't care. No one does." Caulden lowered himself just onto the arm of the chair and folded his arms. "This little firestorm he generated diverted attention from some other problems we had. Better yet, we used it as cover to clean up some problems – LaRoy for example – and bring others back in line. Nothing like the fear of getting blown up to make you cooperate with the real agenda."

It was sinking in fast and Alyn was soaking it up. If ever there was a person prepared to take the pledge, it was Alyn Nuary.

"And so we're back to the lieutenant?" she asked appropriately.

"Indeed we are. This is what I foresee. You will arrange for–" One of two phones the major carried vibrated. "One minute, darling."

He answered. "Major Caulden... Yes... When?... A subpoena?" Caulden spoke to Nuary. "Did you issue a subpoena for Lieutenant Auburn?"

"No."

"Who was it?..." The major stood up. "He's no process server. He's an investigator for some backwater swamp in Florida..."

"Marcus Pete?" Alyn said softly. "He was here yesterday looking for her."

"And who else?... Jesus, was she having a party?... A baby shower? That's funny, Standish. Maybe you can tell jokes at the enlisted man's club in Iceland during your next tour!... No, skip it. There won't be another watch tomorrow night. She's headed out... None of your business. That's 'need to know.' Tell her shit, shower, and shave. Get her packed."

Caulden hung up. "What is it with these little shitheads from Tampa? They are a persistent bunch, I'll have to say that. Pete paid a visit to our Lieutenant."

"That can't be good."

"What did you say five minutes ago? 'No one has access to her.' Isn't that about right? Christ. Well, she doesn't have the phone, we know that. No matter what she might have told Pete, it's hearsay three times over. You'd have to go to hell and back twice to get any court to listen to it.

"Oh, here's another gem for you, Director Nuary, straight from the swamp. Florida. Is it the hot weather down there or what? I remember you had Meyer look into a restaurant down there – relatives of our boy, ex-Ranger Ciampiano. One guess who just showed up to visit Lieutenant Auburn."

"That old man? The waiter?"

"None other, and he brought another guinea named Testiani. She claims to be Ciampiano's mother. What a cluster fuck. Arrange for an interview of the supposed mother. That baby might be just the trigger we need to flush Ciampiano."

The major went to the door, but left it closed. "Okay, Alyn, we're clear now on whys and who?"

"Crystal."

"Good, because here comes the how. Now is when it's apt to get cloudy again, but I need you to keep your eye on the prize. Eye on the prize, girl. Eye on the prize. People like to think the first ones are the hardest, but it's not so. Every job is different. Not harder, easier, nothing. Just different. Do just what I tell you, and you could be the first female Director of the FB of I."

She squirmed her ass deeper into the chair and folded her hands on her lap, covertly pushing her fingers into her crotch. "I'm finding this strangely erotic."

"I thought you might. Listen close," he said as he stepped back toward her with a tight menace in his eyes. "You only get one shot at an opportunity like this."

————————————

27

The following morning, Marian spent several hours on the phone. She leveraged favors from every old case and called in markers from anyone who owed. When she hit a wall, Mr. Guzimon retreated through the adjoining door between their hotel rooms and made a side call to Tampa. Soon the phone in Marian's hotel room would ring and the logjam would have been miraculously cleared. It went this way until a knock at the door announced a courier with sealed documents from the local court. Marian hugged her uncle and clutched the papers that provided her custody of baby Sam.

Marian gave the epitome of what a true sigh of relief was. "Not this time," she said as her eyes began to glisten. "This time I do the thing I should have always done."

"Ah, you're a good girl, Marian. *Brava ragazza.* I knew this thing all this time."

With one quick stop in between, Marian and Mr. Guzimon were back at the Marine's chair outside Karen's room. Under 'Relationship,' Marian penned, 'grandmother.'

The maître d' pointed to the spot with the pen. "What goes in the space? 'Relationship.' What is *mio* relationship to the *bebè martello?*"

"You are his great uncle, but he'll be no Hammer. He will be a good boy."

"*Zio grande?*"

"*Si.*"

"*Grande?* The big uncle. *Inglese? Superiore?* Superior?"

"Umm... *Si.*"

Marian smiled at the Marines and went inside.

"Superior. Super uncle," the maître d' said as he wrote it. "I like this. The Super *Zio. Si. Bene.*"

He walked into the room to find Karen looking fresh, showered, and dressed in a light tan prisoner's jumpsuit standing next to the bed. Marian was holding the baby and listening.

"The Marines said I should be ready to go. Apparently I am being relocated. I don't know where. If they knew, they'd tell me. How did it go for you?"

"It's done. We have temporary orders here that you need to sign in front of a witness. We'll petition you to court at the next available date for a formal decision, but this will suffice. He's your boy – always will be – but it gives me temporary custody. No one can touch him."

Karen latched onto Marian around her son. She kissed Marian's cheek and lowered her head to Marian's shoulder. For the first time in recent memory, Karen felt the care of a mother and gave the love of a child in return.

Mr. Guzimon put his hand on Karen's shoulder and patted. "Ah. Our Marian is a good one, she is. *Benissimo*."

As an answer, Marian turned and thrust the baby into *Zio's* hands, then threw her arms full force around Karen and hugged her for all she was worth. Karen burst into tears of joy, remembrance, longing, and fulfillment. She would miss love, in both the strong and fragile hugs of Sams – big and small – but found, in Marian's arms, a love she had groped aimlessly for her entire life. Marian felt a teeming sense of love recovered.

The maître d' walked baby Sam out into the long hallway and left the women to their embrace, longings, and shared tears. The Marines nodded and smiled. *Zio's* chin went higher with each glance from the soldiers. At the far end of the hall, he spoke gently as he somewhat roughly bounced the baby up and down in his arms. "*Voi siete il Siciliano*. You are Sicilian, *Po' Martello*. *Della famiglia, Ciampiano*. *La città di Ficuzza*. *Provincia di Palermo*." He held little Sam in one hand and mesmerized the baby with a waving finger the Marines took as a playful scolding. "You must go back to your home, little boy. There... there you will find the rest of your family. From Ficuzza, you find your father. I will teach you as long as I can, *Piccolo Martelletto*. As long as I can."

A phone rang somewhere nearby. One of the Marines answered it, but Mr. Guzimon couldn't understand what was said from afar. He drifted with little Sam back to Karen's room and peeked inside to gauge the condition of his extended family. The women were sitting on the edge of the bed looking at printed copies of the photos Marian had taken the day before.

"You hold on this. My number is on the back," Marian said as she pointed to a photo. "And I will put this one in his crib."

A steady stream ran down Karen's face and fell from her chin between rests on Marian's shoulder.

"I'll find out where you've been moved to and we'll arrange to visit."

"I breast feed him, Marian. How will he manage?"

Zio had stepped inside and handed the delicate bundle to Marian who took the baby gently and instantly put him in Karen's arms.

"He's half a grown boy already. I know Ciampianos. He'll eat anything you put in front of him."

Corporal Standish stepped into the door. "Lieutenant? Time to make way, ma'am."

"Come here, please, Corporal." Karen handed Sam to his grandmother and wiped her face with her hands. "I need a pen," she said and Standish yanked one from his pocket before Marian could reach for her purse. "Corporal, I need you to sign these documents," Karen explained as she wrote her name on several papers Marian had brought. "That you are a witness... that I signed these. That's all... You're not attesting to anything. Only that you saw me sign these... under no duress. That's how any question might be posed. I am under no compulsion to sign these papers. Understood?"

"Yes, ma'am."

When she had finished and the corporal had signed and initialed as directed, Karen abruptly hugged him. "You've been very kind, sweet, actually. I appreciate it. Little Sam does too," she smiled and wiped her face again. "Thank you so much."

"You're welcome, ma'am."

Marian followed up Karen's hug with a one armed version of her own while still holding Sam. The maître d', eyes on him, shuffled his feet and looked at the floor, the baby – anywhere but the uniform – yet found the strength to stick out his hand.

"*Grazie,*" he said with hesitation as he shook hands with the corporal. Mr. Guzimon then leaned over and whispered in Italian to the baby. "He is *militari. Non la polizia.* I think it is okay."

A small entourage had formed in the hall and escorted Karen to a waiting van. She rode in a wheelchair, still sore and tired, holding Sam on her lap and a photo in her hand. Karen had long been resigned to her own fate and was now comforted by the knowledge of her baby's. Social service workers had appeared to take little Sam, but were quickly thwarted by the court papers, though *Zio* thought his tart dismissal of them in a rapid Italian diatribe had done it.

The goodbyes were short – quick hugs and kisses hastened by the running engine of the white van with heavy metal screens over the windows and behind the front seats. As other Marines took custody of

Karen, Standish told them in no uncertain terms to treat her right. One produced handcuffs.

"She has to wear them for transport," he told Standish before it was questioned. "It's not us."

Corporal Standish took the cuffs and locked them as loosely as possible on Karen's thin wrists being careful to not disturb her photograph.

"When you get to your next duty station," Karen told him before she stepped up into the van. "You stay safe."

"Yes, ma'am. Thank you."

"I don't suppose you can tell us where she's going," Marian asked as she held the baby while the Marines fastened Karen's seatbelt over her lap.

"No, ma'am."

"I understand," she said. "We'll find you. Now that we've got this little guy taken care of, we can focus on you. Things will work out. I made some calls regarding the charges and a bond hearing."

The door was sliding closed between them.

"Okay," Karen said as the door latched closed. She waved meekly through the steel mesh grate with both hands held together by the handcuffs as the van sped away, the photograph of her and baby Sam clamped in her fingers.

No one paid any attention to the van as it wound through the streets of the base. It sauntered through the main gate and headed for downtown DC. The Marine guard questioned the driver. "I thought we were going to the court?"

"We are. Federal court, not military. It's an FBI case, not ours, even though she is. Confusing, isn't it?"

Simple papers, with the right boxes checked and the right signatures attached, got the van in the parking garage beneath the courthouse when a tank couldn't have breached the many barriers and levels of security. Karen, holding her picture and another simple form provided by the guards, was walked to an elevator. The ride up several stories was quiet. She was grateful not to have seen any media trucks camped around the building though she was prepared to find reporters outside the courtroom. She was pleasantly disappointed when the elevator doors opened and no one waited with a microphone or a camera.

It was only a few steps to the courtroom. The parking garage, elevators, and this court had been, by design, easily accessed and secured.

As a Marine held open the door, Karen noticed the stage of the courtroom was missing several actors. A judge was already seated at the bench, but there was no bailiff. There was also no one at the prosecutor's table. Nor was her attorney present. She assumed they were in one of the adjoining rooms in conference as she took her seat at the defendant's table and waited. The fact that there was no court reporter present wasn't immediately disconcerting. Presumably he or she was with the attorneys taking down the give and take of pre-trial motions, until Karen realized the stenographer's machine was sitting unattended and had not accompanied the operator to a sidebar.

The Marines stood a few feet behind her.

The judge referred to a few papers on his raised bench. "You are Lieutenant Karen Auburn?"

Karen quickly stood. "Yes, your honor."

"Sergeant? Remove those cuffs while in the presence of the court, please. It's prejudicial."

The Marine complied.

"Thank you, your honor," Karen said as she waited while the confusion deepened.

"This is a bond hearing," the judge said suddenly and Karen thought of Marian. "The single charge of Conspiracy against you notwithstanding, it is the disposition of this court that you — having been deemed not a flight risk, with an exemplary record as a member of the Judge Advocate General's Office, and in that capacity, having a clear knowledge of the consequences should you fail to comply and appear before this court at such time as duly ordered — are to be released on your own recognizance pending such additional circumstance.

"Lieutenant Auburn? You are free to go. Your dress whites are in the anteroom across the hall."

As abruptly as he began, the judge had ended the thirty second hearing. He was up and walked out the back of the courtroom to his chambers leaving Karen full of questions. The lawyer in her was ready to ask for a meeting with the judge to ask how she could be bonded out before being officially charged, where her counsel was, in fact, where the prosecution was. And the court reporter? Who would have a record this hearing took place at all? But she looked at the picture in her hand instead. She would go in search of her baby instead of answers. The answers could find themselves.

Despite the many shortcomings of the court, the judge had been right about her clothes. The white maternity uniform she had been wearing when she was arrested was in a brown paper bag on a conference table in the room across the hall. The Marines told her to leave her jumpsuit in the corner on the floor and disappeared. Karen locked the door and got changed, still confused, still looking at the photograph now sitting on the table as she dressed.

The maternity uniform fit only slightly better than the tan jumpsuit. The baby had taxed it to its limit, but it felt better against her skin, and the support of her shoes around her still swollen feet, much more comfortable than the plastic sandals she'd been wearing since the day she was arrested. Her jewelry, purse, and phone weren't in the bag, but her military ID and wallet were. She had them and the precious picture in her hand when she stepped with great care out of the conference room, quite expecting to be advised a mistake had been made.

The hall was empty. Karen thought of the stairs, but her feet and body begged for the elevator. She pushed the call button and waited, glancing over her shoulder and around her for the jig to be up. In the elevator, she adjusted her poorly fitting uniform. She took a wad of the waist and scrunched it into her right hand and held it as inconspicuously as possible on her hip.

The foot traffic on the street level of the courthouse was vigorous. Security officers and Capital Police manned scanners and examined documents of those with business in the building. The exit had no such scrutiny, just one officer to insure people traveled only one way. Karen walked right by him.

The street was not congested, not even busy except for a consistent stream of people coming to the court bearing reams of legalese within bulging tied legal folders. In the days and weeks to come, of all those people, police found no one who could unequivocally say they heard the shot. The man just behind Karen, thought she had tripped and fallen. When he instinctively reached to help her he saw the blood spouting from her neck with such force it sprayed several feet across the gray granite steps.

Two or more people walked by her, oblivious, so focused on their own issues waiting within the building. Called by the shouts of the man kneeling beside her, others gathered. Some were repulsed by Karen's gapping throat, the incredibly rapid pooling of the rich dark blood contrasting against her bright white uniform, and turned away. A greater number stood transfixed by her slight trembling, her gasps, the twitch of her bluing lips, and the involuntarily incessant blinking of her wide eyes, as though she was caught in disbelief. In less than thirty seconds all movement stopped. The picture of her and baby Sam was still caught in her rapidly cooling blanched fingers. Anyone who later said otherwise, was only recounting seeing the rigidity of Karen's muscles give way to death.

Her face was ashen. The lips that kissed her son goodbye less than an hour before were suddenly gray blue. Soon they would be cold. Her eyes were still. The lids sagged slightly over the next several minutes causing some alarm. Gawkers thought that despite having had most of her neck ripped away by a high caliber rifle bullet fired from a hundred yards away, the woman on the steps of the federal courthouse was still alive. That wasn't true. Karen never made a sound as she was thrown to the stone stair. She felt an impact and a tearing, but no pain. Her eyes saw the sky through the tower of buildings from an angle the most daring photographers seldom captured. There was no sound. Just the feeling of slipping – of that last moment rarely caught before one drifts to sleep.

———————————

28

The Capital Police had to muscle their way through the forest of cell phones held up to film Karen's ill-fitting uniform. It had been stolen, someone reported, hence the poor fit. Sidewalk denizens made reports as sound as any network anchor. None of the talking heads knew anything else to say except to play crude videos of Karen's body over and over and over again while they scrolled a banner that screamed 'Breaking News – Military Terrorist Killed.' When a neatly folded letter beside her body was collected along with Karen's ID, wallet, and picture of baby Sam, the ghouls who masked their true intent to blatantly shock and offend by saying, "This is extremely graphic. You may wish to look away or remove children...," shifted into hyper-drive and aired pictures of the document next to Karen's body from nine different angles. Media soon had poor photos of the letter. They enlarged and cropped it live in order to scoop their like-minded competitors, until the letter could be read easily. As another "aid to the public and increase your ability and right to know...," the note was transcribed and aired alongside the bloody videos until it was agreed, a new watermark or an all-time low, had been eclipsed.

Marian sat on the edge of a hotel bed with her spoiled makeup collected on tissues and napkins all around her. Mr. Guzimon was cramped into the corner, unconsciously as far from the television as he could be and still see. One hand was clamped over his mouth. The other was wrapped in the folds of his shirt under his arm to keep him from lashing out at something. The baby was swaddled tightly, sleeping on the bed when the message on the letter found at Karen's side ran for the umpteenth time.

In the Shadow of Justice

The military terrorist you released has been called to account for her misdeeds. In the shadow of your justice system, the shadow of your federal court, we exercise our right to defend our Nation, "...against all enemies, foreign and domestic."

Jack Aaron was in the corner of Marcus's office in a pose remarkably similar to the maître d', nine hundred miles to the north. He was quiet as a live news cycle played through the computer on Marcus's desk. The investigator's words stumbled from his mouth with the rhyme and reason of a stream of consciousness.

"I just saw her yesterday," Marcus muttered. "She just had a baby. Released on her own recognizance. ROR? In a federal case? You ever hear of that? How does a terrorist get ROR'd? Honest to God, I just saw her..."

"That lieutenant was no terrorist," Jack said through his hand. "She never helped no terrorist. Nothing even close, Petey. Not even close..."

They watched another few minutes as the anchors interviewed experts on long range ballistics and people who shared their support of The Illuminati against those that didn't.

"Did you get the package from her?"

Marcus answered by opening his desk and taking out Karen's phone. He sat it down as if it was fragile.

"And?" Jack asked.

The hesitation was to give Marcus time to take an SD chip from his pocket. He tossed it to the corner of his desk toward his boss. "It's there. Just like she said."

"How many copies did you make?"

"There's one in the evidence room downstairs. I have one and that one. That's yours." He pulled out a small padded envelope. "And one in here ready to go to FDLE for analysis."

"Did you go through it?"

"I'm no Helfer Oakes, but it looks right to me. I found the page he snuck out to Karen. I'd say he's right. It's Rand. Helfer called it from the very beginning."

"Yes he did."

"And now he's dead."

"Yep."

"And the lieutenant helped him get it to us."

"And now she's dead."

"Yep," Marcus said, sounding much like his friend and mentor.

Jack took a step from the corner and picked up the chip. "What do we do with this?"

"Pretend it's a suppository for Clayton Rand?"

Jack smiled. "Maybe. Or we could bury it. Let it go away."

"You think its trouble?"

"Trouble? It's a magnet for bullets."

"I never knew you to shy away from–"

"I ain't. I never said that. Just thinking out loud over here."

They were quiet. Jack wandered around the room.

"You could be right," Marcus said as a picture of Karen, smiling in her crisp white Naval uniform in front of an American flag came across the screen. "We've had enough trouble maybe."

Jack stopped walking. Marcus realized he was staring at him. "What is it?"

"We'd never bury it deep enough."

"What do you mean?"

Jack pointed at the phone. "Say someone puts together that she sent that to you. You could become a terrorist, a dope dealer, get caught in the sack with a dead thirteen-year-old girl. Hell, Petey, these bastards will do anything." He pointed to the streaming news. "Next week that could be your picture."

"No way. It'd never stick."

"I'll bet that's what Karen told you in DC, didn't she?"

It was a revelation that took a few minutes to touch bottom.

"Let's mail this," Marcus said as he flicked the corner of the small package addressed to FDLE on his desk.

"FBI won't like it. Might look bad on your application."

"Fuck them," Marcus said without looking away from Karen's picture on the computer screen.

Jack shook his head then reached across and put his hand on Marcus's shoulder. "I'm sorry, Petey."

"For what?"

"I fanned the flames pretty hard on this," Jack said as he patted his friend's shoulder and stepped away. "I feel like I got everybody wound up in this thing we can't stop."

Marcus stretched his neck and rolled his shoulders. "You never took any of us any place we didn't want to go."

"I bent a few rules," Jack said as he stopped on his way out the door.

"You've nothing to be sorry about. You didn't kill anyone."

The DA looked at the chip in his hand then across the suddenly wide gulf of the room to Marcus. "Nope... Not yet."

"Hey, boss, where're you going?"

"Going to see a guy about a dog."

Jack walked into The Columbia Restaurant and went straight to the long bar. Before he was in his chair, the back room had been advised the District Attorney was out front. Jimmy reached for the cheap whiskey in the well behind the bar.

"Boilermaker, Jimbo."

When the frosted mug of beer and the shot of whiskey arrived, Jack was sitting, thinking as he spun a simple black flip phone around and around on the bar. Jack tossed the shot back and chased it with a long sip the cold beer. Next to the empty shot glass the phone spun like a compass. The DA watched it spin and guessed where it would point when it stopped. Several tries later, it pointed to the stool next to his, just as Don T walked up. He sat down without a word.

"If it's not the boss himself," Jack proclaimed. "You didn't have to come out. Nice of you to say hello though." Jack drank heavily from the tall glass. "Oh, that's good. Jesus, what a day. How've you been, T?"

"I'm old."

"Horseshit. You're only a couple years older than me. We're just kids." Jack almost finished the drink. "You know why I come here?"

Don T shrugged.

"You have the coldest beer in Tampa — maybe the coldest in Florida. By God, that's good. It's so damn cold it should be frozen. How do you get it so cold? What's the secret?"

Another shrug.

"Same old talkative self, aren't you? It's good to know there's some things you can count on in this world — ice cold beer at The Columbia and Don T doesn't spout enough to fill a thimble."

The Don smiled just a little.

"It doesn't matter," Jack said he finished the beer. "I believe I'll have another. Join me?"

"Water please, Jimmy, and another Boilermaker for the DA."

"Water? C'mon. What? You can't be seen fraternizing with the enemy?"

"You're not the enemy, Jack."

"If I was, I'd have to say I wasn't any good at it. Have I ever taken anybody down outa this place?"

"I don't remember."

"I do. Never. Never made one thing stick in all these years."

Don T shrugged and Jack laughed. The drinks were settling on fresh coasters.

"Maybe I should try harder," Jack said as he downed the second shot and took another sip of beer.

The Don merely nodded and raised his water before all the glasses returned to the coasters.

"You know why I came here, T? The real reason?"

"Campaign contribution?"

"Oh, that's funny, that is. You're a goddamn riot. 'Campaign contribution.' You'd like that – get your hooks into me. Then you'd start asking for favors – get your cronies out of jail. Shit like that. Ain't happening." Jack pulled out his money clip and flipped a twenty on the bar. "And I buy my own drinks too, thank you very much."

The smile on his host's face was growing. Jack took another drink.

"So, you want to know why I'm here or not?"

The predictable shrug came.

"It's like talking to myself in here." Jack looked at the bartender, purposely as far away as he could be. "Jimmy? The boss always so talkative?"

Jimmy shrugged.

"Shit..." Jack looked at the Don and pointed over his shoulder at the barkeep. "You teach him that?"

Don T smiled. "He's a good boy."

"Alright. Okay. That's why I'm here. A good boy. I came to ask a favor."

"You ask me a favor?"

"He speaks! Yes, you old guinea bastard. You. I need something and I think you got it."

"Alright."

"There was a kid worked here. Fifteen years ago. Sam Ciampiano."

"Fifteen years is a long time."

"You'd remember this kid. I do. I knew his old man. Same as you. You better than me. Sam Ciampiano Sr. Ring any bells?"

"I don't hear any."

"I don't hear any... You're on fire tonight, you know that, T? You and Guzimon should work up an act. You don't remember him?"

"Lots of kids worked here. I don't remember."

"I figured that. How about his old man? Remember him? They used to call him, The Hammer. For reasons that will remain unsaid at the moment."

"No... I don't re–"

"Okay, I call 'horseshit' on that too, but whatever. Since you don't know them, you can just listen as I tell you a story. How's that?"

The Don sipped his water and nodded.

"Here goes. The old man, Sam Sr. – let's say, just for fun – he works around here for years. I'm just saying. Just for shits and giggles. He works around here forever. He does a lot of dirty jobs. Jobs no one else wants or jobs nobody else can do. He does a lot of damage to people. Good guys, bad guys. A fighter. Borderline psycho. Hard case. Toughest guy I ever knew. But say what you want, he's a stand-up guy. No matter what you did to him, he kept his mouth shut. Maybe he got roughed up. Did a skid bid in state prison over a horseshit charge. Was threatened, or his family maybe. He never says a word. Ever. I know. I chased him up a few alleys back in the day. Nothing can flip him. Tough, tough guy.

"Anyhow, he hooks up with this teeny bopper. Her name was Testiani. I know, I know. No chimes going off in your head. I coulda guessed that. Next thing you know Testiani pops out a kid. Little boy. That'd be Sam Jr., see?

"This baby performs some sort of miracle. Sam Ciampiano Sr. stops. Runs a little book, probably does some things I don't know about, but stops living the high life and raising holy hell. No more crazy stuff. Why? Because he lives for this little kid.

"You listening?" Jack took a quick sip, but didn't wait for an answer. "So... now the kid grows up and goes to work here. Just like young Jimmy down the end of the bar. Your, 'good boy.'

"Young Sam, as near I can tell, stays out of what we'll call, 'the family business.' Keeps his nose clean. No trouble. But trouble finds him, see? And he's in a jam – a big one. A real big one. A monster. Who's he go see to get out of it? You."

Don T took a sip of water and stared at Jack as though he was half listening to a homily.

"And you want to know why I think that? I know you do. All those years chasing his father around, chasing you. It dawns on me – who's better at making people disappear than Don T? Am I right?" Jack leaned back smiling. "Right? That's like... the house special. Poof! Gone! People do the wrong thing, skim a few bucks, say the wrong thing to the wrong guy. And, poof! They disappear. You're like a magician."

The Don folded his hands and leaned on his bar. There was a slight smile, but nothing else to show he'd even heard.

"I know, I know, I know. You don't know shit. I got that before I came in the door. But here's the favor. This kid – our 'good boy' – Sam Jr. He's about one news cycle away from coming totally off-the-goddamn-wall-un-fuckin'-glued. I'm talking about nuclear meltdown, Grade A yellow cake, C 4, ballistic, bat-shit crazy. He's got the tools, the smarts, and worst of all, he's got the genes for damage and destruction. You know what I mean?"

Jack gave himself and the Don a break and had a long draw at his mug. "Oh, that's good. You see the news today, T?"

"I don't watch TV."

"What do you do?"

"I like a good book."

"You like to read? Read the paper. You'll see a story about a young lady – a Navy lieutenant – in Washington some dumbass shot. It's this New Illuminati thing. Oh, it's not your style. Maybe somebody had a good idea, wanted to do the right thing. Set a few things aright. Do what's wrong, but for the right reason. You know what I mean? Cheat a little. Use a marked deck to win back money for the orphanage someone stole from the kids. Sounds right, right?"

Jack edged out on his stool toward his host and leaned on the bar next to him. "But you can't do that" he continued. "You can't make it up as you go. It's a runaway train. The next guy cheats to raise money for some horseshit idea instead of the orphanage. And the next guy starts using the marked cards to put a couple bucks in his pocket. Gas money. Just gas money to get me to the game so I can win money for the orphanage. See how it goes? Two more steps and they're just a bunch of thieves as bad as the guys they started out after. Follow me?"

Don T nodded.

"Why am I telling you this? You know it already. Even about Ciampiano. You already know, don't you?" Jack grinned. "Why you sneaky guinea-greaseball-mother–"

Jack stopped, looked at the Don then finished his beer. He saw Jimmy coming out of the corner of his eye. "No thanks, Jimmy. I'm all set."

The empty glass went to the inside edge of the bar. "I don't know if he's across the street or on the moon, and guess what? I don't want to know. Someday I'd like to have a beer with the kid, maybe. Tell him stories about his father. But he'd have to be alive to do that, wouldn't he?"

Jack stood up and tucked in his unruly shirt and ran his fingers through his hair to straighten it out some. "Put a collar on him, T. Chain him to the floor. Straightjacket. Whatever it takes. You'll be saving his life. That's the favor I'm asking. If he steps out from cover, they'll kill him. Somehow you hold him down until you can put that baby in his lap. I'm telling you. It'll be another miracle, Don T. Another miracle. Just like his father."

Jack took a step toward the door. "See you around."

The Don didn't touch it, but pointed to the phone on the bar. "Don't forget your phone, DA."

"Oh, thanks. It ain't mine." Jack came back, picked it up, and slipped it in his pocket. "It ain't even a phone. It's a recorder."

The Don just shrugged.

"I'm kidding, you old sonofabitch. Think about what I said, will you?"

Don T almost unnoticeably nodded with eyes that were remarkably less tight. "You should stay, Jack. Beat the dinner crowd. The soup is especially good today."

Jack watched his powerful host for a count and felt the whiskey warming his stomach. "Thanks, T. Thanks for everything. But I gotta go see a guy about a dog."

29

It was only a matter of blocks and an equal number of minutes before Jack was at Clayton's door. He didn't ring the bell, but looked up at the camera.

"You know I'm here. Open up in the name of the law."

There was no answer and no electronic clicks from the other side of the door so Jack turned around and kicked backward with the heel of his shoe so hard the heavy door rattled. Beneath the noise, Jack heard the electronic sliding of the locks and the door opening.

"That was all recorded, Mr. Aaron. The DA kicking my door should play well on the news. When's the campaign start again?"

"Knock yourself out, Rand. We need to talk."

"I've nothing to say. You know that. And it's my understanding the FBI has nothing to say either."

"That'd be true, but they don't have this." Jack pulled the phone from his pocket. "Or this." He dug deep until he found the small SD chip. "Wanna talk now?"

"No. Goodbye, Mr. Aaron."

"You don't recognize this phone? I found it. Found it in Sam Ciampiano's mailbox. You sent it to him so you could chat about your Illuminati horseshit. Your prints are on the inside cover," he lied. "Where you took that little tab out that covers the battery. More importantly, you and I talked on it one night. Remember that? It was a curious call. Short, but enough to triangulate back to this house."

Jack stepped back and looked around. "It's a nice house. Security is a little tight for me. Sort of reminds me of a prison. Now... now that could be good. Might make the adjustment for you a little less traumatic. What do you think?"

"I think you're blowing smoke and better leave."

"Fair enough. Fair enough, but maybe you should take a look at this." Jack held out the chip. "Go ahead. It won't bite you. Well, that's not really true. It will bite you. In fact it's gonna bite you. It's gonna rip your throat out. Just like that lieutenant's in Washington."

"Goodbye," Clayton said and began to close the door.

Jack's shoulder hit it in a drive that would have made an NFL lineman proud. Once prompted, the door's weight kept it going and though he stumbled, when Jack righted himself he was inside.

"Nice place. I'd forgotten how nice it was," he gasped as he caught his breath.

"That little trick was recorded too. That's breaking and entering."

"I know the law, Rand."

"This building is classified a government installation. Enjoy federal prison, Mr. Aaron. They love former cops in there."

"Whatever. Why don't you call your buddies in the FBI, CIA, wherever. I'll wait." Jack opened the refrigerator and took out a Miller. "Want one?"

Clayton stared at the blind boldness standing in his kitchen as Jack twisted off the top and purposely dropped the cap on the floor.

"Go ahead. Call them," Jack reiterated on the strength of The Columbia's whiskey. "Tell them about the phone and this chip. Tell them it has the dead congressman's hard drive on it. Tell them you fucked up and the file points right back to you and this 'federal installation.' That'll impress 'em." Jack took a long drink. He looked at the bottle. "This could be colder. You might want to check the settings on your icebox.

"What'll it be, Rand? You calling your handlers? Here," he tossed Clayton the cheap pay-as-you-go phone. "Use this one."

"You're lying," Clayton said as he caught the cheap phone and set it on the end of the long granite counter.

"Naww. You don't believe that. You know it's all true. I'd never kick your door in if I was full of shit. I could get in trouble," he grinned.

"And so? What do you want?"

"You."

"To do what?"

"To go to jail, I think. But I doubt I could get you there quick enough."

"How's that? You can't put me in jail over that phone. Not even with that hard drive. It'll get squelched. It'll vanish. Maybe you'll vanish."

"That's not very nice. Sounds like a threat. But you could be right about you playing some kind of get-outa-jail-free card. Still, it is enough to get you killed."

"Come again?"

"I got some questions first. Or maybe you'd call them observations. This Illuminati thing – oh, I like the name by the way. Very clever – all this house cleaning. I get it. Hell, I agree with it. I might even send in a tax deductible donation to your cause if I could. It's funny," Jack said as he drank Clayton's beer and wandered around the kitchen. "I was just talking to an old friend of mine about it. Maybe it started as a good idea, but you didn't see the end game, did you? I know. You didn't. I think that's always the hard part. Any damn fool can start a fight. It's ending one that gets touchy. But what I think doesn't matter to you. You could care less. I'm nobody. Just a local DA. You know I have to play by the rules. Pretty much, know what I mean?

"Anyway, I'm not tricky enough to play the games you play. But you know who else isn't very tricky? Ciampiano. He ain't tricky at all. What he is though, is pissed – branding iron-red-hot-psycho-pissed, or he's about to be, and pissed ain't good somebody like Sam. And it's even worse for the one he's pissed at. You putting any of this together, Einstein?"

Clayton just watched him meander with steps and words.

"You know who Mary Shelley is?" Jack stopped walking and asked. "Of course you do. You're a smart guy, Rand. I think I'll start calling you Mary Shelley. After all, you wrote the script, didn't you? Or should I cut out the horseshit and go right to Dr. Frankenstein?"

"And this means what to me, Mr. Aaron?"

"That monster you created? Ciampiano–"

"I didn't create anybody. People were ready to do whatever they did. You said you agreed with it yourself."

"But being ready to do something and doing it, that ain't the same. It ain't the same thing at all." Jack tossed the SD card on the counter next to the cheap phone and pulled out his small revolver. Clayton's eyes widened. "Relax, Rand. I'm not gonna shoot you. Unless I have to."

He opened the cylinder and emptied the revolver's bullets in his hand, but immediately put one round back in the gun. The rest of the bullets went in his pocket except one. "Let me explain it to you this way," Jack said as he closed the cylinder on the pistol and seemed to weigh it in one hand versus the weight of the single bullet in the other. "The difference between thinking about doing something – talking about it, maybe even agreeing with it – and actually doing it, is the difference between me throwing this bullet at you," Jack held out his hand and showed him the bullet between his finger and thumb. Then he cocked the pistol and pointed it in Clayton's face. "And shooting this one at you.

See the difference? Same bullets. I throw one. I shoot one. Same bullets. Think there's a difference now, Rand?"

"What do you want?"

Jack lowered the gun and resumed walking. "That monster of yours, Ciampiano. I have an idea where he is. Well, not exactly, but sort of how he got there. And yeah, I don't know where he is, but I know where he's going."

"Where's that?"

"Right here. He'll be along. And he's going to kill you. I'm not too smart, I think I said that already, but that nice lieutenant who took one in the neck? She loved Ciampiano enough to risk everything to protect him. And my guess is he's a stand-up guy who loved her right back. Then they have this little baby, see? You probably haven't put that together yet." Jack smiled and lied again. "Handsomest little baby boy you ever saw. Anyway, that little boy's daddy is coming here. This house. He's coming to kill you."

Clayton laughed and tried to hide the anxiousness wrought on by the gun and its owner, both of which appeared to be half-cocked. "You're a dreamer. We're old friends. I've known him since we were kids."

"Yeah, that's right. The Newsboys. I forgot that. If it was just him, you might be right. He'd take it on the chin. He's a soldier. Goddamn best we can make. Knows the game. Knows the rules. Knows there ain't no rules. But it's not just him anymore. The lieutenant got killed by those wingnuts you turned loose. You know, I heard there was one of your Illuminati triangles carved into the butt end of the bullet they carved out of her spine. They must have hand loaded that round special. Almost took her head off. Jesus, can you imagine that? Awful. Just awful. Ciampiano isn't gonna like that. That's why he's going to bury you."

"I didn't turn anybody loose. We're done here. Get out."

Jack was speeding up, but held the revolver at his side. "Try telling Ciampiano that through the duct tape around your mouth. Tell him you didn't do it when that first shovel full of dirt hits you in the face."

"You're crazy, Aaron."

"Maybe," Jack continued. "Oh..., but maybe Ciampiano won't have to kill you. Somebody else might whack you first. See, people get their wires crossed all the time. That's the problem with a scheme like yours. It's like that picture of that pyramid thing you put together, except, it's a Ponzi one. Sooner or later it doesn't pay off. Someone uses it as an excuse to do whatever it is they want to do – profit, eliminate the competition. All kinds of ideas start coming into their heads. That's what my friend and I were just talking about. That's the flaw. And people can justify it all if they twist it around enough.

"Or, worse yet, somebody makes a mistake. Like what happened to the lieutenant – Sam's girl and that baby's mom. That's why, as strange as this sounds coming from a guy like me, we can't do things like what you did."

Clayton shook himself free for a moment and looked Jack square in the eye. "Yes we can. We did. We will. And we'll do it again."

"True. Somebody will, but it won't be you." Jack gently released the hammer on his revolver and put it away. "In a couple of hours a sealed indictment will be opened at the county courthouse. Local, not federal. I've indicted you. The Illuminati will do the rest. Or Ciampiano will. You see how this works, Shelley?"

"They won't let you indict me."

"Who's 'they?' The FBI? CIA? Shit, they probably want to shut you up more than anybody. But they'll have to take a number to kill you. They can't stop the indictment or the coverage. I've already made the press releases. You'll be front page news by morning. It's too late."

"It'll all be dismissed," Clayton smiled a confident protest.

"Probably, but think of the headline – 'Millionaire Businessman Indicted,' for... whatever. Just fill in the blank. It doesn't really matter anymore, does it? And wait until they get a load of what's on that hard drive," Jack said as he pointed to the table. "'Government Operative Orchestrates Killing.' Oh, the talk shows are going to have a ball."

"I never killed anybody."

"I don't care, Shelley!" Jack shouted and slammed his beer down on the black granite so hard the bottle broke. Beer and glass ran across the counter and onto the floor. "And those people you think you didn't create won't care either. People believe what they hear – believe what they want to. 'Government,' 'Millionaire,' and 'Indictment' in the same sentence? That's enough. You're a dead man."

"It won't work, Jack!"

"Maybe, but remember you said that if they leave you for Ciampiano. Remember it when he drags you out into the Green Swamp. All those bugs and snakes. Jesus." Jack forced a quiver, noticed he'd cut his hand, and flicked away pieces of glass off the cuts before rinsing his hand in Clayton's sink and wiping his hand on his pants. "Gives me the willies just thinking about it." Then he smiled. "Oh, the duct tape will keep the dirt out of your mouth. Your eyes? Not so much."

Jack went back to the heavy steel door and ran his hand along its wide edge. "That is a helluva door, Rand. Helluva door. I'd keep her locked tight if I was you." He looked back at the broken glass and beer trickling onto the floor and smiled. "Sorry about the mess. Have a good night, Rand. Sleep tight now."

Jack's hands were buried in his pockets as he walked toward the car. He jingled the bullets like loose change and thought of what he'd said. He hoped he was wrong. He hoped Ciampiano wouldn't come.

Inside, Clayton was on the phone. His computer was scrolling the SD card.

"So, what do I do now?"

"First, you stop opening the fucking door! I thought you were a genius? Christ..."

"Can you get to him?"

"Of course we can, but there's limits to everything. ROI. Return on Investment. We can't shut up the entire DA's Office very well, can we? The return wouldn't be worth it."

"Well, how about Sam?"

"What about him?"

"Can you stop him?"

"We don't even know where he is. Maybe he's outside your door right now."

"That's not funny. I didn't kill his girlfriend. It was probably you. Maybe I'll send him after you and your incompetent FBI."

"Why don't you do just that?"

The phone air was filled with nothing but exasperated breathing.

"Rand. Pull yourself together."

"Easy for you to say. My life turns to shit tomorrow if those indictments come out."

"You should have thought of that before you turned into Captain America and tried to save these animals from themselves."

"But Sam. Can't you find him? Tell him it wasn't me, wasn't us? Back off him or something."

"No. He's a loose end."

"He's the best. You should have recruited him."

"Maybe we did."

"You sonofabitch. He's okay then? I'm okay?"

"No idea. We watch the people who are watching the people who are watching the people."

"Goddamn it, Major!"

"Don't call me that."

"Is he with the good guys?"

"There aren't any good guys."

"There should be. There was meant to be."

"No, there is only the game. Some winners, some losers. No one starts out good or bad. It's... It's a process. Except in this game – some people start out with hotels on their property and stacks of $500 bills under the edge of the board. The thing is, no one really knows who owns the hotels or whose money it is. People think that funny colored five hundred dollar bill is the solution, but it's nothing. Less than a drop in the ocean. The Bank. Who owns The Bank? That's the real power. The Bank just watches the pieces run around the board thinking they're living their little lives, when they're only making the wheel turn for The Bank."

"Jesus, what's the point then?"

"Power, that's the point. Who has it? Who wants it? And who thinks they can get it. You ever hear of a guy named Frederick Douglas?"

"Of course."

"You know what he said? So damn true. Sums it all up."

"I don't need a history lesson."

"He said, 'No power was given up voluntarily.' You get it, Rand? We need the game. That is why it must be played. It's the only reason. Goodnight, Clayton."

———————

30

Before sunrise the steel door was witness to a line of media trucks, replete with their mast antennae, parked in front of Clayton's house.   He sat stammering in front of the monitors at the onslaught taking place outside.   By dawn the national media was on the story like a rabid dog at the throat of a helpless child.   Clayton watched live videos of his house and heard the helicopters overhead.   Somehow they'd gotten pictures – from high school and fund raisers – and attached scrolling details, most of which were inaccurate.   In his mind, Clayton remembered what seemed like years and years ago when he had watched a similar crucifixion of the county commissioner who burned the Cypress trees and inadvertently sent the first bolts of lightning through the monster's body.

A ping brought Clayton's attention to his computer's monitor.   He had a message.   A small silent envelope faded on and off in the corner.   It was a familiar, but dated process.   A single click launched a blazing scan.   The message was released and opened on his monitor.

"To those whom much is given, much is expected."   And *their sins will find them out.   We're coming.*

Clayton rubbed his face hard then his hands began to tremble over the keyboard that had been the scalpel and provided the stitches that held his creation together.   The choking fear welling in his mind as he stared at the silent glowing monitor was the same as Dr. Frankenstein had felt when he looked for a soul in the eyes of his monster – eyes he had sutured into place with brilliant hands that, like Clayton's, were now powerless.   Frankenstein stepped toward him.   The digital letter and Mary Shelley's lumbering brute would only be satiated by a death.

———————

EPILOGUE

The bright blue and orange heavy wooden boat lurched up and down like a violent rocking horse until it cleared the clamor of the Adriatic surf. The oars shivered in their locks as Sam pulled against them far harder than he needed. There was no rush against the quiet life he had drawn. The motor sat quiet, its prop not even in the water. Working the oars was good exercise and kept his body firm in the absence of polished chrome weight machines and barbells. The burn in his back and thighs felt good and reminded him of times in military gyms the world over when contests of reps and heavy bench presses raged with the screaming encouragement of like-minded soldiers. But here the sea was quiet except for the slipping and straining of the oars and the lapping of the cold water.

In time, the ebbing tide and the breeze took over and was easing him along gently out over the still moonlit black water. Sweating from his workout, Sam rinsed his head in the sea that reached up the side of his boat. The water this far out was silent in comparison to the crashing coast. It rolled gently in a calming rhythm under the boat. It was quiet. The darkness of the sea was discernible from the night sky only by the appearance of stars on the horizon and their scattering above. The dark enveloped him like a cloak. He was invisible to the world. He was hidden, while his troubled heart stumbled against memories of her then staggered back up and pushed ahead, away from the specter of recollections that would haunt him until his last breath.

Relieved of his rowing, Sam baited and lowered his line into the deep then waited, rested, and began to plan. In some parts of the world, this day was nearly spent. For Sam, this was just the beginning.

THE END

If you enjoyed *Return to Power , The New Illuminati – Part 2,* promote my work by sharing with family and friends. Also, please post a review @ Amazon & Goodreads!

Thanks so much,

David-Michael

www.ingramcontent.com/pod-product-compliance
Lightning Source LLC
Chambersburg PA
CBHW050912250626
47155CB00001B/200